Painful Reminders

Book One
Cari Daniels
Series

Betty,
Maybe someday
you'll be autographing
your own books!

Sherry Martin-Legault

Sherry Martin - Legault

P

Outskirts Press, Inc.
Denver, Colorado

Painful Reminders
Book One Cari Daniels Series
All Rights Reserved.
Copyright © 2009 Sherry Martin-Legault
V2.0

Cover Photo © 2009 JupiterImages Corporation. All rights reserved - used with permission.

Outskirts Press, Inc.
http://www.outskirtspress.com

ISBN: 978-1-4327-2434-4

Library of Congress Control Number: 2009924055

Outskirts Press and the "OP" logo are trademarks belonging to Outskirts Press, Inc.

PRINTED IN THE UNITED STATES OF AMERICA

Dedication

This book is lovingly dedicated to my husband, Stephane, and to my children, Amanda, Joshua, and Joseph, who have all believed in me from the beginning.

Thanks for listening to all the plot lines.

Acknowledgements

Thanks to the friends who read over the manuscript for me: Jani, Lori, Miriam, Nat. Your help and enthusiasm were greatly appreciated.

Thanks to the L.A.P.D. staff who answered my technical inquiries when I was in my research phase. Any errors are entirely mine.

Thanks to all my friends in the medical profession, and law enforcement, for putting up with my many questions through the years.

Chapter 1

Cari rubbed the back of her neck as she headed towards the nearest water fountain. She blinked her brown eyes several times in order to refocus her vision. She'd just spent hours bent over papers. *I'm so glad that exam is over with. I almost don't care if I passed it or not.* A slight smile lifted the corners of her lips. *Almost. It's not everybody who makes the rank of Sergeant around here. I just hope that I'm one of them.*

"Hey, Cari, how'd it go today?" asked Officer Mike Patterson, her patrol partner of the past several years. He crossed his arms as he leaned against the wall.

"I don't really know, Mike." She shrugged, both in reply and in an effort to loosen the stiff muscles between her shoulder blades. "I'm trying not to think about it." She grinned at him. "But I'll bet you've never wondered for a second about anything you've had to do."

"Oh I've wondered all right." He smiled back at her. "Like both times that Julie was pregnant. I did plenty of wondering then."

"All set for Thanksgiving?" She leaned down and took a few sips of the tepid water. She wiped some errant drips from her chin as she straightened once more. "I know Julie's been baking up a storm for at least a week already. When do Michael and Christa get in?"

"Tomorrow afternoon. Yeah, I'd say we're all set. But it won't seem quite the same without you there this year."

Cari felt her cheeks flush slightly as she rubbed her neck. "I guess it will be kind of different, won't it?"

"Does Mark even know how to cook a turkey dinner?" he teased. "I didn't think that doctors had much time for kitchens."

"Actually, Mark is a wonderful cook." She frowned. "Probably better than I am." She shrugged again. "Oh well, some guys have all the luck. Good looks, great job, and knowing how to cook."

"And having a beautiful fiancée to protect him." He gave her a wink. "Set a date yet?"

Cari shook her head. "Not yet. We've both been pretty busy and we haven't had much time to discuss that." She shifted her weight and rubbed the small of her back. "Maybe this weekend. We both booked off of most of it."

"Well, we'll sure miss not having you over, but I'm not too old to remember what it was like to spend some time alone with my fiancée. I'm sure you'll have a great time."

Cari yawned. "Writing that exam was not 'a great time' I'll tell you. I've been studying for weeks for that. It'll be so nice to just sit at home and do nothing tonight."

"I'm sure it will. Well, see you tomorrow."

"Bye, partner."

Mike laughed. "Hey, maybe you'll soon get to call Mark that."

"Let's hope so. Isn't that what marriage is about?"

<hr />

Cari arrived at Mark's house at precisely four p.m. on November 28th, 1991. Her blonde hair was loose around her shoulders, rather than pinned up, like she needed it on the job. She was wearing a cream colored cotton sweater, and a knee length denim skirt. A pair of leather sandals adorned her feet. At five foot nine, and 140 pounds, she made an impressive sight, but few people realized how difficult it was to buy clothes that fit properly. She was just about to ring the doorbell when she heard the deadbolt turn. She smiled as Mark opened the door for her and whistled.

"My, my, you're looking awfully good today, Officer Daniels." He stepped back as she entered the small foyer. Then he kissed her cheek before closing the door.

"You're looking pretty good yourself, Dr. Hamilton." She sniffed the air. "Mmm, it sure smells good in here. When do we get to eat?"

Mark frowned at her. "Are you always so ravenous, Cari? Or just when I'm the one doing the cooking?" Before she could reply he pulled her into a firm embrace. "Dinner will be ready in about an hour. Why don't you put on some music while you're waiting? Then you could help me set the table."

"Oh, so I have to work for my supper do I?" she protested, even as she put her arms around his neck and kissed his slightly rough cheek.

"Well," he murmured just before kissing her lips, "maybe we can make some allowances." He pulled her closer and kissed her again.

Cari felt a bit uncomfortable and tried to pull back. "Mark, I think something is burning on the stove."

"Nice try," he whispered. "There's not even anything turned on right now. On the stove at least." He kissed her again, almost hurting her mouth.

"Mark, please . . ." Cari pressed against his chest. "Enough. Okay?"

He released her with a sigh. "Why don't you sit down and think of a date when you can put me out of my misery?" He rubbed his long fingered hands over his face. "All these false starts are getting kind of annoying." Without another word he headed towards the kitchen, leaving Cari alone with her thoughts. Troubled ones.

What's the matter with him today? He's never been so — so pushy before. Should I say something? Or maybe even leave? Shaking her head, she slipped off her sandals and went into the living room. She randomly selected a CD and soon music filled the room. But her thoughts were still muddled. *For Pete's sake, we aren't a couple of teenagers! I'm 30 and Mark is 35. So why is he acting like a pouty high school senior?* She shook her head again. *Maybe it's just because I'm too tired.* Her shift the evening before had been particularly rough. *I'm probably just overreacting about this. It's not as though he's never kissed me before.*

Cari sat down on the leather recliner and went over the coming months in her mind. *January isn't a great month for a wedding. February is almost too mushy. March is spring break and we'd both be too busy. April is Easter. May? May could work.* She yanked her purse into her lap and rifled through it, looking for a pocket calendar. *May 1992. Saturday the 9th or 16th?*

"How about May the 9th?" she called without looking up.

"No need to shout," Mark said as he put his hands on her shoulders.

Cari jerked forward and turned to look at him. "How many times have I told you not to do that to me?"

"Relax," he said in a silky tone. "I just happened to be right behind you, but you didn't notice. And, by the way, May is no good. I'll be at a medical convention in Seattle. Besides, that's still six *long* months away. How about Christmas Eve? That's much more reasonable." He caressed her cheek as he talked.

"Are you crazy, Mark? That's only a month away. Neither of us could get organized that fast. And with our weird schedules it'd be even worse." She shifted slightly and looked up at him with a smile. "Besides, aren't I worth waiting for?"

He didn't answer, other than to mumble something about the potatoes boiling over, and left the room.

Cari was more on edge than ever. *We haven't been engaged that long, have we? Only a few months. Why is he in such a hurry? Kids?* She could feel her cheeks turn crimson. They hadn't even talked about that yet. *He's already 35. Maybe he really does feel the need to quit dragging his feet. Do I want to have a baby right away? What about a possible promotion?*

Am I ready to set that aside right now? She bit her lip as she continued to think it over. *I guess I have been the one holding back in this relationship. I'm not afraid of marriage, am I? Am I?*

Supper was soon ready and Cari was relieved to see that Mark's mood had reverted to one of cheerfulness, rather than tension. She praised his cooking, helped with the dishes and then joined him for hot cocoa in the living room.

"How about February?" Cari remarked, sipping around the mound of whipped cream on her drink. "That's only 3 months away. We should both be able to book time off then. Shouldn't we?" she asked with a smile.

"Well, maybe," he replied, setting his empty mug on the coffee table in front of him. He put his left arm around her shoulders and drew her closer to him. "Why wait, Cari? We could just elope. Why fuss with a wedding at all?"

Cari stared at him with her mouth partly open. "What is the matter with you, Mark? I'm trying to be reasonable and--" Her sentence was cut off as Mark grabbed her mug, spilling some cocoa onto her sweater. More spilled when he set the mug on the table.

"I'm tired of being *reasonable*, Cari. That's what's the matter. And you don't seem to be getting the point too well. Let me help you out." His left arm tightened around her as he grabbed her left hand. He shifted his weight, forcing her backwards on the sofa. He began to kiss her, pressing his mouth on hers.

Cari squirmed and tried to free her hands. She almost panicked when she realized that his grip was actually hurting her. She tried to move her head to the side, but that proved just as useless. She braced her left foot on the floor, in an effort to shift her weight. It didn't help. Her heart was hammering in her chest when Mark paused to take a breath. "Let me up!"

Mark only grinned at her. "Why? Would you rather go to the bedroom?"

"No! I want to--" She jerked as she felt his hand lifting her sweater. "Mark, please--"

He deftly slid her onto her back, shoving her right arm between the cushions and the sofa back. He still held her left wrist with bruising force. "I'm tired of waiting, Cari. And I know that you are too, even if you won't admit it."

She tried to shake her head, but Mark's mouth came back down on hers. She almost gagged when she realized where his left hand was. She was startled by her own reaction to his touch and became frantic to free herself. He easily held her down.

"You can fight me, Cari, but you won't win. Just relax and enjoy yourself."

"Let me go! You're hurting me." Tears coursed her cheeks as she looked into his eyes. She barely recognized him as the same man that she'd so willingly agreed to marry a few months before.

"Then quit trying to fight," he replied. His left hand roughly gripped her face. "Don't make me hurt you."

Cari trembled violently at the rage she saw in his eyes, and in the tight lines of his normally smiling mouth. *He'd do it. He's willing to hurt me. Oh, God, why didn't I leave sooner! I don't want him to hurt me. I don't even want him to touch me anymore.* "Please don't hurt me," she whispered.

Mark released her face and stared down at her for a moment. "Are you going to cooperate?"

Cari couldn't make herself say the word 'yes' but she managed a slight nod.

"Good."

Cari closed her eyes and did whatever he told her to, trying not to be sick. After what seemed like an eternity to her, Mark abruptly got to his feet. Cari was too stunned to move. When she finally opened her eyes, Mark was staring right at her.

"Get up and get out of here," was his blunt remark.

"Why?" she asked in disbelief. She forced movement back into her taut limbs and tried to sit up. "Why?"

"I have to get up early for work."

"You what! You force yourself on me, and then you casually tell me to get out." She sat up and self-consciously adjusted her clothes.

"You weren't even worth the effort," he remarked derisively. "Glad I found out before the wedding."

Mounting rage mingled with smoldering shame as Cari got to her feet. "How does raping me tell you what our marriage could have been like?"

He took a step towards her and Cari tensed, still unsure of his potential behavior.

"Get out of my house. But give me back the ring first."

"You're insane, Mark." She shakily removed the diamond from her left hand. "How do you intend to explain this?"

"I don't." He suddenly grabbed her by the shoulders, a mocking smile on his handsome face. "Who would believe that your loving fiancé would rape you? Besides, you came here willingly, knowing that we'd be alone. You could never prove that I *forced* you into anything. Just as likely that people would think that *you* seduced *me*. Isn't that right, *Officer*?" He took the ring from her and went to get her purse. "Good night, Cari. And, 'Happy Thanksgiving'."

⸺⪢◉⪡⸺

Back in her car, Cari leaned against the steering wheel and wept. *Why, God? Why! Why did I come here? Why didn't I leave when I saw how he was acting? What should I do now? Report it? I can't. I know I can't. It's always been so easy to tell other victims to press charges. But I can't do it myself. I could go to the Sexual Assault Center. No, they know me too well there. I could go to the hospital. No, he didn't really hurt me. Just some bruises. I need to go home. Take a shower.*

She started her car and pulled out of the driveway. Despite the tears in her eyes, she made it home safely. Then she showered until the water turned cold. She crawled into bed, curled up in a ball, and stared at the wall until morning. And for the first time since entering the Police Academy, Cari called in sick.

Chapter 2

Since Cari had Saturday off she didn't need to contact anyone. But she was expected at Mike and Julie's for lunch on Sunday, so she gave them a call early that morning. It was Julie who answered the phone.

"Hi, Cari. How are you feeling?" Julie asked right off.

"Not too well yet, Julie," she replied truthfully. "I think I better stay home if I plan to make it for my shift tomorrow. Sorry about lunch. I really wanted to see Michael and Christa. I guess I'll have to wait for Christmas."

"So what's the matter? Food poisoning? I thought that Mark was a better cook than that."

Cari could hear the teasing in her friend's voice, but she fished for a way to respond. "No, not food poisoning. I'm just – I'm just sick. And I'm really tired." Three nights of horrible dreams had seen to that.

"Cari?" Julie's tone altered slightly. "Is there something more to this than a virus? You haven't been sick enough to miss work in the whole ten years that I've known you. What's going on?"

Cari grew frantic, and her sweating palm made it difficult to hold the phone. She bit her lip. *What can I say? She's bound to figure out something is wrong between me and Mark.*

"Mark and I broke up, Julie," she said in a rush. "And it was pretty awful." Just mentioning that much made her stomach reel. "I'm still stunned, I guess." *That's an understatement.*

"Oh Cari! I'm so sorry to hear that. I had no idea."

"Neither did I. Look Julie, I think I just need to be alone today. I'll try to come over on my next day off, okay?"

"Sure. I understand. But if you need somebody to talk to, you know where to find us. We'll be praying for you."

"Thanks. I know that I'm going to need it." She swallowed against a fresh onslaught of tears. "I'll see you in a few days."

"All right. Bye."

"Bye."

Cari set the phone down and put her hands up to her face. *Well, they know enough, I hope. I guess that's what I'll just have to tell everybody else too.* She moaned. *If that's all I need to say, then why do I still feel so sick?*

⸺◉⸺

Mike noticed how pale Cari was as soon as she arrived at work. That, and the dark circles beneath her eyes, despite her use of extra makeup. But as soon as he commented on the tenseness of her posture she got defensive.

"Yes, I know I look awful. I haven't slept enough since Thursday. And I'll admit that I'm anxious to get this shift over with. But I *don't need* unwanted advice or remarks. Okay?" She slammed her locker door for added emphasis. "Just back off!" She headed from the room and exited the building.

Once at the cruiser, Mike spoke up again. "Mind if I do the driving today?" *You'd better agree with me on this, Cari. You're too shaky to drive yourself.*

"Go ahead," she replied. She got in on the passenger side and slammed her door.

"Cari, look--"

"Mike, don't! Not one word. Not one question." She blinked

a couple of times but a tear still managed to slip past her lids. "If you do, I'll fall apart. Just let me do my job and go home. That's all I can handle right now."

"Okay," he said with a sigh. "For now. Maybe even tomorrow. But sometime soon, we *will* talk."

"Thanks, Mike. I just need some time."

He turned the key in the ignition. "Let's roll, partner."

⸺◦(◉)◦⸺

Cari got through her shift without mishap, but she was exhausted when she reached her apartment. With a sigh she remembered that she hadn't done laundry for several days. She went to her closet and dragged her basket of dirty clothes out and carried it to the kitchen. She got her washer filling with water, scooped in some detergent and began to pick out some clothes from the basket. Halfway through the pile she covered her mouth and tried not to gag. Her sweater and skirt were in the basket. The seemingly harmless cocoa stain increased her nausea.

Cari went to the sink and leaned against the counter. *They're just clothes! Why should that matter? They need to be washed just like the rest.* She shook her head. *There's no point. I know I'll never wear them again anyway. I can't. All I'd be able to think of* -- She wretched into the sink as the washer stopped filling. She splashed some cold water on her face, rinsed her mouth, and gritted her teeth. Then she picked up the skirt and sweater, and shoved them into the kitchen garbage can. The rest of the clothes went into the machine, and she closed the lid.

Cari went to her bedroom, sat on the bed and looked in the mirror at her reflection. She was startled by what she saw. *I can't go on like this. I have to get past it. I can't let what Mark did control the rest of my life. I have to pull myself together. I need to sleep. Do my job. Stop yelling at Mike.* She crossed her arms over her chest, in an attempt to still her trembling. *I won't let this destroy me. I'm not a different person than I was. I can still be a good cop. I* will *be okay.* She continued to look in the mirror as fresh tears streaked down her ashen cheeks. *I just don't know* when.

―――――――――― ((◦)) ――――――――――

"You're looking better today," Mike said once he and Cari were alone in the cruiser. "You must have gotten some sleep last night."

Cari appreciated his concern, but all she could manage was a slight nod. She jerked when he touched her hand, and looked into his compassionate face. She fought the tears with a vengeance. "Yeah, I slept. I'm gonna be okay, Mike. Really." She felt him gently squeeze her hand. "Just keep praying for me, okay?"

"Sure thing. How about right now?"

"I—I don't know, Mike. I'd likely just mess up my makeup again." She tried to withdraw her hand, but he wouldn't release it.

"I'll keep it short." He immediately closed his eyes. "Dear Lord, I thank You for giving Cari rest last night. I pray that You'll surround her with Your peace, and that You'll give her direction each day. Amen." He looked at her and smiled. "Short enough for you?"

"Fine. And thanks, Mike."

"Any time, partner."

―――――――――― ((◦)) ――――――――――

Julie's hug lasted just a bit longer than usual when Cari arrived for supper. "Now that I've seen you for myself, I can quit grilling Mike about how you're doing." She gave an extra squeeze before releasing Cari. "I've been driving him crazy all week."

Cari smiled as she moved towards her favorite wing back chair in the den. "I have really appreciated your prayers, Julie." She swallowed hard. "You'll likely never know how much." She sat down and put her feet up on the ottoman. She laughed for the first time in a week as she recalled their long-standing joke. "If you guys would just give me this chair, I wouldn't have to keep coming over here so often."

"And that's precisely why I *won't* give it to you," Julie replied. "As long as the chair is here, I know that you'll keep coming back." Julie sat down on the beautiful walnut rocker. "So, put me out of my misery. Are you over the worst—or do you still need a shoulder to cry on?"

Cari looked at her friend and tried to come up with an adequate response. She shrugged. "I feel like there shouldn't even be any tears left. And I—I'm not sure that I'm ready to talk." She glanced up at Mike as he entered the room, coffee in hand. "But, on the other hand, I think my *partner* won't let me leave without some sort of explanation."

"Smart girl," Mike remarked as he stretched out on the leather sofa. "We're all ears."

"I guess I knew something wasn't quite, well, *right*, when I got to Mark's." She began to wring her hands, and she avoided looking at either of them. "I stayed anyway, and supper was fine. It was after that." She realized that she was trembling again and forced her muscles to relax. "We argued about the date for the wedding. He didn't want to wait around anymore. He suggested eloping." She swallowed again as she tried to keep a tight rein on her emotions. "It got worse after that." She fought the rising nausea. "He asked for the ring back. No, actually, he *demanded* the ring back. And he told me to get out." She shrugged. "And I've been a mess ever since."

"I can't believe he did that!" Julie whispered. Her green eyes glinted with an emotion that Cari couldn't quite define. "That has got to be one of the cruelest things I've ever heard of."

Mike was still sipping his coffee, apparently deep in thought. "Well, to be strictly honest, ladies, I'm not totally surprised."

"What?" both women replied at once.

"What do you know that you haven't been telling, Michael Patterson?" Julie demanded, an indignant look on her face.

"Well, Mark and I talked a fair bit, you know, and I always got the impression that he was as tense as a teenaged guy. He was looking forward to getting married, but he always complained about the 'hassle' involved with the actual wedding. It seemed to me that he was more interested, or even *preoccupied* with the honeymoon than the marriage." He looked directly at Cari. "Frankly, Cari, I'm kind of relieved that you found this out now, before he hurt you any worse."

The irony of his statement hit Cari like a sledgehammer. *Why didn't you tell me this sooner, Mike? Now it's too late. Mark couldn't have hurt me more than he already has.* She put her hands up to her face and tried to regain her composure. Her friends remained silent. After several moments, she lowered her hands to her lap. "Thanks for being so honest, Mike. But I wish you would have said something before now." She tried to keep anger from her tone. "I had no idea what Mark was saying to you. He'd certainly never let on to me. Or, if he did, I never caught the hint."

"I'm sorry. I didn't realize that he'd actually break off with you. He never said he was interested in anyone else, either. He only talked about you. I don't doubt that he loved you. I think he just let his emotions, and maybe his hormones, get in the way. If I had thought it was my place to say something, I would have. But you're a big girl, Cari. I was afraid you'd yell at me for interfering."

Cari slowly nodded. "I think I understand, Mike." She tried to smile. "But from now on, please *interfere* if you think I'm in for a surprise. I don't *ever* want to go through something like this again."

"Deal. I now have official permission to 'butt in'. Don't forget later on," he teased.

"I won't, Mike," she replied wistfully. "I won't ever forget."

———— ⊃«❖»⊂ ————

Cari stared at her calendar and counted the days for the fourth time. Then she turned and leaned against the wall. *God, please let me be wrong. Just over tired. Too strung out emotionally. I have to be wrong!* But she had every reason to believe she was right, especially when she wretched for the tenth morning in a row.

———— ⊃«❖»⊂ ————

"So, partner, have you checked the bulletin board yet?" Mike asked with a grin as he and Cari neared the locker area.

She looked at him in confusion. "Bulletin board? Why would I?"

Mike's smile faded. "Are you feeling okay, today, Cari? You've been awfully quiet."

"I'm okay," she lied. "But why should I be looking at the bulletin board? Are we getting a raise or something?"

"Some of us are," he replied. "Why don't you just go take a look?"

"All right," she snapped. "Since you won't give me a straight answer." She turned to go, but Mike caught her by the arm.

"Cari, what's the matter with you?"

"I'm tired and I want to go home." She looked at his hand on her arm. "Let go of me, Mike."

"In a minute."

"No. Right now."

He released his hold. "Cari, the exam marks are posted on the board."

Still nothing registered with her. "And?"

"The Sergeant Exam marks."

Cari felt as though he'd hit her. She stared at him as his words sunk in. *How could I forget the exam? I studied so long for that.* "And?" she asked again, this time with curiosity taking hold.

"And you scored the highest mark, that's what. Why don't you go see for yourself?"

Cari leaned against the nearest wall. "I don't believe it!" she whispered. "I mean, I studied. I thought I did okay. But I had no idea that I'd do so well." She looked at Mike again and grabbed his sleeve. "You're not just teasing me, are you?"

"No, I'm not. And I'll gladly escort you to the board so you can see for yourself."

She managed a quick nod, and soon found herself staring at the test results. Several other officers were around her, and most of them congratulated her, even those who had received lower marks. Mike kept a steadying hand on her shoulder. "I still can't believe it."

"Well, maybe it'll sink in when you get your next pay check," he laughed. "Ready to go home now –*Sergeant* Daniels?"

"Yes. Yes I am."

⸺◦《◉》◦⸺

Cari received official recognition the following day at the division roll call. But the excitement she had anticipated just wasn't there. A more pressing issue was nagging at her. One that she couldn't pass off with a handshake and a 'Thank you, Sir'. And she wondered how much longer she could put off those 'test results'.

Chapter 3

It was December 20th, 1991 when Cari pulled up in front of the *Sexual Assault Center*. It was 4:30 p.m. and she knew that when she came back out to her car, her life would be changed, one way or another. And she strongly suspected *how* it would change. She placed her hands on the steering wheel and rested her forehead against them.

"God, this is one test that I sure don't want a positive result on. Help me through this, please. I don't know what else to do. And if the test is—if it's positive, then please, *please* help me." She sat up, wiped her eyes, and opened her door, bracing herself for an uncertain future.

———◦《◦》◦———

Cari sat on the table in the examining room, watching her friend, Dr. Lewis. The doctor removed her latex gloves and tossed them into the waste basket. Then she turned back to face Cari.

"Yes, Cari, you are pregnant. Not too far along, but you are."

Cari felt her shoulders slump. "It's been three weeks," she murmured. "November 28th. Thanksgiving Day." She wrapped her arms around herself. "I never even thought about getting pregnant. I just wanted to forget. To get on with my life. What do I do now?"

Teresa Lewis approached Cari and put her hands on her shoulders. "Well, first you cry. Then you go over your options. You consider your job. You think about who you want or need to tell. And maybe you consider pressing charges against the man who raped you." Cari stiffened. "I only said 'maybe'. No one can force you to. That's your choice. But, it you think there's any danger of him hurting another woman, then please consider it. Okay?"

"I don't know what he'd do. I just remember how shocked I was. And how scared. It was like he was a different person. But even if I thought he might do this to someone else, I don't think I could prove anything in court." She choked on her tears. "And he knows it, too."

"Okay. I want you to get dressed. Then come and sit in my office and we'll work through this together. One step at a time. Nobody is going to rush you. I'm not the only doctor on call tonight. Ask as many questions as you need to. Stay as long as you want. All right?"

"Thank you, Teresa."

The doctor patted Cari's shoulder. "I'm just glad you came to me, Cari. You've helped so many other girls when you've volunteered here. Now let *us* help *you*." She took a step back. "I'll see you in a few minutes."

Back in the office, Teresa went over Cari's options with her. "If you choose abortion, Cari, I can't help you."

Cari immediately shook her head. "No. I wouldn't. I *couldn't.*"

"Glad to hear it. I rather suspected that when you came here. Okay. What about adoption? There are several agencies that I could put you in touch with. Either private or open adoption. I'm sure you know that there are many couples who would love to have a baby come into their home."

Again Cari shook her head, though not as forcefully as before. "No. If I'm going to carry this baby for nine months, I don't think I could give it up." She leaned forward in the chair. "I mean, it's not like I'm sixteen or something. I'd be 31 by then. I have my own apartment, a car, and a good job. I could provide for this baby. Couldn't I?"

Teresa smiled and reached for Cari's trembling hand. "Only you can answer that. If you want to keep this baby, I won't try to talk you out of it. But other people might. Have you thought about your church? Are you prepared for what people will say? The questions they may ask. You might even want to start going to a new church, one where nobody knows you. Just think of an answer before the questions start coming."

"I have to tell Mark," she breathed. "I don't know how I'm going to do that, but I know I have to. And I have to tell him before I go to anybody else. We go to the same church. It's been so awkward for the past couple of weeks, even being in the same building with him." She got up and began to pace.

"You could write him a letter. Or call him. Or meet him in a public place. You set the terms, Cari. Don't let him intimidate you."

"I think I have to do this in person. I guess I need to *see* for myself how he reacts. Somehow a letter just wouldn't be good enough." She sat down again. "Am I making any sense?"

"Yes, you are. You're a lot more rational than you may be feeling right now. Okay, other than Mark, who do you want to know?"

"Mike and Julie. They're like my parents. Especially since mine died two years ago." She toyed with the collar of her sweater. "I know they'll do anything that they can to help me. And my pastor. He'll need to know. Other than them, I guess I'll have to tell my boss, won't I?"

"If you plan to go on maternity leave it'll definitely be necessary," Teresa said with a smile. "What about work? Will you keep on patrolling? Or will you apply for a desk job, seeing as you just got promoted?"

"I'm still getting used to that idea. I really don't see myself as the 'desk' type. But I obviously can't work a beat. I'll have to see what the powers that be have to say about it. I'll likely do some kind of administrative duty. That's normal procedure."

"Fine. So, see what your bosses have to say about it, and work from there."

Cari yawned. "I think I'd better get home. I barely make it past supper without needing to lie down. Is that normal?"

"For many women it is. But I do want you to start taking some prenatal vitamins. Especially with the kind of work you do. Get as much rest as you need. And try to eat properly."

"Breakfast is a write off at the moment," Cari commented with a frown. "I'm surprised that Mike hasn't mentioned my lack of interest in coffee and donuts either." She shuddered just thinking about it. "I'm okay for lunch and supper."

"Good. But at least try for a mid-morning snack until the nausea settles down. It's very important for you and the baby."

Cari's right hand instinctively went to her still flat abdomen. "I'm really pregnant," she whispered. She looked at Teresa. "I've never been so scared in my life."

———— ‹‹()›› ————

"And you actually think that I'm the father?" Mark asked with obvious outrage.

Cari leaned back in her chair. They were in a crowded restaurant, but she still didn't feel totally safe with him. "You *know* you are, Mark. Nobody else *could* be."

He shook his head as he gripped the edge of the table. "You can't prove that."

"Not at the moment," she replied. "But after the baby is born it would be easy enough."

"You wouldn't dare! I'm not about to pay child support for some kid that may or may not be mine."

"I don't want you to," she retorted. "I just came here to tell you

I'm pregnant. I figured if you could change my life so drastically, I could at least let you know." She slid her chair back and moved to get up.

"Wait a sec. Who else knows so far?"

"Just my doctor. Why?"

"Then you could still get rid of it. Forget it ever happened. Our whole relationship was a mistake."

Cari stared at him in amazement. "I can't believe you said that! You're an obstetrician. You deliver babies every week. And now you want me to abort your own child?"

"I don't know that it is mine! Besides, that shouldn't make any difference."

"Oh yes it should, *Doctor* Hamilton. But I can see that it doesn't." She got up from her chair and slung her purse over her shoulder.

"Cari?"

"What?" She looked into his eyes.

His familiar grin replaced his previous scowl. "Merry Christmas."

Chapter 4

Cari knocked on the door with the nameplate reading 'Lieutenant Harvey Steele'. She rubbed her sweaty palms together while she waited for a reply.

"Come in," he called.

Cari turned the knob and leaned against the door. She tried to take a deep breath, but found that she couldn't.

Lieutenant Steele looked up from the pile of papers on his desk and smiled. "Well, Sgt. Daniels. Just the person I need to see. I've been going over possible assignments for you. Have a seat please."

Cari reached for the back of the nearest chair and managed to sit down. "There's something I need to tell you, Sir, before any assignments are given. Something you need to read first." She withdrew a folded sheet of paper from her pocket and passed it to him, unable to keep her hand from shaking. "This may change your plans."

Lt. Steele took the paper, a frown on his face. He remained silent while he read, though his brows furrowed. When he'd read it, he set the paper on his desk, and removed his glasses. "Well, to say that I'm surprised would be an understatement, Cari. Knowing you for as long as I have, and knowing your firm, and even vocal stance on this very topic, I'm not even sure where to begin." He rubbed his forehead before putting his glasses back on. "Is there anything you'd care to tell me about this letter?"

"Yes, Sir, I would," she stammered. "I just – could you please give me a moment?"

"Of course. Take as long as you need." He leaned forward on his elbows and clasped his hands together.

"I – I was raped, Sir," she whispered. "About a month ago. I just found out Friday that I'm – that I'm pregnant."

"I rather suspected that, Cari," he replied in a fatherly tone. "Like I said, I've known you a long time. Can you tell me why you didn't report the assault when it happened?"

Cari nodded her head. "It was my fiancé, Sir. And I – I didn't think I'd be able to prove anything." She blinked to keep back her tears, but she couldn't prevent her hands from trembling. "I – I was scared. And confused. I just didn't think I could make it through the questioning, let alone court." She shook her head. "I wonder now how other women are able to do it."

"You're going to go through with the pregnancy?"

Cari jerked her head up. "Yes, Sir. That's why I brought the letter to you."

"That's what I assumed, but I needed to know. Have you told Mike yet?"

She shook her head. "N—not yet. I'm going over there tomorrow night."

"He'll miss having you for a partner, you know. He's been waiting for you to be reassigned since your promotion."

"I know. We've talked about that, Sir."

"What about here at the station? I can assign you to desk duty, or administrative work, that's not the problem. I just wonder, would it be easier for you if you went to another division?"

Cari frowned. "I don't understand, Sir."

"Well, to be plain, what are you planning to tell the other officers and staff about your pregnancy? Have you even thought about that yet?"

"Yes, Sir, all weekend. But I'd rather not transfer. I think that would be even worse. At least here people already know me, and what I believe. Not that I intend to tell them exactly what happened, but the majority at least know that I was engaged. I'm hoping that the rumor mill won't go too wild."

"All right, no transfer. How are you feeling, physically? Any problems?"

Cari shook her head. "Just the normal kind. Nausea when I get up. But that should pass after a couple of months." She straightened her shoulders. "I'll be fine, Sir."

"I certainly hope so. For the time being, however, I want you to take a few days off."

"But, I -- "

"Hear me out," he replied, his upraised right hand stopping her flow of words. "It's obvious that you're tired. Under a great deal of stress. You still have people to talk to, and I have to decide on an appropriate assignment for you. Take a few days to think things over, Cari. If you decide you'd like a transfer, I'll understand. But I don't want this to be impulsive."

"Sir, I've never been impulsive in my life," she protested. "But I'll take your advice." She got to her feet and reached out her right hand. "Thank you, Lieutenant. I appreciate your concern."

He shook her hand, even as he got up. "You're welcome, Sergeant. Now, let's plan to discuss this again next week. By then we should both have some clear direction to follow."

Cari nodded, released his hand, and left the room.

———— ≈«◉»≈ ————

Christmas Eve arrived in all its usual pageantry, but Cari hardly noticed. She was consumed with the momentous change in her own life. By the time she stepped into the den at Mike and Julie's, little else seemed to matter.

"I need to talk with all of you," she said, including Michael and Christa in her statement. Her sober expression must have been obvious for Mike simply nodded as he reached for Julie's hand. They sat down on the sofa. Christa moved to the rocker. Michael chose to sit on the floor in front of the fire. Cari remained standing. Her gaze finally rested on Mike.

"There isn't any easy way to say this, so please bear with me." She bit her lip. "I haven't been totally honest with any of you about some things. Now there's no way around the truth." She noticed that Julie edged a little closer to Mike. "When I went to Mark's on Thanksgiving Day, we didn't just argue about a wedding date." She blinked furiously, but the tears came anyway. "He raped me." She heard Julie gasp and Michael mumbled something. "I begged him to stop, but he threatened to hurt me. I have no idea what he would have done to me, but I was terrified. So, I – I stopped resisting."

Cari moved to the wing chair and slumped into it. "Then he told me to get out. And he wanted the ring back. He told me that I could never prove rape. He was maybe right. I didn't tell anybody. Until this week. But I'm pregnant. I told Mark yesterday, and he – he suggested an abortion. He won't even admit that the baby is his. I went to Pastor Hiller this afternoon. He wants me to keep coming to church, but he's going to ask Mark to attend elsewhere."

"I'm so sorry, Cari," Mike said, tears in his eyes. "That's why you missed work. And why you were so edgy. And then you forgot about the exam results. I should have known there was more to it than a broken engagement." His expression took on a note of grief. "What I said about Mark's attitude – I was dead on, but I didn't know that he'd hurt you. Can you ever forgive me?"

"You didn't know, Mike. He was like Jekyll and Hyde. Everything was okay, and then . . ." She shook her head. "It just didn't register until it was too late."

"Scary," whispered Christa. "Makes me want to stay clear of the guys at school. Even the Christian ones." She shuddered.

"I didn't mean to scare you, Christa. I just wanted you to know the truth." She forced a smile. "I'm sure not all guys are like Mark.

Just be more cautious that I was."

"But you're a cop and he still fooled you! How am I supposed to figure them out?"

"I guess I was blinded a little by my own feelings. I guarantee, I won't let it happen again."

"What about the baby?" Michael asked. "Are you going to resign from police work?"

"No. But I'll have to switch to a desk job. And then take a maternity leave."

"If you let anybody else baby sit for you, Cari, I'll never speak to you again," stated Julie with her usual intensity.

Cari actually laughed, and the hovering tension eased. "I was hoping that you'd offer, Julie. But I wasn't sure if you'd be willing to play 'Grandma' just yet."

Julie looked and Michael and Christa for a moment before grinning. "Only for the 'adopted' ones, Cari. The other two better wait a few years."

"Amen to that," Michael replied. "I have every intention of being an old man before I even consider marriage."

———•((0))•———

"I've decided to assign you to the reception area, Cari," stated Lieutenant Steele. "Belinda Franco has just left for her own maternity leave, and the position is available. You'll be able to stay off your feet part of the time, and the shift will be consistent." He smiled as he passed her a folder of information. "There's a new officer that you'll be working with. She's a rookie, but she's not your average officer. Take a look for yourself."

Cari glanced down at the folder and opened it. "Officer Pamela Martin. Just completed her academy training. Excelled in the obstacle course and physical training." Cari lifted an eyebrow. "Really? It says here that she's only 5'7", and 125 lbs. That's a bit of a surprise."

"Keep reading. Police work is her *second* career choice."

"Bachelor of Science in Nursing. Two years in the trauma unit at *Cedars Sinai*." Cari raised her head. "And now she wants to be a cop too? A little ambitious, is she?"

The Lieutenant smiled. "She seems to enjoy the challenge. She said it was the only way she could combine her two greatest goals, healthcare and police work."

"So why didn't she become a paramedic, or something? Besides, how does she combine these two things? Isn't scheduling a nightmare?"

"Actually, she only needs to maintain a minimal amount of hours at the hospital in order to keep her nursing license valid. And once she completes her police training, she'll be able to work around the shift schedules."

"Is she good at paperwork?"

Lt. Steele laughed. "She's done plenty as a nurse. As a matter of fact, her reports are not only thorough, they're legible. She's also excellent at interacting with the public. Don't let her size or her looks fool you. She scored higher than several of the male rookies during the physical training."

Cari felt herself smile. "Oh, that should have been interesting. I remember doing that with the driving course. And the target range." She closed the folder. "Okay, you've got me really curious now. When do I start?"

"Right after the holidays are over."

—»«◊»«—

"So, I lose you to a desk," Mike joked over lunch. "I feel like I'm being jilted." He smiled but Cari could see the sober look in his eyes. "I'll really miss working with you. You're one of the best partners I've ever had. I'm not eager to break in a new one."

"Sure you are, Mike," she replied with a cheeky grin. "Then you can con them into buying all the coffee for the first six months." She toyed with her paper napkin. "Besides, I'm getting kind of used to the idea of being a mother. I'm scared witless, but I'm somehow excited too." She shrugged. "I know that doesn't make any sense."

"It doesn't have to." He placed his hand on her arm. "I'm just glad that you're working through this."

Cari bit her lip. "Well, I wasn't ready to crawl under a rock, so I guess I'll just have to see what happens."

"Just know that you've got friends who are praying for you."

"I'm counting on that, Mike. More than you know."

Chapter 5

"Go ahead and take your lunch break, Pam," Cari said to the rookie officer who was working the desk with her on April 4th, 1992. "I'll be fine for a half hour. It's been really slow this shift anyway."

"Are you sure, Sergeant? I mean, I could wait."

"I'll be fine. Besides, Officer Patterson is planning to meet me here when I take my break. So, just go ahead. If I need you for something, I'll just page you."

"All right, Sergeant. Thanks." Pam got up from her chair. "I won't be long." She eased away from the desk, though she glanced back at Cari a couple of times.

Cari smiled. She enjoyed working with Pam Martin. Actually, the woman fascinated her. Just as Lieutenant Steele had told her, Pam's work was neat, efficient, and she was great with the public. It didn't hurt that she'd aced the obstacle course either. *Glad she's on our side. She's not short on brains, or work ethics.* She'd been keeping tabs on Cari's health since they'd started working together.

Cari worked for a few minutes before she heard someone come into the station. She raised her head and smiled. That is until she was met be a fierce scowl.

A young man, perhaps in his late twenties, stood near the desk. He was dressed casually, though his clothing appeared to be expensive. His neck muscles were taut, his eyes somewhat glassy. He was about six feet tall, maybe 150 pounds.

"How can I help you, sir?" Cari asked, her voice steady, but her manner cautious.

"I want my car," he hissed. "It got towed, and I want it back."

Cari frowned. "I'm sorry, sir, but your car wouldn't be here. Did someone call you about it?"

"Yes, and they said to come *here*!"

"All right, calm down, sir, and I'll see if I can figure out the mix up for you. What kind of car is it?"

"A '92 Jag. Dark green. Custom plate that says *RICHBOY*. And I want it now."

Cari was starting to wish that Pam would cut her break short, or that Mike would stroll in early. Neither happened. "Let me check on the computer, and I'll see where it was taken." She turned slightly, to be able to glance at the monitor. After a moment, she found the information. "Okay. It's not here, it's at the next division over." She turned her head, but he wasn't standing in front of the desk anymore.

The man was directly behind Cari's chair, obviously having gone around the desk. He grabbed her by the shoulders and spun her around.

"I want my car right now! Do you hear me?" He shook her so violently that her head snapped back and slammed against the unyielding wood of the reception desk.

"It's not -- " Her words were cut off when he jerked her up out of the chair and threw her against the desk, cracking a couple of ribs on her left side, and knocking the wind out of her. Before she could even react, he brought his knee up into her groin, pulling her towards the impact. Her knees buckled, but he delivered a second blow. Then he shoved her to the floor.

Cari tried to focus her vision and take a deep breath. Both proved difficult. She was on her right side, her holstered .38 beneath her. She couldn't get onto her back, since she was pressed against the desk. Just as she tried to ease up from the floor, she saw his booted foot coming at her. She covered her face with her left arm. The boot caught her in the ribs, breaking the ones that had already cracked. A second kick filled her mouth with blood and vomit.

"I'm going to dance on your grave, pig. But first I'm going to put you in it."

"Hey! What are you doing?" Mike yelled. "Get out from behind the desk."

"Make me, pig!" the assailant yelled right back. He kicked Cari a third time, further pulverizing her left side.

"Cari!" Pam screamed as she entered the room, dropping a cup of coffee onto the floor.

"Freeze!" This from Mike, his voice closer than before.

The final kick caved in the left side of Cari's chest, and her heart skipped crazily. She wanted to scream, but she couldn't even breathe.

The sound of the shot, and the tumbling over of the assailant brought no relief for Cari. The assault was over, but her fight was just starting.

Pam rushed over to Cari, hesitated a second, then checked for a pulse on the assailant. "He's dead," she stated, her voice calm and authoritative. "Call for an ambulance, Officer Patterson. Then come and help me." She knelt down and touched Cari's face. "Don't give up on us, Cari." She checked her pulse and frowned. Then she looked up at Mike, who was now towering over both of them. "Call somebody and get them to bring a stack of towels from the locker rooms, and grab the first aid kit. Move it."

Pain pressed in upon Cari. So many kinds, and in so many parts of her body. Hot, piercing, dull, hammering, pulsating. She felt as though her head would explode from lack of oxygen. She clawed at the bloody floor by her face. *I can't breathe! Why can't I just pass out? I can't stand this pain.*

The room was filling with officers, who'd no doubt heard the shot. Pam was still issuing orders, heedless of rank, or lack thereof.

"Somebody give me a hand over here. She's got a flail chest, and she won't be able to breathe until we can get it stabilized."

It was Lieutenant Rawlins who complied. He knelt down and did whatever Pam instructed. A moment later, despite excruciating pain, Cari was able to get a couple of gulps of air.

Sirens wailed, and medics soon entered the area. Pam was still giving orders.

"Flail chest. Multiple fractures of ribs and sternum, possible cardiac tamponade, damaged kidney and spleen. Heavy internal bleeding. Pulse rapid and irregular." She paused a second. "Pregnant, approximately 20 weeks. Get the other vitals, stat, and set up an EKG."

Cari closed her eyes while they worked. They cut off her clothes, something that would have humiliated her in other circumstances. Monitors were attached. IV's were started in both arms. Through it all, breathing was nearly impossible.

"We have to open her airway or she'll never make it to the hospital," Pam stated.

"Begging your pardon, officer, but are you qualified to do this type of thing?" one of the medics dared to ask.

Pam sighed. "Yes! I also work in the trauma unit at *Cedars Sinai*. Now get the kit, and an ambubag, and let's get busy."

Cari opened her eyes in time to see the scalpel in Pam's hand. Her body went rigid. Pam smiled and touched her shoulder. "C'mon, Cari, we're only trying to help you. Give me a few seconds, and you'll be able to breathe better. Trust me, Sergeant."

Cari closed her eyes again, but she could feel everything they were doing. A moment later, she realized that Pam had been truthful. The first rush of air from the ambubag was a blessed relief. *If only my heart would quit skipping and fluttering.*

"Okay, let's get her out of here," Pam ordered.

Just then, the EKG squealed, and all Cari could hear was Pam yelling "CPR!"

Pam Martin and two medics frantically fought to keep Cari alive on the way to *Cedars Sinai.*

"She's gonna need open heart surgery as soon as we can get her there," remarked the attendant who was holding Cari's ribcage and monitoring the EKG.

"I know, but we're all she's got for the time being," Pam murmured. "What's the ETA?"

"About two more minutes."

It took them three, and Cari went into cardiac arrest again just as they wheeled her into the trauma unit. An ever growing group of personnel worked to keep her alive.

"We've got a pulse, but it's not steady. Get those scans, stat. Get Dr. Wilson prepped in OR 3. And Dr. Steinbach, too. We may have a cerebral hemorrhage, here. We need more blood. Use type O if we have to. She's lost too much already."

Cari survived the surgery, but her heart stopped in both the OR and the Recovery Room. A temporary pacemaker was attached to her battered chest, in an effort at stabilizing her condition. Her skin was ashen. Her heavily bandaged ribs moved rhythmically with the force of the ventilator. Twin IV's kept fluid pumping into her arms. An EKG monitor was still hooked up to her. An automatic BP cuff kept track of her vital signs. And two nurses hovered nearby, checking her every few minutes. Her unstable condition had landed her in CCU, but she didn't wake up long enough to find out.

"What, exactly, is wrong with Cari's heart, Doctor?" Mike asked as he spoke with Dr. Ken Wilson. "She's always been extremely fit up to now."

"Her heart lining was damaged by the bone fragments from

her ribcage, Officer Patterson." He shook his head. "Her chest looked as though she'd been in a car wreck. I still can't believe she sustained so much damage from a few kicks. What was the maniac wearing?"

"Hiking boots with steel toes and sole plates." Mike shuddered. He looked up at the surgeon once more. "I've never seen anybody with such a broken chest before. Will it even heal properly?"

"We can only hope so," the surgeon replied. "She's got more than enough pins and plates in there to set off a metal detector now. But we'll have to keep taking x-rays to determine how much healing is taking place."

"She's lost so much blood. How long will it take her to recover from that?"

"Months, most likely. Maybe a year." Dr. Wilson picked up his fountain pen and rolled it back and forth in his hands. "Frankly, it's a miracle that she even made it here. Not many would have. Her kidney was almost beyond repair. Her spleen was lacerated. She's got a long road ahead of her – and that's if we can get her heart to cooperate."

"Will she need more surgery?"

"I don't think she could survive any more right now. We'll do what we can with drugs and the pacemaker."

"Can I see her, please? Even for a minute."

The doctor shook his head and put down his pen. "I'm afraid not. Her condition is so unstable. We just can't allow it. Once we transfer her to ICU, then brief visits will be possible. Sorry, but that's the best that I can tell you."

Mike got to his feet, overwhelmed with the enormity of Cari's condition. "She lost the baby, didn't she?" he asked in little more than a whisper.

"I'm afraid so. Her body simply couldn't sustain it after the kind of traumatic injuries she received." He smiled slightly. "But, if she can make a full recovery, she should be able to have children in the future. That's one part of her that wasn't injured."

Mike nodded and turned towards the door. "Will you let me know if there's any change in her condition?"

"Certainly. Since she listed you as her emergency contact we'll be keeping you posted. Try not to worry, sir. If she's managed to pull through so far, she still stands a decent chance."

"I hope that you're right, Doctor."

Mike didn't see Cari for the next ten days.

Mark Hamilton looked down at Cari's face and blinked back the tears pressing at his lids. *She looks awful. How did she even survive? Her x-rays are such a mess. And her heart still isn't responding properly.* He steadied himself against the metal rail of the bed. *And the baby. It was a perfect little boy. What's she going to say when she can talk? What will I say? What can I say at this point? 'Sorry for getting you pregnant, Cari'? Maybe I should just stay away from her, like the last four months.* He shook his head. *I'm sorry, Cari. I don't know if that will make any difference to you, but I am sorry.*

Cari was aware of two things when she woke up: agonizing pain throughout her body, and constant noise. Voices, machines, buzzers. It hurt to swallow, to breathe, and to even move her hands. Tears slipped down her cheeks to the thin pillow beneath her throbbing head. *I'd rather be unconscious if it hurts this much to be awake.* She opened her eyes with a start when someone gently touched her cheek. She recoiled when she saw that it was Mark Hamilton. *Go away! I don't want you here. Leave me alone.* She frantically scanned the room and saw that a nurse was still with her. *He won't hurt me if we're not alone, will he?*

"Shhh. It's okay, Cari. I just wanted to see how you're doing," he said, in the soft tone she hadn't heard in months. "This is the first time I've seen you awake." He wiped away her falling tears. "I guess the pain must still be pretty bad." A brief smile curved his mouth. "I'm glad to see that you're such a fighter."

Cari squeezed her eyes shut as the pain around her heart grew worse. She could feel beads of perspiration forming on her face. Mark's hand moved away, only to be replaced by a cool cloth.

"Take it easy," he soothed. "Try to relax."

How can I relax with you touching me? She tried to turn her head, but the ventilator tubing constricted her movement. Mark seemed to get the message anyway.

"Okay," he sighed. "I'll go for now. But when you're feeling better, we need to talk."

Cari opened her eyes and was stunned to see tears in his.

"I'm sorry, Cari. For everything." He glanced at the nurse and then turned to go.

Cari moaned as the pain surged through her body. *No! I can't forgive him, God. Not even if he is sorry for what happened.* The nurse stroked her hand. *Can't somebody stop this pain?* She fought it until exhaustion closed in upon her senses.

Chapter 6

Mike hardly recognized Cari as he stood next to her bed in ICU. She was so pale, and her face seemed almost gaunt. She'd lost several pounds already, and he'd been warned that she'd likely lose several more. She was still hooked up to almost all of the equipment, except for being down to one IV. She tried to smile when she noticed him standing there, but she wasn't able to speak yet. She was being weaned from the ventilator, but the tube was still in place.

Mike reached for her right hand and held it in both of his. "You must be going crazy with all this noise," he said, fishing for anything to start a one-sided conversation. "I know how much you like peace and quiet." He felt her fingers clasping his. "Julie is bugging me to come in here, too, but I told her it just wouldn't be fair until you could answer some of her questions. So she's holding off until you're moved to another room." He saw her moving her lips and tried to figure out what she was trying to say.

" 'Don't wait'? Is that what you're saying?" He thought she formed a 'yes'. "So, you don't want Julie to wait. Well, I guess I'm out voted then. She'll likely be here tomorrow."

"Just another minute or so, sir," said the nurse as she came in. "Ms. Daniels tires very easily."

Mike tried not to laugh as Cari frowned at the nurse's back. He squeezed her fingers. "I have to get to work anyway. But I'll be back as often as I can." He watched her lips again and then he smiled. " 'Pray'? We've been doing little else, Cari. And we won't stop now." He glanced at his watch. "I'd better get moving." He leaned down and touched her face. "See you later, Partner."

"You'll have to come home with us after they let you out of here," stated Julie as she held Cari's hand. "You'll need lots of TLC, and I'm just the person to dish it out."

Cari stared at her friend and tried to think of a way to protest. Then she realized that protest would be futile — even if she could talk. If Julie had a plan in mind, not much would keep it from happening. So she smiled slightly. *I'll be glad to go anywhere when they let me out of here.*

"Michael and Christa have been calling every day from school. They're both worried about you. And Mike keeps complaining about breaking in a new partner. He's anxious to get you back." She frowned. "But the doctors just keep telling us we'll 'have to wait and see' how much progress you make." She sighed loud enough for the nurse to hear her. "Won't you be glad to sleep in a regular bed again? I know I always hated sleeping at the hospital. And think of what it'll be like to drink a nice cup of tea." She gently touched one of the bruises from Cari's IV. "*Anything* tastes good after too long on these."

Cari tried to nod her head enough to agree with Julie. *I barely remember what water is like, never mind food. And I'm tired of feeling like a pin cushion.*

"Actually, despite his complaining, I think Mike kind of likes his latest partner. He's in his mid thirties, I think. A widower with two kids. He just transferred from Sacramento. I guess he wanted a fresh start in a new place. I haven't met him yet, but I will soon.

Mike says they'll be coming to church this week." She grinned at Cari. "Imagine that — another Christian paired up with Mike. Isn't God good to us?"

Cari's eyes filled with tears. *I want to believe that, Julie. But I'm stuck in this room. Everything hurts. I can't talk. And Mark — I don't want to forgive him, Julie. How can I? But I'm still alive, aren't I? I could have died. I should have died I guess. Oh, I just don't understand any of this.*

"Hey, I didn't mean to make you cry, Cari. I'm sorry." Julie touched her cheek. "I'd better go before they refuse to let me come back again. I'll see you in a couple of days. And try not to worry too much. You'll have a chance to say some of the things that are bottled up right now. Just hang on until then."

Cari continued to cry until after she was given the next dose of medication. Then she drifted into a sleep filled with troubling dreams.

⟝ ⟨⟨◉⟩⟩ ⟞

"His name is Rick Benson," Mike said when he visited Cari the next time. "He's a really nice guy. It's too bad about his wife. She was only 33 years old. I think he moved out here for the sake of his kids, though. Seems they've been having a hard time adjusting to the loss." He sighed and muttered more to himself than to Cari. "I can't even imagine what it would be like." He looked up at her and grinned. "Don't you just love listening to your visitors shooting off their mouths this way? I bet you've got all sorts of things stored up for later on. Then you'll get even with us."

He shifted his weight from one foot to the other. "Seriously, it's great to be working with another Christian. Rick's been asking about you each shift."

Cari raised her eyebrows in surprise. *We've never even met each other.*

"We pray for you on our breaks." He looked at her intently. "I don't believe in coincidence, Cari. I think God brought Rick into the picture to help all of us. He needs new friends. And I'm sure you're glad for any prayers on your behalf. And, if you wouldn't mind, I'm pretty sure that Rick would come and visit you too."

Cari tried to shake her head. She also mouthed a distinct 'No!'. She made a gesture with her right arm, taking in the machines, as well as herself. 'No.'

"Okay, I get the message. I won't let him near you right now. Maybe once you can talk again. Or when you come to our place. I shouldn't tease, I guess, but I don't know what else to do when you can't yell at me, or give me a whack on the arm." His smile brightened his blue eyes. "Take care. I miss having you around."

Cari gripped his hand a little tighter. 'Thanks', she mouthed.

⸺ ((◉)) ⸺

It took another week in ICU before Cari was fully weaned from the ventilator. She was thankful to be moved to a private room, and less noise, but she was quick to discover just how much effort it took to breathe on her own again. And she was still confined to the bed. The slightest exertion messed up her heartbeat, and her right leg was hard to move. Her doctors had told her it would be weeks before she could walk properly, possibly months. She could whisper, but barely loud enough to be understood. And every sentence left her wondering why she'd made the effort at all.

Mike and Julie were finally allowed to visit her at the same time. They came in with a small cactus plant. It had a gorgeous pink flower in full bloom. Julie set it on the window sill before sitting near the bed.

"Thanks," murmured Cari. "It's pretty."

Julie grinned. "Oh, don't thank us. Rick sent it home with Mike and asked us to bring it over to you. There's a note to go with it. Would you like to see it?"

"A note?" Cari asked in surprise. "He doesn't even know who I am."

"Oh, he'd like to," Julie replied with a conspiratorial look at Mike. "He was over for lunch on Sunday, with his son and daughter. Mike and I told him lots about you. And showed him a few pictures. He'd definitely like to meet you."

Cari was more flustered than ever, and Mike was quick to notice.

"Julie, enough teasing," he said softly. "Just let her read the note."

Julie was immediately contrite. "Sorry, Cari. I just wanted to see you smile. And maybe to peak your curiosity a little. I guess I wasn't being fair." She reached into her purse and withdrew a very plain looking card. Cari managed to hold it in her left hand and open it with her right.

'Dear Cari;

I thought you'd likely seen enough flowers and bouquets by now, so I wanted to get you something a little different. I had another reason too. Cacti have always fascinated me. As a matter of fact I've done a fair bit of research on them. I think they're a good example for Christians. You see, even when we're caught in the middle of a 'prickly' situation, God can still make something good come out of it. So, when you look at the cactus, try to think about the pretty flower that manages to grow in the middle of all those prickles. I hope you're soon well enough to have another visitor. Mike and Julie make you out to be slightly less than an angel. I haven't met anyone that nice in quite a while.

God bless.

Rick Benson.'

Cari set the card down and kept her hand on top of it. *No way am I letting these two read this!* "Please tell him 'thanks' for me," she said to Mike. "But – no 'visitors' yet."

"What?" Mike asked.

"He'll know what I mean." Cari sighed and closed her eyes. "I'm sorry guys. I'm not very good company today." She winced as she shifted position. "I think I'd better try to rest."

"Okay," Julie replied. "We'll come back in a couple of days. Don't wear yourself out trying to entertain us."

Cari smiled, but she was too tired to even open her eyes again. "Thanks," she mumbled. She never even heard them leave the room. She fell asleep thinking about cacti with pretty flowers on them.

Cari was staring at the cactus when Mark entered her room. She immediately shifted position and regretted doing so. "Why are you here?" she asked through gritted teeth. "I don't want to talk with you."

Mark didn't move any closer to her, and he looked as nervous as she felt. "Fine. But will you please at least *listen* to me? Then I promise to leave you alone. Okay?"

She hesitated. *Why now? Why couldn't he have come to me months ago?* She bit her lip. *Would it have made a lot of difference? I didn't want to see him then either.* "Okay. Talk." She reached for her water glass with a trembling hand. She managed to get it to her mouth and take a sip, but she had trouble returning it to the tray. Mark stepped over to the bed and took the glass from her. Then he sat down on the chair.

"Thanks," he said. He passed his hands over his face, which was glistening with sweat. Then he placed them in his lap. "I won't even ask you to forgive me at this point, Cari. I know that I don't deserve it. But I need to tell you how sorry I am. For hurting you like I did. About the baby," he whispered. "It was a boy." He looked right into her eyes. "Did anyone tell you that?"

She shook her head, not trusting her voice.

"I was the one they called into the Trauma Unit. I was filling in for another doctor that shift." He wiped his face again. "The other surgeons were busy enough just trying to keep your heart going.

They asked me to do a quick D&C." He swallowed and cleared his throat. "You'd already miscarried, and they were trying to get you ready for the OR." He put his head down and remained silent for a few moments. "I knew it was my baby, Cari." He looked up again, tears in his eyes. "Oh, I'd told myself a pile of lies since Christmas, but I always knew you were carrying my child."

Cari bit her lip and clutched at her blanket with her left hand.

"There was nothing wrong with him. He was a perfectly formed little boy. But I guess your whole system had suffered too much shock. Your heart kept stopping, and you couldn't breathe. Neither could he." He made no effort to brush away his falling tears. "I will never forget that day."

"You wanted me to have an abortion!" she rasped. "So you got what you wanted after all." She turned her head away.

"No, I didn't, Cari. Haven't you listened to a thing I just said? What I said at Christmas was just to hurt you. I knew you would never consider it. I was pretty sure that you'd decide to keep the baby."

"Yes, I was going to do that, Mark," she said with a stony glare. "With or without your help."

"I would have offered to help."

"Now's a convenient time to say so! When you'll never have to." She moaned and braced her left side with her right hand.

"Cari, I was keeping track on my calendar. I had figured out the due date. I was thinking about child support payments. Or maybe a trust fund. But I knew you didn't want to have anything to do with me."

She closed her eyes and tried to steady her breathing. Her heart was skipping again and she was no longer wearing the pacemaker. Her temples were throbbing.

"I still don't!" she cried. She opened her eyes but couldn't focus. She was determined to have her say though. "It's so easy for you – to be sorry now, isn't it? But we could have been -- married by now, if you hadn't -- " She gasped for air as her vision darkened.

Her hand went limp. The pain in her chest grew unbearable. "Mark – get – somebody."

Mark grabbed the buzzer lying next to her. Then he reached for the oxygen mask above her bed. He turned it on and fastened it around her face. "Take some deep breaths," he ordered, "before you black out completely." He put his left hand on her carotid artery. "Deep breaths! Your pulse has gone crazy again."

Cari heard footsteps but kept her eyes closed.

"Get Dr. Wilson, stat! Get an EKG monitor in here. And bring the crash cart just in case." The footsteps hurried away again.

Cari didn't know how long it took for her doctor to return with the nurse. She was too busy trying to breathe. She felt a cold stethoscope touch her chest, and she heard the man swear.

"We'll need the pacemaker again," he fumed. "We might still be able to keep her from going into arrest." Her breathing gradually eased. He tapped her cheek lightly, and she opened her eyes. Her vision was still slightly blurred, but no longer dark. "What are we supposed to do with you, young lady? You don't want to wear that glorified Walkman for the rest of your life, do you?" She could make out the concerned edge in his tone.

"No," she whispered behind the mask.

"Good. Then I suggest you behave yourself. I don't want to have to send you back to CCU."

Mark cleared his throat. "I'm afraid that I'm partly responsible, Ken. I got her –*agitated*."

Dr. Wilson folded his arms across his broad chest. "Well, this could be interesting, but I don't have time to discuss it." He looked back down at Cari. "I'm going to have the nurse give you a mild sedative. Then I expect you to rest for the remainder of the day. I'll schedule the procedure for the morning. And no visitors either. Is that clear, Sergeant Daniels?"

"Yes, Sir," she replied.

"Fine." He touched Mark's arm. "That goes for you too, Mark. Especially if you're the one who got her pulse messed up in the first place."

"I'm going," he assured his colleague. "Just as soon as Cari is resting comfortably."

Cari stared at Mark and Dr. Wilson frowned.

"All right. Or for ten minutes. Whichever comes first."

"Got it. Thanks, Ken."

Dr. Wilson wrote the medication order on Cari's chart, spoke with the nurse and left the room. Cari was given an injection shortly afterwards. Her breathing eased and she closed her eyes. After another few minutes, she felt the mask being removed and she looked up at Mark rather drowsily.

"I'm resting," she mumbled. "Go away."

He hung up the mask and shut off the oxygen. Then he patted her shoulder. "I'm going." He squeezed her arm gently. "And I won't bother you again until you get out of here. Okay?"

Cari yawned and closed her eyes. "Okay." She was getting very sleepy. "Later." She heard him leave the room. *What did I just agree to?* She licked her dry lips. *I'm not sure I meant to do that.*

Chapter 7

Cari opened her eyes to find Pam Martin entering the room. Instead of her LAPD uniform though, she was wearing nursing scrubs.

"Hi, Sergeant. How are you feeling today?" Pam approached the bed and casually picked up the chart. She frowned. "Back to the pacemaker again? What happened?" She rehung the chart on the footboard.

Cari wasn't exactly sure how to answer that. Just how much did hospital staff know about her former relationship with Mark? "My pulse went erratic again yesterday. Dr. Wilson wasn't happy. He's restricted my visitors for the moment too." She managed a smile. "But I guess you got around that little detail."

Pam smiled as she stepped forward and leaned against the side rail. "Yeah. I'm on my break at the moment, but I'm working till midnight. So, back to my first question. How are you feeling?"

Cari rolled her eyes. "Tired of being tired. And the days and nights have started to blend together for me." She licked her lips. "What about you? How's it going back at your *other* job?"

Pam didn't answer right away. "Actually, it's been a bit of a strain lately. I really pushed the envelope the day you got hurt. The brass still doesn't know what to do with me: tell me 'thanks' or 'you're finished'." She shrugged. "It'll be a little easier once they decide.

For the moment, I'm still on the schedule, and the payroll. But, I'm up for my next six month review shortly."

"Keep me posted." Cari shifted position and immediately felt pain shoot through her chest. She closed her eyes and exhaled slowly.

"Take it easy. You have to move in stages."

"I keep forgetting that," Cari muttered. "I can't get used to feeling so awkward." She looked at Pam once more. "Sorry to complain so much. I'm sure you could use a better break than this."

Pam laughed. "Oh right. I could sit in the nurse's lounge and listen to the other girls talk about which doctors they think are the cutest. No thanks. This is fine." She glanced at her watch. "I don't have long though."

"I really owe you, you know? If you hadn't been working with me that day--"

"Somebody else would've taken care of you."

Cari shook her head. "I don't think so. Mike was in shock, and the rest of the officers weren't much better. You actually knew what to do for me. I'm sorry I haven't thanked you before now."

"You're welcome." Pam looked at her watch again. "I'd better go. I'll try to stop in again soon. Make sure you get some rest. Dr. Wilson is the best cardiologist we've got. You want to stay on his good side."

"I know. Thanks for coming."

"No problem."

————))0((————

"I've been in the hospital for five weeks, Doctor. When will you let me out of here?" Cari asked as she sat up in bed. "I promise to behave. Besides, I won't be on my own for a while either."

Dr. Wilson studied her face for a full minute before answering her. "You're not ready yet, Cari. Even with the pacemaker, your heart isn't remaining stable. And we're still pumping you with antibiotics so you won't lose your left kidney. Your ribs are starting to heal, but slowly. And you can't put any weight on your right leg yet. Do you need any more reasons?"

Cari sighed as she leaned back against her pillow. "At least I'm breathing okay these days," she asserted. She gnawed on her bottom lip. "Dr. Wilson, I'm going crazy in here. If you've never been a patient, you can't possibly understand what I mean. I'm used to long shifts, and regular work outs in the gym. Bed rest and physiotherapy just aren't the same."

He smiled at her but shook his head. "I admire your spunk, but there's no way you're leaving yet. When you can walk with crutches, and when your heartbeat doesn't falter every time you get out of bed, then I'll consider it. And not a moment sooner." He gestured to the abundance of floral arrangements all around the room. "I suggest that you have more visitors from now on. Talk. Read. Play board games. It won't seem so much like a prison in here. But we'll still be able to keep a close eye on you."

Cari sobered at his words, and voiced a question that had been plaguing her for some time. "Doctor, will I be able to return to work, or is the heart problem a permanent one?"

He came and sat on the edge of her bed, and took her hand in his. "Cari, I've always tried to be straight with my patients. The truth of the matter is: we just don't know. At this point, we hope that further surgery won't be needed, but I can't guarantee that. There doesn't seem to be any infection, which is good. But, you could be using that pacemaker for quite awhile yet. Maybe until you've fully recovered from your other injuries. As for your job, well, I'd plan on an extended sick leave. Your benefits will cover all your expenses. You'll still receive most of your pay, since this happened while you were on duty. And, I happen to know that you have the option of taking a desk job when you return. I'd advise you to consider it. You may never be able to regain the stamina and energy level that you had previously."

"Sorry I asked," Cari murmured. "But thank you for not beating around the bush. If I'm headed for a career change, it's better to know in advance."

"I suppose so." He released her hand and stood up. "Well, I'd better get back to *my* job. Think about what I said. This doesn't have to be a prison."

"I give up, Cari!" Christa complained. "You beat me at *Scrabble* every time. Pick on somebody else for a change." She gathered the squares and holders into the box. "Where do you come up with some of those words, anyway?"

"I study the *Scrabble Dictionary* in my ample 'spare time', that's how," Cari remarked with a bored sigh.

"Well, I still think that you cheat," the 20 year old said with a pout. "Michael isn't even this good, and he's an English major." She grinned. "But I bet you couldn't beat Rick Benson, though. I think he's got the dictionary *memorized*. He always gets the highest score when he comes over." She eyed Cari as she folded the board and laid it in the box. "So, when are you going to quit hiding and let the guy meet you? I mean, it's not like it'd be a blind date or something. And he's really nice. If he wasn't so *old*, and didn't have two kids, I might be kind of interested myself."

"I don't know who is worse – you or your mother. You two have pestered me about letting Rick meet me every time you come here! Enough already. I'll eventually see the guy. I just don't want it to be in a hospital. Okay?" She smiled at Christa. "Even if he is as good-looking as Julie makes him out to be."

Christa laughed and covered her mouth. "Well, he is kind of cute." She shrugged. "Then again, so is his son, who is only sixteen. The looks must run in the family. At least on the male side. His daughter doesn't look much like him at all. She must take after her mother." Christa's expression sobered. "It must be awful to lose your mom when you're only ten. Tammy is pretty quiet when they come over. But she likes to be in the kitchen with Mom, just like I used to."

"I remember," Cari replied with a sigh. "Where have the years gone? You're already finished two years of college, and I'm a Sergeant." She frowned. "Well, sort of. And Michael was a bratty 12 year old the first time I met you guys. Hard to believe, isn't it? He's so well-behaved these days."

Christa giggled. "*Most* of the time, anyway. But he can still be a tease when he wants to. Like Dad." She looked at her watch. "I need to get home. I promised Mom I'd get the car back in time for her to go to the store for groceries."

"Thanks for coming. And for losing so graciously."

Christa rolled her eyes as she picked up her backpack. "Next time we play something else. Preferably something without letters. See you later."

"Bye."

Cari looked out the window after Christa left, and considered their conversation. *Okay, God, what am I supposed to do about Rick Benson? I have everybody breathing down my neck about this guy. Should I just meet him and get it over with? Or should I wait?* She thought back to what Christa had said about 'hiding'. *Is that what I've been doing?* She grinned. *Maybe he's worth meeting if he can play* Scrabble *as well as I do.*

⸺◉⸺

Cari made it the full length of the parallel bars in the therapy room without stumbling. She smiled at the therapist. "Next step: crutches. Then I'm getting out of here."

"That's what we're aiming for, Cari. But don't try to rush. It'll be harder to balance with the crutches. It'll take getting used to."

"I'll learn," she insisted, even as her arm began to tremble on the bars. Jill brought the wheelchair over and helped Cari into it. "Thanks. Man, I had no idea it could be so hard just to walk again." She shifted on the chair and put her right hand over her heart. "So far, so good," she said with a sigh. "No crazy rhythms for the past week. Here's hoping it'll keep behaving."

⸺∙«◉»∙⸺

"I'm going to let you go home tomorrow, Cari," Dr. Wilson said the last Friday of May. "But with a few strings attached. Namely, you still have to use the pacemaker. Secondly, we'll be sending a portable EKG with you. I want you to send a reading in to me every day for another month, at least. And I expect to see you back here once a week as well. Got it?"

"Is that all?" Cari asked warily.

"No. That was just for starters." He grinned at her. "I want you to keep track of everything that you eat and drink for the next month. You need to start putting some weight back on. And record every dose of medication, even over the counter drugs. And don't forget to take the vitamin supplements. Any questions?"

"How early can I leave tomorrow?"

Dr. Wilson laughed as her patted her shoulder. "Right after my morning rounds. Will that be soon enough?"

"After 7 ½ weeks in here, I think I can wait another day," she said with an audible sigh. Then she reached for his hand. "Thank you for taking such good care of me, Dr. Wilson. Even when I wasn't very cooperative."

"You're welcome. Now pay me back by making a full recovery. Deal?"

"I'll do my best."

⸺∙«◉»∙⸺

"I can't believe I'm exhausted after a *ride* from the hospital," Cari complained as she entered Mike and Julie's guest room. "I can't wait to lie down and rest, and I've hardly done anything." She laboriously made her way to the bed and eased to a sitting position. "You may soon regret having me here. I might prove to be lousy company." She leaned the crutches against the wall next to the bed.

"Well, you might get sick and tired of us too, so we'll be even. But I figure we can all give it a try." Julie fluffed up the top pillow. "Now, you take a nap while I fix some lunch."

"Yes, Ma'am," Cari replied with a tired smile. "That thought is getting more appealing by the second."

"Then quit thinking about it and do it. See you later." Julie went to the window, closed the curtains, and left the room.

Cari lay down and closed her eyes. *How can I be so tired? It's been almost two months. On the other hand, I could have died. So, I think I'll settle for tired. Thank You, God, for friends like Mike and Julie. There's no way I could manage on my own yet. And I don't know how long it'll be until I can. Thanks for taking care of me. Please continue to strengthen my body. I promise not to tell You to 'hurry' either. Oh, this bed is so soft after the one at the hospital. And nothing is covered with vinyl either. And I don't smell antiseptic. This is wonderful, God. But I'm so tired.*

Cari buried her face in the soft pillow and fell asleep. Julie had to wake her for lunch over an hour later.

————)(◍)(————

"Would you like to be alone while we go to church?" Mike asked. "Or would you like one of us to stay here with you?" It was Saturday night, and Cari had made it through the afternoon, but she was fading fast.

"I think I'll be fine on my own." At the skeptical look on his face she grinned. "I promise to just laze around all morning. Okay?

I haven't been all by myself for two months. That's utterly amazing. I'll probably be listening for footsteps all morning. But I'm sure I'll be fine."

"I'll take my pager, just in case you need us to come back early."

Cari reached for Mike's hand. "I'll be fine, Partner. Don't worry so much. The worst is past. I'm on the road to recovery."

"Thank God for that," he sighed. "You had me going crazy at first."

"I thought that's what I did when we were working together," she teased. She squeezed his fingers. "I don't know what I'd do without you and Julie."

"Then don't try to find out." He got up from the sofa and passed the crutches to her. "Off to bed with you, Sleeping Beauty. You look like you're been up all night."

She made a face as she struggled to a standing position. "Thanks a lot." She moved a few feet and then stopped. She laughed softly. "So, if I'm Sleeping Beauty, when does Prince Charming come along on his white horse?" She turned her head and saw a smug look on Mike's face.

"Actually, he drives a white *Mustang*, and he'll be here for lunch tomorrow. So I suggest you have a nice, long nap in the morning."

Cari nearly choked. And she debated about throwing a crutch at him, but didn't want to hit any of Julie's china figurines. "I'll get you for this, Mike Patterson," she warned. "I'm not sure when, but I will."

"I'll remember that, Cari – at your wedding reception." He laughed out loud as he sauntered out of the room.

Cari fumed for a moment, until she realized that her arms were weakening on the crutches. "I'll get you, Mike," she muttered to herself. "You and your whole match-making family."

Chapter 8

Cari woke up Sunday morning with a headache. She had a pillow over her face when Julie came in to tell her that breakfast was ready.

"Hey, Sleepyhead," she called. "Are you planning to greet the world some time today?"

Cari mumbled beneath the pillow and heard Julie approach the bed.

"Cari? Are you okay?" Julie's joking tone had changed to one of uncertainty. "Cari?"

Cari moved the pillow from her face and squinted her eyes at the light coming in from the hallway. "I didn't sleep too well, Julie. And I have a very bad headache." She swallowed as she thought of the bacon and eggs in the kitchen. "I – I think I better pass on breakfast at the moment." At Julie's look of protest, she added, "I'll be sure to have something later on. Please don't worry." She eased herself to a sitting position and rubbed her forehead and temples. "I just need to take something for my head and try to go back to sleep."

"If you say so," Julie replied. "But don't tell me not to worry. I'm a mother, remember?"

Cari tried to smile as she reached for her pain medication. "Okay. You worry and I'll sleep."

"Fair enough. Here, let me get that for you," she offered, as Cari reached for her half empty water glass.

"No. It's okay. I need to go to the bathroom anyway. I'll just take the pill while I'm in there." She reached for her crutches as she turned and let her feet touch the floor. She bit her lip as her right thigh stiffened. "I can see that this is going to be a long day," she muttered. She got up and braced herself. "Ten feet suddenly seems like a major undertaking."

"Want me to get Mike?" Julie asked.

"No way! He'd insist on staying home. And I'm sure I couldn't get any rest if I knew that he was here just to watch over me. Just tell him I'm tired and need to sleep in."

Julie frowned while Cari made her way to the bathroom door. "How did you two ever get along so well as partners? You're as bull-headed as he is."

Cari would have laughed if her head hadn't been pounding so loudly.

———— ⚜ ————

Cari was still awake when the others left for church, so she decided to get up and have some breakfast. *Maybe I'll sleep later.* She made her way to the kitchen and found a place setting left for her. There was a glass of juice, a muffin, and a bagel. And the *Coffee Butler* jug was sitting next to an empty mug. She smiled as she maneuvered onto the chair. *Julie, you'll spoil me rotten while I'm here.*

After breakfast, Cari went to the den. *I may as well watch some TV. I can't seem to sleep anyway.* She lay down on the sofa, remote in her left hand, and started to channel surf. She settled on a church program she sometimes watched. She made it through the congregational singing, a lovely solo, and the Scripture reading. Then she promptly fell into a deep slumber.

Mike and Rick were discussing the sermon illustration, Julie was asking Tammy if she'd mind setting the table for lunch, and Christa was telling Michael and Ricky to quit complaining about her driving when they rode with her. None of them even thought of Cari at first. Not until the table was set and the potatoes mashed did Julie notice that the television was on in the den, but that Cari hadn't acknowledged their presence. She almost panicked as she went to get Mike in the living room. She interrupted him in the middle of a sentence.

"What is it, Sweetheart?" he asked. He got up from his chair.

"I – I'm worried about Cari," she replied, casting a quick glance in Rick's direction.

Mike smiled as he touched her arm. "So what else is new? You worried all through church."

"Mike, we've been home over half an hour already, and she hasn't come out, or said anything. The TV is on in the den, but --"

"I'll go check on her, Julie." He gave her a kiss on the cheek. "I'm sure she's just fine. She said she was tired this morning." His ready smile didn't hide the concern mirrored in his own eyes.

There was a 1950's western on the television when Mike entered the den, Julie at his heels. He stopped short when he saw Cari on the sofa, the remote loosely held in her left hand. He stifled a laugh. "She must have dozed off quite a while ago. She hates westerns," he whispered.

"Oh well, nobody's perfect," Rick said from right behind them.

Mike turned around and grinned at him. "A little *eager* to meet her, Rick?" he chided. Then he sobered. "Seriously, I don't think she'd appreciate that the three of us stood here like this watching her sleep. Kind of an unfair advantage."

"Yeah, I guess so," Rick replied. "Are you sure she's okay?"

"She's still breathing. And she certainly looks comfortable enough. I guess we might as well leave the TV on. She'll likely wake up if we shut it off. Let's go have lunch."

"Then she'll end up eating by herself," put in Julie. "That wouldn't be right either. Maybe we should wake her up."

"Or just wait a bit longer," Rick suggested. "Oh, oh. Now we're in trouble."

"Why?" Mike asked. Rick pointed towards Cari. She had just pressed on the remote and hit the mute button.

"Are you three going to stand there talking all day, or are we going to go and eat?" she remarked casually. None of them answered. She shut off the TV and set the remote on the table. Then she carefully sat up, moving some strands of hair out of her face. She looked from Mike to Rick, then back again. "And by the way, I don't *hate* westerns. I just haven't seen too many *good* ones." Her gaze moved back to Rick, and he shifted his weight, looking rather uncomfortable. "I prefer the ones with strong heroines, not helpless females." She picked up her crutches and got off the sofa, with only a slight grimace. She moved towards them and Julie stepped aside. "And I rarely lose at *Scrabble*," she said as she left the room.

Rick whistled softly as he watched her retreating back. "You didn't warn me that there were nerves of steel beneath that beautiful smile."

Mike only laughed. "You'll have your work cut out for you, Rick."

His partner grinned. "Oh, I don't know. I haven't lost a game of *Scrabble* in a very long time either."

"I wasn't referring to a board game."

"Let's go and eat lunch," Julie said with a sigh. "You two could stand here yakking all day."

Out in the kitchen, Cari was introducing herself to a shy young girl she presumed to be Tammy Benson.

"Hi. I'm Cari Daniels," she said with a smile. "I'd shake hands but I might fall over if I tried that."

The girl seemed small for her age at first, but then Cari realized that she just wasn't standing up straight. "Hello. I'm Tammy. My dad, Rick, works with Officer Patterson."

"I know. I've been hearing a lot about him."

"All good, I hope," Rick said from behind her.

Cari's smile froze for a few seconds, and the hair on her neck bristled. Then she turned her head. "So far, yes."

"Hi. I'm Rick Benson."

Cari had noticed his looks when she was in the den, but she found him even more handsome up close. He was only a couple of inches taller than she. He had dark brown hair and green eyes. A mustache. Squared jaw line. Probably weighed about 175 pounds. Cari swallowed. *Looks are definitely not everything. Mark's a handsome guy too.* She looked down at the floor, feeling slightly sick. *It's only been six months. It's too soon to even be noticing another guy.* "Excuse me," she murmured. "I'd better sit down."

"Sure. Didn't mean to get in your way." He stepped aside and put his arm around Tammy's shoulders. "Ready for lunch, Kiddo?"

"I guess so," she replied, eyeing Cari across the table. "But I'm not very hungry today, Dad."

"Oh. Any particular reason?"

"Nothing I want to talk about." She continued to look at Cari until the woman blushed.

Cari felt increasingly uncomfortable. *Lord, I feel like I'm on display or something. And that poor girl is watching every move I make. She must wonder if I'm after her dad. How can I make her feel more at ease around me? For that matter, how can I relax around them?*

The others gathered at the table and sat down. Cari was introduced to Ricky, and found out just how much he looked like his dad. Then Mike said grace. And Cari started into a very different afternoon than she expected.

Chapter 9

"That's not a word!" Rick protested as he and Cari engaged in a closely matched game of *Scrabble*. "You made it up."

"I did not," she asserted. "You're just mad that you haven't thought of anything worth 40 points."

"I have so. I was just trying to be nice to an invalid," he teased.

Cari glared at him. "Watch it, Benson," she warned. "There's nothing wrong with my arms, and this is a pretty small table."

He looked at her and laughed out loud. "I can see why Mike misses having you for a partner. It must have been easy to stay awake with you in the patrol car."

"Boy, you're really asking for it, aren't you?" Cari glanced at Tammy, who was quietly working on a puzzle on the coffee table. "Tammy, would you mind looking up my word? Your dad is sure I'm cheating, and we need a third party to check it out for us."

Tammy looked from one to the other. Then she came to the card table and picked up the dictionary. "What's the word?" she asked, with little apparent interest.

"This one," Cari said as she pointed to it. She watched the girl flip through the pages. She eventually paused at one and ran her finger down the column.

"Well?" Rick asked with obvious impatience.

"It's a legal word, Dad," she said. Then she closed the book, set it down on the table and went back to the puzzle.

Cari was no longer interested in the game. "Umm, Rick, I'm getting kind of tired. Do you mind if we stop?"

"Dad never likes to quit before a game is finished," Tammy remarked without even bothering to look up. "Used to drive my mom crazy." She put the last piece into the puzzle. "My mom could work on the same puzzle for weeks, not really caring if it got done. She just liked trying at it. I never do well at *Scrabble*, but I can always finish a puzzle." She got up from the floor and surveyed her work for a moment. Then she began to take it apart and put the pieces back into the box.

Cari was baffled. *What was that little speech about? Is she trying to tell me that I don't fit in? Or is she just crying out for her dad to notice her? This is way out of my league.* "Excuse me. I think I should go lie down." She reached down to get her crutches.

"I could get those for you," Rick offered. "It must still hurt to bend over like that. Broken ribs can be painful for a long time."

"Actually, I'm getting pretty used to it."

"I'd like to help anyway," he added in a soft voice.

"Okay. Thanks." Cari moved back her chair and braced her left foot on the floor, and her left hand on the table. Just then the table leg gave out and she lost her balance. Rick dropped the crutches and steadied Cari instead. He gripped her upper arms and easily kept her from falling. His hold was firm, but gentle. His face was just inches from hers.

"You okay?" he asked, concern clearly etched on his handsome face.

"Yes," Cari whispered. "Thanks. But I – I think I'd better just get my own crutches from now on. It's likely safer."

"Sure. Why don't you just sit down and I'll hand them to you? I don't think that you could reach them where they fell."

"All right." *Just let go of me.* He helped her ease down to the chair once more. Then he picked up the crutches and passed them to her. "Thanks." Cari was soon on her feet, a firm grip on the handles.

"It's been nice meeting you." She looked at Tammy, who seemed to be ignoring her. "All of you." She bit her bottom lip. "Excuse me." She left them as quickly as she could manage and went to her room.

Once on the bed, Cari thought over Tammy's remarks. *I wonder what her mother looked like. Maybe Rick isn't paying enough attention to her because she reminds him of her. Something is eating away at her. And she's far more comfortable around Julie than she is with me.* She closed her eyes. *I'd like to help her, God. I think. But I have absolutely no idea how to do that.*

Rick went to bed early that night, but he couldn't sleep. He was puzzled by both Tammy's comments and Cari's reactions. *What was she talking about? Scrabble and puzzles? And she stared at Cari to the point of rudeness, and then tried to ignore her. Cari tried to be nice to her, but gave up after Tammy's little speech. Are they afraid of each other? Is Cari just not feeling well enough yet? And what is Tammy's problem? She said it was nothing she wanted to talk about. Maybe I should have pressed a little more.*

He turned over onto his other side. *She's a very beautiful woman. Underweight maybe, but very pretty.* He smiled in the dark. *And very determined to say the least. She wants as little help as she can get away with.* His smile faded. *Especially from me. Unless it just seemed that way. Maybe today just wasn't a good time.*

He sat up when he heard a light rapping on his bedroom door. "Come in," he called.

Tammy came into his room, her arms crossed over her chest. Rick switched on the lamp and saw tears on her cheeks.

"What's the matter, Sweetheart? You should have been asleep hours ago. Tomorrow's a school day."

"I didn't come in here for another lecture, Dad," was her bitter retort. She turned as though to leave.

"Tammy, wait. Sorry. What is it you need?" He patted the bed beside him and she sat down. She stared into his eyes for a long time.

"I need a mom, Dad," she choked out. "A big sister even. And I don't have either. My head is full of questions, and I can't ask a *guy*. Not even you. I don't know any of my school teachers well enough. I don't even have any friends here, Dad. Maybe I'm not a little girl anymore, but I still need a woman around me."

Rick reached out to her and pulled her against his chest. "I'm sorry, Tammy. I should have known, but I didn't. I'm not sure of the best way to help you though. Maybe I could arrange for you to spend more time with Mrs. Patterson. She works at home part-time, but I don't think she'd mind having you come over after school sometimes. Do you want me to ask her?"

"I like Mrs. Patterson, Dad, but right now that other lady is living with them too."

"You mean Cari? Don't you like her? You just met her today. What's the problem?"

"I don't know! Maybe because of how she looked at you while you were playing *Scrabble*. Like she was checking you out or something. And I'm not sure that she liked you too much."

Rick was thankful that his daughter couldn't see the blushing of his face. He'd had no idea that Cari had been watching him; much less that Tammy had seen her doing it.

Tammy wasn't through. "And when you kept her from falling, she looked kinda – well, angry maybe. Or scared. I'm not sure. But most people would have been relieved." She shrugged her slim shoulders. "She hardly talked all afternoon."

"Tammy," Rick countered, "neither did you." She was silent for several moments. "Well, Mike did tell me that Cari was engaged to a guy last year, but he broke up with her. So, maybe she doesn't trust guys too much right now."

Tammy sat up straight and looked at him. "Do you wish she would?"

Rick cleared his throat before answering. "I honestly don't know.

I still miss your mom. Very much." He swallowed the lump that was growing in his throat. "But that doesn't mean I don't notice other women. I thought that Cari was nice. I'd like to get to know her better. But that may be all that ever happens." He gave her a kiss. "Now, I think we'd both better get some sleep. We have to get up early."

"Okay." She got off the bed, but turned to look at him again. "Could you talk with Mrs. Patterson? I really need somebody right now."

"Sure. I'll talk to her."

"Thanks, Dad." She left the room and closed the door.

Rick still sat in the quiet room with the lamp on. *Oh, Lord, what am I going to do with a growing daughter and no wife to help raise her? Please give me wisdom. Ricky seems to be doing okay, but I feel like Tammy is slipping away from me somehow. Please help me, Lord. Help me to make the right choices.* Even as he prayed, he thought of Cari Daniels. *What if she really doesn't like me?*

"I'd love to have Tammy come over after school, Rick," Julie said as she spoke into the kitchen phone. "How about Mondays, Wednesdays, and Fridays? Then she can stay for supper, and either I'll take her home, or you or Ricky could pick her up. Okay. And I know that summer holidays are coming up too. Just let her know that she can still come. All right. I'll be looking forward to it. Bye."

Cari looked up as Julie set down the receiver. "Well, you sure must like company. Both your own kids are home right now. Me in the guest room. And now you're taking on another challenge." She shook her head as she reached for her coffee mug.

"Cari," Julie remarked as she sat down at the table, "Tammy lost her mom two years ago. She was only ten at the time. Now she's twelve, almost thirteen. Do you see the difference? She needs somebody in her life to balance out the feminine side. Her father and brother love her, but that just isn't enough. You could help her too."

"Me? The kid hardly spoke to me on Sunday. I think she sized me up and found me seriously lacking. She made me nervous, Julie. Besides, I was an only child. I didn't even have a lot of friends when I was growing up."

"But you did have both parents, didn't you?" her friend chided. She clasped her hands together. "Cari, are you forgetting that you were prepared to be a mother – to your own child? Boy or girl?"

"Of course not!" Tears stung Cari's eyes. "How could I forget? And what does that have to do with Tammy Benson?"

"She needs a mother too. Maybe not 24 hours a day like an infant, but at least some of the time. And I don't think it has to just be *one* either. I'm sure that Christa could take her shopping sometimes. She likes to be in the kitchen with me. Please think of some way that you could interact with her, Cari." She reached for her hand. "It doesn't matter how little it may be. But that girl needs us."

"I'll think about it, Julie. But I won't commit myself to anything."

"Okay. But Cari, don't just *think* about it. Please *pray*. I think Tammy is carrying around a lot of hurts that she hasn't been sharing with anybody." She gently squeezed Cari's fingers. "Just like somebody else that I care about. Those emotions, whatever they may be, have to be dealt with eventually. In all of us."

Chapter 10

Tammy arrived on Wednesday at 4:00 p.m. She looked unsure of herself when Julie met her at the door. But within a half hour she was busy helping to prepare supper, and talking about her day at school.

"We're supposed to write an essay about someone in a challenging career. The girls are supposed to interview a woman, and the guys get to interview men. How sexist is that?" She sighed as she set plates on the table. "It'd be easy if I could just do it on my dad. I don't know a lot of women. My mom was a -- " She cut off her sentence abruptly. "But I can't ask her," she whispered. She immediately withdrew into her quiet shell once more.

Julie put an arm around her shoulders. "What did you mom use to do, Tammy?"

"She was a nurse. In the Cardiac Unit at the biggest hospital in Sacramento. She was a supervisor, and she really loved her job, you know. And I used to just sit and listen to her describing the different cases." She shrugged. "I sometimes think that I'd like to do that kind of work too. But I don't know."

"I think that I could arrange for you to meet a nurse, from *Cedars Sinai*, Tammy," Cari said as she approached the table. "I was in CCU for over a week, then ICU." She sighed. "And then a private room for a month. I had a lot of different nurses while I was there, but some of them worked pretty consistent shifts. Some of them were so nice that I gave them thank you notes when I left." She leaned against the counter. "I know they were very important to me while I was there. People must have felt that way about your mom too."

Tammy looked at Cari but didn't say anything. Julie stepped away from her and went to the stove.

Cari tried again. "Just on the police force, I know women chopper pilots, scuba divers, K-9 trainers, investigators. Those are all challenging jobs."

"What about your job?" Tammy finally asked. "It's challenging, isn't it?"

Cari considered the question for a moment. Then she answered honestly, "That's how I wound up in the hospital for two months. However, not all shifts are that risky, or dangerous. Sometimes we drive around a lot, or do mounds of paperwork."

"When did you become a cop?" Tammy drew a little closer to Cari. "Was it hard?"

"I went to the Police Academy almost eleven years ago. And, yes, it was hard. There weren't a lot of women on the force at that time. There's more now. It was very demanding physically too. Still is for that matter. Before I got hurt, I was working out in the gym at least twice a week, sometimes more. It seemed like there were constant tests to write." She smiled. "Last year I wrote my Sergeant's exam. It took weeks to get ready for that one. But it paid off."

"My mom was always studying too. She said that medicine was constantly changing and she had to keep up with it, especially as a supervisor." She looked down at the floor. "My dad cancelled all of her nursing journal subscriptions last year. I guess he couldn't stand having mail come with her name on it anymore." She moved a little closer to Cari, almost within arm's reach. "As long as those magazines were coming in the mail, I felt kind of like Mom was still – *around*."

Cari had tears in her eyes. *Julie was right. This kid is carrying enough hurts for a dozen people. But how do I help her, Lord?* She reached out her right hand towards Tammy. "I kept all of my mom's perfume when she died. It reminded me of her. What she wore when she went out with my dad or the fragrance that was for church. I still have them."

Tammy moved against Cari. "I still have a couple of the journals, in with my stuff. Dad doesn't know."

Cari rested her hand on Tammy's back. "That's okay. We all need something to hang on to. It's okay." She could feel Tammy trembling. "Next time you come over, bring one of the journals. And I'll let you smell some of my mom's perfume." The girl was nodding vigorously. "Right now, though, I think we better clean up our faces. We don't need some guys bugging us about that, do we?"

Tammy looked up and tried to smile. "No. Guys just don't understand crying, do they?"

Cari and Julie both laughed at her insight.

"Not too many," Julie replied. "So if you find one who does, marry him."

———— •《◊》• ————

When Friday rolled around, it was actually Cari who met Tammy at the door. They smiled shyly at each other and headed towards the kitchen. They munched on cookies with Julie, and washed them down with glasses of milk as they talked. Finally Cari pointed to Tammy's backpack.

"Did you bring it?" she asked.

Tammy blushed. "Yeah, I did. Do you still want to look at it?"

"Sure," Cari answered. "Especially if there are any articles about heart dysrhythmias, or busted ribs. I could relate to those kinds of topics."

"I haven't looked at them for a while," Tammy remarked. "I

can't remember what's in this one."

"That's okay. We'll just check it out together." She reached for her crutches. "But first I'll go get something from my room. I'll be back in a few minutes."

Tammy simply nodded and unzipped her pack.

Cari returned to the table with a small bottle tucked into the pocket of her jeans. She withdrew it and set it on the table. "This one was my mom's favorite. My dad bought it for her a few years ago." She sat down and uncapped the bottle. A rather heady scent permeated the kitchen. Tammy wrinkled her nose and Cari laughed. "I didn't say it was *my* favorite. I much prefer subtler scents. But I guess it suited my mother. She was kind of bold and high energy." She replaced the cap. "But I think she wore it so often simply because my dad bought it for her. She always made a big deal of anything from him."

Silence prevailed for a few minutes, each deep in thought. Then Tammy slowly slid a magazine in Cari's direction. "There is an article about dysrhythmias, Ms. Daniels. Maybe you'll learn something from it."

Cari looked at her and smiled. "Maybe I will. But please call me 'Cari'."

"Okay."

Julie continued to make supper while Cari and Tammy discussed the article. Cari even lifted the edge of her sweatshirt to show the girl her portable pacemaker control. Tammy seemed fascinated by it.

"So that little box has helped to keep you alive?" she asked in apparent wonder.

"More than once so far. My heart seems to be starting to behave again, but I still have to wear this for at least three more weeks. Then Dr. Wilson will let me know if that's enough. I certainly hope so," she finished with a sigh. "I'm getting tired of having cords and Velcro attached to me all the time."

"Was it scary in the hospital?" Tammy inquired in a very soft voice, not looking at Cari.

"Yes, especially at first. I faded in and out a lot, but every time I was awake I was in so much pain I didn't think I could stand it. And all the tubes and machines made constant noise." She smiled again. "And I couldn't even talk for the first two and a half weeks. That drove me crazy! You see, I had a tracheotomy tube in my throat, and it was hooked up to a ventilator. Talk about uncomfortable! But my chest was such a mess; I just couldn't breathe on my own."

"Wow! Dad told us you were hurt pretty bad, but nothing like that. No wonder you still look so tired." Tammy's eyes widened and she put a hand over her mouth.

"It's okay, Tammy. Trust me, I know I don't look my best these days. But I'm a whole lot better than two months ago. Yes, I'm still tired. I lost a lot of blood, and it could take a very long time for my body to build up again." She grinned. "And my ribcage reminds me of the 'Tin Man', but I'm getting better, slowly."

Tammy lowered her hand. "Sorry about that. I'm always getting in trouble for saying whatever comes into my head."

Cari raised her eyebrows in mock surprise. "Oh, really? I thought I was the only one that happens to." She closed the medical journal. "We better put our stuff away and set the table. Your dad and brother will be here soon." *And I sure don't want to get you in trouble with your dad. Actually, I don't want to get* myself *in trouble with your dad, either.* She tucked the perfume back into her pocket and got up from her chair.

"Cari?"

"Yes?" She steadied herself as she looked down at Tammy.

"Thanks a lot."

"You're welcome."

Chapter 11

"How's the essay going, Tammy?" Rick asked as he gave his daughter a quick hug. He knew that she'd decided to write about Cari. He was rather interested in the final product himself.

Tammy looked a bit uncomfortable. She glanced at Cari with a pleading expression in her eyes. Cari smiled back at her before answering Rick.

"Well, I don't know how much has actually been written down so far, Rick. However, the interviewing process has been interesting for both of us."

Rick watched his daughter visibly relax. "Oh. Glad to hear it. But," he patted Tammy on the shoulder, "it does have to be handed in next week. I suggest you get it together over the weekend."

"Sure, Dad. No problem. I'll work on it tonight and tomorrow. Then Cari can check it over with me on Monday. I'll have it ready for Mr. Reed by Tuesday."

"Sounds good to me." Rick knew that she took her work seriously, so he wasn't sure why he was on her case about the essay. *Likely just because of the subject of the essay.* He looked at Cari and smiled. "You're looking a little steadier this week. How are you feeling?"

"Like I'll be really glad to get rid of these crutches permanently.

However, I'm still stuck with them for another three weeks. Then I get to upgrade to a cane."

"Well, at least that will leave you with one hand free," he countered. "That'll help, won't it?"

"I guess so. But I'd much rather be walking *entirely* on my own," she sighed.

Just then Mike entered the kitchen, without his usual smile in place. Cari noticed immediately, and asked about it before Rick could signal her not to.

"Why so glum, Mike?" she asked. "If I was frowning like that, you'd be giving me the third degree right now. What's up?"

"I'd rather not discuss it for the moment," Mike replied with a rather cool tone of voice.

Cari persisted. "That excuse didn't work for me too often." She looked to Rick then. "You're his partner these days. Do you know what's going on?"

Rick hesitated before answering. "Yes, I know what's going on. I also know that it's none of my business, Cari."

She stared at him for a moment before frowning. "Fine. Maintain your vow of silence then. It's time for supper anyway."

Rick watched her move to the table and saw her wince as she sat down on the chair. Her jaw clenched as she touched her right leg. *Mike, you'd better clue her in before she finds out from somebody else. She doesn't look like she'd appreciate that too much.* "C'mon, kiddo," he said to Tammy. "We need to eat and run tonight. Ricky's got a game at the school."

"Cool," Tammy replied. She hastened to the table and sat down next to Cari. "Maybe by the fall you'll be able to come to some of the games. Ricky is really good – at every sport." She made a face at her brother. "He can be an annoying jock sometimes, but I guess I'll keep him."

Cari laughed out loud, and Rick was amazed at his daughter's remark. She never teased in public, and rarely at home. *I guess being around Cari is good for her after all.* He sat down next to Tammy. *Now, if I could just get to know Cari better myself. But I don't see that happening any time soon.*

—————=◦((◦))◦=—————

Cari joined Mike and Julie in the den after the others had left. She fixed her gaze on Mike.

"Okay, Partner, spill it. I realize that you probably didn't want to talk in front of Tammy and Ricky, but you don't have that excuse now. So, what's up?"

Mike reached for Julie's hand and gently caressed it. He didn't even look up at Cari when he spoke. "There might be an inquest, Cari. And, since I've never been part of one, personally, I'm kind of edgy about it."

"Inquest? About what?" When he didn't reply, she tried to think of what he could mean. Her eyes widened. "For shooting the guy who tried to kill me?"

"Yes," he replied softly, finally looking at her. "There seems to be some question as to whether or not I was justified in using 'Deadly Force'. Someone from the guy's family is after a public inquest, and they just may get it." He released Julie's hand. "I've been going over it for days, Cari. I don't see that I could have done anything else." He shook his head.

"Mike, this is crazy! The guy was *killing* me. I had no way to defend myself – since I couldn't even breathe, let alone fight. You and Pam Martin tried to get him to stop. You yelled for him to. What more do they want? Having me *dead?*" She noticed that she was trembling and tried to take a deep breath as she leaned back in the chair. "The guy was out of his mind. Don't they understand that?"

"That's precisely their point, Cari. They figure that since he was high on crack, he wasn't responsible for his actions. And, hence, I should have just tried to restrain him, not shoot him."

Cari closed her eyes, and the whole incident played over and over in her mind. *'I'm going to dance on your grave, pig! But first I'm going to put you in it.'* She could almost feel each blow from his boot. She moaned without even realizing it. "Who was he?" she suddenly asked. "I don't even remember his name."

"His name was Kyle Richards. He was 27 years old. A graduate of Harvard Law School. He was working for the family firm here in L.A. *Richards & Richards*. He's from a long line of lawyers."

Cari put her hands up to her face. "Mike, if they go after you in this, what will they do about me? Try to prove that I was negligent? He caught me off guard. And promptly beat me to a pulp! Was that my fault? What if he'd gone for my gun? He could have killed all of us. Has his family considered any of that?"

"I'm sure they have, Cari," Mike said with an audible sigh. "And you'll very likely be expected to testify about this whole incident too."

"*Incident?* Is that what it's called? I thought it was attempted murder. Or, at the very least, assaulting a police officer. I would have done the same thing you did."

He tried to smile. "Maybe. "Let's hope that we never have to find out. For now though, we need to prepare ourselves in case this whole mess goes to court, or worse, to the press. We could come out looking like a couple of idiots, not professionals."

"I can't believe that this is happening, Mike."

"Well, you'd better, Cari. How else can we be prepared?"

Cari had nightmares most of the night. She relived the assault over and over. It always ended the same: with her trying to breathe, and a shot being fired. By morning she was in tears. *God, help us through this. Mike and I just can't handle this on our own. Please help.*

———◦《◉》◦———

Cari worked on her typed statement for hours on Monday

morning. She was trying to be certain that every detail came through loud and clear. *I have to. Mike and I could both lose our jobs if I don't do this right.* By the time Tammy arrived, she was rather distracted, but glad to take a break. Tammy timidly handed her the rough draft of the essay to read over. Cari sat at the table, mug in hand.

Society's Soldier

By Tammy Benson

For my interview I chose someone that I've come to admire. Her name is Sgt. Cari Daniels. And she has one of the most challenging careers around. She's a member of the Los Angeles Police Department, and has been for almost 11 years now. She's told me all about what it was like when she started, being one of the few women at the Police Academy. She's always tried to work her hardest to prove that she's just as good an officer as the men she has worked with.

For example, she has studied hard for every test and exam since she started, and has done well on all of them. Several months ago she attained the rank of Sergeant, with top marks. She has made a habit of working out, and swimming, in order to stay in shape physically. And I happen to know that she's a whiz at Scrabble, *which helps to keep her mind sharp. She's taken up rally driving through the years, so that her reflexes are always ready when she's behind the wheel of the patrol car. She's also taken computer and business classes so that she can readily deal with the mounds of paperwork that come with her job.*

Sgt. Daniels has not tried to glorify herself, or to glamorize her job. However, I have gained a new appreciation for both. Just two and a half months ago, she was assaulted while on duty. She was severely injured and has only recently been released from the hospital. Even though she will still be recovering for a while yet, she's looking forward to returning to work. Or, to the 'front lines' if you will. She has no intention of quitting.

What have I learned during the past week? Well, I'm not sure that police work is what I'd choose as a career, but I might change my mind when I'm older. I've learned that whatever career we go after will demand a lot of time and effort. Quitters just won't achieve as much. I know that I need to study a lot of different things, in order to keep more options available. I know that I don't want to settle for just the minimum requirements. I always want to do the best that I possibly can. I've also learned that police officers deserve more respect than they've been getting lately. Maybe they don't make great inventions, or travel in space, or discover cures for diseases. But they do help to keep our cities and towns safer places.

Thanks, Sgt. Daniels, for being so dedicated on the job. And for taking the time to help me with this assignment. I'm glad that women like you help to look out for girls like me.

"This looks great, Tammy," Cari remarked with a smile. "I'll have to hire you to do all my PR in the future." She put her arm around the girl and gave her a slight squeeze. "I'm sure your dad will like this. You kept it short, but to the point. I hope that's what your teacher was after though."

Tammy nodded. "I quote: 'Just give me some basic facts about the person and their job. I don't need a book. One page should be sufficient.' I think I've got enough, don't you?"

"Sure." Cari handed the essay back to Tammy. "Now, I think we both deserve some of the brownies that Julie made this afternoon."

Chapter 12

Cari stared at the official document in her hands. *An inquest. This is going to be awful. What kind of questions will we have to answer, Lord? How on earth can we even prepare ourselves for something like this? It's one thing to hear about other cases. It's quite another to be caught in the middle of one.* She folded the sheet of quality stationary and placed it in the envelope. *Just two weeks to get ready for — for what? Why is this even happening?* She set the letter on the bed next to her and reached for her cane. *Maybe I shouldn't move back to the apartment until the inquest is over.* She knew that Mike and Julie wanted her to stay, but she was anxious to get back home again. She gritted her teeth as she stood up. *I need to go home. I can think more clearly when I'm by myself.*

It was the end of June already, and nearly three months since the assault, but Cari was still walking with a severe limp. Pain shot through her right groin almost every time she even moved her leg, much less put weight on it. She was finished with the pacemaker though, for which she was exceedingly grateful. She could actually wear blouses tucked into her pants or skirts now, and she didn't tire quite so easily anymore. She was gradually improving, though some days it still seemed as though she was far from her goals.

"Want me to help you pack, Cari?" Julie asked as she entered the bedroom with a stack of clean clothes. She set them on the bed and looked at her friend. "I know you're planning to go home in a couple of days, but I thought I could at least help you to get organized." Julie sighed as she sat down on the bed. "Do you have any idea how much I'm going to miss having you around?"

Cari smiled at her as she opened the closet door. "Well, I know how good it's been for me to stay here. And I'll miss all of you. But it's been three months, Julie. I want to go home. I think I'll feel more like I'm on the road to recovery once I'm sleeping in my own place again, and cooking my own meals." She pointed a finger at Julie. "Though you have spoiled me rotten since I got here. I think the only cooking I've done was to make some toast for myself. It'll be a challenge just to make some soup or something."

"I suppose I shouldn't pester you, Cari, but I'll likely still worry about you. And call you every day." Her lips curved downward. "Well, maybe just every other day."

"That'll be fine. And you're welcome to come and visit, you know. You could bring Tammy with you sometimes, too. I'll miss spending time with her."

"Well, that shouldn't be a problem. She's finished school for the summer. I'm sure Rick would be just as glad for her to visit you at your place, just as long as she's spending time with one of us females." She stood up again and joined Cari at the closet. "So, what do you want packed?"

⇒ ((◉)) ⇐

Cari crawled into her own bed for the first time in months with a sigh of relief. *Oh, it's good to be home.* Exhaustion quickly took over and she slept right through until morning, when Mike called her and turned her world upside down.

"They got a hold of *what?*" she cried into the phone, hoping that she hadn't heard him correctly.

"Your medical records."

"But how could they do that, Mike? And why do they want them?"

"They're still trying to make it look as though you were distracted, and unfit for duty that day."

"Mike, what can they find out from those files, besides my injuries that is?"

He was silent for a long time. "Cari, you miscarried that day. So, obviously they could prove that you were pregnant at the time. They might make an issue out of that."

Cari suddenly felt incredibly cold. She pulled the quilt up under her chin. "Mike, they just can't do that to me!" She thought of Rick and Tammy. "Have you told Rick about the baby?" she demanded.

"No, lf course not, Cari."

"Sorry. I didn't mean to yell at you." She bit her lip. "But he's going to find out now, isn't he?" She swallowed as she tried to think logically. "So, I was pregnant. That didn't affect my job performance any. Did it?" A wave of uncertainty mingled with nausea. "This isn't fair, Mike. How do we fight against this kind of thing?"

"We can pray. Besides that, I honestly don't know. But Cari, maybe it would be best if you told Rick about the baby. You don't want him to find out at the inquest, do you?"

"I don't want him to find out at all!" she wailed. "Or Tammy. I just can't tell him."

"Do you want me to?"

"N—no. I don't. Let's just see what they try to use at the inquest, Mike. Besides, Rick has no reason to be there."

"Okay, if you say so. But I think that you're selling Rick short. He might understand, Cari."

"How could he? Besides, the medical files don't mention *how* I got pregnant. And I'm not prepared to tell *anybody* that." Her face flushed even as her teeth chattered.

"There's always a time for honesty, partner," he prodded.

"I'm not *lying* about anything, Mike," she retorted. "I'm just not *telling* anything." *And I have no intention of telling anything in the near future either.*

———◦((◦))◦———

Mike prayed for Cari as soon as he hung up the phone. *God, I know that she's still hurting, but I'm afraid that the inquest is simply going to force her hand in this. Why won't she share the truth while it's still under her own control? What will she do if a lawyer asks her who the father was? I don't think she's considering all the possibilities. This inquest won't be easy on either of us. But I think that Cari may suffer much more from it than I do. I'm willing to resign if I have to. But Cari is still young, and wants to pursue her career. What would she do, Lord?*

Please help her to get the rest that she needs between now and the inquest. Help her to think clearly and logically. Help her to remember anything that will be important. Please give her strength each day. And Lord, please help her not to run from the very people who would like to help her through this whole situation. Help her to lean on You, God. And I'll try to do likewise.

———◦((◦))◦———

Cari sincerely wished that she could enter the court room without her cane, but she knew that she simply wasn't steady enough yet. She adjusted her blouse and skirt, thankful that she had finally regained most of her lost weight, and that her misshapen ribs weren't obvious beneath her clothing. She had debated about wearing a blazer, until she recalled that this was the month of July, and anything but cool weather. *This will just have to do, at least for today, and for as many days as this inquest is going to take.*

She saw Mike and Julie approaching her, holding hands. Julie looked strained. Mike looked determined. Cari forced a smile to her lips.

"Well, I guess this is it, guys. Ready to take on Goliath, Mike?"

she asked.

His eyes regained some of their normal spark. "Let's go to it," he replied. "I don't know how many *stones* we've got, but David only needed one." He reached for the heavy door and pulled on the brass handle. Then they walked into the combat zone.

Chapter 13

Mike was sworn in first, and was allowed to give an account of the *incident* before being cross examined by the Richard's lawyer, Jerry Neilson.

"Is it correct, Officer Patterson, that you were not actually standing close to Mr. Richards and Sgt. Daniels at the time of the alleged assault?"

The lawyer representing Mike and Cari got to his feet. "Objection, Your Honor! There is no question whatsoever that an assault occurred."

"Objection sustained. Counsel will drop the word 'alleged' from his remarks."

"Yes, your Honor. Officer Patterson, will you please answer the question?"

"No, I was not standing close to them. Cari – Sgt. Daniels and Mr. Richards were on the far side of the reception desk. I was entering the building." Mike was already tired of repeating the details over and over.

"So, you would have been how far from them? Fifteen, maybe twenty feet?"

"Yes."

"So you did not, at that time, have a clear view of the al – assault?"

"No, I did not."

"When did you become aware of a problem? Did Sgt. Daniels call for help?"

"No. Just as I was entering the building, I heard a loud *thud*. I looked up and saw Mr. Richards behind the desk, where only officers or support staff is allowed to be."

"And what did you do at that point, Officer Patterson?"

"As I've already told the court, I asked Mr. Richards what he was doing and told him to get out from behind the desk."

"And what was his response?"

"He said, 'Make me, pig'."

There was murmuring in the courtroom.

"And so you decided to shoot him?"

"No! I ordered him to 'freeze'."

"What about Officer Martin? When did she enter the exchange?"

"Just before I drew my weapon."

"And did she say anything?"

"She screamed Cari's name."

"Could you *see* Sgt. Daniels, Officer Patterson?"

"No, but --"

"Then how did you know where she was?"

Mike tried not to lose his temper as he carefully went over it in his mind. "I knew she was *supposed* to be at the desk, and that Mr. Richards must be confronting someone."

"But until Officer Martin entered the room, you couldn't *see* anything?"

"No."

"When you drew your weapon, did Mr. Richards listen to your command to 'freeze'?"

"No, he did not. Instead, he gave Cari – Sgt. Daniels, another kick."

"You couldn't *see* his foot, could you?"

"No, but --"

"So, you're only *assuming* that he kicked her again."

Mike didn't answer at first. He looked over at Cari and saw she was trying not to cry, though tears glistened in her eyes. "Yes, at that moment."

"So, you discharged your service revolver?"

"Yes."

"And the bullet hit Mr. Richards in the heart, killing him instantly."

Mike swallowed hard as he heard Mrs. Richards weeping openly. "Yes."

"Then what did you do?"

"I immediately went to check on Sgt. Daniels."

"And found her in what state?"

"Severely beaten and barely alive."

"Did you check to see if Mr. Richards was still alive?"

"No, but --"

"You intentionally ignored Mr. Richards in favor of your former partner?"

"No!" Mike insisted. "Officer Martin is also a registered nurse. She had already confirmed that Mr. Richards was dead. We then focused our attention of saving Sgt. Daniels' life."

"So, Officer Patterson, you've already admitted that you couldn't *see* the assault take place, yet you resorted to *deadly* force in regards to Mr. Richards. Was Mr. Richards armed?"

"No."

"Was he threatening *you?*"

"No."

"Was he threatening Officer Martin?"

Mike hesitated at that one. "No."

"And you couldn't actually see what he was doing to Sgt. Daniels?"

"No."

"No further questions, Your Honor."

Mike's head was pounding from fatigue and the incessant

questioning. He rubbed his face with his hands.

The Department lawyer, Bill Craddock, approached Mike.

"Officer Patterson, will you please tell us how long you have been a police officer?"

"For 23 years."

"The whole time with this force?"

"Yes."

"In those 23 years, have you ever drawn your revolver on a suspect before?

"Yes."

"How often?"

"Twice."

"Under what circumstances?"

"While apprehending an armed robbery suspect. And during a hostage taking incident."

"Did you need to fire your weapon in either instance?"

"No. Both suspects surrendered immediately."

"So, in the incident involving Mr. Richards, what proved to be the difference?"

"He was showing no intention of ceasing the assault. His behavior remained aggressive."

"So, at that moment, your 23 years of experience led you to believe that your only option was to fire your weapon?"

"Objection, Your Honor," protested Jerry Neilson. "Leading the witness."

"Objection sustained. Please rephrase your question, counselor."

"Yes, Your Honor. Officer Patterson, what made you decide to fire your weapon?"

"I believed it was the right choice."

"Why didn't you employ your baton, or attempt to get a hold on Mr. Richards?"

Mike closed his eyes as he replayed those moments. *Why didn't I? Maybe I could have tried. Why didn't I? Because of Cari.* "I was trying to protect Sgt. Daniels."

"How long did you and Sgt. Daniels work together?"

"For seven years. But I've known her since she enrolled at the Academy."

"Would you have done the same for *any* fellow officer?

"Yes."

"No further questions, Your Honor."

"You may step down, Officer Patterson," the judge said.

Mike stood and got out of the witness box. He made his way to the table and tried to smile at Cari. But his heart wasn't in it. The other lawyer looked completely confident. *What is he gonna try when Cari takes the stand? And how will she handle it?* He sat down at the table and Cari reached for his hand.

"Thanks, Mike," she whispered.

"You're welcome – I hope." His hair bristled on the back of his neck as Mrs. Richards continued to weep. He lowered his head and closed his eyes. *I killed a man, Lord. I was doing my job, and trying to protect Cari. But I still killed him. How would Julie handle it if somebody shot Michael?* He rubbed his now trembling hands over his face, noticing the wetness on his cheeks. *God, resigning is starting to look like the best choice available. If I could spare Cari from the stand, I would. Please be with us, God. I'm not sure we've got any stones left.*

Chapter 14

The judge called a lunch break, and Cari and Mike eagerly left the court room with Julie. Unfortunately, Mr. and Mrs. Richards entered the hallway at the same time. Cari and Mrs. Richards eyed each other for a moment before Cari looked down at the floor. Her right hand trembled on the grip of her cane.

"He was only 27!" the woman cried in a choked whisper. "You had no *right!*"

Cari felt tears rushing down her cheeks as Julie placed a warm hand on her shoulder. "C'mon, Cari. Let's go find a place to rest." Cari tried to nod.

They moved down the hallway towards an empty room their lawyer had reserved. He soon returned with strong coffee and some sandwiches. Cari didn't touch a thing. She sat at the table, her head down on her arms. *I can't do this, God! I'll fall apart when they start asking me questions. I can't remember everything clearly anymore. It's been three months already. And I was in so much pain at the time. I might say the wrong thing. And what about Mike? He's so pale. And Julie looks worried. Bill isn't saying anything – good or bad. You could have stopped this from happening. Why didn't You? What if I have to resign? What else would I do? Police work is all I'm trained for.*

I'm tired, God. I don't feel well. I haven't been sleeping right for days. How am I supposed to stay alert and not mess up during cross examination?

She remembered Dr. Wilson's reluctance when he'd signed the medical consent form. Cari had pointed out that he didn't have much choice. At best, she could have delayed the inevitable. There still would have been an inquest.

"But you're not strong yet, Cari. Your heart has been doing all right for the past few weeks, but you haven't been exerting yourself either. A court case is highly stressful. Please be careful. Get enough rest. Eat properly. Try to remain calm. And if you feel so much as a flutter from your heart, get over here immediately."

So far, she hadn't followed any of his advice.

⸺⸱◉⸱⸺

Back in the court room, Cari took the stand. Just mounting the small steps to the witness box was a chore. Her right leg was not cooperating in the least. She was sweating, but her hands felt cold and clammy. She swallowed as she focused her attention on the Richard's lawyer. Bill Craddock walked her through an account of the assault, but then it was Jerry Neilson's turn to question her.

"How long have you been with the LAPD, Sgt. Daniels?"

"Almost 11 years." A slight flutter in her chest caused her to clench her right hand.

"And you worked with Officer Patterson for seven of those years?"

"Yes."

"Can you tell the court why you didn't call for help as soon as you realized that Mr. Richards might pose a problem for you?"

She closed her eyes for a moment and tried to think of the best way to answer his question. She took a breath. "He didn't seem threatening at first."

"What do you mean?"

"I mean that I could tell he was upset, but until I turned away from him, I didn't realize that I was in danger."

"Why did you turn away?"

"To look up the needed information on the computer."

"And what did Mr. Richards do at that point?"

I've already told you all this! "He moved around the desk and came up behind my chair."

"And you didn't look up and notice his movement?"

"No, I --"

"You were busy with the computer?"

"Yes."

"Had anyone else ever managed to sneak up on you like that?"

Cari couldn't believe he was getting away with this type of question. She clenched her hand tighter. "No."

"And you say that Mr. Richards grabbed you by the shoulders?"

"Yes."

"Was that when you realized that you might have a problem situation?"

Cari gritted her teeth. "No, that realization became clear when he slammed my head against the desk."

Jerry Neilson looked down at his notes at that comment, but several people in the room murmured in response to it.

"Why didn't you call for help?"

"I was trying to stay conscious. Before I could say anything, he picked me up and shoved me into the desk."

"And you still didn't call for help?"

"I couldn't breathe."

"And why was that?"

"Because some of my ribs cracked when I hit the desk."

"How much do you normally weigh, Sgt. Daniels?"

"About 140 pounds."

"And Mr. Richards weighed close to the same. Yet you say that he picked you up and threw you?"

"Yes."

"You offered no resistance?"

"No."

"But you've already said that you're a trained police officer. Why didn't you react and attempt to protect yourself? Surely you could have kicked Mr. Richards or--"

"Objection, Your Honor. Speculation."

"Sustained. Rephrase you question, Counselor."

"Yes, Your Honor. Was there no way to defend yourself, Sgt. Daniels?"

"I couldn't breathe," she repeated. "It's hard to think when you can't breathe."

"Did Mr. Richards make any attempt to grab for your firearm?"

"No."

"Or your baton?"

"No." She put her hand to her chest and squeezed her eyes shut for a few seconds.

"Sgt. Daniels, how did Mr. Richards catch you off guard while you were checking the computer?"

"I don't know," she whispered, pain building in her chest.

"Speak up, please. What did you say?"

"I don't know," she replied somewhat louder.

"Was there anything different about that evening, Sgt. Daniels?"

"What do you mean?" she asked in confusion.

"How many times have you dealt with, shall we say 'irate' individuals?"

"Hundreds."

"And you've never had a problem before?"

"I've never been *attacked* before," she clarified.

"So what was the difference?" he persisted.

Cari's breathing was no longer steady. She licked her lips before answering. "I don't know what was different."

"Were you more tired that usual? Not feeling well?"

"Objection! Leading the witness."

"Sustained. Counselor, I advise you to stick to a legitimate line of questioning."

"Yes, Your Honor." Jerry went back to his table and picked up another file folder. He returned to the witness stand. "I'd like to submit to the court a possible reason for Sgt. Daniels' confusion, or lack of attention that evening. It's the initial medical report from the *Cedars Sinai* hospital." He placed the folder on the judge's bench.

"Please don't do this!" Cari whispered, tears gathering in her eyes. "That report has nothing to do with my work." She gripped the door of the box with whitened knuckles. Her pulse was pounding off rhythm in her ears.

Jerry went on without mercy. "It clearly states in the report that Sgt. Daniels miscarried while in the emergency room. She was said to be approximately 20 weeks pregnant at the time."

Cari's tears streamed down her cheeks. "Why are you doing this?"

"Were you tired that evening, Sgt. Daniels?" he continued, ignoring her distress.

"No! I was not. I was not 'distracted' or 'confused' either. I was attacked by Mr. Richards." Her breathing was now ragged.

"You will control your outbursts, Sgt. Daniels," admonished the judge. "Counselor, you may continue."

"Sgt. Daniels, have you missed many shifts since you joined the police department, due to illness?"

Cari looked into his face and saw how much he seemed to be enjoying himself. She felt increasing nausea. "Only once," she replied woodenly.

"And when was that, Sgt.?"

Cari didn't answer. She knew how he would twist her words. The pain was growing in intensity.

"When, Sgt.?"

"The day after I got pregnant." She put her hands up to her face and tried to block out the excited conversations in the court room. *Why, God? Why like this?*

"Your Honor," Bill interjected, "I request a brief recess, in order for Sgt. Daniels to regain her composure."

"I only have a few more questions," Jerry remarked.

"Recess denied. You may continue, Counselor."

"Sgt. Daniels, why were you still working that far into your pregnancy? The records from the division indicate that you could have taken an earlier maternity leave, especially if you had used your accumulated sick leave."

"I enjoyed my job," she replied.

"Were you physically, emotionally, and mentally capable of *doing* that job properly?"

"Yes!" She closed her eyes again as her pulse went crazy.

"Sgt. Daniels, you've already been warned by this court," the judge reminded her.

"I <u>was</u> fit for duty. I was doing my job. But someone on crack can be unpredictable." She was getting dizzy.

"You only *assumed* that Mr. Richards had been taking drugs, didn't you?"

"After all my years of police work, I've become quite capable of recognizing the signs."

"If you were so certain of the *possible* threat from Mr. Richards, why didn't you request assistance?"

"I knew that I wouldn't be alone long anyway."

"You thought you could handle the situation alone, because there really wasn't a threat from Mr. Richards at all. Isn't that right?"

"No!" Cari blinked a few times. "Oh, God . . ." she gasped as she slumped forward in her chair.

Chaos broke out in the court room. Suddenly hands were reaching for her.

"Cari! Can you hear me?" It was Mike and Cari struggled to answer.

"Hospital --"

"Court is adjourned until further notice. Bailiff, get an ambulance. Get Sgt. Daniels from the witness stand immediately." The judge's orders were quickly followed.

Mike readily lifted Cari from the box and laid her gently on the floor. "Hang on," he urged. He had a hand on her wrist. "Your pulse is haywire, Cari. Why didn't you say anything?"

She shook her head. Someone had wet a handkerchief and was wiping her face with cold water. She opened her eyes and saw Julie.

"Don't you dare die on me, Cari Daniels!" she whispered.

"My heart — it hurts." She clenched her jaws as the pain worsened again. She suddenly heard doors slam, and squeaky wheels moving along the wooden floor towards her. "Dr. Wilson warned me – not to come."

"Cari, stop talking," Mike ordered. "Let the medics get you to the hospital." Even as he said it, the two men lifted Cari to the stretcher. A blanket was placed around her and the straps fastened. A noisy oxygen mask was placed over her nose and mouth.

"I'm going with her," Julie stated.

"She's going to be all right, isn't she?" inquired a very pale Mrs. Richards.

Julie met her gaze as she got to her feet. "Only God knows that for sure, Ma'am. But I hope so."

Chapter 15

Cari passed out on the way to the hospital. Her heart kept beating, but her pulse was only 45 and dropping when she was whisked into ER. Julie waited in the hallway, pacing back and forth. She saw Dr. Wilson running down the hall and into the room where Cari had been taken. She could hear him yelling orders to all of the personnel, but Julie didn't understand it. She *did* understand that Cari was in trouble.

Cari came to after an injection of adrenaline. An oxygen mask was still covering her mouth, and the familiar IV tubes were running into her arms. She looked up into Dr. Wilson's face and saw how worried he was.

"I don't care what that judge, or the whole LAPD says, Cari. You're *not* going back into that court room; now or later. I won't let you kill yourself for the sake of an inquest." Cari tried to say something but he shushed her. "No talking, Cari. I'm keeping you here overnight. And probably longer than that. I don't even want you to *move*. Do you understand me?"

She blinked a response, since he'd just told her not to move.

"And if your heart won't stabilize with medication, we'll have to go in with a permanent pacemaker." This time Cari tried to talk. He put his hand on her shoulder. "Only if we have to. We'll wait and see."

Cari closed her eyes. *I don't want to be here. I want to go home. I want to forget about the inquest. About ever being pregnant. About any heart trouble. I just want to forget.*

Forgetting became easier a few minutes later, as more medication filtered through her system. She fell asleep before she was ever moved to CCU.

⬥

Back in the court room, Mike was facing Jerry Neilson, his face taut with anger. "You *knew* her heart had been damaged. Why didn't you allow a recess? What did this prove? That you're an expensive bully?" Mike allowed himself to be led away by his attorney.

"How could you treat the poor woman like that?" Mrs. Richards was asking her own lawyer. "You never told us how badly she'd been hurt. A damaged heart for goodness sake! Were you hoping for some sort of confession before she died?"

"Mrs. Richards, I suggest that you keep your voice down," urged Jerry, still looking very much in control.

"I'll do nothing of the kind, Jerry. I happen to be the one who signs your pay checks. *I suggest* that you bear that in mind." She stepped closer to him. "I also suggest that you make a motion to withdraw from this inquest. I no longer want you here. You may have an impressive record of wins, but you're certainly lacking when it comes to common decency."

"What are you saying, Mrs. Richards?" His cool reserve had now melted.

"I made myself clear enough. I want you off the case. As a matter of fact, I'm going to ask that it be thrown out altogether. And give me those medical files, Jerry. I want to return them to Sgt. Daniels personally, if that's possible. If I had had any idea what you had planned to do with them --" She glanced over at Mike as tears coursed her cheeks. "Whatever was I thinking? I nearly cost that man his job." Mike looked back at her at that moment. "Life just doesn't always boil down to what is *fair*. Kyle was spaced out on crack. And he tried to kill Sgt. Daniels. And I knew all that before I dragged these poor people into here."

She turned back to a still startled Jerry. "Leave your files here with me. I'll handle this myself. I didn't get a law degree for nothing. And by the way, Jerry, I wouldn't be looking for a hefty bonus this Christmas if I were you. We don't reward wanton disregard in our firm."

He swallowed as he loosened his silk tie. "Yes, Ma'am."

Cari's condition worsened overnight. Due to the trouble with her heart, her other vital organs were affected as well. Her left kidney began to shut down. More fluids were pumped into her. Other medications were tried. She grew restless and had to be restrained with padded wrist straps. She mumbled even when she was asleep.

"She's not responding to treatment, Officer Patterson," stated Dr. Wilson. "I'll wait another 24 hours, but if there's no improvement, we'll have to go in and check for damage. And she may very well lose a kidney in the process."

"People can survive with only one, can't they?" Mike asked hopefully.

Dr. Wilson frowned. "Most can, yes. But Cari's whole system sustained trauma. I don't think that one kidney would be sufficient to filter infections, etc. As it is, she'll have to be hyper vigilant for the rest of her life. If she so much as gets the common cold, either her kidney or her heart could suffer further damage."

"Will you please let me see her?"

"Yes, I will. She's so restless that I think someone close to her may be beneficial at this point."

"Thank you."

"But just for a couple of minutes. I can only bend the rules so far."

"I understand."

A few minutes later, Mike stood next to Cari's bed and reached for her right hand. She turned her head in order to look at him. He squeezed her fingers.

"Hi. Dr. Wilson let me sneak in here, but just for a couple of minutes. But I figure that's long enough for a quick prayer." He watched tears trickle down her cheeks before he closed his eyes. "Dear Father, please be with Cari. Especially during the next 24 hours. Help her to regain her strength. Please let her heart rate return to normal. Please give Dr. Wilson and the other staff wisdom. And please give Cari peace, so that she can rest while she's here. Amen."

"Thank you," she whispered. "I'm so scared, Mike." Her face contorted as her heart rate faltered again.

Mike looked at the monitor as a nurse hurried over to the bed.

"I'm sorry, sir, but you'll have to leave now." She touched Cari's other hand. "And you have to stop talking right now, Ms. Daniels. Dr. Wilson wants you to be as quiet as possible."

Cari nodded but looked at Mike.

He gave her fingers another squeeze. "You're not alone, Cari. Don't forget that." He released her hand with great reluctance and left the room.

"How is she?" Rick asked as soon as Mike stepped into the den, his arm around Julie.

Mike looked from Rick to Tammy. The young girl appeared terrified.

"She's not doing too well," he answered honestly. "But I was allowed in long enough to pray with her."

"Is she going to die?" Tammy asked.

Mike and Julie sat down on the sofa before he responded. "Dr. Wilson didn't say that, Tammy. But Cari is very sick. He doesn't even want her talking or moving right now. She needs to completely rest, and hopefully the medication will work like it's supposed to. But Cari told me that she's scared. So, we should all pray that she'll be able to relax properly."

"I'm scared too," Tammy whispered, mostly to herself. "Mom went to the hospital, and she died there." She leaned against her dad and he put both his arms around her.

"Shhh. That wasn't the same, Sweetheart. Besides, Cari has already shown how much of a fighter she is. She made it through almost two months in the hospital before. This time it might only be a few days. You should be thinking of ways to help her when she gets back home."

Tammy's head came back up and she looked into Rick's face. "Do you think I could maybe stay with her for a few days? I know how to cook enough to help out. And I could do her wash too."

Rick glanced at Mike and Julie, and they both smiled. "Well, we'll have to see what Cari thinks of the idea, but it's okay with me. Maybe you could send her a note and let her decide."

"All right. I'll work on one when we get home." She turned back to face Mike and Julie. "I didn't mean to ignore you two. I was just worried about Cari."

"That's okay, Tammy," Julie replied. "We're all worried about her."

Chapter 16

Dr. Wilson did not resort to surgery, but he kept Cari in CCU for a full week. When it came time for her release he sat on her bed and held her hand, as he'd done before. He smiled at her as he began to speak.

"You'll have to be making some choices about your future, Cari. Your body simply won't be able to withstand the stresses of police work anymore. Even if we did give you a pacemaker, kidney infections could put you right back in here again. And I'm sure that pacemakers and dialysis don't hold much appeal at 31 years of age."

"I don't know what else to do," Cari said with a sigh. "I'd resigned myself to life behind a desk full of paperwork. But at least that was still something familiar. What options do I have?"

"Plenty. And you'll have lots of time to think of them too. As a matter of fact, I've already spoken with your superiors at the Department, and the Insurance rep. You are entitled to full disability benefits, since there is truly nothing you could be doing related to police work. So, don't fret about your financial situation. You need rest. Time to build up your strength. And I expect to see you every month for the next year, whether or not you experience any flare ups."

"Yes, sir," she replied with a smile. "And thank you for handling so many of those things for me. I wouldn't even know where to begin. I always paid for my benefits, but I never needed to use more than the dental coverage until April. This is all new to me."

"Just as many other things will be." He stood up as he squeezed her fingers. "I have every confidence that someone as strong as you will do just fine in the future."

"Thank you, Dr. Wilson. I just hope that you're right."

━━━━◄◐►━━━

Rick and Tammy picked Cari up at the hospital to take her home. She smiled at Tammy as she recalled the note the girl had sent along with Mike.

> *'Dear Cari;*
> *I want to let you know that I'd be glad to help you when you go home. (I have Dad's permission.) I could cook and clean for you during the day, and run errands if you need anything. Since it's not school right now, I could help you most days. (Dad said not on Sundays or his days off, though.) Either Dad or Ricky would drop me off and pick me up. Please say yes. I'd only mope around and worry about you if you refuse. Please let me know A.S.A.P.*
> *I'm praying for you. Tammy'*

Cari had cried when she'd read the note, and it hadn't been too hard to give an immediate answer. She'd grown to enjoy Tammy's company since the end of May. And, she had to admit, cooking and cleaning were not too easy just yet. And that was before her present trip to the hospital. Dr. Wilson wanted her to lead a *very* sedentary life for the next several weeks yet. She needed all the help she could get.

"Ready to tackle my laundry, Tammy?" Cari asked as they reached the elevator.

"Sure thing," replied the girl. "I even know how to iron. Right, Dad?"

Rick laughed. "The neatest creases you've ever seen."

"Great. My clothing will vastly improve in no time."

Once at her apartment, Cari headed straight for her couch and sat down. "Same song, second verse," she muttered. "I'm still so tired. This is pathetic." She looked up to find Tammy tidying up the magazines on the coffee table. Rick was standing by the door, looking unsure of himself. "Why don't you sit down, Rick? Let's see if Tammy knows how to make a pot of coffee."

"Of course I do," replied the teen. "It shouldn't take me long." She was soon puttering around in the kitchen, getting out mugs and spoons. "Hey, Dad, I think you'll have to go and get some milk. This stuff is no good. Yuck! There are lumps in it."

Cari could hear the lumpy liquid being poured into the sink.

"Yes, Ma'am," Rick answered. He moved back to the door.

"There's a convenience store downstairs," Cari told him. She reached for her purse.

"Never mind," he said. "I'll pick up some other stuff while I'm there. See you shortly." He was out the door before she could reply.

Tammy entered the living room, hands on her slim hips. "You realize, of course, that Dad's idea of 'groceries' are *Twinkies* and *Joe Louis*. He also likes nachos and salsa. If you're lucky, he *might* remember the milk." She shook her blonde head and went back to the kitchen.

Cari dissolved into laugher, placing a hand on her still sore chest.

Sure enough, Rick returned with two magazines, a book of crossword puzzles, plenty of junk food, and no milk. Tammy scolded him none too gently, and went to get it herself, muttering all the way. And Cari thought of how young Rick looked with flaming red cheeks.

"Thanks for the ride home, guys," Cari said as she walked Rick and Tammy to the door. "And for all your work, Tammy. You make a wonderful housekeeper."

"Thanks, Cari." She gave her a quick hug. "Now, if we could just teach Dad how to buy *real* food, we'd be all set."

"Hey! Will you lay off? It's not my fault that I'm a junk food junkie."

Cari considered his physique and marveled at how he stayed in such good shape. *Then again, I used to be able to do that too.* "It's okay, Rick. We'll let you drive, and Tammy shop, and I'll make the list. Deal?" To her surprise, Rick and Tammy both suddenly grew sober. His hand gripped the knob a bit tighter. "What's wrong? What'd I say?"

Tammy blinked a few times, her blue eyes glistening. "My mom always made the list, and Dad and I would go to the store. Now I make the lists."

"I'm so sorry," Cari whispered. "I didn't know."

"It's okay," Rick sighed, looking weary. "Change can be a good thing sometimes. Let's go, Tammy. We need to get home. See you later, Cari."

"Sure. Bye."

"Bye Cari." Tammy gave her another quick hug. "And don't worry about us. We'll be okay."

⤐ ((◉)) ⤏

Rick sat in the living room long after Ricky and Tammy went to bed. He replayed the afternoon over and over in his mind. Having coffee with Cari. Watching Tammy bustle around, making herself at home. *She's growing up so fast. Too fast. And she needs a mother. Thank God for Julie and Cari. They've helped her so much lately. I wonder what they find to talk about.* He shook his head. *Maybe I don't want to know.*

He got up and shut off the TV. He hadn't been paying attention to it for the past hour anyway. Then he sat down again. *I wonder how Cari is really doing. She hides her feelings so well sometimes. I know she's going to retire from the force. I wonder what she'll do then. Will she stay here? I guess so. Her doctor is here. And Mike and Julie. But how will she fill her time? And when will she get her strength back? I know she used to be in top shape. Now an afternoon of company leaves her drained. She's got a long way to go.* He sighed as he shut off the lamp. *But does she want to do it alone?*

"I've got Dr. Wilson's report right here, Cari. Along with the reports from the Department appointed doctors and specialists. I'd still like to hear it from you." Lt. Steele removed his glasses and leaned forward in his chair. "I want you to tell me why your career as a cop is over."

Cari nodded, and swallowed hard. "Yes, Lieutenant." She'd gone over it in her mind a dozen times already, but this was the real thing. "It's not just the physical aspects, Sir, though my days of doing the obstacle course, or jumping a hurdle are over." She gestured to her cane. "But, more than that, it's the stress. The life and death decisions. The ever-present deadlines. My body, especially my heart, can't take that kind of pressure anymore."

She shifted in the chair and winced. "I thought maybe I could. I was willing to do desk duty again. Something. But after the inquest, I knew that wasn't realistic. I'll never be able to give enough to this job again, Sir. There's permanent damage. I may still end up with a pacemaker. But even if I don't, I won't put other officers at risk, just because I'm determined to hang onto a dream."

She licked her lips. "I'm glad I lived that dream as long as I did. Some officers don't get to have ten good years on the force. And I've been blessed with good partners too." She smiled as she looked at him. "And superiors. But I know it's time to let go."

Lt. Steele slowly nodded his head. "Thank you for your honesty,

Sgt." He patted the large folder on his desk. "The doctors all say much the same. You should be able to find some other work, after you've had more time to recover. But not something as stressful as police work. Office work maybe. Consulting of some kind. Shorter hours." He smiled. "Maybe it's a good time to think again about marriage and children." He held up his hand so she wouldn't interrupt. "I know, all of that is too soon, and maybe too painful right now, but don't rule it out completely."

He got to his feet and then sat down on the edge of the desk. "I want you to know that I respect your decision. However, I sincerely wish it could be different. I always hate when good officers retire. I believe you could have gone a lot further in your career with the force. I wish you well in whatever else you pursue. And, actually, I have a suggestion about that. Why not go into investigative work? You have a natural aptitude for it. Years of experience in law enforcement. You could set your hours."

"But, Sir, I – physically, I don't know that I could do it."

"I have a friend who's an amputee, Sgt. and he's done very well at it. Just promise me to give it some thought."

Cari nodded. "All right. I'll consider it. But not until I'm strong enough to function on my own."

"Fair enough. Let me know when you're feeling up to it, and my wife and I will take you out to dinner."

Cari nodded once more. "Thank you, Sir, I'd enjoy that." She paused. "Mike told me that Pam Martin was given a commendation for her actions at the time of my assault."

"Yes, that's right."

"Has she been promoted yet, Lieutenant? I mean, I know she broke a lot of rules, calling superior officers by name, ordering them around, but it *was* a medical emergency. I still think she's got the making of a great cop."

"It takes one to know one. I agree with you. Officer Martin was reprimanded for her breech of protocol, though all of her superiors attributed it to the crisis nature of the situation, and on the whole, her reports still came out looking quite good. Yes, she's been promoted to Police Officer II, and I believe she'll do well. She's going to give some instruction at the Academy in first aid. She's already shown how capable she is in that regard." He laughed. "After what she did for you before and after the medics arrived, I think most officers in this division would be more than happy to work with her."

"I'm really glad to hear that. I think she might be a good candidate for Juvenile Narcotics. Her medical background could be a real plus."

Lt. Steele laughed again. "Still thinking like a supervisor, are you? As a matter of fact, I've already been approached by Detective Macklin about that. Her youthful appearance could be very useful too, in undercover operations."

Cari's eyes suddenly misted with tears. "I'm really going to miss this," she admitted. She took the tissue he offered and dried her eyes. "I never wanted to be anything but a cop."

"Except for maybe a rally driver," he teased.

She laughed at that. "No steady income with that. Just a lot of fun."

<hr>

Cari stepped out of the shower and reached for her towel. Once she had it securely wrapped around her, she went to the mirror and picked up her brush. She shifted her weight to her left leg as she looked at her reflection. She paused the brush in mid air. *I look awful. I'm still pale as a sheet, after all this time. Am I ever going to look healthy again?* She brushed out her hair and dried off. Then she limped slowly to her bedroom and got dressed. She sat on the bed and leaned against her pillows. *I'm exhausted and all I did was have a shower. This is ridiculous!* She fell asleep before any further complaints came to mind.

Chapter 17

Tammy stood at the door with two bags of groceries in her hands, and a grin on her face. "Dad and I stopped at the store on the way here. Now I'll be able to make you a decent meal today. How are you feeling?" She said all that as she marched towards the kitchen to put the food away.

"I'm kind of tired," Cari replied as she locked the door. "But that's not news. How are you?" She inched towards the kitchen and sat down at the table. She watched Tammy work as the girl talked.

"Oh, I'm fine. But something is bugging Dad. He was really quiet this morning. He hardly said two sentences at breakfast." She shrugged as she closed a cupboard door. "He gets in these – these *moods* once in awhile." She opened the fridge to put away a jug of orange juice. "Usually it's because he's been thinking about Mom too much. There, that's finished. Should I do some more laundry this morning?"

Tammy's energy level made Cari envious, but she shook her head. "Not yet. I'd like you to sit down and talk to me. Okay?"

"Sure. About what?" Tammy plopped down in a chair, put her elbows on the table, and placed her face on her hands.

"About your mom, if you don't mind." Cari watched the girl's expression, but didn't see much change.

"Well, okay. But what do you want to know?"

"Anything. What did she look like? What did you used to do together? Things she liked to do or see. Anything."

Tammy licked her lips. "Well, she looked a lot like me." She made a face. "Or I look like her. Whatever. She had blonde hair and blue eyes. She was kinda short. Great figure." She smiled. "She used to blush every time that Dad would whistle at her. They met in high school, by the way. Umm. She liked to watch old movies. You know, the really sappy ones that make you cry. She read loads of books. About almost anything. She used to say that was one way she never felt like an idiot. She had read *something* about *many* things, so she could make a decent comment if she was asked."

Tammy shifted position. "She was really smart. Always top of her class in school. Better marks than my dad actually, and she used to tease him about that. She loved going to the beach. Not to swim or suntan though. She liked to just sit and listen to the waves. She told me once that it made her think of God's heartbeat. I never forgot that." She was silent for several minutes, but Cari didn't interrupt.

"She used to worry about my dad sometimes, especially if he was working the night shift. Rather ironic, isn't it? My dad never got hurt at work, and my mom was killed at home." Her eyes were suddenly wet.

Cari reached over and took her hand in hers. "What happened, Tammy? Do you want to talk about it?"

"She was shot by some guy on drugs," Tammy blurted out. "He stole some money and shot my mom. Dad found her when he got home. She was still alive then, but she died in the hospital. I never even got to say 'goodbye' to her." She put her head down on her arms and wept. "I miss her so much sometimes. She was always ready to listen. I love my dad, but he's always ready with an *answer*. Do you know what I mean?" she asked with her head back up.

"Yeah, I think I do. Guys are like that, Tammy. They want to be able to *fix* everything. And it's hard for them when they can't." She had tears in her own eyes. "Mike is one of my best friends, but it took him a long time to learn that I didn't always want advice, just a sounding board. Maybe you should ask *him* to speak with your dad. That might help."

"Maybe." Tammy wiped her eyes and got a tissue from her pocket and blew her nose. "I didn't mean to sit here and bawl like that," she apologized. "Sorry."

"Don't be. You have no idea how much I cried when my parents died. Or even in the past few months. Pain and I have become close companions."

"How did they die?"

"They were killed in a car accident. A head on collision. The other driver was killed too. He was a 17 year old stoned on pot." Cari shook her head. "Drugs make such a mess of peoples' lives."

"Wasn't the guy who beat you up on drugs too?"

"Yes he was. Crack."

"It's so hard not to hate them, isn't it?" Tammy asked, staring intently at the table. "I mean, *they* make the stupid choice to do drugs, and *we* have to pay for it." She clenched her fist. "They never even caught the guy who killed my mom. At least Mr. Patterson shot the one who hurt you."

Cari was stunned by the outburst, but even more by her own feelings. *I've hated like that too. I've struggled with the same things. I've been so relieved that Kyle Richards is dead. I never even thought of it as hate. And what about Mark? I hate him too, don't I? I won't let go of the pain. Part of me wants to make him pay for hurting me.* She covered her face with her hands for a moment.

"My dad doesn't hate the guy. He *prays* for him. He said that's the best way to keep from hating him. You can't pray and hate at the same time. I've tried to pray, but it's so hard. Hating is so easy." She frowned. "How did we get off onto something so morbid, Cari?" She moved to get up.

"Tammy, wait a minute. Everything you just said is so true. I've never once tried to pray for the people who hurt me. And, yes, it's much easier to hate. But that doesn't make it *right*. They made bad choices that affected our lives. But we still choose whether or not to hate them for it."

"Yeah, I guess you're right." She flicked her bangs out of her face.

"Thanks for saying what you did. I needed a reminder like that." Cari shifted on the chair. "*Now*, how about some coffee? You did such a fine job yesterday."

———

Cari lay awake long into the night. She couldn't forget her conversation with Tammy. *God, you know that I don't want to forgive Mark. I know that he apologized. I think I could even believe that he meant it. But I still hate him for what he did. How do I let go of that? How?*

'By letting me give you something better.'

Cari sat up in bed and wrapped her arms around her knees. *What?*

'I'm still here, Cari. I've never left. Just trust me. That's what I'm asking you to do. I have something so much better than hate to give you. Trust me.'

Cari wept until her sides ached. "Okay, God. I – I'll let go of the hate. I'll trust You." Her whispered words seemed to echo in her room. "I'll trust You."

Chapter 18

Cari had been home a week when she received an embossed envelope from *Richards & Richards* law firm. Her hands shook as she opened it. *What is this all about?* She already knew that the inquest had been thrown out. *Are they going to try for a law suit instead?* She removed the sheet of stationary and read it over twice, not comprehending.

Dear Ms. Daniels;

I hope that you will take the time to read this simple note. I assure you that you have nothing to fear from myself, or this firm. On the contrary, I wish to apologize for ever being foolish enough to drag you into court at all. Unfortunately, a grieving mother does not always think clearly. I had given Mr. Neilson free reign while preparing the case for us. I greatly regret the outcome of my negligence.

In short, I humbly apologize for any grief that this brought to you, both physical and otherwise. That was never my intent. I have already taken the liberty of speaking with Officer Patterson, and he advised me to write to you rather than to see you in person, at this time. However, at your earliest convenience, I would like to meet with you. I have a matter that I wish to discuss with you, that I hope could prove beneficial to us both. My card is enclosed, along with my personal phone number. Please contact me as soon as you feel up to it.

I wish you a complete recovery.
Sincerely,
Rebecca Richards

What on earth is this all about? What could she possibly have to say to me?

'Trust Me.'

Cari closed her eyes for a moment. *Okay, I'll call her. But I have no idea what to say to the woman. None at all.*

Cari reached for her phone and looked at the prestigious business card clipped to the bottom of the page in her hand. She pressed each number and waited. She was ready to hang up after the third ring, but just then someone answered.

"Hello? Rebecca Richards speaking." She sounded formal but pleasant.

Cari's hands began to sweat as her throat went dry.

"Hello? May I help you?" Still no hint of irritation.

"Mrs. Richards, this is Cari Daniels. I – I just received your note."

"Just a moment, Ms. Daniels. I'm going to go close my door." Cari could hear footsteps moving away and returning. "Ms. Daniels?"

"Yes."

"How are you doing? Officer Patterson informed me that you've been resting at home." She sounded genuinely interested in the answer.

"I – I'm doing all right, I suppose. Very tired though. And, frankly, I'm quite bored." *Why did I say that?*

Mrs. Richards laughed. "Well, I hope to be able to alleviate some of that boredom for you, Ms. Daniels. When could I meet with you?"

Cari swallowed as her mind raced. Thankfully, her heart didn't follow suit. "Well, I – that depends on *where*." *My apartment is way beneath this woman's league.* "I haven't been out much since--" she hesitated as she scrambled for an intelligent response.

"I understand. Actually, it might be best if I could just come to see you at home, if you don't mind. This is a rather private matter anyway. Would that be all right with you?"

Cari cast a frantic glance around the room. *There's only so much cleaning that Tammy can do with this place. It'd still look pretty much the same.* "Next Friday?" she stammered. She heard pages flipping.

"Morning or afternoon? I have an engagement in the evening."

"M-morning, I guess."

"About ten o'clock?"

"That would be fine." *Liar.* "Mrs. Richards?"

"Yes?"

"What is this all about?" *There, I've said it!*

There was another laugh. "Nothing sinister, I assure you. But I'd much rather discuss it next week."

"All right."

"Goodbye, Ms. Daniels. Thank you for responding so promptly. It only confirms my previous opinion of you."

"Ah, thank you. Goodbye." Cari hung up then and closed her eyes. *There is no way that I'll sleep next Thursday. A wealthy woman, that I do not even know, is coming to see me about something she won't discuss over the phone. I'm going to go crazy!*

'Trust Me.'

—◦◦◦—

Julie brought Tammy over on Thursday afternoon and helped clean the apartment. She laughed at Cari's panicked features.

"Will you relax? The woman, contrary to what you may think, is not a tyrant. She's actually very nice. She took Mike and me to the most expensive restaurant I have ever been in, and treated us with the utmost respect. We had a wonderful time." She sat down opposite Cari. "And she apologized for the things that she had said to Mike at the inquest. She was very sincere, Cari. Trust me, it'll be fine tomorrow."

"But who's going to make the coffee?" Tammy asked with a grin. "I think I have you spoiled, Cari. You only drink it when I'm here."

Cari laughed. "Well, kiddo, I haven't forgotten how to do *everything*. I think I can manage a pot of coffee." She bit her lip. "But would you mind getting out my good cups and saucers for me? And buying some cream downstairs?"

"And some napkins, and a good tablecloth, and some petit fours? Really, Cari, is the woman that much of a snob?" Tammy wrinkled her nose in obvious distaste. "Would you just like me to come in a maid's uniform and wait on you?"

"Don't you dare, you cheeky little kid! But you're probably right. Why am I making such a big deal out of this?"

"Because you're scared," Tammy reasoned. "So, where's your purse? I need to go buy that cream for you."

"It's in the bedroom. You know where I keep my change purse." Tammy went to get it and Cari rolled her eyes when she looked at Julie. "I don't know what I'd do without her, Julie. I'll be lost when she goes back to school in September. She's helped me to maintain my sanity."

"Anything else, Cari?" Tammy asked as she moved towards the door.

"Yeah," Cari answered with a grin. "I've got a craving for a *Twinkie*."

Tammy groaned as she unlocked the door. "Oh brother! You've been around my dad too much." She was still muttering out in the hall.

Chapter 19

C ari jolted up off the couch when the buzzer sounded. She made her way to it and answered, while bracing her now painful side. "Who is it?" she asked, already knowing the answer to that.

"Ms. Daniels? It's Rebecca Richards. May I come up now?"

"Sure." Cari pressed the button for the door and waited, trying not to be sick. When she heard footsteps in the hallway, she swallowed. *I will not throw up. I will not throw up.* She then heard what could only be described as a *polite* knock on the door. She turned the knob and opened it. Then she stared in surprise.

There stood Rebecca Richards, clad not in a designer suit, but in blue jeans, a cotton sweater and a sports jacket. Her dark hair was loose around her shoulders, and she wasn't wearing much make up. She looked much closer to 40 than the 50 she must be.

Rebecca smiled at Cari. "May I come in, or would you rather talk in the hallway?" she asked with a note of humor in her voice.

"Please excuse me, Mrs. Richards." Cari backed up and allowed Rebecca to enter. "Please make yourself comfortable." She closed the door and bolted it. "Would you like some coffee?" she asked as she turned around. She found Rebecca looking at her collection of books.

"You have wonderful taste, Ms. Daniels. Have you read all of these?" She gestured to the bookcase.

"As a matter of fact, I have. I've had a lot of *spare time* lately. And reading is something that doesn't tire me too quickly."

Rebecca turned around and smiled. "Well, yes, I'd love some coffee. Why don't we just sit in the kitchen? Then you won't have to worry about carrying anything back and forth."

Cari blushed at the woman's foresight. She still had a pronounced limp, and she had indeed worried about carrying hot drinks. "That would be fine. Right this way." She went to the kitchen and pointed towards the table, which had been beautifully decorated by Julie and Tammy the day before.

"You have a lovely apartment. It reminds me of the one I lived in before I married Luke." Rebecca gave a low, unladylike whistle. "That would have been almost 30 years ago already. Time flies, doesn't it?" She pulled out a chair and sat down.

Cari managed to pour the coffee without spilling it, and joined Rebecca at the table. She stirred the cream into her coffee before looking up. Then she bit her lip before speaking. "Why are you here, Mrs. Richards?" Cari blushed as soon as she spoke.

Rebecca laughed as she touched Cari's arm. "It's all right, Ms. Daniels. I haven't really meant to be *mysterious*. I just wanted to talk about this in person. Don't worry. I don't bite." She laughed again. "Though some of my associates may try to tell you different." She took a sip of coffee and smiled. "This is wonderful." She set the cup down. "Now, shall we get right down to business?"

"Please do," whispered Cari, trying not to let her mind wander to countless possibilities.

"I'd like to offer you a position at the firm, Ms. Daniels."

"You what? I'm not a lawyer."

"I realize that. Lawyers we have in abundance, Ms. Daniels. It's something else that I have in mind. Would you care to hear about it?"

"Sure." Cari clasped her trembling hands together in her lap.

"What I would like to have you do is take over the security

department for me."

"Security? What kind of security?"

"Well, we have a large office building. There are closed circuit monitors in all the hallways, though not in the offices themselves. We also have a security officer for each floor, two on mine. They patrol the hallways and make sure that only people cleared through the front office are around. All of my staff wears ID cards, so it's not too difficult to distinguish a client." She drank more coffee before continuing.

"I'm sure you can appreciate that we deal with a great number of confidential matters at our firm. Many well known people hire us to represent them. We cover all aspects of law, both criminal and civil."

Cari nodded, but she ignored her coffee.

"Well, sometimes our clients are involved in rather—*tense* disputes. They may have private investigators following them, etc. We like them to feel comfortable when they come to us."

"Hence, the security. But what would you want me to do? It sounds pretty well organized already."

"On the contrary," Rebecca sighed. "In the past six months alone we've found people trying to enter my office, as well as several others in the building. Somehow, despite our precautions, they're getting through." She got up and refilled her coffee cup, motioning for Cari to remain seated. "I'd like you to devise some extensive training sessions, for *all* of the staff, not just the security department. And then, if you're willing, I'd like you to work in the front office."

Cari was stupefied. *'Trust Me.'* "But I'm not qualified for that kind of position."

"You most certainly are, Ms. Daniels. Ten years of police work. You've gained the rank of Sergeant. You've taken computer and business courses. You're somewhat familiar with the legal system. And you're highly observant." Rebecca looked down at the table and fingered her napkin. "I noticed that in court. You described my son, Kyle, in more detail than *even I* could have. You remembered numerous specifics. Oh, indeed you are qualified."

"But, I still don't understand. Why are you offering me this position?"

"It's not just a good will gesture, it that's what you're thinking, Miss Daniels. Yes, I enjoy helping people when I can. However, when it comes to the firm, I don't let personal interests get in the way. Not *usually*. Kyle, unfortunately, was the exception. Luke and I knew he was using drugs. We just didn't realize how heavily. If we'd known, we – well, I *don't* know what we would have done." Her dazzling diamond ring caught the sunlight as she moved her hand. Then she looked at Cari once more.

"I've been looking for someone for months, Ms. Daniels. But my *gut instinct*, if you will, kept me for hiring anyone. Then I met you, albeit under unusual circumstances. You're talented, resourceful. You obviously have a fighter's spirit in you. You're alert, and you *ask questions*. I hate when the people I work with simply nod their heads as though they understand everything. You don't learn as much that way. Will you at least consider the position?"

"Y-yes, I'll consider it, Mrs. Richards, but you have to realize that I'm far from well at this point. My doctor would have a fit if I suggested *any* job." She smiled as some of the tension left her shoulders. "Actually, you could say that he has me on *probation*. I'm not even sure when a short walk won't leave me worn out. I don't know what kind of an answer I could reasonably give you."

"A simple 'yes' will do for now. We'll work from there."

"But --"

"You did say that reading doesn't tire you too quickly?"

"Yes, but --"

"I happen to have a briefcase full of security reports down in my car. I thought you might like to look them over for the next few weeks. Then, by the time you actually come to the office, you'd have a bit of a head start."

Cari laughed for the first time. "I see why you've been so

successful in law, Mrs. Richards. You have got *persistence* down to a fine art."

"My husband calls it *persuasion*. But thank you just the same. What else would you like to know about the job? I can see that your head is just about ready to burst."

Cari felt her cheeks flush once more. She clasped her hands a bit tighter. "Well, now that you mention it . . ." She tried to get her thoughts in order. "Who would be my immediate supervisor?"

"I would. Actually, we'd meet regularly to discuss any security matters, either good or bad."

"And who would I be responsible for? Or, should I say, how many?"

"About twenty-five. And I'll warn you now, Ms. Daniels, some of them don't really appreciate working *with* women, let alone *for* them."

Cari grinned at that. "Somehow, that doesn't surprise me. It isn't a whole lot different in law enforcement. How many hours per week?"

"That's entirely negotiable, especially given your physical limitations. You could start off as part time, and increase your hours as you're able to, at full salary, of course." She went on to name a figure that left Cari speechless. "And you'd have a company car, if you'd like. Or, you may keep your own, and take an equivalent benefit on an annual basis. Many of our employees choose to do that."

"What kind of car?" Cari asked as she thought of her rusted '82 Camaro.

Rebecca looked at her and whistled again. "I did have you pegged right! You choose the vehicle, provided it's within the price range offered. We regularly deal with BMW."

"This job is looking better all the time."

"Mind if I make a suggestion?"

"Of course not."

"Don't rush out and look for a new apartment. This one is

decidedly *homey*. A great place to relax. Luke and I have a huge house. We can entertain the entire staff easily. But there's only one room in the whole house that I can truly *relax* in, and that's the library. Don't change for the sake of a job, Ms. Daniels. Just continue to be yourself. You'll never regret doing so."

Chapter 20

Cari called Julie as soon as Rebecca left her apartment.
"I still can't believe this, Julie! I wasn't even thinking about a job yet, and she practically dropped this one into my lap. What do you think Mike will say about it?"

"He'll probably figure that you're the best person for it — when you're well enough, that is. Just make sure you take time to recuperate, Cari. No more stints in the hospital please."

"I hope not. Actually, I have a huge pile of notes to go through for the next while. That'll keep my brain occupied, while my body starts to catch up."

"You *sound* excited about this. *Are* you?"

"Yes, I am. I'm shocked. And I'm not sure why she chose me, but I'm looking forward to it. You know how much I enjoy a challenge."

"That I do. Speaking of which, have you talked with Rick in the past couple of days? Mike said he hasn't been quite himself this week. Tammy only shrugged when I asked her about it yesterday."

"Well, no. I don't see a lot of him. He usually just drops Tammy off and picks her up. When he does stay long enough for a coffee, he only talks about his shift. Not about himself. I guess he's kind of a quiet person. Isn't he?" She realized just how little she knew about Rick.

"Not according to Mike. Something must be bothering him. Oh, well, he'll talk when he's ready, I suppose. We can pray for him regardless."

"I better go and lay down, Julie. I'm not used to having such exciting mornings anymore."

"See you later."

"Bye." Cari hung up but didn't head for her bedroom. She was still puzzling over Julie's question about Rick. *I wonder what could be bothering him right now. Is he still in one of his 'moods' that Tammy talked about?* She shook her head. *I'm getting too tired to figure out anybody else's moods. I have enough trouble with my own.*

"Well, you must be following my orders this time," Dr. Wilson commented as Cari rejoined him in his office. "No major problems?"

"Not at the moment," Cari replied. "I still limp like a rodeo reject, but at least I'm walking on my own, and I can finally drive my car again." She grinned. "It's so nice to only have to consult *my* schedule now, and not with other drivers."

"Just don't push yourself."

"When do you think I'll be ready for some office work – even part time?" she queried, hoping that he wouldn't yell at her for even suggesting the idea.

"That depends on a few things."

"Such as?" She sat slightly forward on the chair.

"Such as: how many hours, sitting or standing, stress level, and your eagerness to start."

"Well, I get to name the hours. Combination of sitting and standing. I'm not sure about the stress level at this point. And I'm eager to start – in maybe a month or so."

He put his hands together and rubbed them back and forth. He was no longer smiling. "Doing *what*, exactly?"

"Supervising security at a law firm. Some teaching, some monitoring, some reception work. And lots of reports to type up and file."

"Sounds like it might be feasible. When did this come about?"

"Just recently. And I can wait as long as you insist upon. The job is waiting for me. But I'd like to have some sort of time frame in mind."

He consulted the calendar on his desk. "How about the beginning of September? Part time only, mind you. You might be able to handle full time by October, but don't try to hold me to that."

Cari felt her shoulders relax. "Thank you. I'm sure that will be fine. At least I have something to aim for."

"So, how are you doing emotionally? That's not as easy for me to examine." He smiled at her again. "Severe trauma such as yours causes more than physical pain."

Cari looked down at her hands for a moment, considering how to answer him honestly. "Well, I have good days and bad ones. At this point the good are starting to outweigh the bad. However, I still have moments when I'm so frustrated I could scream. Or when the pain is so intense that I wonder if my life will ever return to normal." She swallowed before going on. "And in another month it'll be the due date for the baby I miscarried." She bit her lip. "That won't be easy either. But I'm spending more time with friends than I ever did before. Even making some new ones. And now I have a new career to look forward to. So, all in all, I guess I'm doing okay."

"Glad to hear it. And thank you for not just giving me the traditional 'I'm just *fine*, Dr. Wilson'. I never fall for that."

"No, I don't suppose you would."

"Well, I'll see you again at the end of the month and give you a definite answer about work. All right?"

"Great. Thank you." Cari got up from the chair and tried to

loosen up her right leg. "I always have enjoyed rodeos," she said with a laugh. "I could always pretend." Then she made her way from the office, limping as she went.

⟫⟨◍⟩⟪

Rebecca Richards came to visit after hearing from Cari at the end of August. She brought along her husband this time. He was a tall, thin man in his mid-fifties. Dark hair, grayed at the temples, and a warm smile. Cari liked him immediately.

"Nice to meet you, Mr. Richards. Please come in. Would you care for some coffee?"

"No thank you, Ms. Daniels. We've just had lunch." He and Rebecca sat on the sofa and his wife opened her briefcase and withdrew a file folder. Cari saw that her name was on it.

"I thought it might save time if you filled these out at home. Then you can just bring them into the office next week." Rebecca passed the folder to Cari. "All the standard job forms, as well as company guidelines, protocol, safety regulations, etc. If you have any questions just give me a call at the office."

"Thank you."

"Ms. Daniels, I wanted you to meet Luke today because you'll seldom see him at the firm. He's already semi-retired, and only handles a few cases a year from his home office." Rebecca smiled warmly at him as she reached for his hand. "That's why you'll report directly to me. Luke is pretty much just a figurehead at the firm. Chairman of the Board. But most of the decision-making is up to me."

"I understand," Cari replied respectfully. "It sounds like you two have worked out a very agreeable relationship through the years."

"That we have," Luke put in. "We've had almost thirty years to hammer out the details. Becky always has been the better administrator. I prefer handling an actual case. So, I've let more and more of the control pass over to her. I still have an office with a name plaque on it, but I'm rarely there to make use of it."

"Luke also encouraged me to hire you," Rebecca added. "He figured that if a woman could head the company, one should be able to head a department."

"Well, I plan to give it my best shot," Cari said. She immediately put a hand over her mouth. "I'm so sorry I said that. It was a very poor choice of words." She hated the pained look that had crossed Rebecca's face.

Luke was the first to recover. "It's all right, Ms. Daniels. I won't say that Kyle's death never crosses my mind anymore. But we don't harbor any resentment towards you for what happened, or towards Officer Patterson. We can see now how little choice you had under the circumstances."

"Thank you," she whispered.

"And since Kyle's death, we've instituted a *Zero Tolerance* policy at the firm in regards to drug use. If we suspect that any employee is using any, we insist on a drug test by a private lab. If the test is positive, the employee is let go. So far, we've lost three promising young attorneys. So, we're trying our best to make something positive come out of our son's mistakes. Hiring you is another of them."

"Well, I certainly hope that I don't disappoint either of you."

"I have no fear of that," Rebecca answered with a smile. "And I'm seldom wrong."

———— ◦《◉》◦ ————

Cari had Tammy spend the whole of Labor Day weekend with her. Rick was working, Ricky was camping, and Cari thought it would be fun to do something together before the school year resumed. Tammy was excited at the prospect. She brought a bag full of junk food and pop with her.

"Who all are you expecting?" Cari teased. "A small army?"

"Nah. Just an ex cop and a giggly teenager."

"Okay, but what on earth do we start with?"

"That's easy. First we have the popcorn. Then the chips and pretzels. Then some of the sweet stuff."

"I see you have it all planned out. Do I get to do anything?"

"Sure. You get to pick all the movies we're going to watch."

"Thanks."

They had a wonderful time the whole weekend. When Cari took Tammy home on Monday, Rick invited her in for supper. She was about to decline.

"Don't worry, I'm not cooking. I'm just going to order some pizza. How about it?"

"Well, okay." Cari entered the house for the first time, and was immediately met by a family photo of the Bensons. "Your wife was beautiful, Rick," she said before catching herself. She turned to look at him when he cleared his throat.

"Yeah. Everybody always thought so – me included." He cleared his throat again. "So, how do you like your pizza?" He had a pen in his hand to write down her answer.

"Anything but anchovies." He scowled. "What?"

"That's two strikes against you then."

"What are you talking about?"

"You don't like westerns either." His scowl was replaced by a grin as Cari continued to stare at him. "Too bad, seeing as you walk like you just came off a ranch."

"You take that back, Benson!"

"Why should I?" he asked as he picked up the receiver. "I'm the one paying for supper." He pressed the buttons and ordered two pizzas, one with anchovies and one without. Cari was still fuming when he hung up. "If you're trying to intimidate me with that look, it won't work, you know."

"And why not?"

"Because I've already planned how I'm going to cream you at *Scrabble* tonight."

"Well, Rick, still think you can 'cream' me at this game?" Cari asked two hours later. "I've used all my letters, and I have 100 points more than you do. *Nobody* is that good."

Unlike the first time they had played, Tammy had sat and watched the whole time, checking for any words that they accused each other of making up. She seemed to be enjoying herself immensely.

"Are you ready to admit defeat yet, Dad?" she asked with a cheeky grin.

Rick didn't even look up at her. "Not yet," he mumbled.

Cari looked at her watch. "Rick, I really should be leaving now. I actually have a job to go to in the morning." He still didn't look up. She tried again. "Officer Benson, are you ready to call an end to this game, or will I have to charge you with resisting arrest?" Tammy giggled. Rick still stared at his remaining five letters. Cari gripped the corners of the board and jerked it up. Letters slid over onto Rick's side, and right into his lap.

He jumped up from his chair. "What'd you do that for?" He finally looked at her.

Tammy was hysterical now. Cari tried not to laugh.

"Rick, you are by far the most obsessed *Scrabble* player I have ever met. I'll gladly take you on again sometime. But you really better learn when the game is over." She got up from her chair, and grimaced at the familiar stiffness in her right thigh.

Tammy stopped laughing when Cari sucked in her breath. "Are you okay, Cari?"

"I'll be fine, Tammy. I've just been sitting for too long, that's all." She took a step and halted.

"You are *not* fine," Tammy insisted. "Want me to help you to your car?"

"Sure. I'd appreciate that."

"We could drive you home," Rick offered, apparently forgetting about the game.

"That won't be necessary, but thanks anyway." She put an arm around Tammy's shoulders. "Okay, Kiddo, let's go." They got as far as the front door before Cari admitted defeat. She looked at Rick. "Is the offer still open? I don't think this leg is going to cooperate."

"Sure. But why don't we wait for Ricky to get here? Then I'll drive you in your car, and Ricky and Tammy can follow. We'll come back together afterwards."

"That sounds like a lot of bother. I should just --"

"You should just wait for Ricky to get here," he insisted.

Cari frowned as she regarded Rick. Then she laughed. "Good thing they only shoot lame horses, and not the cowgirls. I'd be in serious trouble otherwise."

———— ◦((◦))◦ ————

An hour later Rick was escorting Cari to her door. Her leg hurt more than ever.

"Thanks for the ride, Rick. I appreciate it." She unlocked her door and opened it.

"You're welcome. Anytime." He touched her arm and she turned around. There were tears in his eyes. "I'm sorry for kidding you about your leg before supper. I guess I had no idea how much it still bothered you."

"That's okay." His tears and apology made her uncomfortable. That, and the fact that they were alone for the first time ever. "Hey, I joke about it," she said with a smile.

"You do it to hide the pain. I did it to tease you. That isn't the same at all. I'm really sorry." He released her arm and stepped back. "Good night, Cari."

"Goodnight. And thanks for driving."

"Sure. See you later."

"Bye." Cari entered her apartment and closed the door. Then

she leaned against it. And suddenly she thought of Julie's remark to Tammy months earlier, about men understanding tears. *"Most men don't. So if you find one who does, marry him."* Cari closed her eyes and clearly envisioned the anguished expression in Rick's eyes when he'd apologized. *I think I just met another man who understands tears. Mike is married already, but Rick isn't.* Then she remembered the family photo at the Benson home. *Or maybe in his heart he still is.* She shook her head and straightened up. *Men who cry just don't fit into the puzzle right now. I have a new career to think about.* She got halfway to her bedroom before she paused mid stride. *But he sure has gorgeous eyes.*

Chapter 21

Cari took her cane with her on Tuesday morning, seeing as her right leg was still sore from the previous evening. *So much for first impressions.* She entered the underground parking area of *Richards & Richards,* showed some identification, and then waited while the attendant called up to Mrs. Richards' office. He spoke for a moment and then smiled.

"Your spot is just over there, Ms. Daniels. Close to the elevator and stairwell. I put up the sign on Friday."

"Thank you --" she took another look at his ID card, "Ted."

"You're welcome."

Cari found the spot readily enough and parked her car. Then, cane in hand, and briefcase in the other, she headed for the elevator. She got off on the first floor and found Mrs. Richards waiting for her.

"Good morning, Ms. Daniels. Ready for your first day?"

"Yes I am. What would you like me to do first?" Cari noticed that she was attracting a fair bit of attention, discreet of course.

"You can follow me and have you ID photo taken. Your card should be ready by lunch time. Then just come up to the conference room and I'll introduce you to some of the other partners."

"All right."

The picture was taken and the two took the elevator to the tenth floor of the building. Cari was again thankful that she wasn't afraid of heights.

"Right this way, Ms. Daniels." Rebecca moved gracefully, yet purposefully ahead of her down the plush hallway. It was obvious that only the senior partners were on this floor. She stopped at a clearly labeled door and opened it. Then she waltzed in, a smile on her face. "Ladies and gentlemen, I'd like to introduce you to our new Security Manager, Ms. Cari Daniels."

Cari followed her in, and was met by a few smiles, some sober expressions, and a couple of leering glances. She set her jaw as she approached the empty chair that Rebecca indicated to her. She set her case on the table and her cane on the floor next to her chair. A round of introductions followed. *I'll never be able to learn all these names, never mind another couple hundred employees.* She smiled politely at each one, trying to regain her confidence. *It's the cane. I feel better when I don't need to use it.*

"Ms. Daniels, while I think of it, John Maxwell is the person you'd go to any time that I'm on vacation, or unable to be reached." A man directly opposite Cari smiled at her. She guessed him to be around forty, and he had cultured good looks. His smile was both open and unnerving. Cari returned it briefly and then looked away. Rebecca brought her back to the matters at hand.

"As you all know, I've hired Ms. Daniels to fine tune our Security Department, and hopefully to prevent further problems here at the firm. She's spent the past several weeks going over files pertaining to each incident. And she's come up with a few suggestions for us. Go ahead, Ms. Daniels."

"Thank you." She looked at the brief case, but decided she might drop files before she got them opened. She also wasn't sure about standing in front of all those executives. She put her hands together and got into her topic.

"As Mrs. Richards has already stated, I've been going over each incident report. I believe that I've found a common thread, as it were, to link them all." John Maxwell crossed his arms and leaned back in his chair. "I strongly suspect that someone in the security department is *purposely* allowing people into the building. What I haven't figured out yet is *why* they would do so. Perhaps speaking with some of you would aid in my investigation. You see, I need to have a better idea of some of the cases that were being handled at the time of these incidents." Some of the lawyers shifted in their chairs, and a couple frowned severely. Cari was undeterred.

"I recognize that you take matters of confidentiality very seriously as attorneys. However, I'm still requesting the information. So far, no thefts have taken place that we know of. But, there is always the possibility that if someone could slip into an office for a few minutes, they could *look* at a file, or perhaps photograph it."

"Surely you're not suggesting espionage, are you?" Steven Hawkings complained. "This isn't a movie set, even if we are in LA." A few members snickered at his comment.

Cari gritted her teeth for a few seconds. "Mr. Hawkings, I'm certain that you're aware that almost *any files* could be subpoenaed."

"Of course I am."

"Then wouldn't it be simpler to work *with* me, rather than *against* me?" She smiled sweetly as she watched his facial expression take on a distressed tinge. She noticed John Maxwell wink at her and she lowered her gaze. "My job here is to find where the breeches in security are. Frankly, some of them are very simple. For instance, do all of you, and your staff, lock the offices when you step out, even briefly? Do you leave files on your desk, or your briefcases unlocked?" Several throats were cleared on that question. "Do you leave your Rolodex on your desk, or lock it into a drawer when you leave?" More furtive glances around the table.

"I'm not trying to tell you how to run your business practices. I am trying to point out potential problems, before they become an issue. Secondly, I've been asked to design a training program for *all* staff members to participate in. I plan to cover things such as observation techniques, which shouldn't be too difficult for a group of top notch lawyers." They didn't seem to appreciate her remark. "Gathering accurate information is extremely important. Self-defense is another area that could be covered." She caught of whisper of: 'Doesn't look like she passed that one herself.' Cari clasped her hands a bit tighter, and tried not to blush or lose her patience.

"Finally, I would like a list of *anyone* who should not be allowed into this building. For example: former spouses, boyfriends, girlfriends, anyone who wasn't happy about a former case outcome, especially if they ever uttered any threats."

Steven Hawkings muttered again, "That'll be an extensive *list*. Where do you plan to keep it? Tacked up on the bulletin board?"

Cari slowly rose from her chair and braced her hands on the table. "No, Mr. Hawkings, I do not intend to post it for all the world to see. I'll enter it into the main computer in the front office, complete with pictures, if possible. Furthermore, Mr. Hawkings, you may not like me personally, or care for what I'll be doing here, but I'm not about to let you stand in my way. I intend to do my job to the best of my abilities – with or without your assistance." She felt a trifle guilty when some of the others smirked, but only a trifle. She sat down once more and looked at Mrs. Richards. Rebecca was smiling, a glint of humor in her eyes.

"Thank you Ms. Daniels. I'm sure that if anyone has any questions later that you'll be more than happy to answer them." Cari nodded. "For the time being, I suggest that we all get back to work." She looked across the table. "John, will you please show Ms. Daniels to her office? I'll bring her the keys a bit later."

"Certainly," he replied, with a roguish grin.

Rebecca got to her feet and everyone else followed suit. Cari was still reaching for her cane when John said, "Allow me." She looked up into his face as he passed the cane into her right hand. Then he straightened up and helped her glide her chair away from the table.

"Thank you," Cari murmured. She got to her feet and picked up her briefcase. Pain shot through her right leg and she clenched her jaw.

"How long has it been now?" John asked. "About five months, isn't it? I'd say you're doing remarkably well."

Cari met his gaze with a questioning one of her own. "How did you--"

"My dear Ms. Daniels, have you already forgotten who you're working for? Several of us in this room attended Kyle Richards' funeral. As a matter of fact, I was one of the pallbearers." Cari felt the color draining from her face, just as John put a steadying hand on her right arm. "I don't hold grudges, I assure you. I knew the boy was headed for trouble months before he died. I even tried to help him." He shook his head. "He didn't want to be helped."

"Why are you telling me this?" she wondered aloud.

"Just trying to give you the lay of the land." He chuckled deep in his throat. "You've already picked a fine match with Steven Hawkings. He's a male chauvinist bar none. He works here for the salary, not the boss. And he doesn't like *anybody* telling him what to do, about anything. He's a fine lawyer, but I've often questioned his methods. You likely made some of the women a bit nervous. They sometimes think they're in a field unto themselves. They forget that other women are just as skilled, or clever." He released her arm and took her case from her hand. "Or as beautiful. Shall we go?"

"Y-yes, thank you, Mr. Maxwell."

"Please just call me John. I save the 'Mr. Maxwell' for the court room." He led her to the door and held it open for her. "By the way, my office is the one next to Mrs. Richards', if you need me for anything. Your office is down on the first floor, right in the line of defense."

"Are you *always* in such a good mood?" she asked as they entered the elevator.

He raised his eyebrows and seemed to ponder her question. "I think I'll let you find that out for yourself." He winked again and Cari looked at the carpeted floor.

Oh, Lord, what have I gotten myself into with this job?

Chapter 22

C ari was ready for a break when Rebecca Richards entered her office, ID card in hand. She smiled as she set it on Cari's desk.

"How's it going so far?" she asked. "Making yourself at home in here?"

Cari laughed softly as she let her gaze travel the room. She had a huge desk. Matching file cabinets, a sophisticated computer system. A few expensive prints adorned three of the walls. An oak wall unit covered the other, complete with a large TV and VCR. "At *home* you ask?" She tilted her leather swivel chair. "There's more money invested in this room than my whole apartment."

Rebecca seated herself across from Cari. "How are you feeling? Had enough for your first day?"

Cari sighed. "That obvious, is it? As a matter of fact, I'm quite tired – even if it is only lunch time."

"Don't force yourself to stay this afternoon, Ms. Daniels. Set a pace that you can handle."

"I suppose you're right, Mrs. Richards. I had no idea I'd tire this quickly. I think I'd better limit my hours this week, and start to increase them after that."

"Sounds sensible to me." She crossed her legs and folded her hands in her lap. "How did you feel about your introduction this morning?"

Cari felt a flush creeping up her neck and across her face. "I'm not too sure. It seems that I didn't exactly endear myself with too many, especially Mr. Hawkings." To her amusement, Rebecca rolled her eyes.

"Don't waste your time trying to impress him, Ms. Daniels. Steven Hawkings is as conceited as they come." She grinned. "Actually, I rather enjoyed watching him squirm this morning. That's an all too rare occurrence, I'm afraid." She leaned forward slightly. "All in all, I thought you handled yourself very well."

"Thank you."

"Now, would you care to join John and me for lunch, or would you prefer to head home right away?"

Cari debated briefly. "I'd be glad to join you. Thanks for asking."

"Fine." Rebecca got to her feet. "You can just follow in your own car. Then you won't need to come back for it later."

"All right. When would you like to leave?"

Rebecca glanced at her diamond studded gold watch. "In about ten minutes, I'd say. John and I will meet you downstairs. Your parking spot isn't very far from mine." She turned towards the door.

"Mrs. Richards?"

"Yes?" she turned her head, her left hand on the brass door knob.

"Is John Maxwell married?" Cari asked, hoping she wasn't breaking any company protocol. To her relief, Rebecca flashed a warm smile.

"No, he isn't. He's managed to resist all efforts at match making. Why do you ask?"

Cari fiddled with her desk set. "Well, to be honest, he was so full of flattery this morning, that I wasn't sure what to think of him." She met her employer's gaze. "If I'd found out he was married, well, I --" She shrugged.

"Well, he's not attached in any way, Ms. Daniels." Then she

laughed as she opened the door. "And by the way, John Maxwell never wastes his flattery on anyone. Whatever he said to you this morning, he meant it." She stepped into the hallway. "We'll meet you downstairs in a few minutes."

Cari stared at her closed door in confusion. *What have I gotten myself into? I should have skipped lunch.* She squared her shoulders and got up from her chair. *Well, Mr. Maxwell, I have no intention of ending your long standing record. You can remain a bachelor for the rest of your life. I'm just here to do my job.* She bit her lip. *So why am I thinking about every word he said to me, and how considerate he was?*

————————

At the restaurant, John treated the ladies with utmost courtesy, pulling out their chairs for them, and making certain that they were comfortable. Cari was thankful that she had worn her best skirt and blazer. The restaurant was decidedly upscale. Rebecca and John seemed familiar with the menu, and offered her a few suggestions. She finally opted for a Caesar salad, with lemon glazed chicken breast. And she munched on the sliced French bread that had been brought to their table.

"So, Ms. Daniels, how do you think you're going to like this new position?" John asked just before he took a sip of ice water. "Not as exciting as police work, I'm sure."

"Actually, it's quite similar in some respects. But, I've discovered, there will be even more paperwork that I was accustomed to." She shifted slightly and winced. "Which just might be a good thing."

"If you don't mind my asking," he went on, "just how extensive was the injury to your leg?" At Cari's increasing color, he added, "I'm sorry. That's none of my business. I'm sure it'll have no bearing whatsoever on your performance." He looked at the bread basket and selected another slice.

"I don't mind, exactly," Cari replied. "Goodness knows enough people have asked me about it. I'm sure more will too." He met her look and gave a slight nod, indicating that he was listening. "It's not exactly my *leg* that was injured. It was a couple of blows to the groin area. That tore the ligaments and muscles. It also caused a femoral hemorrhage. So, surgery was necessary to repair some of the damage. That's why the pain hits my thigh so often. That or a stiffness that makes walking on it difficult."

"Hence, the cane," he remarked. "Thank you for your honesty, Ms. Daniels." He smiled at her. "I'm afraid that I've always wanted to know all about people's injuries."

"Maybe because you specialize in insurance claims," Rebecca suggested. "But, unfortunately, that was only one of many injuries Ms. Daniels suffered. It may prove to be the most troublesome or persistent however. I've been told that muscles and ligaments can take a long time to heal."

"That's what my doctors have told me," Cari said. "It could be a year, or longer, before my limp isn't so noticeable." She picked up her glass and smiled, somewhat uneasily. "But I'm sure there are more interesting things that we could be talking about."

"Indeed, Ms. Daniels," John said. "You could tell us what you've gleaned so far in your investigation. You could hardly go into any detail this morning."

Just then, their lunch arrived and Cari spoke between bites of food. John and Rebecca asked questions occasionally, but for the most part, they just listened to what she had to say. The time passed quickly, and it was soon time to leave. Rebecca picked up the tab, despite Cari offering to pay for her own meal.

"Nonsense," Rebecca said. "This was a business lunch. I always take care of those. I'm just glad that you were able to join us." She patted Cari's forearm. "Now go home and get some rest. I'll see you on Thursday."

"But I was going to be back in the morning," Cari replied.

"That won't be necessary," Rebecca insisted. "You need more time. The work will still be waiting on Thursday. And, you'll be better able to deal with it."

Cari glanced at John, but he only smiled and shook his head slightly. Cari backed down. "All right. I have some things at home that I can go over. I'll see you Thursday morning, then. Goodbye. And thank you for lunch."

"You're welcome."

"Good day, Ms. Daniels," John said.

Cari walked to her car and got in. *Yes, I'm tired. Yes, my leg is killing me. Yes, I need to rest. But I* don't *need to be babied, do I?* She started the car and checked for traffic. *But, she is the boss, and I don't think she likes to be argued with either.* Cari smiled. *And I think I like her better all the time.*

Chapter 23

Tammy gave Cari a call when she got home from her first day of school. She asked Cari all about her new job, and sounded very impressed when she described her office.

"Wow! Sure beats the old metal desks they've got down at the police station, doesn't it?"

"I guess so. How was school? This is your first year at this one, isn't it?"

"Yeah. It was okay, I guess. But it always takes me a long time to make new friends. And there are a couple of guys who were whistling at me in the hallway." She sounded exasperated. "I mean, get real, I'm only thirteen years old."

"Well, you are a very pretty girl, Tammy. Try not to let it bug you too much."

"I just ignored them today."

"Smart girl. How would you like to come over after school tomorrow? I'll be home all day."

"Sure. But I better check with Dad first. He might have the day off. I'll call back later and let you know."

"Fine."

"How's your leg doing today? Dad was still worried about you on the way home last night."

"Was he?" That surprised her. "Well, you can tell him that I made it through the morning without too much trouble." She didn't mention about needing her cane to do it.

"I'll tell him. Well, I better go see what I can start for supper. I'll call you after I talk with Dad. Bye."

"Bye." *I wonder why he was worried about me. Maybe I looked worse than I thought last night.*

※

"So, are you going to have a uniform and a gun and stuff?" Tammy asked when she visited Cari on Wednesday after school. "Most security people do, don't they?"

"Yes. Actually, my boss gave me the choice. But, since I've been wearing a uniform and a gun for so long, it'll probably feel pretty normal to keep doing it. And I'll have a radio on me, too. And a master key for every room in the building." Cari paused as she considered the amount of responsibility she was about to assume. "I'll get used to it eventually." She looked at Tammy and smiled. "What about you? Any more whistles today?"

Tammy shook her head. "Nope. But they're almost always looking at me." She shrugged. "Dad said young guys just act that way because they don't know how to treat girls. He told me not to worry about it." Her eyebrows furrowed. "Did guys ever whistle at you when you were my age?"

Cari was taken aback by the question. Then she thought about it for a moment. "I can hardly remember, Tammy. It's been a long time since I was thirteen. I guess in high school guys tried to get my attention. I usually just ignored them."

"What about now?" Tammy pressed. "Do guys ever make you feel, well, *uncomfortable*?"

Cari felt the color leaving her face and looked down at her hands. Thoughts of Mark Hamilton flashed through her mind. *And what about John Maxwell? He commented on my being 'beautiful'.* She looked up again. "Yes, sometimes guys can still make me uncomfortable. Even as a cop. But I try to just be myself. It never helps to get paranoid about stuff like that." *Even after what Mark did to me.*

"Thanks. It's always so easy to talk with you."

"I'm glad you think so." Cari got up from the couch. "Ready for a snack? I've still got some junk food left from the weekend."

"All right!"

⸺◉⸺

Cari spent most of Thursday gaining a better understanding of the security monitoring system at the firm. There were cameras on each floor, in the lobby, the parking area, and the stairwells. She was wondering if they should also be installed in the elevators. *Slip ups are happening somewhere.* She found out how to load the tapes, and edit them; where they were stored, and who had access to them. She also spent part of the time at the front desk, meeting some of the clients as they came and went. She tried to hide her surprise as she realized how well known some of the people were. Movie stars, publishers, producers, writers. *This should be anything but a boring job.*

Cari was on her way to Mrs. Richards' office when she ran into Jerry Nielson in the elevator. They looked at each other, but said nothing. Cari finally tried to ease the tension.

"Good day, Mr. Nielson."

"Hello, Ms. Daniels."

The elevator stopped at the top floor and Cari got out. So did Jerry, but he went down the hall in the opposite direction, whether to avoid her or to see someone, she wasn't sure. She went to Rebecca's office and knocked on the door. There was no answer, so she checked her watch. *Four o'clock. I'm sure that's what time she wanted me to meet with her.*

"May I help you with something, Ms. Daniels?"

Cari turned and saw John standing at the door to his office. "I was supposed to meet Mrs. Richards," she replied. "She doesn't seem to be here, though."

"She probably just stepped out for a moment. Would you like to wait in my office, rather than going back downstairs?"

Cari considered her growing fatigue. "Thank you. I suppose I could just keep calling her office until she gets back." She walked over to him, no cane, but limping badly. She stopped short when she saw him frown at her. "Is something the matter?"

He shook his head and unlocked his door. "Just can't fathom how you're walking at all. I twisted my knee once and thought I was crippled for life."

She suspected that was only part of the truth, but she didn't pursue it. She followed him into his office and looked around in admiration. Unlike her office, all of the furniture was glossy cherry wood. There wasn't a hint of clutter or disorder in the whole room. Even the coffee mugs were neatly arranged on a tray. She smiled.

"I see you're impressed," he commented. "Please, have a seat." He pointed to his chair behind the desk. "I'm sure Rebecca will be back shortly." He set his briefcase on the floor next to his massive desk. "If you'll excuse me, I just need to go and change for an appointment." Without waiting for her to reply, he went to the washroom adjoining his office and closed the door. She soon heard an electric razor going. She felt ill at ease and reached for the phone. Still no answer.

Cari got up from the desk and began to look at the hundreds of books on the floor to ceiling shelves. They were not all legal material. She noticed Shakespeare, Tennyson, Byron, Dickens and Dickenson. *No wonder he talks like he does.* She was still looking at them when she heard the washroom door open, and she quickly turned around.

"Do you enjoy reading?" he asked with a ready smile. "You're welcome to borrow some, if you'd like." He was wearing a fresh shirt and suit. He'd even changed shoes.

Cari wondered who he was going to meet with – a client or a

dinner date. "Yes, I enjoy reading," she responded before her mind wandered any further. "I see you have a number of the classics."

He smiled as he came closer. "You can blame my English professor at Harvard for that. She made them come alive for me. I've been collecting ever since. Any luck reaching Rebecca?"

Cari shook her head. Then she looked at the brass clock on his desk and frowned. "I wonder if she forgot."

"Not without a very good reason. She has a remarkable memory." Just then there was a knock on the door. John opened it and there stood Rebecca.

"I was hoping to find you here, Ms. Daniels." She stepped into the room. "I'm so sorry I missed you earlier. Luke called from home about something he needed from his office, and I lost track of the time."

"That's all right," Cari said. "I've been browsing through Mr. Maxwell's library while I was waiting."

"Good. Thank you, John. Now, shall we go to my office?"

"Certainly," Cari answered. She limped around the desk and to the door. Like John had done earlier, Rebecca frowned. Cari felt herself tense.

"Is your limp as painful as it looks?" Rebecca asked.

"Well, I – I'm not sure," Cari stammered. "I try to ignore it as much as possible."

"And that's why you jaw is clenched?" Rebecca looked at her as though expecting an honest answer.

Cari felt cornered. "Yes, I suppose I do that sometimes, but not always."

"Ms. Daniels, when Luke and I told you about drug testing, did you assume that would also include prescription pain relievers?"

"Well, yes. So, I've only been taking it at home." Now she was more flustered than ever.

John entered the conversation then. "Ms. Daniels, one thing that Rebecca can't stand to see is people in obvious pain. From now on, take your medication whenever you *need* to, including here at work. I'm sure it'll make your job easier."

Cari looked from one to the other, and then at the plush gray carpeting. "I'm sorry. I suppose I should have clarified the information last week."

"No, Luke and I should have done that." Rebecca reached over and touched Cari's arm. "I didn't mean to embarrass you. I just don't want you to endure needless pain."

Cari brought her head up and tried to regain her usual composure. "Thank you, Mrs. Richards." She moved to leave the office.

"Stop by any time," John said. "You could choose a few books to take home with you."

"Thank you. I'll do that." She forced a smile that she didn't really feel and went out to the hallway. *I feel like a complete idiot! It's a wonder I haven't been fired already. I better get my act together — and soon.*

Chapter 24

Cari discovered another employee who liked her about as much as Steven Hawkings. His name was Pete Willis and he worked in the Security Department. He was clearly as chauvinistic as Hawkings, but more outspoken in his feelings.

"I happen to like this job, Ms. Daniels," he practically snarled at her as he sat in her office. "But I can't for the life of me figure out why they hired another woman, let alone as the supervisor. You don't even have any experience in security, do you?"

Cari did not appreciate his question in the slightest, or his general attitude. She gritted her teeth. "If you have a problem with my level of *experience*, Mr. Willis, I suggest that you take it up with Mrs. Richards. She's the one who hired me." To her relief, he made no further comment. "I asked you in here, Mr. Willis, because I've been speaking with each member of the Security Department. And, seeing as you've been here the longest, you may be able to offer some assistance."

He frowned, obviously confused. "With what?"

"Well, for instance, what changes do you think we could make in order to prevent more incidents from occurring? Extra cameras? More staff? Any ideas?"

"Well, I – I guess I haven't thought about it too much." He shrugged and nervously fingered his radio. "None of the incidents have been *major* anyway," he reasoned. "I don't think we need more staff." He leaned forward in his chair. "And why more cameras? Where would we put them?"

"In the elevators."

"I don't think all these lawyers would appreciate that, Ms. Daniels. Right now the only place they have any real privacy is in their offices or the washrooms, or the elevators. I doubt the clients would like it much either. They already get followed around and filmed everywhere they go."

Cari considered his statement for a moment. "You could be right," she conceded. "But if we leave things as they are, we still have to tighten our security measures. If you think of ways that we could do that, I'd be glad to hear them." She got up from her chair and extended her hand.

Pete looked at her hand before standing. He shook it, though he obviously didn't want to.

Cari forced a smile. "Thank you for coming. I'll see you on Friday morning, when I begin the seminars for the staff."

He rolled his eyes. "Look, Ms. Daniels, after five years on this job, do you seriously think I need a refresher course?"

Cari gritted her teeth once more. "Yes, Mr. Willis, I do. I was with the LAPD for eleven years, and I went through many *refresher* courses." Her eyes narrowed slightly. "And I wouldn't bother to call in sick either. You'd only have to take the course later."

"All right, I'll be there." He moved towards the door, but turned at the last minute. "But I'll likely be bored out of my skull." Then he was gone.

Cari sat down at her desk and closed Pete's file, but she didn't put it away. *What is the matter with that guy? If he hates working for a woman, why is he here? Then again, he may have been hired before Luke Richards retired. Well, he certainly doesn't like me. He's smart, though. A trifle too cocky, but a thinker. I'd much rather win him over than fight with him. I doubt that he loses an argument too often.*

She got up and put the file folder into her briefcase and snapped the locks. She smiled as she recalled his parting remark. *Well, Mr. Willis, I'll do my best to keep you from being bored.*

———⟨◦⟩———

Indeed, by lunch time on Friday, Pete Willis was wishing that he'd kept his mouth shut. Cari had him participate in some of her 'Observation' lessons, and he didn't do too hot on any of them. When she had someone pose as a robbery suspect, he only got half of the physical features correct. When she flashed a series of license plate numbers on the screen, he could only recall a few of them. Likewise, when she held up photos of vehicles, he couldn't keep all of the colors straight. He couldn't complain about her being *unfair* though. She asked everyone the questions. They all made errors. However, Pete had always prided himself on his observation skills. He was quickly finding out that those skills were sadly lacking.

Cari's closing remarks soothed his ego just a little. "I didn't have you go through these exercises so that you would all feel stupid," she said. "But, I do hope that you'll make the effort to work on these things. For example, when you drive home, notice a few license plates, and see if you can write them down when you get there. Learn to *observe* people without *staring* at them. Call up an auto body shop or a car dealer for a current listing of paint colors." She held up two large glossy photos. "As you can see, there's a big difference between gloss and metallic." She set them aside.

"I'm also not out to make anybody feel guilty. What I am aiming for is to make *Richards & Richards* a firm that both employees and clients can feel safe in. I can't do that alone. But, I hope, we can all work together on it. Thank you for your time and patience. The next session will be in two weeks." She grinned. "Now go have some lunch."

Chairs moved all over the room as employees got to their feet. They all cleared out, except for Pete Willis. He approached Cari, feeling none too comfortable.

She looked up and smiled. "Can I help you, Mr. Willis?"

"No. I mean, not really. I just wanted to tell you that I guess you were right." She cocked an eyebrow and waited for him to continue. "I guess we *all* need refreshers once in awhile. Maybe I've been getting a bit careless." He looked down at the floor for a moment.

"Thank you," she replied. "I'm glad this morning proved useful."

His head came up and he saw that she was still smiling, but she didn't look as though she was *gloating*.

"Maybe you could help me to prepare the next session. I'm not as familiar with patrolling hallways and stairwells. I wouldn't mind some *experienced* personnel giving me a few tips."

Pete felt heat rising from his neck to his face, and he hoped that there was no color showing with it. "Sure," he said. "I could help you with that."

"Good. I'll talk with you next week sometime." She gathered her various materials together. "Maybe on Tuesday. I won't be in on Monday." She dropped one of the photos and squatted down to pick it up. Her face went pale as she did.

"You okay?" Pete asked. When she didn't answer right away, he squatted down next to her. "Ms. Daniels, are you okay?"

She gave a quick jerk of her head.

"Want me to help you up?"

"I'll be fine," she murmured, still not looking at him.

Pete was sure that he saw tears in the corner of her eye. She reached up her right hand and gripped the edge of the conference table. Then she pulled herself to her feet. Her face was completely white.

Pete tried a different tack. "Female. Caucasian. Blonde hair, brown eyes. Approximately five-eight. One-thirty pounds." She was staring at him now. "Visibly distressed."

"Very good, Mr. Willis," she said, her voice quiet. "But I'm five-nine, and 140 pounds."

Pete crossed his arms as he watched her knuckles whiten. "The rest stands, Ms. Daniels."

"I told you that I'll be fine." She was looking more agitated. "You may leave now."

"Suit yourself," he said, uncrossing his arms. "But maybe you'd better sit down for a few minutes before you try to walk out of here. I'm sure you don't want to faint in the hallway – on camera, at that."

She sighed as she leaned her weight against the table. "Thanks for the advice. But I'm meeting Mrs. Richards for lunch in a few minutes."

"I can let her know you'll be delayed," he offered. He noticed color returning to her cheeks.

"Mr. Willis, I'm quite capable of using a telephone myself." She clenched her jaw and straightened to her full height. "So, would you please leave?"

He could hear the note of anxiety in her tone, though she managed to keep if from showing on her face. "All right, I'll leave. What time do you want to meet on Tuesday?"

She looked puzzled for a few seconds, but recovered quickly. "About ten o'clock."

"See you then." He turned and headed for the door, wishing that she wasn't so stubborn, while at the same time admiring her grit.

Cari was still leaning against the table when the telephone rang. She carefully turned around and reached for it. "Hello? Cari Daniels speaking."

"Cari, it's Rebecca Richards. I'm afraid I'll have to cancel lunch today. I just received a call from a client who can't meet with me at any other time before next week. Sorry for the inconvenience."

Cari tried not to sigh with relief. "That's no problem, Mrs. Richards. Actually, I'm still tidying up in here. Then I think I'll just order something to my office. I have a lot of work to do." *I'll find some if I have to.*

"Fine. I'll see you next week. By the way, how did it go this morning?"

"Very well, I think." She was trembling more than before and braced her right hand on the table.

"Good. Bye for now."

"Goodbye." Cari hung up the phone and made her way to the nearest chair. She was still sitting there an hour later when John Maxwell came in.

———«(◉)»———

"What are you still doing here, Ms. Daniels? The session was over before twelve, wasn't it?" He approached her with his long legged stride and sat down on the edge of the table. Then he studied her face. His smile faded. "What happened?" He glanced at her right leg, which was stretched out in front of her.

"My leg acted up," she admitted. "But not until the session was over, thankfully."

"So, that's why you're still sitting here?" he asked. "Can you even get up?"

"I've been too tired to even try." She put her hands up to her face and sighed. "This is so ridiculous. I go to see Dr. Wilson on Monday morning. I was all set to tell him how little trouble I've been having since I started working again. Now this!" She blushed as she looked up into his face. "I – I'm sorry. I'm just thinking out loud, I guess."

"We all do that, Ms. Daniels. Now, the question remains: can you get up from that chair?"

Cari put her hands on the arm rests, braced her left foot and got to her feet. "I'm up," she said through gritted teeth.

"Next question then. Can you walk?" He got off the desk and put a hand on her right arm. "Ready to give it a try?" She nodded.

She took a couple of steps and said nothing, but John could see the tautness of her shoulders beneath her uniform. "Okay. Third question. Would you like a ride home, or do you want to hide out in your office for the afternoon?"

Cari looked at him, her face pale. "My office, please. Could you just --"

"Help you there? Certainly. Actually, I wasn't going to give you the option." He helped her to the door. "However, I will let you choose lunch. I was all set to go for some Chinese food myself. I could just get extra."

"Sounds fine, thank you." She paused at the door and closed her eyes. "All I did was squat down to get something off the floor. I can't believe it hurts this much after almost six months." She opened her eyes when John touched her cheek.

"Next time, just ask someone else to pick it up for you. Six months is not very long." He moved his hand away from her face. "Ready for a late lunch?"

"Sure," she replied, a slight smile curving her lips. "I love Chinese food."

"Glad to hear it." He reached behind her and opened the door. "Let's go."

Chapter 25

"Feeling any better?" John asked as he gathered up the garbage from their lunch.

"Yes, thanks," Cari replied. "But, I'll admit, the thought of a hot Jacuzzi is real appealing at the moment." She rubbed her right thigh before getting to her feet. "Thanks for getting lunch. I appreciate it."

"Ready to head home now, are you?" At her nod he added, "Are you sure you can drive?"

"I'll be okay." She gritted her teeth as she removed her jacket from the rack near the door. "Sore, but okay."

"Well, I guess I'll have to take your word for it, but I'd much rather drive you home myself."

Cari thought of the long weekend when Rick Benson had needed to do just that. Somehow, this was different. Rick was a friend. John was a fellow employee. Almost like a supervisor. It didn't seem quite right. "Thanks for offering, John. I'm sure you must have plenty of work to do."

"I do, but it'll get done whether or not I take you home."

"I'd have to come back for my car," she reasoned. "Trust me; I'd rather just manage on my own." To her surprise, he didn't smile when she did.

"Independence is a wonderful trait, Ms. Daniels. Stubborn

pride, on the other hand, is not. Which is this?"

Cari frowned at his keen insight. *This guy should have been a cop instead of a lawyer.* "A little of both," she conceded. She opened her door and turned the lock, a none-too-subtle hint.

"Have a good weekend," he said, still unsmiling, as he stepped past her into the hallway.

"Thank you."

————)(◉)(————

Cari's weekend was anything but 'good'. She regretted driving before she was halfway home. A soak in the apartment complex Jacuzzi offered no relief either. She needed extra medication just to sleep that night. She spent Saturday trying to get her muscles to loosen up. She missed church on Sunday because she didn't want to face any more sympathetic glances. By Monday morning she wasn't as stiff, but Dr. Wilson frowned at her anyway.

"What did you do to yourself?" he asked. She explained briefly and his frown worsened. "You're barely *walking* and you try something like that? What were you thinking?"

"I was *thinking* that I needed to pick up the photo," was Cari's irritable reply. "Not that it might be something that I couldn't do yet." She sighed in frustration. "I felt fine otherwise. It's just this stupid leg that won't cooperate with me."

"This 'stupid leg' as you call it, could very well have cost you your life six months ago," he informed her. "The injury was extensive, and the hemorrhage hard to control. By the time you reached the hospital, you didn't even have a pulse in it." He put his face closer to hers. "Do you realize the implications of that, Miss Daniels?"

Cari shook her head, startled by his outburst.

"Then I'll tell you. You could have lost your leg. Lack of circulation destroys the tissue very quickly. And, after the surgery, the threat of a blood clot was a major concern as well." He crossed his arms and stepped back from the examining table. "I realize," he went on, his voice calmer, "that you had enough other injuries to think about. But, please, don't take your leg so lightly. You're very lucky to still have it."

Cari felt sick, even as tears blurred her vision. "Why didn't you tell me this before?" she wondered aloud. "Nobody did."

"Like I said, you were already thinking about your heart and chest injuries. Now, those seem to be healing well. Let's concentrate on your leg. You like swimming, don't you?"

"I used to. I haven't gone since March. Why?"

"Water therapy is very good for damaged muscles. It builds strength without causing further injury. Hasn't your physiotherapist suggested it to you?"

"Maybe she did," Cari replied. "But I don't remember."

"Ask her about it." He put a large hand on her arm. "I'm sorry if I startled you before. I'd just hate to see you lose the ground you've worked so hard to regain."

"I understand, Doctor." She couldn't help but think of John's remark about *stubborn pride*. "I guess I should have been more careful."

"Well, let's have a listen to your heart and lungs, shall we? I can tell by your breathing that they've improved considerably since I last saw you."

⚬《●》⚬

A rather subdued Cari went to work on Tuesday morning. She met with Pete Willis, and they discussed the next training session. She appreciated his input, and made a point of telling him so. He didn't seem to *like* her any better than at first, he just didn't *resent* her quite so much. She met with Rebecca after that, and went over what she had been doing so far, as well has her plans for the next while. Her boss was more than pleased.

"I knew you were the right person for the job, Ms. Daniels."

After leaving Mrs. Richards' office, Cari knocked on John's door.

"Come in," he called.

Cari opened the door and found him at his desk, looking as handsome and well organized as ever. *He's got to have a few flaws, somewhere.*

He was in the middle of something and didn't look up at first. "Be with you in a minute," he murmured, still writing in an open file.

"Mr. Maxwell, this is hardly a good example of office security," said Cari with a grin. His head jerked up in a most undignified manner. "First of all, you didn't ask who was at the door. And you didn't even bother to see who entered the room." She pointed a finger at him, as though he were an errant child. "You definitely need to work on that, sir."

John laughed as he got to his feet. "I stand corrected, Ms. Daniels. I'm afraid I was quite engrossed in my files. I'll try to be more prudent in the future. Please, have a seat." He tried not to be obvious, but she saw him looking at her right leg as she approached the desk and sat down.

"If I'm disturbing you, I can come back later," she offered. "I should have asked."

"I'm grateful for the interruption," he assured her. "Now, to what do I owe this pleasure?" He sat on the edge of his desk, rather than his chair.

"Actually," she said, "I came to invite you for lunch." He was still smiling, so she went on. "I owe you lunch." She swallowed. "And I also owe you an apology. You see --" She stopped when he raised his right hand.

"Apologies are much better over good food. As for owing me lunch, fine. Shall we eat out, or in?"

Cari was once again taken aback by his frankness. "Out, if you don't mind." She felt herself begin to blush. "I'd rather not start any rumors by eating lunch in my office – with male staff members. I'd rather be seen in public." She put a hand to her flaming cheek. "That didn't come out right!"

"No need to be embarrassed. And I whole heartedly agree with you. Friday was quite an exception. I knew you weren't in any shape to go to a restaurant just then. As a general rule, highly visible settings are what I aim for. You'll find that Rebecca Richards does the same. So, where would you like to go?" he asked, slipping off the desk in a graceful move.

Cari sighed. "Well, where do three piece suits and security uniforms *both* fit in?"

"*Langers*," he replied readily, removing his jacket from a hanger on the back of his door. "Corned beef on rye, coleslaw, dill pickle, and a *Coke*. How about you?"

"The same," she said as she got to her feet, careful of her right leg. *Just how much do I have in common with this guy, anyway? He sure is full of surprises.* She stood by the door. "Uh, Mr. Maxwell, aren't you forgetting something?" She casually pointed to his desktop, where an open file still sat, next to an open briefcase.

"Well, well, Ms. Daniels, I can see that Rebecca hired the right person for your job. However, I also believe someone else might not prove to be quite so distracting." He quickly put his things away. "Shall we go?"

—⋙«◉»⋘—

Cari offered to drive, and John didn't argue, but he did insist on opening the door for her and closing it once she was buckled in. Then he moved around to the passenger side and got in. He gave her some brief directions to the deli and they left. Once they got there, John came around to her door again, making Cari blush. She decided she needed to say something.

"Look, Mr. Maxwell, I appreciate your chivalrous treatment of me, but I – I'm just not used to it. Frankly, it makes me kind of nervous."

"All right. But you don't realize how much you're asking, Ms. Daniels. My mother would have my head if she saw me stand back while I let a woman open her own door." He shrugged his broad shoulders. "Let me know if you change your mind. Otherwise, make sure you stay clear of my mother."

Cari laughed out loud and covered her mouth until she could control herself. "If it's going to be that much of a hardship for you, then by all means, take care of the doors."

He bowed slightly. "Thank you. I'll be able to eat my lunch in peace now."

"Oh, let's get inside!" she scolded.

"So, after I got that lecture from Dr. Wilson yesterday," concluded Cari, "I knew that I owed you an apology. I'm sorry if I offended you. I know you were just trying to be helpful."

"Apology accepted." He finished the last of his soft drink. "Does this mean that if I notice your limp worsening, etc. that I'm allowed to comment? Perhaps even offer assistance?" He looked deadly serious, but Cari still smiled at the way he phrased his question.

"Yes, I suppose it does. However --"

"I somehow thought you'd issue a disclaimer." He munched on his dill pickle.

"I don't want to be babied, Mr. Maxwell. Most of the time my leg isn't too bad. Friday was an exception. A mistake that I don't intend to repeat."

"Certainly, Ms. Daniels. You have my solemn promise that I will not hound you in any way about your physical well being." He grinned as he finished his pickle and picked up the tab. "But I also won't let you pay for lunch out of a sense of guilt. I've enjoyed your company." She was about to protest but he simply shook his head. "You drove, so I'll pay for lunch. Next time I'll drive and you can pay. Fair enough?"

"You must drive your opponents crazy in a court room," she sighed.

He laughed as he stood and helped her with her chair. "I often do," he admitted. "Though, most of them don't take it as graciously as you do."

Chapter 26

By the end of October, 1992, Cari was getting accustomed to working full days, as well as doing water therapy and weights to strengthen her right leg. She was more comfortable in her position, and was having lunch with either John or Rebecca on a weekly basis. She'd conducted two more training sessions, which had been well received by the staff. She was enjoying her new BMW immensely, as well as her pay increase.

Things were also going well between Cari and Rick. She and Tammy got together a couple of times per week, including supper at the Bensons' ever other Friday night. She and Rick usually played a game of *Scrabble*, which Cari usually won. She was also developing an interest in puzzles, and helped Tammy to assemble several of them during her visits. Ricky was seldom home, but Cari enjoyed his company when he was. He was soft spoken, and rather shy. But he had a wonderful sense of humor that he sometimes let show.

"What will you be doing for Thanksgiving, Cari?" Tammy asked when she stopped by after school.

Cari tried to stifle the sudden wave of panic that crept up her spine. "I – I'm not sure. I guess I haven't even been thinking about it."

"Not think about Thanksgiving? It's my favorite holiday – except maybe for Christmas. Well, what did you do last year?"

Cari got up from the couch, mug in hand. "I think I'll get some more coffee," she said, mostly to herself. *How do I answer her question? She's getting to know me almost too well.* She went to the kitchen and filled her mug.

Tammy followed her and stood next to her, hands on hips. "Okay, what gives? I thought I asked a pretty simple question."

Cari set her mug down on the counter, knowing she might drop it otherwise. Then she forced herself to answer Tammy question. "Last year was not a great occasion, Tammy. I had supper with my fiancé, and then we got into a big argument. And he broke off the engagement." She shrugged. "So, I guess that's one of the reasons that I haven't felt much like celebrating anything. It's kind of like a bad anniversary." She forced a smile. "What will you guys be doing?"

"Going over to the Pattersons' place. Julie said she'll even let me help to stuff the turkey. I figure the guys will watch sports all afternoon."

"Likely, though you can usually pry them away with the smell of the food, and some pumpkin pie with whipped cream."

"Why don't you join us?" Tammy asked. "I'm sure Julie won't mind."

"I'm not sure, Tammy. I've been getting kind of tired lately. It might be nice to stay home and read a good book. I don't know." She placed a hand on Tammy's shoulder. "Please don't worry about me. I'll be fine."

———— ((●)) ————

"Any plans for Thanksgiving?" John asked as he and Cari ate their corned beef sandwiches at the deli. She shook her head. John's eyebrows furrowed. "No family to go and visit?"

"No. My parents died almost three years ago."

"Sorry to hear that. I'm sure my parents wouldn't mind if you tagged along with me."

Cari almost choked on her piece of bread. Then she shook her head. "I couldn't do that, John."

"Why not?"

"I – I just couldn't, that's all." She reached for her drink and took a sip.

"That's not much of an answer, Cari."

"Well, it's the only one you'll get from me," she stated rather coolly.

"All right." As was his habit, he ate his pickle last. "For the moment."

⬥

Cari picked up her phone on the third ring. It was the day before Thanksgiving, and she was relaxing at home. That shattered with the call.

"Hello?"

"Cari? It's Mark." The receiver began to slip out of her hand.

"Why did you call me?" She sat down on the couch and tried to regain her composure. "What do you want?"

"I'd like to see you, Cari."

"Well, I don't want to --"

"Just give me a chance, please. We could meet at any restaurant that you choose, as public or as private as you want."

Cari gnawed on her bottom lip. "What do you want, Mark? Why should I meet with you?"

"I just want to talk with you, Cari. If you want, I could try to bring my pastor with me."

"What?"

"Look, Cari, would you meet with me?"

"All right," she agreed, afraid he might keep phoning otherwise. "There's a *McDonalds* not too far from here." She looked at her watch. "I'll meet you in an hour, okay?"

"Do you want me to bring my pastor?"

"No. We can meet alone."

"Thanks, Cari. See you in an hour."

Cari hung up the phone and stared at her trembling hands. *Why did I agree to meet with Mark? Am I just curious about why he would call me again after so long? And why would he offer to bring a pastor with him?* She stood up. *I guess I'll find out tonight.*

———)(●)(———

Cari spotted Mark at a table in the corner. She went to buy a cup of coffee and then joined him. She got right to the point. "Okay, Mark, I'm here. Why did you call me?"

"Do you remember when I came to see you in the hospital?"

"Yes. That was months ago." She took a sip and burned her tongue.

"I know. And a lot has happened since then, Cari. That's why I called you."

"What do you mean?" In spite of her tension, she was curious about what he would say.

"After I spoke with you in May, I started to go to another church." His cheeks reddened slightly. "Pastor Hiller had made it clear that I was no longer welcome to attend the same church as you." He cleared his throat. "I only went for a couple of Sundays before I realized that I needed to do a lot more than just tell you that I was *sorry*. I needed to somehow make restitution for what I did." He gripped his cup a little harder.

"I started by talking with Pastor Larson. I confessed to him what I'd done – without naming you. I mentioned the pregnancy and the miscarriage. And I asked him what I should do. He told me to pray about it until I felt I had some clear direction from God. That's why I've taken so long to call you." The corners of his mouth curved upwards. "I guess I'm a slow learner." He immediately sobered. "I also didn't like what God was telling me to do."

"And what is that, Mark?" Cari felt compelled to ask. She saw tears begin to glisten in his eyes.

"Cari, if you want me to, I'll go with you to the station, and turn myself in for assaulting you."

"What?" she whispered. The thought had never even crossed her mind.

"I'm also willing to pay damages, if you'd like to file a civil suit." He put his trembling hands in his lap. "I know it can't make up for what I did, but --"

"Mark, I can't report it! Very few people ever knew what really happened." She noticed that her coffee was getting cold. "And I don't want your money either. I don't need it."

"I thought that might be how you'd react, Cari. But I still needed you to know. I can't change the past. I can't undo the hurt. I can only acknowledge my guilt, and try to make up for some of the pain I caused."

Cari clenched her hands into fists and looked down at the table. "Mark, months ago, soon after I got out of the hospital, God dealt with me about my unforgiveness." She raised her head, and a single tear slid down her right cheek. "I struggled with it. I didn't *want* to forgive you. I didn't think you *deserved* it. But God wouldn't let me go. I – I forgave you. I doubt I'll ever be able to forget, but I did forgive."

"Thank you, Cari." He brushed away the tears in his own eyes. "Okay, if you won't press charges, and you don't want the money, what could I do?"

"Give the money to the Sexual Assault Center, Mark," she answered without even thinking. "They can always use the help."

He nodded his head. "Yeah, I guess that would be appropriate, wouldn't it?"

"Yes," she replied. "And much better than giving it to me, Mark. You could help a lot of girls that way."

"I hope so." He looked at their cups. "Would you like another coffee? Or are you in a hurry to get away from me?" His tone wasn't teasing.

"No hurry," she replied. "But I think I'd rather have a milkshake."

"Sure. I'll be right back." He got up from the table and went to order the drinks.

Cari wiped her eyes and blew her nose. *I had no idea why he wanted to meet with me, Lord. Thank You for having me come. I think I'll be able to get on with my life a little easier now.*

Mark was back and set the shakes on the table. "So, how's your new job?"

Chapter 27

Julie answered the door on Thanksgiving Day and found Cari standing there.

"Mind if I crash the party?" Cari asked with a smile.

Julie gave her a hug. "Come on in." She held Cari at arm's length. "But what made you change your mind?"

"I'll tell you all about it when we're alone. For now, just know that God has been busy in more than just *our* lives."

———— ‹‹◉›› ————

Cari had a wonderful time at Mike and Julie's except for one awkward moment when Rick offered her a cup of cocoa. She had refused, a bit harshly. Then she'd tried to explain that she didn't like cocoa. Julie and Mike had looked at her rather strangely, but said nothing. Tammy had eased the tension.

"Don't you know she's hooked on coffee, Dad? I'll go get you one, Cari."

They had each won a game of *Scrabble*, but Cari refused a tie breaker, telling Rick that he might as well enjoy his brief triumph while he could. Then she and Julie had helped Tammy to work on a 1000 piece puzzle.

"At this rate, we'll still be working on this thing at Christmas," Cari sighed. "We've barely got the border together on this."

"'O ye of little faith'," Tammy replied. "This is no sweat for an expert like me."

"Is that so?" Julie remarked. "Well, Miss Expert, how be you go bring out what's left of the pie?"

———— ‹•› ————

"So, how do you feel about your meeting with Mark now?" Mike asked. "You've had a full day to consider it."

Cari fingered the tassel on the cushion in her hands. "It's been really strange, Mike." She met his questioning gaze. "You see, for the first few months, I think I actually *hated* him. Then, I reached a point where I could forgive, but I didn't plan to ever see him again. So, last night, I had no idea what I'd be feeling when I actually sat down at the same table with him. I was nervous. I didn't really know what to say. But I didn't hate him anymore either. And I knew that he was sincere. He's not the same arrogant guy that he was last year."

"He's repentant, you mean?" Mike asked.

"Yes. Back in the spring, I'd say he was *remorseful*, but I don't know about repentant. Now I'm sure. Nothing else would have motivated him to say what he did last night. He took a huge risk."

"And what about today?" Julie asked. "Were you okay?"

"Most of the time." She shrugged. "It's been a year already, and so much has happened – good and bad." She smiled at her friends. "I like my new job, and my car. I work with some really nice people that I likely would never have met otherwise. And I think there's a purpose for me to be there."

"I'm sure there is," Julie replied. She tugged the cushion out of Cari's hands. "Any interesting men?"

"Julie Patterson! Have you got nothing better to do with your time than to try to liven up my social life?" Cari teased. "Actually, one of the senior partners is very nice. I'm sure you'd like him. But, as far as I know, he's not a Christian. We're friends, but I can't see it going past that."

"What if he were a Christian?" Mike asked, a casual tone to his voice. "Would he be serious competition for Rick?"

"Competition? Good grief. Rick is a nice guy, Mike, but that's about it?"

"So why did you agree to go to the Christmas party with him, then?"

Cari felt more flustered than ever. "Well, I figured he might feel more comfortable going with a friend. I don't know." She cleared her throat and looked at the floor. "Besides, Tammy told me that he wouldn't go at all if I turned him down. He doesn't handle rejection well, I was told."

"A *mercy date*, Cari?"

"So, back to this senior partner," Julie primed.

"All right! His name is John Maxwell. He's forty, very handsome, and filthy rich. And the word *gallant* hardly does him justice."

"Well, well. He does sound like serious competition for Rick."

"Enough you two." Cari got up off the couch. "I'm going home to bed. You two can puzzle over my lack of social life all night if you want. I don't intend to lose any sleep over it."

<hr />

"Have a nice weekend?" John asked when he met Cari in the elevator.

"Yes, thank you. I visited some friends of mine. And you?"

"I went to see my parents." He patted his flat stomach. "My mother forced me to sample everything at least twice, of course. It was enjoyable." The elevator stopped at the top floor and they both got out. "Cari, I've been meaning to ask you something."

"Yes?"

"Have you invited someone to the office Christmas party?" His tone was as casual as ever, but Cari noticed a few beads of sweat on his forehead.

"Uh, no, I haven't. I was planning to go alone. Why?"

"Well, I thought perhaps we could go together." Before Cari could even open her mouth he continued. "Not as *dates* of course. It's just that if someone as beautiful as you went alone, you'd have a dozen drunken males, and maybe a couple of sober ones, offering you a ride home. If we went together, we could keep each other company, and you wouldn't have to worry about being harassed." He'd stated it all so logically.

"I don't know about that, John. I was just going to go alone. I'm not used to going out anymore." Then she thought of Rick's invitation. *That's not the same at all.*

"I see." They were at his office door. "Well, would you at least consider it?" He seemed to be aware of her hesitation. "In case you haven't noticed, I don't drink or smoke. Maybe that'll help you to decide."

"John, that's not it at all." She glanced at her watch and frowned. "Look, I have a meeting with Mrs. Richards right now. Could we discuss this after work?"

"Certainly. Good day, Cari."

"Thanks, John. I'll talk to you later."

"John, do you ever go to church?" Cari asked as they stood next to her car.

"Not very often. Why?"

"Well, I've noticed that you have an extensive collection of classical literature, but the Bible is conspicuously absent. Why is that?"

"Well, I don't really know. I mean, I do own one. It was a gift from my parents years ago."

"Do you ever read it?"

"Not lately." He crossed his arms and steadied his gaze. "And what, pray tell, does this conversation have to do with the office party?"

"Actually, quite a lot. You see, I'm a Christian. I suppose I should have told you that weeks ago. In any case, that has a lot of bearing on my relationships. Even casual things like office parties. You're a wonderful man, John, but if we don't share common ground spiritually, there will always be added tension, for me, at least. Am I making any sense?"

"Yes. Just like usual." He leaned against the side of her car, seemingly unconcerned about the dirt that might get on his suit. "All right, you deserve a fair answer on this issue. I was raised in the church. As a matter of fact, my parents still go. I used to memorize Bible verses to win prizes at Sunday School. But, no, I guess I wouldn't call myself a Christian." His brows knit together for a moment. "But I will say this: if a certain young security manager invited me to church, I'd be willing to go with her."

"Really?" Cari was dumbfounded. She'd thought he might get upset with her. Now he was fishing for an invitation.

"Yes. Just let me know the time and place. I'll meet you there."

"Okay." She opened her purse and pulled out a small pad and pen. She wrote down the name of the church, the address, and the time of the morning service. She handed the paper to John and he smiled.

"I've been wondering what it was about you that made you stand out." At her puzzled look he clarified himself. "I don't mean in a negative way. Quite the contrary. Your attitude, your work ethics, your language. I've noticed. I just never bothered to ask you about it. Perhaps I should have."

"If you had, I would have been glad to tell you."

"Cari, does this mean a *no* for the Christmas party, then?" He sounded disappointed.

Cari bit her lip. "I'm not sure, John. Can you let me think about it for a few days?"

"Certainly. It's not as though I have anyone else in mind," he replied as he straightened up and absently wiped at the back of his pants.

"You don't?"

Chapter 28

Cari met John in the church foyer the following Sunday morning. Unlike at work, he was dressed in a two piece suit. He was still extremely handsome, and Cari could tell that some members of the congregation were making assumptions about her relationship to John. She tried to brush aside her misgivings as she shook his hand.

"Glad you could make it," she said. "If you don't mind, I thought that we could sit with some of my friends."

"That'll be fine. Just lead the way." His warm smile helped to put her at ease: until she caught a glance from Tammy Benson. The girl had her eyebrows raised in surprise. Then she turned and looked at her dad. Then back at Cari and John. Cari was thankful to be able to sit down next to Mike and Julie before her color deepened.

"Hi!" Julie said. "Are you going to introduce us?"

Cari did make brief introductions just before the music director began the song service. She found it difficult to pay attention. *I'm not used to sitting with a guy anymore. It's been a long time. And it doesn't help that everybody is likely assuming that he's my new boyfriend.* She reined in her rambling thoughts and joined in with the singing. She noticed that John followed along in the hymnal, but he didn't sing.

During the sermon Cari couldn't help but cast furtive glances at John every few minutes. *I wonder what he's thinking. Will the pastor be able to pierce through his intellectual wall? I know he's a sensitive guy too. God, please help me to just pay attention. I'm sure that I need to hear the sermon just as much as John does.*

When the service was over, Julie immediately invited John to join them for lunch. He looked at Cari as if searching for an answer.

"Did you have any other plans?" she asked. He shook his head. "Well, I usually go to Mike and Julie's on Sunday's, at least most of the time." *Maybe he just wants to go out for lunch. Or go home.*

John turned to Julie and smiled. "I'd be glad to accept, Mrs. Patterson. Thank you for asking. I hope it won't be any inconvenience."

Julie rolled her eyes. "The only *inconvenience*, John, is if you keep calling me Mrs. Patterson. Just Julie would be fine."

"As you wish – Julie." John focused his attention back on Cari. "Shall I follow you over?"

Cari considered for a moment. "Why don't I just ride over with you? Then you can bring me back for my car later."

"Always so logical," he said with a grin. "I'll go bring it around."

"Thank you." Cari watched him as he walked up the aisle towards the foyer.

Julie captured her attention with a tap on the arm. "You weren't kidding, were you? The guy is story book handsome. And the way he talks."

"And he drives a Jaguar," Cari added with a smile.

"Sounds like a pretty stacked deck to me," Mike put in as his arm went around Julie's shoulders. "All that and he doesn't act the least bit arrogant. Amazing."

"But true," Cari said. "I'd better go." Then she paused. "Wait a sec, you guys are the ones hosting lunch. You'd better get there before we do."

"I'm sure you could take a longer route to get there, Cari," said Tammy, who had just stepped up behind her. "So, who's the guy?"

Cari turned around and met Tammy's searching gaze. "He's a

friend from work, Tammy. His name is John Maxwell."

"Oh. Well, I can see that it's a good thing Dad and I are taking Ricky to his volleyball game this afternoon. Dad would be green with jealously if he had to spend much time with that guy."

"Tammy, why on earth would you say something like that?" Cari asked.

"If you haven't noticed for yourself that my dad really likes you, then you aren't as observant as I thought. I better go. See you on Tuesday. Bye." She was gone before Cari could even grasp the brief conversation.

"Try not to worry about it, Cari," Julie remarked. "But she is right. Rick does like you. Maybe more than we thought." Julie looked to Mike but he only shrugged.

"I only work with the guy. And he does not discuss his social life, or lack thereof. Cari's on her own on this one."

"Speaking of on my own, I'd better get out front. John must be waiting by now. See you shortly." She nodded to a few people on the way out, but didn't stop to talk with them. As she expected, John was parked out front, standing at the passenger door, waiting to hold it open for her. "Sorry to take so long."

"No need to apologize." He opened the door and allowed Cari to get seated properly. Then he came around to the driver's side. "I never told you earlier, you look lovely today."

"Thank you." She almost forgot the directions to Mike and Julie's after that.

"I guess I've grown accustomed to seeing you in a uniform at work. A dress makes quite a difference." He pulled away from the entrance area and wound his way through the parking lot, and towards the street.

Once at the house, Mike ushered John to the den, and Cari went to the kitchen with Julie. The table was soon set and Julie called the men to join them. Mike said grace and they began to enjoy the meal.

"You're a wonderful cook, Julie," John commented as he ate his second piece of chocolate cream pie.

"Thank you," she replied. "Would you like some more coffee?"

"No, thank you. A glass of water is fine."

"Do you have any hobbies, John?" Mike asked. He'd already grilled him about his job and family, in a fatherly sort of way.

"A few. I enjoy racquetball, tennis, and horseback riding." He grinned as he brought his water glass to his mouth. "I'm a bit of a jock, I'm afraid."

"Don't let him fool you, Mike," Cari interjected. "He also collects classical literature. And he must *read* it, because he often *quotes* it."

"So, a balanced person, are you?" Julie said. "Mike loves to go hiking. But he always takes along a good book too."

"Hiking, is it? Have you ever gone on a trail ride in the Sierras? The scenery is spectacular."

"No, never done that. Horses and I have never been great friends. I got bucked off when I was about sixteen, and had a busted arm to show for it." Mike shook his head. "Never liked them since. I'd much rather walk on my own two legs."

"I like cross stitch," Julie remarked. "And biking. And trying new recipes." She laughed. "You've been a most accommodating guinea pig, John. This is the first time that I've made this pie."

"Well, I certainly hope it won't be the last."

"I second the motion," Mike declared.

—————«⟨◉⟩»—————

As John pulled up alongside Cari's car, he shut off the ignition and turned towards her. "Thank you for a very interesting day. All of it. But, I also feel that I should settle a question about this morning." He paused a moment. "I'll admit that the church service was interesting. I'd even say that I enjoyed it. But I won't say that I'm ready to make any rash decisions, or to change my life, or lifestyle, for that matter." When he saw that she wasn't going to interrupt, he continued.

"I respect you, Cari, and what you believe. I can see that Mike and Julie share your convictions. But I'm not ready for that. That doesn't mean I won't be at some point in my life. Just not *now*. I hope that you understand."

Cari nodded even as she thought of the verse *'Now is the day of salvation'*. "I understand. No one can make this kind of decision for you. Not now or later. But if you ever want to discuss it again, please feel free to bring it up."

"Thank you. I'll be sure to remember that." Cari reached for the door handle. "Just a minute, please."

"What is it?"

"Have you made a decision about the Christmas party?"

Cari bit her lip. "I'll go with you, John. But absolutely no strings attached. Okay?"

"Certainly," he said with his usual warmth. "Now, let me get the door for you."

Cari laughed. "How could I have forgotten such an important thing?"

Chapter 29

Cari and Julie went shopping for the dresses she wanted for the two Christmas parties. For the police one, she bought a cream-colored, linen shirt dress. It was mid-calf length, with long sleeves. Brass buttons on the front and epaulettes gave it a sophisticated appearance. Julie approved the purchase, but suggested that Cari also get some accessories, such as new shoes or some jewellery.

Cari shook her head. "Julie, I never was much for high heels anyway. At my height, I hardly need to be taller. Besides, anything more than a half inch drives my right leg crazy. Low pumps will just have to do. And I've got enough of those already."

"What about a new pair of earrings, at least? It's such a pretty dress, but why not brighten it up a little?"

"Okay. What kind of earrings? You know I rarely wear any jewellery. I wouldn't know what to pick." *I'm so used to uniforms five or six days a week.*

"Oh, just something simple, Cari. Maybe some gold drop ones. I'll find you something, and I know exactly where to look. C'mon. Let's go." In her obvious excitement, she failed to notice the pained expression on Cari's face.

"Julie, could we please take a lunch break or something? I've got to sit down for a while. My leg is getting sore after walking all over this mall."

Julie was immediately contrite. "I'm sorry. It's just that you're looking so healthy again. I guess I just forget about your leg sometimes." She put a gentle hand on Cari's arm. "Sure, let's go have something to eat. Then I'll drag you to the jeweller's that I have in mind."

Cari had to admit that the new earrings suited her very well. They were small, 24K gold hearts, which were on delicate chains, and simply passed through her lobes and hung nicely. "They are kind of cute," she said to Julie. "But I doubt that they'll go with whatever dress I buy for the office party. That is strictly a formal event." She rolled her eyes. "You should have seen the invitation. Linen paper with gold embossed lettering. It's gorgeous."

"Well," Julie replied, "pearls are always a sure bet. They match just about anything. And you said you were looking for something in dark brown, didn't you?" Cari nodded. "Then pearls will be great. Either drop style like these ones, or some plain studs."

"I think studs." Cari bit her lip as she pondered the idea. "But now you've got me wondering about a necklace, or choker or something. I guess it depends on the neckline." She let out an exasperated sigh. "What a lot of bother for two parties."

Julie ignored the sigh. "A short strand is always nice, Cari. That way, it will look good over a collar, or against bare skin. Try a couple on while we're here."

A half hour later, Cari was leaving the store with two sets of earrings and a small strand of pearls. She was also complaining about the prices. "Christmas specials, my foot! Good thing I make more money that I used to."

"Wait until you buy a gown, Cari," Julie warned. "Then you'll really have something to complain about."

She did. "This dress may be gorgeous, Julie, but it costs as much as a month's rent! This is crazy." But she knew she'd buy it anyway. It was as though the dress had been designed especially for her. It was chestnut brown, with a satin bodice and a velvet skirt. It had a scooped neckline, but was still modest. And the sleeves were short and puffed slightly. The skirt was rather full, and it came with a taffeta lining. Cari knew that the earrings and necklace would accent it perfectly.

The woman who was helping her with the dress spoke up. "Mademoiselle, might I suggest a pair of matching velvet ballet slippers? We also have some small reticules. Would you care to see them?"

"Why not?" Cari said with a sigh. "I want the dress. What's a little more money at this point?" She glanced at Julie and grinned. "Bring on the accessories."

Cari laid everything out on the bed when she got home. She couldn't help admiring the gown. The woman had been right. The ballet slippers only added to the elegance of it. And the purse, only slightly larger than her wallet, was velvet with satin trim, suspended on a dark leather cord. She sat down on the bed and touched the short satin-lined, velvet cape she had purchased, on pure whim, to go with it. *Well, I'll be dressed like a princess, whether or not I feel like one.* Her thoughts began to wander to John Maxwell, and how he might look for the party. She shook her head. *Doesn't matter what that guy decides to wear. He always looks like somebody off the cover of* GQ *magazine. For all I know, maybe he* has *been on the cover of it.*

Cari stretched out on the bed, careful not to wrinkle any of her new clothing. She put her hands behind her head and closed her eyes. *This has been an incredible year. And I can't believe it's almost over. Christmas is in three weeks, and I haven't bought a thing – for anybody else, that is. What on earth do I buy for someone like Rebecca Richards? I mean, she could have paid my bill with loose change. And John, do I get him anything? I'm not used to this kind of job. It was always so simple before. I'd make cookies, take them to division headquarters, and everybody got some. I only bought a gift for Mike. What should I do this year?*

She stared up at the ceiling. *And what about the Bensons? I'm sure I could find a new puzzle for Tammy. Maybe a new basketball for Ricky. But Rick? I've no idea. Besides* Scrabble, *I don't even really know what he likes.* She frowned for several moments. *Some videos of old westerns? That might work. Nothing personal.* She smiled. *Or several cans of anchovies. I might be able to pull this off yet.* She yawned as fatigue crept through her whole body. *But John is totally different. In so many ways.*

＊＊＊

Rick picked up Cari on the 4th and they drove to the party in his white Mustang. Cari found herself comparing it to John's Jaguar.

Rick's voice brought her back.

"Pardon me?" she said, embarrassed that she couldn't even pay attention for more than a few minutes.

"I said that you look very nice tonight. That color really suits you."

"Thank you." She looked away then and thought of the suit he was wearing. It wasn't new, that was for sure. He'd worn it to church before. He looked nice. Handsome even, she supposed. But she wondered now what they would find to talk about all evening.

"You're kind of quiet tonight," he commented as they neared the banquet facility. "Are you feeling okay?" He sounded genuinely concerned.

"I'm fine, Rick. I guess I'm just used to arguing with you across a *Scrabble* board."

He laughed as he turned into the parking lot. "Yeah, I guess so. I'm sure we could think of *something* to argue about, if we tried hard enough."

"What?" she asked as she turned her head and caught sight of his grin, noticing his dimpled cheek for the first time.

"Or we could just try to enjoy ourselves."

Cari continued to watch him as he parked the car.

"Unless we've both forgotten how," he added. He shut off the engine and opened his door. He came around to the passenger side and waited for Cari to get out.

"Did I just miss something important in that last exchange, Rick?" she asked, her eyebrows knitting together.

He shook his head. "I don't think so, Cari." He reached for her arm. "But I do know that neither of us ever goes out with anyone. I'd like it if we could just relax and have a good time."

"Sure," she replied softly. "Let's go." She allowed him to hold her elbow as they approached the building, but he released it as he opened the door. And he didn't touch her the rest of the evening.

———————

"Hey, Cari! Good to see you. How ya doin?" asked one officer after another. She and Rick mingled with dozens of people for the first hour before he steered her towards a chair and a drink of soda water. Just then Lieutenant Steele came over to her and shook her hand.

"Nice to see you up and around, Cari," he said with a smile. "How are you finding life in the security business?"

Cari laughed. "Oh, it's a lot like being a police sergeant, Lieutenant. I wear a uniform, pack a gun and a radio, and I still get to boss people around. It suits me just fine."

"I'm sure it does." He patted her on the shoulder. "Still, we hated to give up such a fine officer." His eyes narrowed. "Having much trouble with your health these days?"

"Some days, yes," she admitted. The Lieutenant joined her and Rick at the small table. "I'm afraid that my right leg is never going to be quite the same, Sir." He nodded. "And I tire easily." She shook her head slightly as she looked at the glass in her hands. "I'll admit that I sometimes miss doing police work. But," she raised her head and met his steady gaze, "I just wouldn't have the stamina for it anymore."

"What about your current job? Isn't it tiring too?"

Cari smiled. "It's *mentally* challenging. Scheduling, training, surveillance, etc. But I'm free to set my pace. I don't face the life and death pressure that I did with the force." She smiled once more. "But I do have just as much paperwork to keep track of."

Lieutenant Steele got to his feet. "Glad you could make it tonight," he remarked. Then he smiled at Rick. "Mike's old and new partners at the same table. Interesting." Then he was off to speak with a few other people.

"So, you seem to really like your new job," Rick said. "I guess I've never bothered to ask you about it before. What, exactly, do you do there?"

Cari spent the next several minutes filling him in. Then Mike and Julie joined them as the caterers finished setting out the food.

———— ◆◆◆ ————

Rick walked Cari to her door when he took her home. He seemed a bit uncomfortable, making her edgy too.

"Thanks for inviting me, Rick," she said as she got out her keys. "I did enjoy myself tonight." She smiled. "And there wasn't even a *Scrabble* board in sight."

Rick didn't return her smile. Instead, he swallowed and then cleared his throat. "Uh, Cari, I've been meaning to ask you something for a while now."

"What is it?" She clutched her keys just a little tighter than necessary as she searched his face.

"I've been wondering if you'd have dinner with me sometime."

"But I already come over every two weeks," she replied, purposely avoiding an answer.

He shook his head. "I mean with *me*. Alone. You know, out to a nice restaurant."

Cari didn't know how to answer. She had been wishing that he simply wouldn't ask her. Now she ran the risk of hurting his feelings: something she really didn't want to do. "Rick, I – it's been a long time since I went out with a guy, over a year, as a matter of fact. And I'm not sure that I'm ready to start dating again." She felt her cheeks flush with color.

"Cari, I haven't even *wanted* to ask a woman out since Karen died. But you're so different. I'm not in hurry to get involved again. But it has been kind of a lonely two years, almost three. And I feel like I can be myself around you." His green eyes were sparkling with rising emotions. "I didn't think it would hurt to ask." He shrugged his shoulders. "Goodnight, Cari. Thanks for coming." He turned to go.

"Rick, wait a minute." He turned back. "I'm sorry. I didn't even give you a fair answer. I'm just not sure what to say." She could feel the keys scraping her palm. "I – I'll have dinner with you sometime. But only if you can understand that I'm not agreeing to anything more than that. Okay?"

"Sure. That's more than fair. Thanks, Cari. I'll call you after I check my shifts. Goodnight."

"Goodnight, Rick." Cari turned and unlocked her door, anxious to get inside, and to be alone with her thoughts. *God, should I have just told him 'no'? But he's so sweet. And we might even have a nice time. Tonight was okay. Oh, I'm just not sure anymore. I hope that I did the right thing.*

Chapter 30

John's gaze swept over Cari twice before he even spoke to her. By then she was sure that her cheeks were crimson.

"My, you look ravishing tonight, Ms. Daniels," he commented, as he took her right hand in both of his. "It's definitely a good thing that you aren't going to this party alone. You would be the object of pursuit all evening." He grinned. "Then again, you still may be. Shall we go?" At Cari's nod, he tucked her arm beneath his and led her towards the elevator.

Cari was doing some covert gazing of her own. John was wearing a tux, but unlike any she'd ever seen, except in old movies. *That's it. It's English cut. Complete with tails. And he thinks that I look nice.* The jacket and pants were charcoal gray. The lapels and leg stripe were both black velvet. He had a waistcoat of silvery gray satin. The ascot was fashioned of black silk. And the shirt was crisp, white cotton. *Julie, wouldn't you love to see this outfit? Most guys don't dress like this for their own weddings, let alone office parties.*

Once at the car, John made certain that none of Cari's gown was in danger of being caught by the door. Then he got behind the wheel, deftly moving his tails out of the way. "All set?" he asked he turned the key.

"Yes," she replied, even as she wondered if it were true. *I'm dressed to the teeth. And John looks like an ad for* Classy Formals. *All this for a Christmas party?*

Cari had been to the Richards' home more than once, but she hadn't seen it decorated for Christmas before. The whole laneway was aglow with twinkling white lights. The double front doors had the biggest wreaths she'd ever seen. All the ground floor windows were also adorned with bows, lights, or in some cases, candles. She sighed as John helped her from the car. "This is amazing."

"Wait until you see the inside," he remarked, taking her arm. "Rebecca has a real knack for making things look inviting." The truth of his statement was borne out just a moment later, as they entered the foyer.

"Oh, my!" Cari whispered. "I feel like I've just walked into a fairy tale." There were more red bows, and garlands, and holly and ivy. The chandelier had mistletoe suspended from it. There were numerous poinsettias, of various colors, all over. Someone took her cape and John led her into the front room. She stifled a gasp when she saw the tree. It was at least twelve feet tall, and packed with ornaments, made of brass, crystal, wood, fabric. It was stunning.

"There you are!" Rebecca exclaimed as she reached for Cari's hand. "And you look simply marvelous. Wherever did you find your dress?" Cari named the boutique. "Of course. They have such wonderful designs there. Come in and have something to drink. Dinner will be served in about an hour. Make yourself at home." She focused on John then. "You're looking as handsome as ever, John. But I'm sure you'll be the envy of most of the men here." She patted his arm. "Have a good time. I'll see you both later."

"Does she *ever* run out of energy?" Cari asked.

John shook his head. "Not that I've ever seen. And I've worked with her for over ten years. Care for a drink?"

"Yes, thank you." They walked over to an expansive bar and to Cari's delight there was some mulled cider. "Ooo. Now it's really starting to feel like Christmas." She took the cut glass mug in both hands and sniffed. "I have always loved the smell of cinnamon, in drinks, in baking, potpourri." She cast an anxious glance at John.

"I'm sorry. I'm standing here rambling like an idiot. You'll regret your choice of escort before too long, I'm afraid."

"Not in the slightest. Besides, I was just about to agree with you." He took a sip of the spicy drink. "Cinnamon has always hinted at the warm, inviting, yet slightly exotic. A bit like the tropical islands, where it first came from."

They spoke with other staff, and Cari received so many compliments on her dress, she was almost glad she'd spent so much on it. Then supper was served and they made their way to the buffet table. Cari could hardly believe her eyes. There was something for every taste; beef, turkey, ham, seafood, both hot and cold, appetizers, salads, soups, crackers, breads, both raw and cooked vegetables. She filled her plate with only a smattering of her favorites. John had his quite laden too. They found a couple of vacant chairs and began to enjoy the food.

By the time everyone had partaken of the main course, some were getting quite drunk. Cari became a bit uncomfortable, and John suggested that they step outside until dessert would be served. She readily agreed. She soon discovered that Rebecca had also been busy in the courtyard. There were several candelabras in strategic locations, casting shimmering streams of soft light around them.

Cari sighed. "It's so lovely out here, isn't it?" She looked up at the star studded sky. She felt John place a hand on her shoulder and she turned to face him.

"It certainly is. Then again, I much prefer the *companionship* of one, to the *company* of a hundred." He reached for her left hand. "Your very presence, dear lady, makes any evening lovely." He brought her hand to his lips and kissed it.

Cari withdrew her hand and looked away, suddenly not so relaxed.

"Is it just me, personally, or all men who make you cringe at a genuine compliment?"

"You always talk to me in such poetic terms, John. I'm just not used to it."

He put two fingers beneath her chin and tilted her head to look at him. "Cari, I'm neither a flirt, nor a tease. I've never dated a woman from the firm, or anywhere else that I've been employed. I despise office gossip, and I don't intend to make you the brunt of it. However, if you expect me to ignore the most interesting woman that I've ever met, you'll be disappointed. I won't push my way into your life, but I won't stand aloof either. I've waited a very long time to find a gem like you."

He lowered his head and Cari closed her eyes, panic and anticipation mingling in her stomach. His lips barely touched hers before he drew back and moved his hand. "Please don't compare me to someone else, Cari. I have no intention of hurting you."

"We'd better go back inside," she murmured, acutely aware of his subtle, spicy cologne.

He smiled at her and reached for her hand. "As you wish. But please remember what I've said."

"I will." *How could I forget?*

——⫷◉⫸——

Cari had no appetite for dessert, plentiful though it was. Her mind was still on what John had said to her. *I tell him distinctly 'no strings attached', and then he turns around and kisses me! The nerve of the man.* She bit her lip. *But he was so gentle. And I'm getting so confused.* She rubbed her slightly throbbing temples. *I have to remember that he's not a Christian. I've got no business fantasizing about him – at all.*

"Headache?" John asked softly. Cari nodded. "Would you like to go home now? I never stay for the dance anyway."

"Yes, please." She looked at him. "But I have no idea where my cape is. Do you?"

"No. But I can find out. Just wait right here." He got up and went to speak with one of the household staff. Cari saw him smile at the young woman, and then he left the room.

"Ms. Daniels? Do you mind if I join you?" The voice above her belonged to Steven Hawkings, and he was very drunk.

"I was just getting ready to leave," Cari replied, looking to see if John was back yet.

Hawkings sat down anyway. "Why waste yer time on Maxwell? You're too good looking for guy like him. An' he's too old for you."

Cari got to her feet rather abruptly, and gritted her teeth against the pain her sudden move brought. "Excuse me, Mr. Hawkings." She took a step, but he grabbed her hand, forcing her to turn around. "Let go of me!"

"Why don't you just sit down an' have a drink?" His smile was nothing short of a leer, and Cari was tempted to slap his face. Instead, she used her free hand to press on his wrist until he let her go.

"Don't ever touch me again, Mr. Hawkings," she remarked, "drunk or sober." Then she turned and left the room, almost colliding with John.

"Hey, wait a minute," he said. "What's the rush? I've got your wrap right here." He carefully draped it around her shoulders, resting his hands there for a moment. "What's wrong? You're trembling."

"Steven Hawkings," she whispered, blinking back a few persistent tears. "Let's go, please." She felt him give her shoulders a reassuring squeeze.

"All right. A hundred and fifty years ago I may have challenged Hawkings to a duel. But, I'll try to let common sense prevail for the moment."

"Please do," she said, looking up into his kind eyes. "Though, the way you're dressed tonight, it's not hard to picture."

They had just come around the corner to the foyer when Cari stopped dead. There, not a dozen feet away from them, were Luke and Rebecca Richards, in a passionate embrace. They were beneath the mistletoe, but Cari could see that they didn't seem to need much motivation. She turned to face John. He was grinning down at her, his blue eyes sparkling. "What's so funny?" she asked.

"Your reaction. Luke and Rebecca Richards have been married almost thirty years. And every year I catch them under that mistletoe, oblivious to everyone and everything around them. I think they're a wonderful example of what marriage *can* be like – even in the world of law and money." He lowered his voice a notch. "Rebecca has been pursued by several men, attorneys and clients alike, since I started at the firm. She either ignores them, or outright tells them to back off. Luke is the same with women. Neither is looking for any excitement outside their marriage, and they make sure that everyone else knows it."

Cari could hear giggling and turned her head. She caught sight of Rebecca wiping lipstick from Luke's neck. She also heard the woman saying, "I'm so glad I married you." And she had no doubt that her employer meant it. The couple stepped away from each other, but still held hands. That's when they noticed Cari and John.

"Leaving us, are you?" Luke asked, looking a little flushed.

"Yes," Cari said. "Thank you for such a lovely evening."

"I'm glad you came," Rebecca said. Then she winked at them. "Have a safe trip home. Goodnight."

"Goodnight," John replied, placing an arm around Cari's shoulders and ushering her towards the exit.

"I *never* saw my parents acting like that," Cari whispered. She looked up as John laughed.

"That doesn't mean they never *did*, Cari." They walked down the front steps. "After all, they had a wonderful daughter like you, didn't they?"

Cari didn't even bother to answer.

⸻ ◦((◦))◦ ⸻

"I upset you earlier, didn't I?" John asked as he stood outside

Cari's door. She nodded. "Why?" He reached out and caressed her cheek.

Cari grabbed his hand with a shaking one. "Please don't do that, John," she whispered.

"You sound frightened. Have I given you any reason not to trust me?"

Tears gathered in her eyes and she shook her head. "No, but someone else did, once. I trusted him too much, and I --" She gulped as the tears began to fall. "I like you, John. I think you're a wonderful man. But I just can't have a relationship with you. I'm sorry." She fumbled with her keys and unlocked her door.

"It's more than the trust issue, isn't it?" She nodded again, unable to speak. "It's because of church, isn't it?"

Cari turned around, her hand on the doorframe. "No, John. It's much more than that. Going to church wouldn't make you a Christian. That's a decision that each person has to make for themselves. And becoming a Christian, just to please someone else – that's not right either."

"False representation," he murmured. "I think I understand. I'm sorry if I offended you. I'll try not to let it happen again."

"Thank you." She wiped at her eyes and tried to smile. "I really did enjoy the evening, John. You were a very nice escort."

He cocked an eyebrow. "*Nice*, she says! Huh! Not at all what I had hoped to hear. Oh well, I shall have to suffer in silence, I suppose. Goodnight, fair lady, and rest well." He bowed at the waist.

"Goodnight, John." She watched him walk to the elevator before entering her apartment. Then she crossed to her sofa, sat down on it, and cried.

Chapter 31

Cari found a 2000 piece puzzle for Tammy and a collection of Roy Rogers's movies for Rick. And she managed to get a basketball signed by one of the famous clients of Richards & Richards. But she still didn't know what to buy for John or Rebecca. She again pulled a few strings with clients, and got a leather bound copy of a rare work by Dickens. And she had a brass candelabra designed for Rebecca. That settled, she focused her attention on her dinner date with Rick.

———))((◉))((———

It was December 20th when Rick took Cari out for supper. They went for Italian food, and were both dressed rather casually. He still found her beautiful. He enjoyed listening to her talk. She rarely mentioned the names of clients, but he knew that she met important people almost every day on her job. She was intelligent, witty, and she had an engaging smile. He was falling hard and he knew it. But he didn't think that she could see it. And he wasn't sure he wanted her to know.

"So, are you all set for Christmas?" he asked while they waited for their dessert.

"Pretty much. You?"

"Oh, I guess so. But, I'll confess, it's getting harder every year. I mean, Ricky and Tammy are both past the toy stage. I just don't know what to get a teenage girl. And ideas?"

"You mean you're this close to Christmas and haven't gotten her anything yet? You'd better hustle," she advised with a grin.

"I know, I know." He waved his right hand in frustration. "But what can I get? One minute she wants to curl up on my lap like a little girl. The next, she's kicking me out of the kitchen while she makes dinner. It's almost scary."

"She looks more like your wife all the time, doesn't she?" Cari asked in a soft tone. "Is that making it even harder for you?"

Rick felt guilty that she'd been able to peg him so readily. "Maybe," he conceded.

"Well, let's see," Cari began, steering back to safer ground. "Has she been admiring anything in catalogues, or on commercials? Has she hinted?" She laughed. "Silly question. Tammy doesn't *hint*, she just *tells*."

"Nothing that I've noticed."

"Does she need any clothes? New shoes?"

Rick shook his head. "I don't think so."

"What about music, or books?"

"Her room is full of them now." He shrugged his shoulders. "I'm telling you, Cari, I've drawn a complete blank this year."

Cari sat sipping her cappuccino, apparently deep in thought. Eventually, she set down her cup and looked at him. "I think I have a possibility, Rick. But you may not like it. I also don't know what you'd normally spend on her." He named a figure and she smiled. "Okay, here's my thought. Why don't you give Tammy a weekend in a classy hotel?"

"What? The kid is thirteen, Cari, not an adult. What are you talking about?"

"Simmer down, Officer Benson, before we get kicked out of here." The waiter set their dessert on the table, asked if they'd like more coffee, and then went to get it. "What I mean is, make a reservation somewhere really nice, feminine even. Have a gift basket waiting in the room, bath products or something. Then I'd take her there for the weekend. I'd pay for the meals. It'd be kind of like an upscale slumber party." She paused while the waiter poured the coffee.

"You see, I've noticed that Tammy is finding Junior High kind of tough so far. Not academically, but socially. She still doesn't have other girls that she spends time with, away from school. And there's the guy issue, too. She's feeling a bit awkward, unsure of herself. Maybe a weekend of being pampered and appreciated for the young woman she is would give her a boost."

Rick sat back and stared at her. She made it all sound so logical, just like – *just like Karen would have. And she's not even a mother. But she was a 13 year old girl once. Maybe it's not such a bad idea after all.* "When?" he asked. "What weekend?"

"Well, I'm pretty flexible on that. Just don't make it too far away, or the anticipation might wear off."

"Okay. How did you come up with such a great idea? It's not like you have kids of your own."

Her smile wavered for a second. "No, I don't. But I did have wonderful parents. My mom and I had a weekend like that when I was starting high school. I never forgot it." She looked down at her cake and began to eat it, effectively ending the discussion.

"Would you want kids of your own – someday?" Rick probed, hoping she wouldn't get upset and storm out of the restaurant. She didn't. But she didn't answer right away. She finished her cake and drank the last of her coffee. Then she met his gaze. Her expression was unreadable.

"Yes, I would – someday. But I don't know when. And I don't know how many. I try not to dwell on 'maybes'."

"What kind of man would ever have been crazy enough to break up with you, Cari?" He didn't realize that he'd spoken out loud until her face went pale. "I – I'm sorry. I didn't mean to say that."

"Do you want an answer, Rick?" she asked, her hands clasped together in her lap, her shoulders tensed.

"Only if you want to give it. I didn't mean to pry like that."

"Maybe it's better for you to find this out now." She looked away for a moment and bit her lip. "I was engaged to a doctor. Last Thanksgiving, I went to his home for dinner. He was acting kind of strange, but I didn't heed the warning signals." Her knuckles whitened. "He raped me. Then he told me to give back the ring and to get out of his house. I did both." She raised her head.

"I'm so sorry," he breathed. *No wonder she's tried so hard to stay clear of guys.*

"That's only part of the story. I got pregnant. I miscarried the day I was assaulted by Kyle Richards."

"Did you ever press charges?" His police instinct was too strong to let the question pass.

"No. I don't know if I could have won a court case anyway. I didn't tell *anyone* until I was pretty certain that I was pregnant."

"So he got off Scott free?" He didn't quite keep the indignance out of his voice.

"Not exactly," she replied, a slight smile touching her lips. "God *arrested* him. A month ago he offered to turn himself in, or to pay a financial settlement."

Rick wasn't sure what to do with the emotions churning inside of him. *This isn't fair, God. First my wife, now someone that I've grown to care about. And why did she have to tell me?*

"Rick, I understand if you're upset." She smiled again. "Mike was ready to beat his head in, too. Never mind what *I* might have done. But it's over. I can't change it. Just like I can't reverse the damage caused by Kyle Richards. But I refuse to give up a promising *future* just because of a painful *past*. Besides, it's been a means for me to help some other girls at the Sexual Assault Center."

She folded and unfolded her cloth napkin. "Look, I thought you should know. I'm not blind. I can see where your thoughts have been heading lately. Tammy saw it before I did. I don't *think* I'm the one for you, Rick. But I don't want my past to be a stumbling block either. If I had kept my mouth shut, and a few months down the road, you – well, it would've been a lot harder to tell you then."

"Mike never told you about my wife, did he?"

"No. But Tammy told me she was shot by a thief on drugs."

"That's only part of the story, Cari." He watched her face as he spoke. "She was raped and beaten before that. She was still bound and gagged when I found her." He looked down at his clenched fist and forced his fingers to loosen again. "I was so thankful that *I* found her, and not the kids."

"Do they know?" she asked in little more than a whisper, her face as pale as before.

"Ricky does. He was fourteen at the time. Tammy was only ten, so I didn't tell her."

"What about now? Shouldn't you tell her? What if she ever found out from somebody else?"

He shook his head. "No way! She had nightmares almost every night until we left Sacramento and moved here. She's had very few since. I'm not about to threaten that now."

"I'm sorry. It must have been awful for you. For all of you." She reached across the table and took his hand. Her own was clammy. "Thanks for telling me. I know that was hard."

He looked down at her hand on his and wished things could be so much different. "I guess Mike and Julie thought we'd be able to understand each other," he said. "They sure have tried to throw us together often enough, haven't they?" He looked up and saw her relieved smile. "Or hadn't you noticed?"

"Hardly! Don't you remember the first day in the den? The three of you standing there talking about me, thinking I was asleep."

Rick blushed slightly. "That *was* pretty bad, wasn't it?" He felt her withdraw her hand, but didn't comment on it. "Well, ready to go?"

"Sure. Just let me go to the washroom first." She got up from the table, leaving him alone with the bill and his thoughts.

She's so beautiful. How could any guy hurt her like that? Especially her own fiancé. And how could she sit here calmly and tell me about it? He picked up the bill and got out his wallet. *And why am I more attracted to her than ever?*

Chapter 32

Cari watched as Tammy opened the ribbon wrapped envelope from her dad. First she stared. Then she looked puzzled. Then she squealed with delight and almost threw herself at Rick.

"Oh, Daddy, thank you! This is such a neat gift." She kissed his cheek as she wrapped her arms around his neck. "Thank you."

Rick looked over at Cari and grinned. He mouthed the words 'thank you', all the while trying to make sense of his daughter's excited chatter.

"Cool!" Ricky exclaimed when he noticed the signature on the basketball from Cari. He glanced at her. "You actually met this guy? Amazing." He read the name again. "Thanks, Cari."

Rick finally opened the set of videos. His initial expression was similar to Tammy's. Then he laughed. "I thought you don't like westerns."

"Only the sappy ones," Cari corrected. "Dale Evans always spoke her mind in those movies. She had guts."

"So, when are you coming over to watch them with me – I mean *us*?"

"Oh, sometime during the holidays, I guess." She laughed herself then. "But you have to provide the junk food."

"Deal."

Cari had just gotten into her car to go home when her Christmas present rang. She picked it up from the mount on the console, and flipped the mouth piece. "Hello."

"Merry Christmas!" said John, the giver of the gift. "Just thought I'd make sure this gadget is working."

"Well, it is, thanks. And Merry Christmas to you." She balanced the phone against her ear and started the engine. "Where are you calling from?"

"My parents'. I always spend a few days with them at this time of year. My mother has to feed all her baking to someone besides my father. How was your day? Did you get a slew of gifts?"

"Actually, no. But I had a great time. And I ate too much of Julie's fudge, just like every other year." *Except last year, when I was struggling with morning sickness.*

"I miss you," he said. "I'm so used to seeing you almost every day."

Cari remained silent as she tried to think of how to respond.

"Well, have a good holiday, Cari. I'll see you in a few days."

"John, wait a sec. I'm sorry. You just caught me off guard a minute ago. It was sweet of you to say such a thing. Thank you."

"No 'I miss you too, John'?" He sounded hurt, not teasing.

Cari bit her lip and squeezed her eyes shut. *I can't lie, can I?* "Yes, I do miss you, John. And it'll be nice to see you again soon."

"Thank you, dear lady, for your honesty. I'm sorry that I twisted your arm to get it. Goodnight."

"Goodnight. And thank you for calling." The line went dead and she put the phone back into the bracket. *Oh, why does he keep doing things like that? I get all rattled, and I can't think straight.* She shifted into drive. *But I do miss him.*

On December 29th, Cari went into work. Sure enough, John was there too. His smile was still warm, though somewhat guarded. He walked her to her office and she invited him in for a moment.

"I was wondering if you'd like to come to the New Year's Eve service at church," she said. "We always have a film, and a time of fellowship afterwards. Then I go over to Mike and Julie's and we play games until we're all too tired to see straight."

John crossed his arms as he casually leaned his back against the wall. "Sounds intriguing, to say the least." Then he frowned. "Am I just a prospective *convert* to you, Cari? You'll only invite me to a church function, or perhaps to a friend's home. Do I frighten you that much?"

"That's not fair!" she retorted, even as she considered the truth of his question.

"Really? Then why not to a ballet, or a movie? Even to dinner? Something unrelated to work or church. You just can't bring yourself to do that, can you?"

"No, I can't!" she admitted as she turned and moved towards her desk. "Yes, I would like to see you come to Christ." She met his reproachful gaze. "If I didn't, I wouldn't be much of a Christian myself. As for not feeling *safe* with you, no I don't. Not because I don't trust *you*, but because I don't trust *me*! You're the kind of man who would be so easy to fall for, John. And I can't allow myself to do that." She braced her hands on her desk and tried not to cry.

"What if I were a Christian?" he asked, his tone no longer biting, or sarcastic.

"I don't know," she whispered.

"It appears as though we both have some serious thinking to do," he replied. "Good day, Ms. Daniels."

Cari listened to him leave, but didn't look up. When the door clicked shut, she sat down at the desk, and covered her face with her hands. *This is too hard! He's too nice. I care about him too much already. I can't keep seeing him day after day like this. But if I try to avoid him, people will start asking questions. What can I do?*

'*Trust Me, Cari. That's what you always need to do.*'

I'll try, God. She wiped at her tears. *I'll try.*

———⋙⋘———

Cari went to the church service, but went home right after, claiming fatigue. It was partially true. She hadn't been getting proper rest during the Christmas season, and she was becoming a bit drained.

Julie was concerned about more than that. "It's guy trouble, isn't it?"

"Sort of," Cari admitted. "Look, all I can do right now is pray for John and do my job. Anything else is just too complicated."

"What about Rick? Is he a problem too?"

"I don't know, Julie," Cari said with a sigh. "I just don't feel what he does, I guess. Not at this point anyway."

"Okay. Go home. Get some rest. And take some time to pray." Julie patted her arm. "God's right in the middle of it all, Cari. Don't ever forget that."

"I won't."

She sat on her sofa, a cup of tea in her right hand, and her Bible open on her lap. She sipped from the cup as she read. Then she set the cup on the coffee table, with the Bible next to it. And she closed her eyes and fell asleep; resting in the assurance that God would take care of her today and tomorrow.

———⋙⋘———

"Happy New Year!" Tammy practically shouted into the phone. "How are you doing?"

"I'm a little deaf, maybe," Cari teased. "But otherwise not too bad. Did you stay up all night?"

"Yup. Then I had some breakfast and crashed until lunch. Then Dad kicked me out of bed, so that I'll be able to sleep tonight."

"I used to be able to do wild things like that," Cari sighed. "But not anymore. Appreciate your youth while you have it, Tammy."

"Oh, good grief! You're what, thirty-one, or something? Hardly over the hill yet."

"Thanks, Tammy, but some days I certainly feel like it."

"I gotta go. Dad wants me to help clean up around here. We got popcorn all over the carpet last night." She giggled. "It's actually Dad's fault – he threw it first."

"Have a good day. Thanks for calling."

"Bye."

Cari just couldn't picture Rick Benson starting a food fight. Or was it that she just didn't want to?

Pam Martin sat across from Cari in one of their favorite restaurants. "You're looking pretty good, Cari. The water therapy and weights must be helping."

Cari stirred her straw in her shake. "They are. I'm still not where I'd like to be though." She shrugged before she took a sip. "But I guess I should be glad for any improvement at this point." She looked up and smiled. "So, how's it going for you? Getting ready for your next promotion?"

Pam leaned back in the booth, nibbling on a fry. "It's always a little hard to tell. They still don't seem to know what to do with me. I don't fit the typical mould, you know. I think some of the guys are intimidated by me, and some of the girls think I'm using an unfair advantage, or something." She reached for another fry. "I'm just trying to do my best."

"You've got what it takes to pull this off, Pam. I happen to know several officers who think you'll advance through the ranks quicker than normal, just because you don't miss anything, and your record keeping is better than most."

Pam rolled her eyes. "Tell that to the ones who still think women should be sitting around at home." She wiped the salt from her hands and crumpled her napkin. "It's not like I'm out to prove that I'm better than anybody else. I just want to do a good job; as a cop and as a nurse."

"You have been doing that for the past year. If anyone can handle the pressure, it's you."

Pam leaned forward and put her elbows on the table. "So, has John asked you out again?"

Cari felt her skin flush, and looked down at her shake. "No. Actually, I think he's pretty ticked right now, probably for good reason." She looked up. "It would make my life a lot easier if he were a Christian."

"Rick is, but that didn't make it easier, did it?"

"Rick is a great friend." Cari studied her friend's face. "You'd be good for Rick."

"No way. I don't date cops and I don't date medical professionals either. My work and personal life are distinctly separate. It's much healthier that way." She took a sip of her soda. "No offense to Rick. He's a great guy. I'm sure some lovely lady will notice that eventually."

"Probably. But it isn't me."

"Me either."

Chapter 33

"What's bugging you, Tammy?" Cari asked as they sat down in her living room. "You've hardly said a thing since you got her today."

Tammy met her gaze, and her usual smile was absent. "Remember those two guys that have been bothering me since September?" Cari nodded. "Well, today they came up with a nickname for me. And they aren't the only ones who think it's funny." She blew at her bangs in obvious agitation.

"Okay, what is it?"

"Piglet," Tammy said with a sigh. "And before you ask, no, it has nothing to do with *Winnie the Pooh*. It's because my dad is a cop – or a *pig*."

Cari reached over and put a hand on Tammy's shoulder. "I'm sorry. Would it bother you as much if somebody besides those two had thought of it?"

"I don't know." Tears began to gather in her blue eyes. "This whole year has been really hard. I wish my dad would just let me study at home. I don't even have any close friends at school." She wiped at her eyes. "But he just doesn't get it. He keeps telling me to hang in there – everything will be okay."

"Would you really like to study at home – or are you just trying to get away from the problem?"

"I'd really like to study at home. Some of my friends in Sacramento were home schooled."

"Maybe your dad is just afraid that you wouldn't have enough help at home, Tammy. I mean, he works some long shifts. And Ricky is pretty busy too. Do you think that you could really do it on your own?"

"I don't know!" Tammy looked down at her hands. "But I'd still like to try."

"Maybe you should just try to get through this year," Cari suggested. "And ask your dad if you could try home schooling next year." She pulled Tammy closer. "Now, are you ready for a snack?"

"Okay."

"Sit down, Jill," Cari said to the young attorney in her office. "What's the problem, and how can I help?"

The young woman was very pretty. She was twenty-seven, had dark hair and green eyes, and a petite build. And she was obviously very agitated. "I need you to keep my ex boyfriend away from me — at least here at work."

Cari nodded in understanding. She knew the relationship hadn't been too healthy all along. "Okay. Do you have a photo that we can put into the computer?"

"Yes. I brought one with me." Jill opened her leather purse and withdrew a wallet size photo, and passed it to Cari.

"Can you tell me why you want him kept away from here? Has he threatened you in any way?"

Jill nodded her head. "I found out at Christmas that he was using drugs. He swore that he'd quit. I believed him." She fiddled with the snap on her purse. "I found out that he was still using them. He tried to get money from my bank account, but I'd changed the PIN on my card. He was so mad at me." Jill looked across the room. "I was so scared," she whispered. "He left when I told him to, but I'm afraid that he'll try to come here."

"Okay, Jill, we'll do our best to keep him away from here for you."

"Thank you, Ms. Daniels." She got to her feet, but Cari could see that she was trembling.

"What about at home, Jill? Is there some way that you can protect yourself there?"

"I had the locks changed this morning. And I'm looking for another apartment."

"Smart lady," Cari said with a smile. "Let me know how you're doing, please." Cari got up and walked Jill to the door. "Even if you just need to talk."

"All right. Thank you."

Cari opened the door for her. "Try not to worry, Jill. You'll get through this."

Jill turned to face her. "I know. I just wish now that I'd never even *met* Trevor, let alone fallen in love with him." She bit her lip. "Excuse me. I'd better get to work. I have an appointment soon."

"Goodbye." Cari waited a moment and then closed the door. *Please watch over her, Lord. She looks like she's barely holding herself together right now. Help her to have a good day. And please help us to do what we can to keep her safe.*

————))•((————

"Would you like to go out for supper?" Rick asked over the phone. "The kids and I just discovered a great new restaurant last week."

"Umm, I'm not sure, Rick. When were you thinking of going?" Cari had brought home several files that she had to go over before the next day.

"Oh, not until Wednesday night."

"Can I get back to you tomorrow night? I'm really swamped with work at the moment."

"Actually, I'll be working tomorrow night," he replied. "Why don't you call me on Wednesday morning? I'll be home."

"All right. I'll call you back then."

"Cari?"

"Yes?"

"How have you been? I haven't seen much of you lately."

"Not too bad. I've just been extra busy."

"So, you're not just trying to ignore me?" He didn't sound like he was joking.

"Rick, what are you talking about?"

"Well, you're still spending time with Tammy, but you haven't been coming over to the house. Any special reason?"

"I've just been busy," she insisted. "And Rick?"

"Yes?"

"I don't appreciate being put on the spot like this. I'm not one of your kids."

"I realize that. I thought you were my *friend* though." He sighed. "Look, let's just forget about supper on Wednesday night. I don't think either of us is in the right frame of mind at the moment. Bye, Cari." He hung up before she could even say anything else.

Cari replaced the phone and picked up another of the files she'd brought home. *What's the matter with him right now? I didn't know guys could be so moody.* She sat there, the unopened folder on her lap. *Have I really been trying to ignore him? Why would I do that?*

Chapter 34

The last weekend of January finally arrived, and Cari and Tammy went to the inn where Rick had made the reservation. They both loved it. The room was fairly small, but cozy. It had twin beds with beautiful quilts on them. The furniture was all antique, and the bathroom had a claw foot tub.

"Flip you for the first soak in the tub," Cari said with a grin. "I haven't seen one like this since I was a kid."

"You go first if you want," Tammy replied. "I still have to check out what all is in this gift basket from Dad." She was sitting on the bed, basket in her lap, removing one item after another. "There must be six different bubble baths in here, and some lotion, a loofah sponge, bath beads, special soaps." She pulled out something flat. "A bath pillow, I think. Want me to blow it up?"

"Please do," Cari remarked as she sat down on her own bed. "My days of blowing up balloons or pillows are over." She patted her left side. "I try to be careful." She looked at the basket. "What else have you got in there?"

"I don't know yet." Tammy dug around a bit more. Then her eyebrows furrowed. "What's this?" she asked as she held up something silky.

"Let's see," Cari said, taking it from her. "It's a silk sleep shirt, Tammy."

"I can't believe my dad actually bought that! He must have told some clerk my size and made her choose one." She shook her head. Then she stared at it a little harder. "Wait a sec," she murmured. "Where's the card? I didn't even read it before unwrapping all this stuff." She rummaged on the bed. "Here it is."

Dear Tammy;

I hope that you and Cari have a wonderful weekend. I tried to pick out some things that I thought you'd like. I just want you to know how special you are. And I wanted to give you something that you're old enough to appreciate. The sleep shirt was your mom's. I'm pretty sure it'll fit you now. I'm glad that I kept some of her things for you. I've never shown them to you, so just ask when you feel ready to look through the other things.

I'm sorry if I don't tell you often enough how much I love you. I guess it's hard for me to watch my 'little girl' growing up so fast. You're going to be a beautiful young woman, Tammy. And you're very special to me. You always will be.

Have a great time.

Love,

Dad

Tammy tried to blink away the tears gathering in her eyes. "It was my mom's," she whispered. "And my dad wants me to have it."

"That was a very thoughtful gift," Cari replied. "Here, why don't you try it on?" She passed it back to her.

"But we didn't even eat supper yet." Tammy gently caressed the soft material.

"Well, haven't you ever heard of 'room service'? You put it on, and I'm going to go fill that tub. After I soak for an hour or so, we'll decide what we're going to eat." Cari grinned again. "And no junk food this weekend, Kiddo. However, chocolate of any kind is allowed. So, go through the menu and pick out what we'll have." Cari turned and opened her suitcase. She reached for her own bottle of bubble bath. She paused and looked in Tammy's direction. She burst out laughing.

"Well, you're the one who told me to blow up the pillow," Tammy retorted, her cheeks warm from her efforts. She put the plug in and passed the pillow to Cari. "Here you go. And if you're not out in an hour, I'll assume that you drowned in there and call 911."

"Don't you dare! Just you wait, Kid. When you get older you'll appreciate the luxury of a long soak." Then Cari sobered. "Besides, my leg is killing me tonight. Just getting in and out could take a few precious moments of my time."

"Okay, an hour and fifteen minutes. I'm getting hungry."

Cari bopped her on the head with the pillow. "Then get unpacked and start browsing the menu."

———•(•)•———

Cari and Tammy enjoyed their meal immensely. And the fudge torte satisfied their craving for chocolate. After they ate, Cari went downstairs and rented a VCR and a movie. They sat on their beds and watched it. It was a gripping story, and they conversed little. But as soon as the movie was finished, Tammy was ready to talk.

"My dad said he kept some of Mom's things – for me. Besides this, I mean. It feels kind of strange. But it's also neat to have something that was hers."

"It was nice of him to think of it, Tammy. Especially since I know that your mom's death was really hard on him. You must be pretty special to him. Some men wouldn't have wanted to keep anything, except maybe some pictures."

"Yeah, I know." Tammy once more fingered the fabric. She smiled. "I guess dads can be full of surprises, can't they?"

"Sometimes," Cari replied. "My dad was a bit like that. He was kind of quiet most of the time. But every once in a while he'd come up with some wild idea. Like a vacation in the hills of Kentucky, or a supper consisting only of ice cream." Cari laughed. "He was a wonderful guy. I miss him a lot." She looked away for a moment.

"That must have been awfully hard on you," Tammy said very quietly. "I mean, losing both parents at the same time. And you didn't have a brother or sister. How did you get through it?"

"I prayed a lot. And Mike and Julie were wonderful. I don't know what I would have done without them."

"Didn't you even have any grandparents?"

"No. They've all been dead a few years longer than my parents. My mom's mother died of breast cancer. Grandpa Carlson had a heart attack. My dad's mother got pneumonia and didn't recover. And Grandpa Daniels was in his late seventies by then. I guess he died of old age."

"At least I still have my grandparents. It's just that they live so far away now. Grandma and Grandpa Benson live in Arizona, 'cause he has really bad allergies. And Mom's parents live in New York. It costs too much to go see them, and they don't visit very often either." She shrugged. "Maybe when I'm older I'll be able to go and see them by myself."

"Where would you rather go, Arizona or New York?"

"I don't know. Both places seem kind of mysterious to me. Mom had tons of pictures of New York. She grew up in an apartment building, but a really nice one. And my dad's parents have a really neat trailer to live in." She shrugged again. "Maybe I'll just have to flip a coin to decide."

"Well, let me know if you opt for New York," Cari replied. "I haven't been there since I was in college. I was considering trying for the NYPD. Then I realized I could end up walking a beat in the snow. I came right back to LA and trained here at home." She smiled as she remembered that trip. "But it sure was an interesting city." She yawned. "Getting tired yet?"

Tammy laughed. "Tired? It's only midnight." She bounced off the bed and headed for the bathroom. "But I guess somebody as *old* as you needs her beauty sleep."

"Thanks a lot! Just you wait, old age will catch up with you soon enough." Cari got off the bed and folded back the quilt and the lace edged sheets. She could hardly keep her eyes open. She positioned the pillows, removed her robe and crawled into bed. "Goodnight, Tammy," she mumbled. She never even noticed her coming back to the other bed. She didn't find out a thing until almost ten the next morning.

The rest of the weekend was also enlightening for both Tammy and Cari. Cari talked about her schooling, her home town, past vacations. Tammy filled her in about her home church, and the friends she'd left behind. She talked about Christmases when she was little. And she told Cari more about her mother. After a small lunch in the quaint dining room, they headed back to Tammy's.

"Thanks so much, Cari. I had a great time."

"Feeling a little better about yourself?" Cari probed. "Ready to face life 'head on' again?"

"I think so." Tammy shrugged. "I mean, I don't feel like taking on the world, or anything. But I think I can just be *me*, and not worry so much about what the other kids think."

"Glad to hear it." Cari squeezed her hand. "You're special, Tammy. No matter what others say, or what may happen. Don't ever forget that."

"Thanks." Tammy stretched enough to give Cari a kiss on the cheek. "I'm so glad I have you for a friend. Bye." She opened the car door and got out.

"Bye." Just as Tammy got to the door of the house, Rick and Ricky got home from church. Both waved to Cari. She waved back just before pulling away. But not before she saw Tammy throw her arms around Rick's neck. *She's gonna be okay.*

Chapter 35

"Cari, would you please go to Jill Harris' office? She was supposed to meet with me twenty minutes ago, but she isn't here yet. And she's not answering her phone." Rebecca Richards sounded a bit puzzled as she spoke on the phone. "She's never been late before, and I'm a little concerned."

"I'll go right away, Mrs. Richards." Cari looked at her watch. It was twelve-twenty. "I'll call you back in a few minutes."

"Thank you, Cari. I'd go myself, but I don't want to miss her in the coming and going."

"Of course. I'll take care of it." She hung up and left her office, heading for the elevator.

On the third floor, Cari saw no sign of Max, the security guard who should have been on duty. *Maybe he's on a break right now. I'll check on that in a few minutes.* She made her way to Jill's office and knocked on the door. No answer. She knocked again. "Jill? Jill, are you all right?" Still no answer. She tried the knob and found it locked. She pulled out her master key and unlocked the door. She called again as she slowly entered the spacious room. "Jill? Are you in here?" That's when she heard the muffled sobs.

Cari opened the door further, checked behind it, and then closed it. "Jill, where are you?" The crying was coming from the direction of the desk, so Cari slowly approached, her hand on the holster of her .38. She noticed that the chair was shoved back against the wall, and a pair of high heels was beneath the wheels. She stepped around the side of the desk and saw Jill, cowering on the floor, curled up in the fetal position. Cari knelt down on the floor close to her, ignoring the pain in her right leg.

"Jill? Are you hurt?" She took careful note of the torn blouse, splattered with what appeared to be ink. Jill's legs were bare, her wool skirt unzipped at the back.

"Trevor got in," Jill whispered. "You told me you'd keep him away." She was obviously in shock, so Cari wasn't about to debate the details.

"I'm sorry, Jill. Right now I'm worried about you. Are you hurt?" Thankfully, Jill raised her face a little. It was slightly bruised and swollen.

"He hit me with my fountain pen," she said through chattering teeth. "He broke it."

That explains the ink. "Jill, I need to get you to a doctor. I could call an ambulance or --"

"No! I don't want an ambulance. And I don't want a hospital." Her trembling worsened and her eyes opened wider.

"You have to see a doctor, Jill. You're hurt. I can take you myself if you don't want an ambulance."

"Please." Jill closed her eyes, but she didn't stop trembling. "He wanted money," she murmured. "And when I wouldn't give it to him, he hit me. I was so scared I didn't even scream." She renewed her sobs. "And he raped me."

Cari had suspected as much, but she still gritted her teeth and tried to keep her thoughts clear. "I'm going to help you, Jill. You're safe now. He's not going to hurt you again. But first I have to call Mrs. Richards." She reached up for the phone on the desk.

"Why? Am I going to be fired?"

"No, nothing like that." Cari touched the hand that had grabbed at her pant leg. "She's just worried about you. She sent me to see if you were okay. She'll want to help you."

"I won't be fired?"

"No. She wouldn't do that." Cari pressed the numbers for Rebecca's private line. "Mrs. Richards, it's Cari. Please come down to Jill's office, but try not to draw attention to yourself. And, if you have a jacket, please bring it down. Thank you. I'll explain when you get here." She hung up and refocused her attention on Jill.

"Okay, Jill, I'm going to help you to sit up." She gently reached out and slid her right arm around Jill's shoulders.

"I'm so cold," Jill sobbed. She managed to help herself to a sitting position. That's when Cari saw more rips in the blouse. She kept her arm around her.

"We'll get you warm just as soon as we can. Try to take some deep breaths. That'll help you circulation to come back." There was a knock on the door and Jill jerked. "Shh. It's Mrs. Richards." A key turned in the lock and Cari called out softly. "Over here, behind the desk, Mrs. Richards."

Quiet footsteps crossed the room. "How can I help?" Rebecca asked as she looked down at the two women. She passed her blazer to Cari's waiting hand. Then she squatted down near them, still looking every inch a lady.

Cari got the blazer around Jill's shoulders. "I'm going to take Jill to a doctor, in my car." She looked at Rebecca. "Is Max out in the hallway now?"

"Yes, why?"

"Would you please go tell him he can finish early today? I don't want anyone in the hallway."

"All right. What else?"

"I'm going to have Kelly remove the tape for this floor. I want you to get it from her, and don't let anyone else touch it, please. I'll review it when I get a chance."

"Of course."

"You won't fire me?" Jill asked in a quavering voice.

Rebecca reached for her hand and held it in both of hers. "Not a chance, Miss Harris. You're one of the finest attorneys this firm has."

"Okay," Cari said, "could you help Jill with her shoes? I'm going to get Kelly to shut off the cameras on this floor and in the stairwell. Then I'll escort Jill down to my car."

"What about your leg?"

"Don't worry. I'll be fine." She relinquished Jill to her boss' care while she called the security desk. She gave Kelly complete instructions. By this time, Jill was on her feet, though far from steady. Cari looked to Rebecca. "Please lock this door, and don't allow *anyone* back in here. I don't want anything to be touched."

"Certainly." Rebecca patted Jill's arm as she straightened up. "You're in good hands, Jill. Ms. Daniels will take care of you."

Jill simply nodded, still looking dazed.

Cari got as far as the door before the younger woman panicked. "Is Trevor gone?"

"I'm sure he is," Cari soothed. "He's probably been gone for almost an hour now. Don't worry. You're not alone. Come on."

They got down the stairwell to the parking level. Cari led Jill to her car and opened the door for her. Then she bent down to speak to her again. "I'm going to get you the blanket that I carry in my trunk. That'll help you to warm up. Okay? It'll only take me a second." Jill nodded, though Cari wasn't certain she understood. She quickly returned with the blanket and tucked it around Jill's shoulders. "You're safe, Jill. And you're going to be okay. You may not think so right now. But you will be. Trust me on that." She closed the door and got in the driver's side.

Once the engine was started, Cari switched on the radio attached to her lapel. "Ted? Bill?"

"Yo." "Yes." Both parking attendants came on almost simultaneously.

"This is Ms. Daniels. I'm going to leave now, and I want both of you to find something to do."

"Come again," Ted said.

"Pardon?" Bill asked.

"I've got company with me. Enough said?"

"Yes, ma'am. I think I have some plates to go look at," Ted answered.

"I'd better check out the log book again," Bill replied.

"Thanks, guys. I appreciate it." She switched off the radio and pulled out of her spot. They were soon out of the parking area and onto the street.

———◦(◦)◦———

"Why did you bring me here?" Jill asked as Cari pulled up in front of the Sexual Assault Center.

Cari reached for Jill's hand. "Because you need help. One of the doctors here is a good friend of mine."

"Won't they make me tell the police?"

Cari bit her lip before replying. "Jill, nobody can *make* you report this. That's up to you. But the doctor will take care of those cuts and scrapes. She might even give you a sedative to help you relax. And she'll listen to you if you want to talk. Okay?"

"Are you sure?"

"Yes, I am."

"I'll go in." Jill closed her eyes for a moment. "I feel so sick, Ms. Daniels. And I'm still so cold."

"Then let's go see my friend."

Once in the foyer, Christy, the volunteer receptionist, greeted Cari and Jill. "How can I help?" she asked.

"This is Jill, and she needs to see Dr. Lewis," Cari replied.

"Go ahead, Cari. She's in room number three right now. I'll bring in the forms later."

"Thanks, Christy." As Cari led Jill in the right direction, her stomach lurched. *Room three? That's where I found out I was pregnant. I can't think about that right now. I need to help Jill.*

Cari literally held Jill's hand while Teresa carefully and gently examined her. Dr. Lewis swabbed the gashes from the pen with iodine, and applied antibiotic ointment to them. She also gave Jill a tetanus shot, since she hadn't had a booster shot since high school. Then she spoke to her again.

"Jill, it's up to you whether or not you press charges, but if you decide to, then I don't want to give you a sedative yet. It could make a difference for giving a statement."

Jill remained silent for a few moments. "I guess I should press charges," she whispered. Then she tightened her grip on Cari's hand. "Will you stay with me? I'm so scared."

"Sure. I'm also going to make sure that Trevor doesn't have a chance to hurt anybody else again, Jill."

"Can I – can I talk to somebody right here?" Jill asked Teresa. "I think I'm too tired to get up."

"No problem. I'll have a plainclothes officer come right to you. That way, we won't frighten any of the other girls that may be here."

"Thank you."

Cari remained with Jill until the report was given, and the rape kit, along with Jill's clothing was handed over to the female officer. Then she helped her to another room, where she was given a warm sweat suit to put on.

"Do you want me to drive you home, Jill?"

Jill immediately panicked. "No! I can't go there until Trevor is caught. He knows where I live."

"Shhh. Relax. Just sit down and try to rest. One of the volunteers can help you find a place to stay for a few days. I don't recommend a hotel right now. You need to be with other people. Do you understand?"

"Yes." Jill sighed as she sat down. "I'm so tired." She put her

hands up to her face. "I think the medication is starting to work."
She yawned.

Cari looked at her watch. It was almost half past three. "I need
to get going, Jill, but I'll have Christy send one of the girls in right
away. Just relax. Nobody is going to kick you out right away."

"Thank you, Ms. Daniels." Fresh tears sprang up in Jill's eyes. "I
don't know what I would have done without you."

"You're welcome. And don't forget, you're safe, and someday,
you're going to be okay again."

"You sound like you really know how I'm feeling."

"That's because I do, Jill. And I'm living proof that you can
survive something like this. Just don't give up. Okay?"

"I'll try not to."

Cari exited the room and bumped right into the broad chest of
Rick Benson.

Chapter 36

"Rick?" Cari managed to get out as she stepped back. She took in his ashen complexion, and red-rimmed eyes. Then she shook her head. "Not Tammy?" she whispered.

He nodded. "A couple of guys at her school. They got her in a dark washroom for a few minutes." His words came out in a rush, a contrast to his normally relaxed speech. "She's so hysterical that we can't even find out *what* happened to her."

Before Cari could reply, she heard Tammy's screams from across the hall. "Don't touch me! I want my dad! Please don't touch me!"

Cari turned and went to the room, not even bothering to knock. Rick was right on her heels. Tammy's outburst came to a halt as she looked at Cari. Then she almost threw herself into Cari's arms.

"I don't want anybody to touch me, Cari. I'm so scared. Please don't let them."

Cari pulled her closer and looked at Teresa once more. "Shh. It's okay. Nobody is going to hurt you, Tammy. Dr. Lewis is my friend. Your dad is right here too. Take some deep breaths. That's it. You're safe now, Tammy. Do you hear me? Nobody is going to hurt you."

"I want to go home," Tammy whined. "I'm scared. I feel sick."

Cari loosened Tammy's death grip on her and looked into her face. "It's okay to be scared. And you can go home pretty soon. But please let Dr. Lewis help you."

"You won't leave?"

"No. I'll even go home with you after."

"And spend the night? I won't be able to sleep alone."

Cari didn't even glance at Rick. "Sure. You won't be alone Tammy." She could see the hysteria easing off. "Trust me. I'll go through this with you. Okay?"

Tammy nodded stiffly, but still clung to Cari. Then she looked at Rick. "Dad, I – I – could you wait outside? I – I don't want you to --"

"Sure, Sweetheart. I'll be right outside the door. And *nobody* is getting past me." He caressed her cheek and then clasped Cari's shoulder. "Thanks," he whispered.

<hr />

Cari wandered to the living room in a daze. She was near collapse, but too wound up to sleep. It had taken hours to settle Tammy, despite a maximum dosage of *Gravol*. She had clung to Cari until exhaustion and frazzled nerves won out. She hadn't been raped, but the two young teens had molested and tormented her, including threatening her with a pocket knife. Now she was in a drugged sleep. And Cari was contemplating food for the first time since breakfast. She found Rick pacing in the room.

"She's sleeping now," she told him and he stopped pacing. "But she might wake up during the night." Cari sat down on the nearest chair and put her hands up to her face. She was trembling with fatigue and knew that Dr. Wilson would have her head for abusing her body this way. She decided against food. She looked up. "Rick, could I borrow a t-shirt and some sweat pants?"

He stared at her. "What?"

"I need something to sleep in. I haven't had a chance to go home for anything."

"Sure. I'll find you something." He left the room for a few minutes and Cari almost fell asleep in the chair. "Here." Rick tossed some clothes to her and she held them in her lap.

"Thanks." She was too tired to move, let alone get up.

"I want to kill those two kids," Rick stated through gritted teeth.

Cari was instantly alert. "You don't mean that, Rick," she said carefully.

He glared at her. "Yes, I do! Tammy was an innocent thirteen year old girl until today. Now she's --"

"She's still the *same girl*, Rick." She got to her feet. "Don't make her feel different. Love her. Hold her. Tell her it wasn't her fault. Listen to her fears. But let her be your little girl. Don't let her stay a terrified victim for the rest of her life."

"I can't even look at her without thinking of them touching her!"

"Then work through it together. If you can't handle it, how will she be able to? She'll have to go back to school eventually. She'll have to face her worst fears. Don't make it worse for her by flying into a rage."

That's precisely what he did. "You think you've got all the answers, don't you? Always free with advice. Always so *logical*. Not everything in life is so neat and tidy."

"Rick, I *know* that. I've had to walk this way myself. *I* was raped. *I* got pregnant. And *I* miscarried. If nothing else, be thankful Tammy was spared that! Jill Harris may not be so lucky. She'll have to wait a few weeks to know for sure. That's a nightmare I don't wish for *anybody*."

He wasn't mollified. "How old were you?" he asked with a sarcastic edge. "Not a kid."

"No, I was thirty instead of thirteen. But it's terrifying at *any* age. Jill is twenty-seven, but she was panicked too. Trevor MacBride knows her number, her address, and he attacked her in her office. She'll be jumping at her own shadow for awhile."

"Tammy is just a kid!" he fumed, stepping closer to her.

"Yes! But with help from her family and friends, and maybe some professional counseling, she'll be able to look forward to the rest of her life." She softened her tone. "Rick, I know that you're hurting. That you wish you could have kept this from happening, but --"

"You don't know *anything*!" he hollered. "You don't know what it was like to find my wife after some druggie had beaten and raped her. Or what it was like to hold her hand while she was bleeding to death on the way to the hospital." He stepped even closer. "Or what's it's like to try to raise two kids by yourself." He lowered his voice but remained just as intense. "Or to wonder if I could have saved Karen's life if I'd gotten home sooner. Or if I might have caught the guy before he even touched her."

Cari broke in, "Or maybe he would have shot you, too, and Ricky and Tammy wouldn't have *either* parent. Or maybe you would have caught the guy and killed him." She held his gaze. "I *do* know, Rick. And I know that the 'maybes' will destroy you – eventually. They'll eat away at you until you can't think of anything else." She reached out and tried to touch his arm, but he moved away. "Let them go, Rick. *Please*. If not for your own sake, then do it for Tammy. She needs your *help*, not your *hate*."

He grabbed her upper arms and put his reddened face close to hers. "I don't *need* your advice or your sympathy, *Miss Daniels*. Shut up and get out of my house!" he yelled as he shoved her backwards.

She stumbled and hit the doorframe. Her right hand went to her leg, even as she used her left hand to steady herself against the wall. She inhaled sharply.

Rick's enraged expression altered. "Cari --" He moved towards her.

Cari straightened to her full height and gritted her teeth. "Don't come near me, Rick! And don't you dare touch me again." Her tone was icy, but her tears were hot. So was the pain in her side. "I promised Tammy that I'd still be here when she wakes up. And I *will* be. So just get out of my way and let me go to her room." She eyed him warily until he moved away from her. Then she walked past him, her limp more pronounced than usual.

"Cari, please. I --"

She turned to face him. "Not now, Rick." She shook her head. "I'm afraid of what I might say." She made her way towards Tammy's room, trying to shut out the sound of Rick's broken sobs.

———— ◦《◉》◦ ————

Tammy wakened several times during the night, hindering Cari's attempts at rest. Cari coaxed some breakfast into her in the morning before approaching Rick. She found him in the family room, his eyes puffy and blood shot.

"Rick, Tammy is awake now. Please go to her. She didn't have a good night." Cari closed her eyes in an effort to slow down the migraine she was getting. "I have to go home and try to sleep."

He didn't answer her, but when Tammy called for him, he left the room.

Cari looked down at her disheveled clothing and sighed. *I need to get changed.* She left the house feeling slightly nauseated. In her car, she leaned her head on the steering wheel. "I'm so tired. And I'm going to be sick. Please help me to get home, Lord." She started the car and backed out of the driveway. She made it home and went straight to bed, fully clothed. She didn't wake up until the middle of the afternoon. Then she had something to eat for the first time in over twenty-four hours.

———— ◦《◉》◦ ————

Cari took a shower after eating a sandwich. When she was drying off, she noticed a darkening bruise running along her left

—— 224 ——

ribs, exactly where she'd hit the doorframe at Rick's. She gritted her teeth. *You're an idiot, Rick Benson!* She got dressed and went to the phone.

"Hello?"

"Ricky? It's Cari. How are you guys doing?"

"Tammy's reading a book right now. I think Dad's trying to sleep. Do you want me to get him?"

For a second she almost considered it. *It would serve him right.* Common sense prevailed. "No. Not if he's resting. I think he was up all night. How are you?"

"I don't know. I mean, I just got back this morning and found out. I guess I'm mostly worried about Tammy. She won't even shut the light off and it's sunny in her room."

Cari thought she understood. She still couldn't drink hot chocolate. "She was assaulted in a dark room, Ricky. She might be paranoid about lights for awhile."

"Oh. I get it. Uh, Cari?"

"Yes?"

"What can I do to help? I mean, when it was my mom, there wasn't anything I *could* do. This is different."

"I'll tell you what I told your dad, Ricky. Just love her. Let her know she's safe. But don't baby her. Help her with her school work for as long as she stays home. Go to counseling with her even. Then you won't have to second guess what she's going through."

"Thanks. I tried to ask Dad but he wouldn't even answer me," he said with a sigh. "I know he's upset, but — well, I just want to help."

"It's okay. Actually, your dad is acting pretty *normal* under the circumstances. He feels like he's somehow to blame. And it's worse because of what happened to your mom."

"He told you?" he asked, sounding rather surprised.

"Yes."

"I better go, Cari. I told Tammy I'd be right back and help her with a puzzle."

"Sure. Just let her know I called. I have to do some work tonight, but I'll try to stop by tomorrow. And your dad has my cell number if he really needs to reach me."

"I'll tell them. Bye, Cari. And thanks."

"You're welcome. Bye."

Chapter 37

Cari's nausea intensified as she and the Richards went over the videotape of Friday morning. It clearly showed Trevor MacBride going to Jill's office at 11:15. He was visibly agitated. He came back out at 11:45, wiping ink stains from his right hand with some tissue, and his face flushed, but smiling.

"Has he been arrested yet?" Luke asked.

"No," Cari replied. "There's a warrant out. The police have checked his apartment, and Jill's too. It looks as though he broke into it – either before or after he attacked her. His prints were all over the place." She shook her head. "Jill is at a women's shelter right now, but she's not leaving until Trevor is behind bars."

"I don't blame her," Rebecca said. "It still amazes me what lengths people on drugs will go to, including Kyle." She looked at Cari with moist eyes. "It's been almost a year now and you still stuffer the consequences." She smiled. "Though you hide it very well behind a smile or a stern rebuke. But you're still in pain, aren't you?"

Cari shut off the VCR once the tape was rewound. "Yes, most days. But I am getting better. I'll always have to be careful, but I'm improving. I rarely need my cane anymore."

"What about your heart?" Luke asked.

"Well, up until yesterday, it's been doing very well. But back to back crises don't help."

"Crises? What else happened?" Rebecca inquired.

Cari briefly told her about Tammy. "As a matter of fact, I'm planning to take a couple of days off. I need to rest and I want to spend some time with Tammy. I hope you don't mind."

"Of course not," her employer replied.

"I'll be going over this tape and the third floor log book too. I want to know how Trevor got past us yesterday. And why Max wasn't around when I went to check on Jill." Her brows knit together. "Heads may roll for this."

Luke laughed. "Were you this zealous as a police sergeant, Cari?"

"No," she replied. "I think I was worse."

—◦((◦))◦—

Rick was civil to Cari when she stopped by on Saturday, but not at all talkative. Until she mentioned taking time off to be with his daughter.

"That's none of your business. I can stay home myself."

Cari bit her tongue in an effort to remain calm. "And what are you going to *do*? Leave her in her room while you pace? She needs *company*, not *rejection*, Rick. Please --"

"*Please* get out of here, Cari," he remarked in a steely tone.

"Why?" she choked, hoping that Tammy wasn't listening to his tirade.

"You're no longer welcome, that's why. And I'd prefer if you stayed away from my daughter, for awhile at least. If she needs any *counseling*, I'll take her to someone else." He turned his back to her and headed for the door.

Cari tried to understand his outburst. She couldn't. "All right, I'll leave," she managed to say. "But I sure hope you know your daughter as well as you *think* you do." She watched him turn the knob and open the door. She picked up her purse and left the house, not knowing when she'd be back. And praying that Rick's rage would subside before he shattered his family completely.

———⊰⦿⊱———

Julie kept an arm around Cari's shoulders as she wept. "He's so angry, Julie. He's just going to make it worse for Tammy, but he can't see it." She lifted her head from her now wet sleeves. "He won't even let me see her right now." She shook her head. "What is the matter with him? Can't he see what he's doing?"

Mike spoke up from his place at the kitchen table. "No, he can't. You said it yourself, Cari. He's *angry*. Blind rage is more like it. Hatred even, and probably a pile of guilt too. He's hurting so badly himself, he wants *somebody* to hurt too. Unfortunately, you were an easy target."

Cari thought of how Rick had shoved her against the wall. Her ribs still hurt. "Will he let either of you go see her?"

Julie shook her head. "I've called, even stopped by, but he just told me that they'd manage on their own. All we can do is pray." Julie managed a smile. "It's been enough in many other circumstances." She gave Cari a hug. "Your being alive is proof of that."

"He's taken all his accumulated sick leave right now, and vacation days, so he can stay home with Tammy," Mike told her. "I don't know if it's going to help or not." He frowned. "And it also means that I get paired with somebody else again."

"You'll manage," Julie assured him. She spoke to Cari then. "How's the girl from work?"

"Jill? I spoke with her this morning. She's still pretty shaky." Cari cleared her throat. "And she wasn't taking birth control pills, so she's scared to death that she might get pregnant. Dr. Lewis told her it wasn't too likely, but she could be wrong – we all know."

"Let's hope not," Julie remarked. "What about the guy who

attacked her?"

"He's in custody, as of this afternoon. So, Jill might go home tomorrow. She wasn't sure if she could handle that yet." Cari rubbed her throbbing temples. "And I'm still trying to find out more about Max, who was so conspicuously *absent* at those times yesterday morning. I'm sure he's involved somehow, but I can't prove it. I mean, the cameras show that he went for a quick smoke break at 11:10. Then, at 11:40, he went to have his lunch. Just a bit curious, wouldn't you say? But I can't *prove* that he let Trevor in and out, on purpose. I think I'm starting to hate my job," she muttered.

"No, you aren't, Cari," Mike said. "You're just frustrated from lack of sleep, and too many things happening at once. Why don't you get out of the city for a couple of days? Sometimes it's easier to think when the problems aren't staring you in the face."

"Maybe," she conceded. "But where? It's not like I know anybody with a cabin or something." She paused. "Well, that's no longer true. The Richards have a four bedroom chalet in the Sierras. John Maxwell has a cabin, I think. Seems to me he mentioned it when he talked about horseback riding in the mountains." She frowned. "It's probably not even accessible by vehicle." Her headache had reached brutal proportions. She looked at Julie. "Mind if I go lay down in the guest room for a couple of hours? I think that's the only way to kill this headache."

"Sure. Go ahead. Why don't you just stay for supper after? Or even overnight. You said you're taking a couple of days off anyway."

Cari shook her head. "Just for a couple of hours. I need to get home after that. But thanks for the offer. I appreciate it." Julie moved her arm and Cari got up from the chair. "Thanks for listening."

"Any time," Mike replied.

Cari grinned despite the pain in her head. "You may regret those words if I ever wake you out of a sound sleep."

"I'll take my chances."

Chapter 38

"You're welcome to use my cabin for a few days, Cari," John told her, "but it may be rather rustic for your tastes."

"Just what do you mean by 'rustic'? Only one TV, and no satellite dish?"

"No. I mean no electricity or running water. And the bathroom is a curtained off corner with a chemical toilet and a basin of water. The heat is from a wood stove, and the light is from lanterns. And there's no phone."

Cari couldn't hide her surprise, obviously.

John smiled. "And, there are some stipulations to this arrangement."

"Such as?" Cari asked as she studied his handsome face. *No guy has the right to look so good this early in the morning, especially on a Monday.*

"First of all, I'll take you there myself."

"I'm sure that's not necessary, John."

"I'm afraid it is. You see, I normally go in on horseback. Since that isn't an option for you these days, then we'd need to go in my Jeep."

"You've got a Jeep?" she wondered aloud.

He laughed. "There are many things you don't know about me. Yes, I have one. And going to my cabin is one of the reasons that I do. I'm not about to wreck my car for the sake of some solitude."

"Okay, so a Jeep is essential. Why couldn't I just rent one?"

"Second point." He held up two fingers. "I have a padlock on the door to the cabin, and only one key, which I don't want lost or misplaced."

"You're suggesting that I'm not careful enough?" Cari was getting just a bit irritated now.

"Not at all. This leads to my third point. I would need to make sure that the woodstove was functioning properly, as well as the chemical toilet. It's a lot cooler in the mountains, and I wouldn't want you freezing just because of my own lack of foresight."

"Oh, all right. I'm sure this chivalrous nature of yours is all your mother's fault. I just need to get away and think for a few days." She rubbed her forehead and frowned. "I need to be alone."

"So I see. Is tomorrow soon enough? I'm afraid that I'll be tied up in meetings the rest of today."

"Tomorrow morning would be fine. And thank you, John. I'm sorry I'm giving you such a hard time about this."

"That's quite all right. I just wanted you to be aware of the details ahead of time." He looked at his watch. "I'd better run. I'll pick you up about seven a.m. tomorrow."

"I'll be ready. Thank you."

"You're most welcome. I hope the solitude helps you as much as it usually does me."

———※◎※———

Cari was once again surprised by John when he met her at her door. He was wearing a plaid flannel shirt, khaki canvas pants, with pockets all over them, and a pair of hiking boots. He looked as though he were ready to go climbing. It took Cari a moment to rein in her thoughts and invite him inside.

"I'll still be a few minutes, John. Why don't you sit down?"

"I'd rather just walk around, if you don't mind."

"Feel free," she said with a slight shrug. "Excuse me." Cari went to her bedroom and tossed another sweatshirt into her bag. She debated a few seconds and then added a pair of jeans. *He warned me that it's cooler up there — wherever 'there' is.* Then she went into the washroom and got a towel, washcloth, toiletries, and a travel size first aid kit. *That should do it.* She carried her bag to the living room, and found John looking through the books in her collection. "I'm all set," she announced, almost sorry to disturb him.

John turned around and smiled at her. "Fine. Do you have some food with you? Or are you planning on fasting while you're there?"

"In the kitchen," she replied. "Thanks for reminding me." She set her bag on the couch and went to get the small box of groceries from the table. "*Now* I'm ready."

"I'll get your things. You just keep the door from slamming into me." He tucked the box beneath his right arm, and picked up the bag with his left. "Ready when you are."

On the street, Cari saw John's Jeep. It was old and rusty. A complete opposite to his sleek Jaguar.

"It runs," he assured her. "It'll get us there and back. Don't worry." He soon had the doors unlocked, the gear stacked in the back seat, and Cari buckled in the front. "I hope you won't miss the tape deck too much. I've never bothered to install one in here."

"I'll be fine," she said, wondering what she'd agreed to in this trip.

━━►«◉»◄━━

"Did you ever see the film *Treasure of the Sierra Madres*?" Cari asked as the Jeep kept right on winding along the roadway, ever higher into that very range.

"A long time ago. Why?"

"Oh, I just wondered if that had anything to do with your cabin being in this area."

John laughed. "Do you think I have gold buried beneath it or something?"

"Not hardly. If you did, why would you bother to work so hard?"

"True. Actually, I built the cabin up here simply because I enjoy the view."

"You built it yourself? Will the wonders never cease?"

"Oh, they might eventually," he remarked with a cocky grin. "But I try my best. Besides, you haven't seen the cabin yet. It may be pretty obvious to you then that a lawyer built it."

"How much farther?" They'd been driving for almost two hours now.

"Less than an hour. Are you bored already?"

"With this kind of scenery, not yet." She leaned her head against the window and closed her eyes for a moment. *Or with you for company. Why can't you be a Christian, John? It would be so easy to fall in — no way, Jose! My thoughts had better get back to the task at hand.* She opened her eyes only to discover John glancing at her.

"Tired?" he asked.

"Not too bad," she remarked. Then she frowned. "Actually, I haven't had enough sleep since Thursday night, I suppose."

"And, this being Tuesday morning already, you must be getting a bit weary."

"Yes, I suppose I am." She smiled as she thought of the stove in the cabin. "I hope you have a good supply of split wood up there. I never was too good with an axe."

"Really? I thought you were good at everything." He looked her way just long enough to wink. Then he shifted his gaze to the road ahead. "If there isn't enough, I'll cut some for you."

"Thanks."

"You don't suffer from altitude sickness, do you?"

"No. At least I never have before. My parents and I often

went on trips to the mountains when I was younger. And I enjoy flying."

"That was before your injuries. Did you think to ask your doctor about this little trip?"

"No, I didn't," Cari snapped, annoyed at his constant logic. "I'll be fine. I'm tired, but I'm not sick."

"If you say so, Ms. Daniels."

"Yes, I do say so, Mr. Maxwell."

Chapter 39

"Well, here it is," John announced as he shut off the noisy engine of his Jeep. "My humble retreat from the rat race." He was soon hopping out and coming over to Cari's door. When she didn't move right away, he looked at her face. Then he noticed her right hand rubbing her thigh. "Sore again, is it?"

"Yes," she admitted without looking at him. "Well, *stiff* is more like it." She turned her head and looked into his eyes. "I'm not sure that I can get out of here," she whispered, a blush creeping into her cheeks.

"Let me help you, then." He slipped his left arm behind her back, and placed his right beneath her knees. "Just hang on and I'll carry you over to the porch."

"No! I just need help out of the Jeep. You don't have to carry me anywhere." She looked somewhat frightened. Or was it embarrassment? In any case, pain still reflected in her dark eyes.

"Do as I say, Ms. Daniels, or I might just leave you sitting here." He watched her bite her lip. Then she slowly put her right arm around his neck. He carefully slid her towards him. As she tilted against his chest, her left arm came around him, and her hands clasped together. He took a step back and paused. *She's so beautiful. Why does she have to cling to her religious convictions so tenaciously?* He frowned as he carried her to the porch. Then he carefully eased her to her feet.

Cari leaned against the log wall. "Thank you," she said, her voice raspy. She tried to straighten up and her jaw clenched. She forced her legs to support her weight, even as the color drained from her face.

"I'll let you inside before you fall over," John said, still frowning. *Why did I let her come up here? She'll probably get sick, or injure herself, or start the whole place on fire.* He removed the padlock and put it into one of the many pockets of his pants. Then he opened the door, allowing the morning sunlight to penetrate the one room structure. "Go on in – if you can." His sarcasm didn't go unnoticed, and Cari's frown matched his.

"Look, John, I appreciate you driving me up here. I even appreciate your help getting to the porch. But I don't need your comments." That said, she turned and limped inside, her right hand on her leg. She got as far as the mission style sofa and gripped it with both hands, her knuckles whitening.

"Suit yourself. I'll bring your things in for you. And I'll be sure to leave just as soon as I check on things." He left the cabin before she even had a chance to turn around. *She's the most stubborn woman I've ever met. Or at least one of the most stubborn. She won't even admit how much pain she's in.* He paused mid-stride. *Then again, she did ask for help from the Jeep. Oh, never mind! The sooner I get out of here, the better.*

Inside the cabin, Cari was trembling. She knew she had to let go of the couch if she wanted to sit on it. But she also knew she might fall if she did let go. She kept one hand on the couch, and took a tentative step around the arm of it. Then a second. She had just seated herself when John came back.

"Well, I see you're making yourself at home. Now, I suppose I should give you the lay of the land, both figuratively, and literally." He set her things on the table by the wall. "You're sitting at an elevation of close to 2,000 ft. If you feel dizzy, lay down until it passes. The terrain around here is meant for serious hikers or those on horseback. I don't suggest trying any of the trails. If you run into any serious trouble, I keep a two way radio in the cabinet by the door." She followed his pointing hand and noticed the placement. "The band is set to connect with the nearest forestry personnel."

John walked over to the woodstove, bringing him within a few feet of Cari. He squatted down and opened the glass front door of the stove. As she'd half expected, there was wood stacked inside, newspaper around it. All that was needed was a match. "I keep the matches in my pocket, usually. Since I won't be staying, I'll leave them in the box you have your food in." He withdrew the small box of matches, got one out and struck it on the stove door. The fire was soon catching, and he closed the door most of the way.

Cari watched his face as the flames flickered to life, and the wood began to snap and crackle. *How can he still be single? He's a wonderful guy. He could offer some woman just about anything she could want.* She almost jumped as the door to the stove clanged into place again. John was talking again, and she'd missed part of what he said. "Pardon?"

He turned to look at her. "I said that the control for the draft is right here on the side. You don't want it burning too hot, but you need enough air to keep it going."

"Sounds like a good rule for relationships," she murmured.

"What did you say?" he asked, one eyebrow slightly raised.

"Uh, n—nothing important," she stammered.

He stepped towards her and she leaned back against the cushion behind her. "I think you did." He crossed his arms. "And I'm not leaving until you say it again."

Cari felt her cheeks flush with embarrassment. She repeated herself, loud enough that he caught each word.

"Very true, Ms. Daniels. I'll have to remember that in the future." He seemed to be studying her with his gaze.

"What else do you need to tell me, Mr. Maxwell?" she asked. "I don't want to keep you too long."

"Oh, I'm sure you don't. The wood is stacked on the porch, and there's plenty to last you a few days." He walked even closer to her, squatted down, and flipped back a small carpet from the floor. She saw a trap door with a metal ring for a handle. "This is where you can store anything that you want kept cool." He flipped the carpet back into place and stood up. He began to smooth his moustache.

"Anything else?" Cari asked, growing uneasy.

"Well, just the matter of where to sleep. You happen to be on the only 'bed' in here, I'm afraid. If you remove the back cushions, it leaves enough space to stretch out. I generally sleep well when I'm here. You should be just fine."

"What about the toilet?"

"It's right over there." He gestured towards a dark curtain. "Do you know how to operate a chemical one?"

"Yes." She was suddenly thankful for all of those family vacations of her past. "I'll be fine."

"Oh, there are blankets and pillows in this chest right here." He nudged it with his boot. Cari had thought it served as a coffee table. "And there are pots and pans in the cupboard above the table. And dishes."

"Where do I get water?" she asked, glad that she'd remembered before he was gone.

"Well, I normally get it from the creek, not too far down from here – but don't you dare try that. I'll go fill the containers and bring them back. Keep one for drinking, and the rest for whatever else you need." He looked at his watch. "I'd better go take care of that, or I'll still be here at lunch time." He walked over to the door, and Cari noticed three collapsible plastic jugs on the floor. One was clearly marked 'Drinking' on the side. John picked up two of them and headed back outside.

Cari took a better look around the room, as the heat from the stove began to reach her. It was about twenty by twenty feet. Each wall had a window, giving the room plenty of daylight. *That reminds me. I have to find out about the lanterns.* Plain navy cotton hung on simple curtain rods. The walls were peeled logs with chinking between them. The floor was rough planking. The kitchen area had a table and two chairs, made of unfinished pine. She finally noticed lanterns hanging on each of the walls. *Oil lamps? Boy, he wasn't kidding about this place being rustic.*

Cari gradually got to her feet. "Time to check out the scenery," she mumbled to herself. She made her way to the door, and onto the porch. She limped past the neatly stacked wood, to the end. Then she propped her elbows on the railing and let her gaze sweep the view in front of her. "This is amazing. I probably won't get any thinking done up here. I'll be too busy looking." She could see for miles. And the smell of pine came to her nose as the breeze picked up. After several minutes, she closed her eyes and simply inhaled.

"I see you've discovered my reason for building right here," John said as he stepped onto the porch.

Cari's eyes flew open and she turned around. "Don't sneak up on me like that!"

"I didn't 'sneak' at all. I was even whistling. You simply didn't notice me. Too enthralled with nature, I suppose." He carried the jugs inside and brought back the empty one. "I'll be sure to yell all the way back this time." He was soon out of sight, somewhere on a winding dirt path between the trees.

Cari looked at her watch. "Almost 11:30 already. I should make some lunch." She frowned. *I wonder if John likes any kind of sandwich other than corned beef. Good thing I brought some of the canned variety.* She went back inside, and set to work. She had two sandwiches, and some cans of *Coke* sitting on the table when she heard John approaching. Sure enough, he was yelling.

"Hey, Cari, I hope you appreciate all this labor I'm putting in," he called out. "You better use every drop of this water while I'm gone." He reached the door and looked at her. "I see you were expecting me this time." He grinned as he set down the jug.

"Yes, thank you. As a matter of fact, I even made you something to eat. Are you hungry?" She gestured to the table even as she sat down at it.

"I most certainly am." He came to the table and surveyed the scene. "Ah, to paraphrase a fine piece of literature: 'a corned beef sandwich, a can of *Coke*, and thou.'" He sat down and sighed. "Too bad there aren't any pickles."

———⊰⦿⊱———

"So, are you sure you want to stay until Saturday?" John asked again. "I could come back on Friday."

"Saturday will be fine. Thank you." She stood on the porch with him, trying not to think of just how *quiet* it would be once he was gone. "Drive carefully on your way back."

"You sound like a nagging wife, you know," he teased. His gaze didn't waver as he gently cupped her face with both of his hands. "I rather like that."

"John, please don't," Cari whispered, all the while wishing that he *would*.

He drew back slightly, but didn't release her face. "Why must you be so difficult?" He let his hands drop to his sides. "Goodbye. I'll see you on Saturday morning, sometime between nine and ten."

"Bye." She watched him go. And she waved as he pulled away. Then she shivered as she became aware of just how *alone* she now was.

Chapter 40

Rick sat up in bed with a start. Tammy was screaming in her sleep again. He got up and went to her room. He sat down on her bed and shook her until she woke up.

"Don't hurt me! Please don't touch me like that! Leave me alone!" she screamed. Rick shook her a little harder. "Dad? Is that you, Dad?" she whimpered.

"Yes, Sweetheart. You're okay. You were just dreaming again." He pulled her into his arms and she sobbed against him.

"I keep dreaming about it, Dad."

"It's only a *dream*, Tammy. It's not *real*." He'd tried this reasoning every other time. It still didn't work.

"I know it's not, Dad. But it *feels* like it is." She gradually quieted. "When will Cari be back? I really need to talk to her."

Rick stiffened. "I don't know when she'll be back. She's busy with her job right now." In reality, he didn't *care* what Cari Daniels was busy with. He just didn't want her around his daughter – or himself.

"But she said she'd help me," Tammy persisted. "She promised, Dad. Why hasn't she been back?" She pulled back and wiped some of the tears from her face.

Rick decided to fill her in, at least partially. "I asked her to stay away for a while, Tammy. To give us time to work through this on our own." He wasn't prepared for his daughter's reaction.

"How *could* you? She's one of my only friends, and you told her to stay away? Why?" She backed against the headboard, and put her arms around her knees. "And you let me think she was just too *busy*?"

"Sweetheart, you don't understand --"

"And neither do *you*! You just keep telling me to forget about it. That I'm going to be okay. You won't even let me *talk* to you. And you haven't been listening to Ricky either. What's wrong with you, Dad?"

Her words cut at him and he couldn't look at her. *What is wrong with me? She needs my help and I just can't give it to her. It's been a week now, and I'm still so angry I could –*

"Just leave me alone, Dad," Tammy murmured. "I'm too tired to think. Just go back to bed."

"Tammy, I --"

"Please, go. I just want to be by myself right now."

"All right, if that's what you want." He stood up, and realized just how tense his neck and shoulder muscles were. "If you need me, just call."

"I've already tried that, Dad," she whispered. "And I'm still waiting for you to show up." She burrowed beneath her covers and closed her eyes.

———※◊※———

Cari couldn't decide if she was eager to go home or not. It was Friday night already. She had slept like a dead person every night at the cabin. She didn't find the intense solitude disturbing in the least. She relished it. And she found it so much easier to think without any distractions. She sat on the couch, Bible in her lap. Tammy came to mind, just as she had many times each day.

Please comfort her, Lord. Please help her to trust You for her safety. And for her sense of worth. Help her to come out of this a stronger person. Help her to rest. Please give Rick wisdom and patience in dealing with her. I know that he's hurting too, but please give him the right words to say to her.

Cari stretched and yawned. *Time for bed.* She soon had the blankets and pillows all arranged on the couch. She readied herself for bed, added some wood to the stove, and blew out the lantern. As she lay in the semi darkness, she thought of John.

Thank You for him, Lord. He's been a good friend. Please keep him safe on his way here tomorrow. And please help me not to be a stumbling block to him. I know that I'm attracted to him. Very much so. Please help me to act properly when we're together. And please continue to speak to his heart. I don't know what it'll take for him to see that he needs You. But I'd like to be part of it somehow.

She rolled onto her side, fluffed the pillow, and promptly drifted off to sleep.

———— ⦿ ————

John hopped out of the Jeep and looked at the cabin. The curtains were open, so he assumed that Cari was up and about. *Even if I am early.* It was only 8:15. He'd started out early, and barely held to the speed limit all the way. *She'll likely yell at me for coming this soon.* He grinned at the thought. *But she's quite something to see when she's miffed.* He headed up to the porch and stopped dead when the door opened.

"I told you not to sneak up on me, John," Cari said. "But you don't have to raise a racket either." With her intense frown, he couldn't tell if she was serious or not. Then she started to laugh. "After a few days up here, I think I'd hear almost *anything* approaching. The peace and quiet has been so refreshing."

Relieved that she wasn't really upset with him, John moved closer to her. "I see you're all in one piece. No mishaps while you were alone?" She shook her head. "So, you really do have a pioneer spirit in you. I've always thought so." She had color back in her face. Her eyes were bright. And she smelled like the mountain pines around the cabin. "You look wonderful, Cari," he remarked softly.

"Would you like some breakfast?" she asked, her right hand going to her throat in a familiar nervous gesture. "If you're this early, you mustn't have eaten yet."

"No, I didn't. And I'd love to have some, thank you." *Is she really afraid, or just not sure of herself?* "What are you making?"

"Pancakes and coffee. C'mon in. I'll just mix up some more batter." She turned and went back inside.

John remained on the porch for a moment. *What an ideal scenario. A beautiful woman, scenic grandeur, good food, and a snug cabin. Too bad she won't let me in on the picture.* He shook his head as he looked off into the distance. *How can I change her mind?* No answers came, so he went inside to enjoy her company, and her cooking.

—◈—

"Thank you so much for letting me use your cabin, John. It really helped." Cari touched his arm as she spoke, without even noticing. "Let me know if I can return the favor sometime."

"Well, you've already made me lunch and breakfast so far. That's a good start."

"Is that a hint for supper?" she asked. She suddenly felt his hand on hers. To her credit, she kept smiling. "I don't know about *making* supper for you, but I could take you out. How about Monday night?" *Why am I doing this? Just because he drove me there, brought me back, and let me use his cabin. And I know that he wouldn't take money, even if I offered it.*

"That sounds like a wonderful idea."

"I'll pick a place and let you know where and when on Monday morning, all right?"

"Certainly. I don't mind surprises when they're sure to be

pleasant ones."

Cari eased her hand from his arm. "Bye, John."

"Have a good day." He nodded just before he turned and made his way back to the elevator.

Cari let herself into her apartment, set her bag on the couch, and checked her answering machine. Sure enough, there were messages. She never got past the first one.

"Hello, Cari, this is Rick. Tammy really needs to see you. Can you please call when you get a chance? Or just come over. I promise not to throw you out again."

Chapter 41

Cari called the Bensons immediately and Rick answered.

"Hi, Rick, it's Cari. I just got your message."

"Oh. I called pretty early this morning."

"I just got home. I've been away for a few days. I still need to shower and change before coming over. How's Tammy."

"Not too good." She could hear the fatigue in his voice. "It's been a horrible week for all of us. And a lot of that has been my fault." He sighed. "I was so bent on handling this *myself*. I can't. I'm not willing to lose my daughter for the sake of my pride."

Cari was amazed at the change in his attitude – until she thought of how many times she had prayed for that change while at the cabin. "I'll come over in about an hour, Rick. Would you like me to bring anything with me?"

"Like what?"

"I have some books about recovering from assault. Have you read anything lately?"

"No, I haven't. It might be a good idea."

"Probably. I'd better go now, or it'll take me longer than an hour."

"Sure. Bye, Cari. And thanks for calling back."

"You're welcome. Bye." She hung up, grabbed the books from beneath her coffee table and headed for her bedroom.

———=«(O)»=———

"I feel like I'm going crazy, Cari," Tammy said as they embraced. "I go to sleep, but I keep dreaming about it. Over and over. I've already missed a week of school, but I'm too scared to go back."

"Well, you're *not* going crazy. And for the moment you can do your school work at home. As for the nightmares, they *will* ease off."

"When?" Tammy leaned back against the pile of pillows on her bed. "I'm so tired."

"Would it help to talk about it, Tammy, either to me, or someone else?"

"I – I think so. I mean, Dad just freaked every time I tried to say anything. I know Ricky would listen, but he's been so busy with school, and helping me to stay caught up." She put her arms around her knees, as though shielding herself. "Maybe it would help."

"Okay." Cari reclined on the bed and put her hands behind her head. "I'm all ears, Tammy. And trust me, no matter what you say, or how you react, I won't be shocked. Okay?" Tammy nodded. "I'll just listen, unless you want to ask me a question." Cari closed her eyes. "Anytime you're ready."

For the next forty minutes Tammy described exactly what had happened to her. Her shock, her fear, her disgust, her anger, and her dismay at her own feelings. As she spoke and cried, Cari felt tears slipping down her own face.

When Tammy was finished, Cari opened her eyes and reached for the girl's hand. "Tammy, when your mom was killed, you were only ten, weren't you?"

"Almost eleven. Why?"

"Well, had she had a chance to talk with you about – well, the *changes* in your body? Did you know what to expect?"

"No. Not really. And Dad never knew what to say. Mostly I found out in health class, or from my friends' moms."

Cari had suspected as much. "Tammy, I want you to listen to me carefully. What I'm going to say is very important."

"Okay."

"Any feelings, or maybe *sensations* would be a better word, any seeming *pleasure* you may have experienced – you don't need to feel guilty for that. Do you understand?"

"But how could I like or enjoy *anything* they did to me? It doesn't make sense."

"Yes, it does." Cari sat up so she could look right into the flushed face of the troubled girl. "God designed each of us to respond to that kind of contact, or touch. And when it's done in the context of marriage, there is nothing wrong with it."

"But --"

"Just a minute. So, since our bodies are made to respond, then it was perfectly *normal* for you to feel what you did. The *response* was normal. It was just too soon, and under the wrong circumstances. Tammy, I don't want you to feel guilty for being a woman. Those guys had no right to touch you, or to provoke any response from you. Do you see the difference?"

"So, none of it was my fault?" Tammy asked, uncertainty in her voice.

"No, none of it."

Tammy's shoulders began to shake and Cari put her arms around her. "They kept telling me I was ready for it," Tammy sobbed. "And I was so mixed up. It hurt and felt kind of good at the same time. I thought there was something wrong with me."

"There wasn't. And there isn't now, either." Cari moved and placed her hands on Tammy's face. "You're hurting, and confused, and scared. But you're still a beautiful young woman. That hasn't changed."

"Where was God, Cari? Why did He let this happen?"

Cari swallowed before trying to answer the very question that she had asked so many times herself. "Tammy, the only answer I can give you is that God has given all of us a free will. And some people choose to do evil things, sometimes to others. But I also know that God is with you. That He loves you very much. And that He wants to help you through this experience."

"How do I forgive those guys? I want to hurt them for hurting me." She choked on a sob. "I know that's not *right*. But what can I do?"

Cari had to look away for a moment, in order to control her own rising emotions. Her experience with Mark was still too fresh. "You forgive because you *need* to, Tammy. Not just because it's *right*. You see, as long as you hang on to the pain, the hurt, the injustice of what happened, the longer those two will have the power to keep hurting you. When you forgive, you're not releasing them from responsibility, and you may never forget what happened, but it won't hurt as much anymore."

"It sounds too easy."

"No, it isn't easy at all. It might be the hardest thing you ever do. But it will also be one of the best."

Tammy brooded in silence for a moment. "This is very *real* to you, isn't it? You're not just giving me answers from a book, are you?"

"No," Cari whispered. "I've lived through the hate, and the forgiveness. And I *know* which is so much better." Cari released Tammy in order to wipe the tears from her own face.

"And you're okay again?"

"Most of the time," Cari replied honestly. "Guys can still make me uncomfortable. And I'm not eager to spend time with the guy who hurt me. But I have forgiven him."

"It was somebody you knew?" Tammy asked with evident surprise.

"Yes." Cari reached for Tammy's hand once more. "And I know you'll find it hard to go back to school. But after you do it the first time, it shouldn't be so bad. You don't have to be a prisoner of fear for the rest of your life. And you don't have to struggle through this on your own either."

"Thanks, Cari," Tammy breathed. "I'm so glad you came today."

"So am I. Now, how be you come out to the kitchen and help me to make some supper?"

"Something *normal* right?"

"Exactly."

———))((———

"Thanks for coming over, Cari," Rick said as they stood by the front door. "And for making supper. We've been living on pizza and burgers for the past week."

"I noticed all the boxes in the kitchen," she replied with a smile. "I'm glad I was able to help."

"And thanks for the books. I've finished one of them already. I wish I'd read it after Karen was killed. I might not have gone so off the handle this time around." He looked down at the floor, his hands shoved into the pockets of his jeans.

"Keep them as long as you need to, Rick. And it might be good to let Ricky and Tammy go through them too. I'm sure they both have lots of questions that they can't bring themselves to ask. A book isn't as threatening."

Rick met her gaze. "You're probably right." He cleared his throat. "I still owe you an apology for last week. I was completely out of line." He paused. "I hurt you when I shoved you, didn't I?"

"Yes," Cari admitted. "But I'm fine now."

"Good. But that still doesn't excuse what I did. I'm sorry."

"I know you are. I knew that as soon as I heard the phone message." She reached out and touched his arm. "And I forgive you, Rick." She smiled then. "Don't ever try it again, though, or I'm liable to fight back."

"I won't."

She withdrew her hand. "I need to get home. Will you be out to church tomorrow?"

"I honestly don't know. I'll see how Tammy is doing. I'm not sure if that would help or hinder right now." He almost smiled. "Though she's better since you got here."

"Good night, Rick. And hang in there. You'll all get through this."

"Thanks, Cari. Goodnight."

Chapter 42

A very tired Cari got to the office on Monday morning. She had visited Jill Harris the night before, and helped the young lawyer begin packing her belongings. Jill had found a new apartment, and wanted to move as soon as she could, but she didn't want movers to pack her things. So Cari had helped. And she'd listened to Jill talk. And she'd offered advice when it was asked for. And she'd gotten home too late for her own good.

"You look horrible," John commented after entering Cari's office. "If you don't mind my saying so."

"Of course I mind!" she retorted, but she knew he was right. "But I was already gone for most of last week. I thought I'd better show up today."

"Why?" he asked, perching on the corner of her desk. "Just a sense of duty?"

"Something like that." She reached for her briefcase and flicked the locks on it. "Besides, I need to spend some time with Max Gardner. He's got a lot of explaining to do."

"You still think he's involved with what happened to Jill Harris?" At her frown, he added, "Sorry. Confidential matter, is it?"

"I'm afraid so." She sighed. "Probably not. Mrs. Richards said to speak with you any time she's not available."

"And?" he pressed, crossing his arms over his chest.

"And, yes, I'm almost certain that Max allowed Trevor MacBride into Jill's office. But I need to *prove* it. And, being a lawyer yourself, you should realize what a daunting task I have before me."

He nodded. "All the more reason to let me help you."

"Help me? How?"

"By allowing me to go over every detail with you. Trevor MacBride may be sitting in jail right now, with enough evidence to convict him ten times over. But Max Gardener is entirely different. If we can prove complicity on his part, he's in plenty of trouble himself. Otherwise, the best we could do is fire him, based on suspicion alone. And I don't think we need a disgruntled former employee bothering anyone, do we?"

"Exactly what I've been thinking." Then she grinned, in spite of her fatigue. "So, how come you're a lawyer, and not a private investigator?"

John laughed. "They don't make as much money as I do. Or dress as well."

"Great reasoning." She studied him for a moment. "So, any idea as to how we can nail Max Gardener?"

"Not yet. But I'll think about it and let you know over supper tonight. Where are we going?"

Cari had completely forgotten, and she was sure that her open mouth must have conveyed just that. "Um, I forgot." She felt her cheeks flush. "How about the *Pacific Dining Car*? I haven't been there for a long time, and nobody makes steak quite like they do."

"All right. What time? And how shall I dress?"

"Oh, you always look fine." She clapped her hand over her mouth. *I can't believe I just said that!*

John grinned like a mischievous little boy. "Thank you, Ms. Daniels. How about semi-formal?"

"Sure. Six o'clock?"

"Fine by me. Shall I pick you up?"

"Why don't I just meet you there?" *It won't seem so much like a date that way.*

"As you wish." He got up from the desk. "See you at six, then. Have a good day."

"Thank you." She watched him leave the room, closing the door behind him. *I should have postponed this whole thing. Or maybe it's better to just get it over with. I don't know. How on earth am I going to last through work and then dinner with John?* She rubbed her hands over her face. *Why does he have to catch me off guard so often? And why does he always have to look so good?*

———◆———

"So, Max, you've worked here for how long?" Cari asked the thirty-five year old man sitting on the far side of her desk. He wasn't on duty, so he was wearing jeans and a denim shirt. He was rather handsome, but Cari didn't trust him. She waited for his answer, no hint of a smile on her face.

"I've worked here for about four years, Ms. Daniels. And I'm sure you already knew that from the personnel files. So, why am I here?" His tone was just short of insolent.

"You're here for several reasons, Mr. Gardener," she replied coolly. "For one thing, I'd like to know why someone with four years of experience would go for a smoke break just a half hour before his lunch break. Any explanation?"

"Look, I got a nic fit and went for a smoke," he replied, sounding annoyed. "An extra half hour seemed too long to wait." He shrugged, a distasteful grin on his face. "But I suppose somebody like you never picked up any bad habits like smoking."

"As a matter of fact, I tried smoking for about six months while I was in high school. But my volleyball coach threatened to kick me off the team if I didn't quit. So I did." She watched a look of surprise cross his face. "But I always managed to wait for my next break. I never tried to sneak out of class for a cigarette."

"What is the big deal?" he demanded, leaning forward on his

chair. "I went for a smoke. I came back to my floor within a few minutes. It's not like I was gone for ages."

"The *big deal* is that someone got on to the third floor while you were having a smoke. Someone who was not supposed to be there. Someone known to be a threat to an employee. And he was able to carry out his threat. And you say that you never saw Trevor MacBride the whole time he was in the building?"

"No, I didn't." He nervously reached for the pack of cigarettes in his shirt pocket.

Cari shook her head. "No smoking in this office, Mr. Gardener. I'm sure you can wait a few more minutes." She smiled but he didn't.

"What else do you want to know?"

"Have you ever met Trevor MacBride before? In the building or elsewhere?"

"Sure, I've seen him. Jill Harris had him at the Christmas party. He looked about as drunk as most of the other guys." He smirked. "Except for John Maxwell, that is. He never gets drunk."

"That's because he never drinks," Cari retorted. "Back to MacBride. You'd seen him before, so you would have recognized him last week."

"Sure. But I didn't see him here." He fingered the pack in his pocket, frowned, and then leaned forward again. "What about Kelly at Front Desk? Wouldn't he have come in that way?"

Cari shook her head. "He didn't come in the front door. Apparently, he entered the parking area, and came up the stairwell to the third floor. He was wearing a hat, and had his head slightly down, so his identity wasn't obvious until he reached the third floor – right after you left to have a smoke." She fingered her pen and began to tap it lightly on her desk.

"Well, what about the parking attendants? Didn't they notice him – coming or going?"

Cari smiled. "Interesting that you should mention that, Max. Ted told me that you radioed down to him to make sure that you'd locked your car. Just before your smoke break. Then, on your lunch break, you came to talk with him in person. He heard a car leave, but he had his back to it, while you engaged him in conversation." She set aside her pen. "Interesting, isn't it?"

"Not very," he remarked, though his agitation seemed to be rising. "Any more questions?"

"Yes. Do you know how much trouble you could be in for aiding Trevor MacBride – especially if you *knew* what his intentions were?" He stood up, but she wasn't quite through. "And did you remember that each other *incident* occurred on the shifts that you were working? Usually on your floor. A few too many *coincidences*, Max. Far too many."

"What are you trying to prove?" He braced his hands on her desk and glared at her. "I do my job, and I do it well. And I won't take the rap if some nutcase gets past the *whole* security department. No way. You won't pin anything on me." He shook his head. "No way." He straightened up.

"We'll see, Max. We'll see," Cari replied evenly, though the hairs on the back of her neck were standing up. "You may go for now. I'll let you know when I need to speak with you again." She looked down at his open file on her desk, but he still had something to say.

"You won't pin anything on me. Not one thing." Then he turned and left the office, slamming the door on his way out.

Cari put her hands up to her face. *I'm sure he's involved. I'm certain of it. But how on earth can I prove it?*

━━━━►《●》◄━━━━

"You look tense," was John's first comment when he and Cari met outside the restaurant. He smiled then. "Lovely, mind you. But tense." He reached for her satin clad elbow and escorted her inside. "Long day at the office?"

"Yes. I had a meeting with Max Gardener. I succeeded in making him very nervous, but he didn't admit to any wrongdoing. It's so frustrating," she said with a sigh.

"Apparently, we only have circumstantial evidence on him so far. We need something more concrete than that." He paused, mid stride. "Have the police asked MacBride how he skirted security so readily?"

"Yes. And all he'll say is that he had 'inside help'. He won't name anyone."

They were shown to a table in the corner, and continued their conversation.

"Maybe he'll have more to say after he's gone through detox. It can be a horrible experience." At Cari's look of confusion, John hastened to add. "I only know about it second hand, Cari. Drugs never appealed to me in the slightest. Waste of time and money." He reached for his menu. "Not to mention that I buried a few careless friends during my time in law school. They thought overdoses were a convenient way to cope with stress."

"How awful." Cari frowned. "Drugs seem to make such a mess of so many lives." She shook her head in an effort to dispel thoughts of Kyle Richards, and her parents, and Jill Harris. "So, what are you hungry for tonight?"

"Just about anything at this point. I skipped lunch today."

"Actually, I'm not very hungry at all," she said honestly. "Maybe I'm too tired. I think some sourdough bread and a Caesar salad will be more than enough." Then she looked at him and smiled. "But feel free to order whatever you like."

"I intend to," he remarked with a grin. "Though it just won't be the same as those pancakes you made up at the cabin."

His words brought a flush to her cheeks. *Why does he have to keep twisting conversations in his favor? I try to keep things* friendly, *and he keeps bringing up the* romantic. Then she smiled behind her tall menu. *Why am I complaining? Most men wouldn't give romance two minutes of their time.* Her smile quickly faded. *If only he were willing to focus on God for that long.*

———⟫((•))⟪———

"Thank you for a lovely meal, Cari. Now, I think you should go home and get a good rest."

"You're welcome. And I intend to."

They left the restaurant, and John insisted on walking Cari to her car. When he placed a warm hand on her shoulder, she turned to face him. His look was sober to say the least.

"Be on your guard with Gardener. Some people get pretty desperate if they're backed into a corner. He just may come out fighting." His free hand clasped her other shoulder. "I'd hate for anything to happen to you."

The kiss that followed was both warm and gentle. Cari's hands went to his forearms as the moments passed. Then she drew back, flushed and uncertain. "I – I'll be careful," she murmured. Then she turned and opened her car door. "Goodnight, John." She got in and closed her door, but her mind couldn't shut out what had just taken place.

I kissed him. He didn't just kiss me. I let him this time. I wanted him to. I have to keep my distance somehow. He's not a Christian. He may never be. She turned the key in the ignition. *I have to remember that. I have to.*

Chapter 43

"How are you doing, Jill?" Cari asked as the young lawyer came back to the firm a week later.

"I'm hanging on right now," she replied, no hint of her former cheerful personality. "That's about all. I'm hoping it'll help to get back to work." She shrugged. "Try me again later."

"Jill, would you like me to go up to your office with you, just this first time back?"

Jill looked immensely relieved. "I kept telling myself that I wouldn't ask you to do that. But, yes, I'd appreciate that very much. Thanks."

"No problem. Ready whenever you are."

Jill led the way to the elevator, but when she got off on the third floor, she hesitated. She turned to face Cari. "I – I thought I could do this. Now I'm not so sure."

"It'll be okay. I'll open the door for you, and go in first if you like. Don't worry."

"I think that's all I've been doing for the past two weeks."

Cari walked beside her to the office door, unlocked it, and stepped inside. She held the door all the way open while Jill entered. "You'll be fine, Jill. It's okay."

Jill looked around the office, and Cari could see the frantic expression on her face as she eyed the desk. Everything had been cleaned after the evidence had been collected, and photos taken. Even the carpet had been steam cleaned. Jill forced herself to walk to the far side of the desk, setting her briefcase down on the dark surface of it. Then she almost slumped into the leather chair. "I feel sick," she admitted, looking at Cari. "That's normal, isn't it?"

"Yes, it is. Don't try to stuff what you're feeling. But don't let the fear take over either. This is still *your* office. You have work to do, and clients to meet with. You're a capable lawyer. None of that has changed. It only will if you let it." Cari approached the desk and stood directly opposite Jill. "It'll get easier each time. It did for me. To work, I mean."

Jill nodded her head. Then she took another look at her desk. She noticed the large bouquet of roses in a crystal vase. She reached a shaky hand towards them, and removed a small card. She read it, and then looked at Cari. "They're from Mrs. Richards. She wanted to welcome me back today." She set the card on her blotter. Then she licked her lips.

"What else is bothering you, Jill?"

Jill clasped her trembling hands together and swallowed. "I – I guess it's easier than I thought it might be. I just wish that I could sleep at night."

"Having nightmares?" Cari asked with understanding.

Jill nodded. "Every night. And I *know* that Trevor is in jail, and can't get to me. It doesn't make sense."

"It doesn't always have to. Just focus on the time when you *will* be able to sleep soundly again. It may take a while. You might need to get some medication from your doctor, temporarily. But it *will* get better. Don't give up."

"I did the right thing – pressing charges, I mean. I'd still be hiding if I knew that Trevor was out there, some place." A shudder passed through her slight frame. "But I dread going to court." She smiled half-heartedly. "Pretty pathetic for a criminal lawyer, isn't it?"

"No, it isn't. I was a police officer, and it took me a long time to start to relax."

"Was he caught?"

Cari shook her head. "No. I never pressed charges."

"Why not?"

"For a lot of reasons that don't make much sense anymore," Cari replied with a sigh. "But I can't change the past." She straightened up. "Think you'll be all right now?"

"I hope so." Jill looked at her watch. "I have a client coming in ten minutes. I guess I'll *have to* be okay. Thanks for coming up with me. I appreciate it."

"No problem. I'll see you later."

———◦((◦))◦———

Max Gardener watched Cari leave work that afternoon, and followed her to her building, just staying far enough behind so as not to be noticed. He parked on the street, and then entered the underground parking area, trying to look as though he had a right to be there. He located Cari's blue BMW a few minutes later. Then he took out his pocket knife and stabbed it into her right front tire. He also damaged the other three tires. Just before turning to go, he took the sharp point of the blade and dragged it across the driver's door, watching the paint flake off. "Let's see how you like that, Ms. Daniels," he muttered to himself.

———◦((◦))◦———

Cari was late for her meeting with John and Rebecca the next morning. She'd called ahead to say she'd be delayed, but she hadn't given a specific reason. When she entered Rebecca's office, John got to his feet, concern on his face.

"What happened? You're never late."

"Somebody slashed my tires – sometime between 5:30 last night and 8:30 this morning." She made her way to the other empty chair and nodded to her employer. "Sorry I'm late."

"Any idea who might have done it?" Rebecca asked.

"This is LA, isn't it?" Cari sighed. "Just about *anybody* could have done it."

"Really?" John asked. "Why wouldn't they just steal the car? Why slash the tires?"

Cari rubbed at her throbbing temples. "I thought of that. I was a cop for eleven years, John. I've made plenty of enemies along the way. I'm sure I'm easy enough to track down." She shrugged. "I've no idea who would have done it. Or why."

John came and sat down where he'd been before. "I have. What about Max Gardener? You told me he got pretty nervous the other day. Do you think he might try to intimidate you somehow, in a way that he wouldn't likely get caught?"

"Maybe, but maybe not. I mean, why would he bother? He knows I can't prove anything right now."

"Exactly," Rebecca put in. "All the more reason. Perhaps he wants you to back off."

Cari shook her head. "I just don't know." She looked from one to the other. "This is getting to be more frustrating than police work." She forced a smile. "Sorry to be such a ray of sunshine around here."

"Cari, is there any chance that you may be in danger?" Rebecca asked.

"I suppose it's possible. But I don't intend to let that get in the way of my job."

"Please be careful," her employer admonished.

"I will," Cari replied. "Just as careful as I can."

◆◆◆

"How do you plan to get home?" John asked as he stood in the doorway to Cari's office.

"Take a cab. That's how I got here. The Auto Club phoned and my tires are all replaced, but the car is at home." She shrugged as she snapped her briefcase shut. "Why?"

"Because I'd be glad to give you a ride home."

Cari looked at him, wanting very much to accept his offer. She shook her head. "Thanks, John, but I'll take a cab." She tried to smile, but his frown squelched that plan.

"Why? Don't you trust me?"

"John, I just – I think it would be better for me to take a cab."

"Fine. I can take a hint. See you tomorrow." He turned away, pulling the door closed.

"Oh, rats!" Cari gritted her teeth and crossed her arms over her chest. *If I could trust you to just be a friend, John, a ride would've been nice.* She sighed as she picked up her case. *But, as it is, I can't even trust myself.*

———

Cari checked her mailbox and found an envelope, addressed to her in pencil, with no return address. She frowned as she headed for the elevator. Once inside her apartment, she carefully slit the envelope with her brass letter opener. It contained one sheet of regular typing paper. The message was pasted on with clippings from magazines.

"I know where to find you."

"What kind of message is that? Or should I say, 'warning'?" She read it again. Then the phone rang, making her jolt. She went to pick it up.

"I know where to find you," the caller rasped. Then only the click of the receiver was heard.

Cari hung up, her pulse skipping. She went to sit down on her couch, and instinctively looked towards her balcony doors. *Whoever it is knows where I live. And that I'm home right now. So, who is it? And why?*

———◦((◦))◦———

"What are you planning to do about this?" Mike asked as he passed the sheet back to Cari.

"Take it to the forensics department. Somebody must owe me a few favors down there." She folded the paper and stuffed it back into the envelope. "Maybe they can trace the type of lead on the envelope, or something. *Anything* that might make some sense. And, I plan to leave my answering machine on all the time. That way I might be able to record the voice." She fanned herself with the envelope until Mike touched her hand.

"This is really getting to you, isn't it? Slashed tires, messages, phone calls. Any idea who's behind it?"

"Oh, sure. One of my own staff, most likely." She sat down on the wing back chair. "But that's not what my gut instinct is telling me. Somehow, I don't think Max Gardener would go to this much bother. I think he would just tell me to my face." She shook her head. "I just don't know, Mike. I'm trying to be logical about this whole scenario, but somehow the pieces just don't all fit. Or maybe they fit too well." She rubbed her forehead.

"Something else is eating at you too. What's up?"

Cari looked up into her friend's face. Into eyes that knew her very well after so many years of working together. "A lot of things, Mike. Jill Harris is hanging onto sanity by a thread. Tammy is still refusing to go to school."

"And?"

"And I think I'm seriously falling for John Maxwell, and he's not a Christian," she blurted out in frustration. She blinked back tears as she turned her head.

"So, that the biggest problem, isn't it?" He sat down on the coffee table and reached for her hand. "How *seriously* are we talking here?"

"He's kissed me a couple of times. Last time it was pretty mutual." She sighed. "And now I'm practically avoiding the guy, which is tricky when we work in the same building." Blinking was no longer enough and the tears began to slip down her cheeks. "If he was a Christian . . ."

"Then what? You'd be hearing wedding bells?"

"Maybe I would." She pulled her hand free and got to her feet. "I try not to dwell on it. I mean, I pray for him. I've invited him to church. But he doesn't feel any *need* in his life for God. At least not right now."

"Well, then I guess we should pray that he will."

"Please do," she whispered.

Chapter 44

Nothing more happened over the next few days, and Cari tried to concentrate on her job, rather than herself. Then Valentine's Day arrived, and with it, several gifts. Rebecca Richards gave her a heart shaped candy dish, filled with cinnamon hearts. John gave her a box of Belgian chocolates. The Bensons gave her a giant cookie with 'For a Special Friend' on it. And *someone* sent her a dozen red roses, but no card. She was baffled. *John wouldn't send something in secret. He's much too open for that. Rick is too shy.*

By the end of the day, Cari had eaten a large section of the cookie, put the dish on her coffee table, and set the chocolates on her nightstand. She had just arranged the flowers in a vase when the phone rang. She waited, letting the machine kick in.

"Do you like my gift? Red is such a good color on you – blood red."

Cari nearly dropped the flowers in her eagerness to set them down. She put a hand on her chest, willing her heart rate to normalize. *Who is it? And what do they want?*

—◉—

"Well, it's not from just *any* pencil, Cari. I can tell you that much.

I'd say it's from a mechanical pencil. Maybe even a drafting one. Very hard graphite, very fine. Likewise, the clippings were from expensive magazines. Absolutely no smudging of the ink and the paper didn't tear easily either. The envelope is top quality, not your generic make. And, maybe the most interesting, the glue used to paste the words on, it's different. It didn't match up to any of the samples that we had here in the lab."

"Thanks, Tony. I owe you one," Cari remarked as she read over his report. "Not much to go on though. What is so different about this glue?"

"I'm not exactly sure. My *guess* is that it's imported. Maybe European. I don't know if you noticed, but it dried completely clean. It didn't mark the paper, front or back."

"Great!" Cari sighed. "I have a very neat and tidy stalker." She involuntarily shuddered as she said the word. "Somebody with expensive taste, by the looks of things." She put the report into her briefcase. "Somehow I'm not too flattered."

———⟫⟪⟨◉⟩⟫⟪———

"How about lunch?" John asked Cari. "It's been a while."

"I'm sorry," she replied. "I have a lot of work to do today. I've been going over some of the cases that were being handled at the times of the other security incidents. There must be a connection somewhere, and I intend to find it."

"That's fine, Cari. But don't you even plan to eat lunch?"

"Well, sure, but --"

"But not with me. Why won't you just admit it?" He stepped closer to her desk. "It's been over a month since we went out for supper. And you've put me off every time I've asked you. Why?"

"Because it's better if I do," she said with an exasperated sigh.

"Better for whom?"

"For both of us, John."

"Really? I beg to differ with you. I happen to think we make a wonderful pair. And, what, pray tell, is so *threatening* about having lunch together?"

Before Cari could answer, her phone rang. "Excuse me, please." She picked up the receiver. "Hello. Cari Daniels speaking."

"I know who you are. But you don't know who I am. How does it feel to be the mouse for a change, instead of the cat?"

"Who *is* this? And what do you want?"

"Oh, now that would spoil all the fun, wouldn't it? But I know where you are. I always know, Cari. I know all about you." The caller hung up, but Cari still held the receiver in her hand until John took it from her.

"What's going on? What was that all about?"

Cari tried to speak, but only managed a hoarse whisper. She swallowed. "Somebody has been harassing me. Messages, phone calls, flowers. I don't know who it is. That's the first call to here, though." She put her head down on her hands. Her heart was thudding and she felt dizzy.

"Have you talked with the police?"

"Mike knows," she mumbled, not raising her head. "I've reported it."

"Max Gardener?"

"I don't know!" she cried, looking at him. "*I* don't know and *you* don't know. And I don't need any more people asking me questions I can't answer!" She was trembling and hated that John was seeing her in such a state. She took a breath and bit her lip.

"Okay," he said, moving away from the desk. "I won't interfere in this, Cari – but only because you've notified the police. However, if you change your mind, and you'd like some assistance, you only have to ask."

"Thank you," she murmured. "And I'm sorry that I yelled at you. If I think of any way you could help, I'll let you know." She tried to smile, but the effort fell short.

"Promise?"

"Yes."

"Just one more question."

"What?"

"What are you doing for lunch?"

⚬

Cari nibbled at the corned beef sandwich, but she wasn't very hungry. She drank her cola, and then chided herself for adding caffeine to an already stressed system. *My sleep is already messed up right now.*

"Has this ever happened before?" John asked, between bites of food.

"What, the harassment? No, nothing like this." She forced a sarcastic smile. "Only the odd death threat after a drug bust, or something trivial like that." She looked down at the crumpled napkin in her left hand. "Nobody this persistent though."

"Any clues to an identity?"

"Someone who seems to know my whereabouts most of the time. Someone with expensive taste." She explained about Tony's evaluation. "Someone who wants me on edge." She sighed as she shoved her half eaten sandwich away from her. "I'm *assuming* it's a male, but I could be wrong about that. The voice on the phone is so distorted that I can't tell for certain." She shook her head. "It's so frustrating. And whoever is doing it *knows* that."

"Do you think there's any connection to what happened to Jill Harris? Or with the attempted break in at the firm?"

"I honestly don't know. But whoever it is, they know my home and work numbers, and my address." She raised her head and met his look of concern. "It could very well be someone from the firm, John. Somebody who accessed that kind of information."

"But what motive could they possibly have?"

"That's what I keep coming back to. I just draw a blank. I mean, I know that not everyone is *thrilled* to have me there, both men and women. But I don't know who would resort to outright harassment."

"You're so tense you look ready to pounce," he commented, though his tone was kind.

"I suppose I am. Puzzles have never been my favorite pass time. I like logic, not back and forth kind of games. I want to know *who* and *why*."

"Have you made a list?"

"For what, or of what?"

"Of anyone at the firm, or elsewhere, who might resort to this kind of tactics. Like Steven Hawkings. He's never tried to hide his dislike of you, has he?"

"No, not at all." She thought back to the Christmas party. "He was pretty bold when he was drunk. I don't know about sober."

"And Max Gardener. He's already feeling a bit cornered."

"And Jerry Neilson. We shared the elevator once, and he looked as though he couldn't wait to get off. I know he got in trouble for how he handled the inquest." Cari looked away again, not wanting to recall such a horrendous experience. "I think he fell out of grace with Rebecca Richards after that."

"Very true. As I recall, she even considered dismissing him altogether. She found his tactics anything but ethical."

"I'll second the motion. She changed her mind?"

"Yes, she did. Jerry apologized profusely, and agreed to discuss future cases with a senior partner after that. No more of the lone ranger tirades. He was put on probation for six months, and he behaved himself the whole time."

"Six months? That would have come to an end last month?"

"Yes." John took a sip of his drink. "Right at the time you started to receive the messages."

Cari shook her head. "It's grasping at straws, John. It could all be coincidental." She rubbed her forehead. "And I'm too tired to think about it right now."

"Aside from the emotional and mental strain, how are you doing physically?"

"Fine, so far. But I don't do as well when I consistently lose sleep." She bit her lip. "My heart has been hammering a lot lately. I have to make myself relax."

"You're doing anything *but*. It sounds like another trip to my cabin might help."

"Thanks for the offer, but I really can't. I need to stick around for the time being." She met his gaze. "Ready to leave?" she asked, reaching for the tab before he could.

"Sure." He got up from the small table and came to ease back her chair. "Just let me know if you decide to get away for a few days. You're welcome to use the cabin. It doesn't get much more *relaxed* than up there."

"No, I'm sure it doesn't. I'll let you know. Thanks." She turned around when he put a hand on her shoulder.

"Please be careful. I hope someone is just trying to annoy you right now. But don't get careless."

"I won't. I can't afford to be."

Chapter 45

The next message came on February 28th. This time the envelope and paper were from a set of stationery – available from any *Hallmark* store. And everything was written with a generic ball point pen. And the sender obviously knew that he/she would be impossible to trace.

"Are you having fun yet? I certainly am. It's been so easy to stay a step ahead of you, Cari. You've met your match this time. And nobody will be able to rescue you either."

———— ※《◉》※ ————

"I went back to school today, Cari," Tammy said over the phone. "I was scared stiff, and I made one of my friends go everywhere with me all day. But at least I did it."

"Good for you. How are you feeling now that it's over?"

"I guess kinda like I'm maybe back in control or something. I mean, it was really hard, but I went. I think it'll be easier tomorrow. At least I *hope* so."

"You'll do fine, Tammy. I'm proud of you." Cari paused as she considered her next question. "How was your dad today?"

"He had the day off, and I called him on all of my breaks. Kinda to check in with him, you know. He was real glad when he picked me up and I wasn't in hysterics." Tammy laughed. "You know, I think it was maybe harder on Dad than it was on me. I mean, he was real tense when he dropped me off this morning. And I don't think he relaxed until he picked me up again. But, that's all normal, isn't it?"

"Yes, it is."

"How are you? I haven't seen you too much lately. What have you been up to?"

"Oh, I've been keeping pretty busy at work. And I've spent some extra time with Jill Harris, the girl from the office. She's doing better, but sometimes she just needs somebody to talk to."

"I can relate. Have you been spending time with that guy, too?"

"What guy?" Cari asked, though she was pretty certain who Tammy was referring to.

"That John guy."

"Actually, not a lot. He's a busy lawyer, and I have my own work to do. But we get together for lunch sometimes. Why do you ask?"

"Just wondering. He seemed kind of old for you, I guess. But, hey, that's none of my business."

"Tammy, John is about 40, I think. And for you, that would seem pretty old. But I'm over 30, so I don't notice the age difference so much."

"Is he nice?"

"Yes. Very."

"Well, he's good looking anyway. And he has a cool car." She sighed dramatically. "I guess you may as well fall for a prince charming like that. My dad must seem pretty dull by comparison."

"Tammy, that's not fair. Your dad is a sweet guy. And he's a wonderful *Scrabble* opponent. But we really don't have a lot in common."

"Besides working as cops, you mean?"

"Sure. That too. But I'm just not, how should I say it? I'm not *attracted* to your dad. And I've tried to let him know that, Tammy."

"Yeah, I know. But, you can't blame a kid for hoping."

"Hoping what, exactly?"

"That you'd fall for my dad and marry him."

Cari didn't reply for a moment. "Tammy, I'll be your friend no matter what happens, but I don't think I should marry your dad just to acquire a great daughter. Okay?"

"Sure. I get the picture. Hey, I better go do my homework before Dad gets on my case. See you later. Bye."

"Bye." Cari hung up and simply stared at the wedding photo of her parents. *I wonder if I'll ever marry anybody. Rick is a Christian, but I'm not interested. I'm interested in John, but he's not a Christian. Why does life have to be so complicated?*

———— ·《◊》· ————

Cari found a note beneath the wiper blade when she got to her car the next morning. Her hand trembled as she picked it up and unfolded it. This time it was scrawled in crayon, on a torn piece of newsprint.

"Don't forget. I always know where to find you. And I know when you're alone."

"Like right now," Cari muttered to herself. She stuffed the note into her pocket and unlocked her car door. Once inside, she rested her hands on the steering wheel and closed her eyes. *I can't let this get to me. I have to stay focused. Alert. If I panic, it won't help one bit.* "I will not give in to fear. I won't."

———— ·《◊》· ————

"Happy Birthday," Rebecca said as she handed Cari an envelope.

"Thank you," Cari replied. "But how did you know it was today?"

"A boss can always check the personnel files, Cari. So, I checked yours. Have a good day." She excused herself and left Cari's office.

Cari opened the envelope and withdrew a gorgeous birthday card. When she opened it, something fell out. It fluttered to her desk top, so she picked it up. She stared at it for a moment, puzzled. Then recognition set in. It was a voucher from the travel agency that the firm always dealt with. She had a choice of Mexico, Hawaii, or Venezuela. It was to be used within the next two weeks. Cari looked back at the card, hoping for an explanation. She wasn't disappointed.

"Dear Cari,

You have more than earned a short break from the rat race. But, I suspected that you wouldn't take one of your own accord. So, I'm insisting upon one. You can choose the location, but the time is already booked. Just call the agent, and make the arrangements. If you don't mind a suggestion: it's almost the end of peak season in Mexico, and it shouldn't be so crowded. There are some lovely resorts down there. Whatever you decide on, I expect you to come back rested. Have a good time.

Sincerely,

Rebecca Richards"

"A trip? Now? Am I that stressed out that my boss is sending me away?" Cari conceded that she likely was. *I do need a break. And this could be even more fun than John's cabin, though not likely as quiet.* She tucked the voucher back into the card and went back to her work, though her mind strayed to beaches and sunshine several times.

⁓⸙⁓

"It's a lovely resort, Ms. Daniels. Very clean and spacious. And it's all-inclusive. All you'll need to do is pack a suitcase and catch the flight. And, of course, take money for souvenirs."

"And you're certain that Mrs. Richards didn't set a price limit on this?" Cari stammered.

The agent smiled. "She's done this before, Ms. Daniels. She likes to take care of her staff. Do you know John Maxwell?"

"Yes, I do. Why?"

"Well, he's been going to St. Moritz each summer for the past several years. And Mrs. Richards always pays for the trip. Consider yourself fortunate to have a boss like her. Not too many are so generous."

"I know. She's also a pleasure to work with." Cari's mind drifted for a moment. "Could I take this brochure with me?" she asked with a smile. "It'll make it seem a little more *real* that way."

"Sure. Go ahead. I'll just type up the information for you, and call the airline about your ticket. It should only take a few minutes."

"Thank you." Cari sat down and browsed through the information once more. Riding, tennis, pools, beach, abundant food, large suites. Even massage therapy was available. *What more could I want?* She knew that she was tired. The trip would probably be wonderful for her. But she still wasn't used to such generosity. *I should be by now. Hefty salary, company car, benefit package. Why not a paid vacation?* She smiled again. *This should be fun.*

———————

Cari boarded her flight and sat back in the comfort of business class. *This is nice.* An attendant offered her a selection of magazines to look at, but Cari shook her head. She closed her eyes instead. *Why not start the relaxing right here on the plane? No need to wait for the resort.*

The flight was uneventful, but the cab ride to the resort was an adventure in itself. The driver seemed very anxious to get there, and drove much too fast for Cari's liking, despite her own love of rally driving. But, she arrived in one piece, and was ushered into the foyer of a beautiful white building. It was typical Spanish styling; lots of tile, bright and airy. And there were colorful flowers everywhere. She checked in without incident and was shown to her suite. She loved it. But somehow it felt strange to be taking a vacation by herself. She shrugged off the discomfort, tipped the young man who had carried her suitcase, and locked her door. Then she stretched out on the king size bed, beneath the ceiling fan.

Cari woke up a couple of hours later, feeling rested and curious. She hastily changed into some shorts and a sleeveless blouse. She put on her sandals, hung her ID card and room key around her neck, and locked her purse into the room safe, keeping some spending money in her back pocket. Then she headed down to the gift shop and out to the beach area. She sat down on a lounge chair, after purchasing a much needed hat from a passing vendor, and watched the waves rolling in. She felt truly *relaxed* for the first time in weeks. Her thoughts wandered to what she would have for supper, and what she would wear.

"Would you like something to drink, Senorita?" asked a uniformed waiter, a tray of tropical drinks balanced on his right hand, and a warm smile on his face.

"Just some club soda with lime, please." He passed one to her. "Thank you. Gracias."

"De nada." He made his way to other patrons, dispensing beverages.

Cari sipped her drink as she got up from the chair. She walked along the deck of the pool. She frowned. *I'll have to see what I can find to swim in. My bikini days are long gone. I certainly don't need to flash my surgical scars to the world. Maybe a full suit with a pair of shorts.* She shrugged. *Who cares? There's nobody to impress anyway.* She realized how much she already missed John. *I wonder what he does in St. Moritz each year.* She shook her head. *That is none of my business.*

Cari went to her suite, showered, and put on a sundress. Then she went to have supper in one of the three dining areas. The food was fantastic, but she was feeling lonely by the end of the meal.

By the time she was finishing her coffee, she had come to the conclusion that spending a week alone at a romantic resort was not such a wonderful idea after all. *It's almost all couples around here, and some families, but few singles.* She left the dining room and returned to the beach. She removed her sandals and enjoyed the coolness of the damp sand. The sun had already set, and there was a reddish glow on the water.

"Do you mind if I join you?" someone asked from behind her.

Cari turned around and saw a man, close to her age she figured. But he wasn't American. At least she didn't think so. He had jet black hair and dark eyes. He had on dark cotton dress pants, and a white, banded collar shirt. And his mustache topped a smiling mouth filled with beautiful teeth.

"I didn't mean to startle you," he said, stepping a little closer. "But I noticed that you didn't have any company either."

French? What kind of accent is that?

"I'm here on business, for my father's art trade." He shrugged. "It's nice, but a little bit lonely sometimes."

"I – uh, I was going to go in," Cari choked out, her throat suddenly dry. *I thought John was handsome. God broke the mould after this one.*

"No you weren't," he replied, his smile never wavering. "But I see that I've made you nervous. I apologize."

"That's all right. I – I mean I hardly own the beach." She fumbled with the sandals in her now sweating hands. "Feel free." She took a step away from him, planning to go back to her suite.

"Please don't run away. I promise not to bite. Won't you stay – even for a few minutes?"

Cari turned and looked at him again. *Your bite isn't what worries me. It's that smile of yours. Has a woman ever told you 'no'?* "Excuse me, but I'm kind of tired. Good night."

"Good night." He nodded his head as though bowing slightly. "But I'm sure we'll see each other again during the next few days." He grinned at her. "Unless you plan to run away every time I come near you."

Cari didn't answer. She just left the beach, sat down long enough to wipe the sand from her feet. Then she put on her sandals and went back to her suite. Once there, she sat down on the bed and closed her eyes. *I may not know his name. But that guy is 'temptation' on two legs.*

Chapter 46

Cari was sitting alone in the dining room, eating her breakfast, when the man from the evening before spoke to her.

"We meet again. May I please join you? There don't seem to be any empty tables at the moment."

Cari looked around the large room, saw he was telling the truth, and then nervously stared at her plate. "Go ahead," she managed to reply. "I'll be done soon anyway." She looked up when he laughed.

"Not unless you plan to leave all of your food on your plate, or to eat *very* fast." He sat down on the upholstered chair opposite her. A waiter came over immediately, and he ordered his breakfast, in lilting Spanish. Then he turned his attention back to Cari. "Perhaps you would not feel so awkward if I introduced myself." He withdrew a business card from his suit jacket. "I'm Gilles Rodriquez." He passed the card to her, and she took it.

"That's a very different combination," Cari said, thinking out loud.

"My mother is from France, and my father from Mexico City. They met at the Louvre." He shrugged his slim shoulders, and put his hands palm up. "And they suddenly lost interest in looking at works of art. They were married before my father even returned home. After less than a year, I was born, followed by several brothers and sisters." The waiter brought coffee and filled both of their cups. "May I be so bold as to ask you your name?"

"I'm Cari Daniels, and I'm from California." *Why did I bother to tell him that? And why is he so willing to talk about his family?* She swallowed. "So, you work for your father, you said. What do you do?"

"I travel a great deal, looking for new artists, and different items to bring back to our stores in Mexico City. I also look for new pieces for my father's private collection." His platter of food arrived just then. He closed his eyes for a moment and began to eat.

Cari sipped her coffee. "Do you only travel in Mexico?" she asked, not wanting to appear any ruder than she may have already.

"No. I go all over the world." He smiled in his stunning way. "But I always enjoy making discoveries in my own country. And you? What is your occupation?"

"I manage a security department, for a law firm." She didn't elaborate further.

"Very interesting." He drained his glass of juice. "How did you get into that type of work?"

"I used to be a police officer, for several years." She looked down at her empty plate. "Then I was injured, and needed to change careers." She fingered her linen napkin, agitation growing within her.

"Was this a recent change?"

Cari met his warm gaze, and saw that he seemed to be interested, not just nosey. "Yes. I started my new job last fall."

"What part of California are you from?" Again, his tone was pleasant.

"Los Angeles."

"A beautiful city." Then his smile tempered slightly. "Though the riots last spring were quite awful. Were you still a police officer then?"

Cari shifted uneasily. "Yes and no. You see, I was injured a few weeks before that, and I was still in the hospital. But it was before I left the force. I watched it on television, like everyone else. And heard other people talking about it."

"I see." The waiter brought more coffee, but Cari refused politely. Gilles lingered over his second cup. "So, you've had a busy year, it seems. Are you here for business or pleasure?"

"Just to relax." Then she found herself smiling. "It was my boss' idea, actually. She thought that I was working too hard lately."

"Ah, your smile is just as lovely as I thought it would be," he exclaimed softly. "Perhaps now you will not try so hard to avoid my presence." He seemed amused by her earlier hesitancy.

"I'm not used to traveling alone," she admitted, again wondering why. "I suppose it'll take a bit of adjustment."

"True," he replied, after a last sip of coffee. "I've been traveling for the business for ten years already, but I still hate to eat all of my meals alone. I'm used to being surrounded by a noisy family. Could I ask you to join me for dinner tonight? It will be a Mexican fiesta, and I could tell you exactly what you would be eating."

Cari smiled once more. *He may be my age, but he seems as eager as a young boy.* "All right," she almost whispered. "What time shall we meet?"

"Oh, about 7:00 I think. I'll be gone all day. We could meet over on the bridge, there." He pointed and Cari's gaze followed the fluid movement of his right arm. "That way, even if it's crowded we should have no trouble finding each other." He wiped his mouth with the napkin and eased back his chair. Then he nodded his head. "Thank you for the company, Senorita. I will look forward to tonight. Buenos Dios." Then he slipped away, as unobtrusive in his departure as in his arrival.

Cari sat there for another few minutes before she got up and headed in the direction of the bridge he'd indicated. *Why did I agree to have dinner with him? Am I really that lonely?* She never came to a definite conclusion.

That night, Cari stood on the bridge at 6:55, clad in a newly purchased Mexican dress, edged in lace. She was also wearing a light shawl that she had found in the gift shop. The air was much cooler than the previous evening.

"Buenos noches, Senorita," Gilles said from just to the left of her.

She turned and saw how handsome he was in a white cotton suit. His shirt was very colorful and seemed to fit the occasion.

"You look dressed for the fiesta. I hope that you enjoy it. Do you like the music?"

"Very much." Then she grinned. "And the food smells wonderful. When do we eat?"

Gilles laughed, deep in his throat. The sound sent shivers through Cari.

"As soon as you like. Just lead the way."

They loaded their plates, and true to his word, Gilles described any unfamiliar foods to her. Some she declined once she knew what she would be eating. Many others she opted to try. Then they found a small table near the pool and sat down. Once again Gilles closed his eyes before eating.

Cari decided to broach the subject then. "Gilles, are you a Christian? I've noticed that you seem to pray before you eat."

"Yes," he replied with a warm smile. "And so are you if I'm not mistaken." Cari nodded. "I thought so when I saw you last night. Most single women would not go to the beach alone. They would be up in the discotheque. And, I'm usually very good at seeking out other Christians."

Cari felt strangely disquieted. *Oh, boy, here we go! This guy is a doll, and a Christian. Now what?* She forced a slight smile. "Well, I'm glad that you introduced yourself then."

"Good. Now, shall we eat?"

Gilles showed Cari pictures of his entire family. His wallet was full of photos. Cari exclaimed over the one of his parents. "Your mother is incredibly beautiful, Gilles. But she certainly doesn't look old enough to have so many children."

He laughed. "Yes, she's beautiful. And she was barely eighteen when she married my father. He is several years older. I suppose that's why he has more gray hair."

"Did she teach all of you French when you were growing up?"

"Oui, and not just the language, but the history, the music, the arts and literature. I have no trouble at all when I visit France. I try to go at least once a year. My grandparents are still living in Paris."

"It sounds like a very interesting heritage." She toyed with a totally unnecessary piece of dessert.

"Do you have any brothers or sisters?" he asked.

"No," she replied with a shake of her head. "I was an only child. And my parents were killed in a car accident a few years ago."

"How very lonely," he remarked with a sympathetic sigh. "I can't imagine what it would be like not to have a big family." He shrugged gracefully. "But, I've never known anything else."

Cari shoved her plate aside and finished her coffee. "I have friends. I'm very blessed in that way."

"Yes, friends are very important." Gilles leaned slightly forward. "Would you like to go for a walk on the beach – with me this time?"

"All right, as long as you're not tired of my company."

"No, Cari, that is not the case."

Once on the beach, Cari slipped off her sandals and walked along beside Gilles. He paused after a few steps.

"Is it hard for you to walk in the sand? I couldn't help but notice your limp earlier. Perhaps you'd rather just sit down."

"I'll be fine. But thank you for asking."

"C'est rien."

"Do you always switch back and forth from one language to another?" she asked. "Spanish, French, and English?"

"Sometimes, yes. Usually, I speak Spanish here in Mexico, French in France, and English wherever necessary. Do you speak Spanish?"

"Si. I studied it all through school. And it was very useful as a police officer in LA."

"Would you like some practice then?"

"Sure. Why not?" She went on to tell him how much she was enjoying the resort, the weather, and the ocean setting. She only made a few minor mistakes.

"Muy bueno," he said, lightly clapping his hands. "You would do very well in my country."

They both grew quiet as they made their way along the beach. Then Gilles suggested that they head back. "The security guards don't like guests to wander off in the dark."

"No, I suppose not," Cari stammered, suddenly ill at ease. The sole of her foot caught on a sharp shell as they turned around. "Oww! My foot." She felt Gilles' hand on her arm for the first time, and tried to ignore the warmth of his touch. "I hit something."

"Let me see." He squatted down and felt her right foot. He muttered something in French that Cari didn't understand. "It's a bad cut," he said, sounding worried. "You'd better sit down while I get help."

"But my dress." Then she was ashamed to be so vain, especially since she could feel the warm blood seeping from the cut.

"Here, sit on my jacket." He took it off and placed it on the sand behind her. "Let me help you." He gently gripped her shoulders and eased her to a sitting position, and none too soon.

"Gilles, I'm getting dizzy," she murmured. "And I feel a little sick." She lowered her face to her knees.

"Give me your shawl."

Cari took it off and passed it to him, shivering in the cool breeze. Then he rolled it up and tied it around her foot, in an effort to stem the flow of blood. "You need stitches. There's a doctor up at the resort. I'll carry you."

"No! Don't do that. Please."

"Can you walk?" he asked, reminding her of John.

"No," she conceded. As a matter of fact, Cari passed out just after Gilles steadied her in his arms.

Chapter 47

Cari came to to the strong smell of antiseptic. She tried to sit up, but a gentle hand pressed against her shoulder.

"Not yet. Wait a few minutes."

She recognized the voice as Gilles' but it took another moment to realize where she was. It was evidently a small examining room.

"Did I faint?" she asked, though she was almost certain that she must have.

"Yes," he replied, reaching for her cold right hand. He began to rub it between both of his.

"How long ago? And what happened?"

"Not very long." He smiled down at her. "But long enough for the doctor to stitch up the cut in your foot. It was deep. That's why so much blood. He says you should stay off of it for a day or so. He has some crutches you can borrow."

Cari groaned. "I hate crutches. I had to use them for weeks when I --" She caught herself before finishing. "Is it really that bad?" She tried to sit up again. This time she succeeded, though her stomach didn't seem too impressed. She saw that her right foot was swathed with a thick layer of gauze. "Some vacation," she muttered. Then she became self conscious about Gilles holding her hand. She looked into his dark eyes and could see his concern. "I – uh – thank you for bringing me here. I guess I might not have made it back by myself." She forced a smile as she withdrew her now warm hand. "But I feel like such an idiot."

"No need. But I'm grateful that you're feeling better." His expression grew more sober. "The doctor said your pulse was very erratic when I brought you in. He was worried." He looked away from her. "He noticed the scars when he used his stethoscope." He licked his full lips. "So he called the *Medic-Alert* number on your bracelet. He has a pain killer for you to take, at least for tonight. And he'd like to see you again tomorrow, to change the bandage."

"Did you see --?" Cari choked out, her right hand going to the bodice of her dress, covering her heart.

"No, I didn't. Just the doctor. Please don't worry, Cari." His face was slightly flushed as he brought his gaze back to hers. "Would you like to go back to your room now?"

"Please," she whispered. "I'm not feeling very well." She rubbed her forehead. "What time is it?"

"Close to 10:30. You must be tired. Let me help you down from there." He put his right arm around her waist and helped her to the floor.

Just then the doctor came into the room. He grinned broadly when he saw that Cari was fully awake. He held out a bottle of pills to her, carefully labeled in Spanish. Then he reached for the set of crutches and passed them to her.

"A bad cut," he remarked. "You'll need these." He smiled again as Cari got the crutches beneath her arms.

"Gracias, Doctor," Cari said. "May I go now?"

"Si. But you must go and rest." He shook his head. "A lot of blood."

Cari felt the color draining from her face and tried to clear her thoughts. "Thank you. What time should I come tomorrow?"

"Any time," remarked the middle aged man. "Just rest. Come when you feel better."

"All right." Cari expertly maneuvered her way to the open door, but she dreaded the stairs leading to her second floor suite. She gritted her teeth. *I should have stayed home! I leave a stalker and cut my foot instead. Some holiday this is turning out to be.*

⸺ ❊ ⸺

Cari was chalk white by the time she reached her door. Gilles couldn't help but admire her determination, but he still worried about her.

"I'm in room number 304 if you need anything, or if you feel any sicker. Please don't hesitate to call me."

"Thank you, Gilles. But you've already been such a big help tonight. I really think I just need to take the medicine and get some sleep. I'm sure I'll be feeling better by tomorrow. Please don't worry about me."

"But I will," he said with a sigh. He waited while she unlocked her door with a trembling hand. "Don't forget – room 304."

She tried to smile, but pain radiated from her gaze. "I'll be fine. Really. Good night, Gilles."

"Good night." He stood there as she entered her room, and closed the heavy wooden door. Then he closed his eyes. *Please be with her, Father. Help her to sleep tonight. Please let her foot heal quickly. And please keep me from worrying about her too much.* He continued to pray all the way up to his room.

⸺ ❊ ⸺

Cari was anything but *fine* during the night. Her foot throbbed when she tried to sleep. The pain killers only increased her nausea. And there had been a message for her when she returned to the room. It was only anonymous voice mail, so there was no way for her to trace the call.

"Having a good rest, Cari? But, you see, I can follow you *anywhere*. And I will. I could be in LA, or in the suite next to you right now.

And you have no way of knowing. Do you? Sweet dreams."

Cari stared at the ceiling, watching the blades of the fan circulating. She rubbed her eyes, but she couldn't relax enough to sleep. At 3:00 she sat up and reached for the hotel stationery. Then she began to list everything that had been happening to her, and the names of *anyone* who might be behind the harassment. At 4:00 she set the papers aside and closed her eyes. *I can't go on like this much longer. This is really making me edgy. There are just too many people that it could be. I need to figure out who would really bother to go to these extremes.*

She got out of bed and frowned as she reached for the crutches. "I'll bet 'a day or so' will end up being the rest of the week. I can't even put any weight on this foot." She made it to the washroom, where she looked at her reflection. "I look awful! No wonder Gilles was so worried about me." Her forehead furrowed. "I wonder if *he* ever went to sleep." She shook her head. *What is the matter with me? Can I not have male* friends – *unless they're married? He's so nice.*

She suddenly realized that she'd been standing there for too long, and she was light headed. She debated between returning to the bed, and simply sitting down on the bathroom floor. She opted for the floor when her vision clouded. Her crutches clattered against the tiles and the side of the tub.

"How much blood did I lose? This is ridiculous." Waves of nausea joined the dizziness. She vomited into the tub. Then she lay on the cool tiles. "God, please help me. I feel so sick." She tried to get up, but couldn't. Tears filled her eyes, and began to trickle down her cheeks. "Please help me." The phone began to ring, several times. Cari was too weak to get up, let alone answer it. Twice more it rang. "With my luck, it's just the stalker wanting to keep me awake anyway."

Someone was knocking on her door. *At 4:30 in the morning? Who on earth is it?* The knocking persisted. Then a voice followed.

"Cari? Cari, are you all right? It's Gilles. Are you all right?"

What is he doing here? How could he have known? But, thank You, God, anyway. "Gilles," she called, annoyed to find that even her voice was weakening. "Gilles, I'm sick. Please get someone to let you in."

"I'll be right back, Cari!"

She could hear his running steps in the hallway. Then she wretched again. She was only semiconscious when he came back.

"Senorita Daniels, may we come in?"

Must be a security guard – or somebody from the desk. "Yes. Please." She listened as a key was turned in her lock, and she thankfully recalled that she hadn't used the deadbolt. The door opened. "In here, in the bathroom."

Heavy footsteps crossed the room.

"Cari!" Gilles cried, kneeling down next to her. "What happened?" He stroked her face. Then he turned to the night manager. "Llame al medico, por favor." The manager nodded and hurried from the suite.

"I'm so sick," Cari rasped. "I can't even get up."

"Let me help you." He placed an arm beneath her shoulders, and the other behind her knees. Then he got to his feet. He made his way to the bed, and carefully laid her on it. "What happened? Did you faint again?"

"No, not quite, but I got so dizzy. And I got sick to my stomach." She closed her eyes when he began to massage her forehead. "How did you know? Why did you come?"

"I couldn't sleep. I kept praying, but I somehow knew that something was wrong. I finally phoned. When you didn't answer, I came down here."

"I'm glad you did," she murmured, feeling somewhat drowsy. "The pills just make me sick. I think I should just take some *Gravol*. I'm so tired."

A different doctor came this time, a young woman. She checked Cari's vital signs and frowned. "You should be in a hospital, Senorita."

"No, please," Cari begged, her eyes wide with panic. "Just give me something so I can sleep. No hospitals."

"If you insist," the doctor replied. "I will give you an injection though, not more pills. And I want you to have some IV fluids. Such nausea makes a person dehydrated very quickly, especially in a warm climate."

"Fine, just not a hospital." A moment later Cari questioned her own judgment. Her pulse began to pound and her heart fluttered. Her hand immediately went to her chest.

"What's wrong?" the doctor demanded.

"My heart," Cari whispered. "It's not – I had surgery last year." The fluttering grew worse. So did her breathing. She began to gulp for air. Her pulse was roaring in her ears, loud and irregular. The pain in her chest grew intense. She heard the doctor ordering the manager to call an ambulance. Then Gilles was speaking to her, but she couldn't distinguish his words. "Help me!" she rasped. Then she collapsed.

Chapter 48

Gilles and the doctor did CPR for two minutes before Cari responded. But even with a pulse, she wasn't conscious. The doctor was furious and went into rapid fire Spanish.

"Why wasn't she taken to a hospital earlier? Surely Dr. Enriquez must have seen how serious her condition was. And where is that ambulance? She needs treatment that I can't give her here." She frowned. "Possibly she should be sent back home." She shook her head. "Not while she is so unstable."

Gilles was praying the whole time. For Cari to recover, for proper medical treatment, for a chance to speak with her again. And he was thankful that he had followed the prompting and come to her room in the first place. He thought of their stroll on the beach. *What if she'd been alone? She may have bled to death out there. She was certainly too weak to get back here. But how can I help her now? What should I do? Take her home?* He raised his eyebrows as he looked from Cari's still form on the tiled floor, to the doctor kneeling beside her.

"Doctor, how soon could we arrange an air ambulance to Mexico City? She would be well cared for there."

The doctor looked at him as though he were crazy. "That's almost as far as Los Angeles."

"True, but it would not be an international problem. If her condition grew worse, she could then be sent to California."

"Perhaps," she conceded.

Cari opened her eyes and looked from one face to the other. Pain etched her face as she inhaled. "What happened?" she whispered.

"CPR," the doctor replied. "Your chest may be quite sore for the next few days." She checked Cari's pulse once more. "We're going to take you to the hospital, Senorita. You need proper care."

Cari closed her eyes and sighed. "All I did was cut my foot." Gilles touched her hand and she tried to curl her fingers around his. "Please call my doctor back home." She swallowed. "He'll need to know what's going on, and my boss." She grimaced and tightened her hold on Gilles' hand. "My purse is in the safe. I have an address book in there." She paled and let her head go to the side.

"Please don't try to talk right now, Cari," Gilled replied. "You need to rest." He saw she was no longer listening. Her hand was limp.

⸺«(》⸻

The ambulance arrived, and Cari was first taken to the local hospital. After being seen by the doctor in charge, it was agreed that she should be flown to Mexico City. Gilles had called Rebecca Richards in Los Angeles, at 6:30 a.m. to let her know about Cari. She had told him not to worry about the expenses. The firm's insurance coverage would take care of it. She asked for the name of the hospital Cari was going to, as well as the closest hotel to it. She told him that if she couldn't come herself, then her associate, John Maxwell, would.

Dr. Ken Wilson spent almost a half hour on the phone to the doctor in Puerto Vallarta. He went over any previous complications that Cari had had in the past eleven and a half months. Then he sent a faxed copy of the same information to the specialist in Mexico City who would be handling the case. Most of the paperwork was handled before the plane was fuelled and ready to fly Cari to the capital. She faded in and out of consciousness several times.

Gilles called his parents and let them know that he would be flying back home that morning. He briefly explained why, and they assured him of their prayers. Then he boarded the King Air 200 with the pilot and medical personnel. And he held Cari's hand for the next two hours.

———))(((0))((———

Cari grew agitated during the descent into the airport. She thrashed around, her eyes tightly closed, mumbling incoherently. The pain in her ears was driving her crazy but she couldn't seem to make anyone understand. Not with an oxygen mask over her face, and her arms covered with a blanket, and strapping. She moaned as the pain grew worse. Then, when she thought she couldn't stand another second of it, everything went black.

———))(((0))((———

Cari spent most of the day undergoing extensive tests. She was given a blood transfusion, as well as other IV fluids. A heart monitor was connected, and nurses bustled in and out of her room every few minutes. She tried to rest but found it impossible. Every time she thought she might be able to fall asleep, someone else came to check on her. She was finally given a sedative, and drifted into a lengthy, dreamless, sleep.

———))(((0))((———

Gilles spent most of the day drinking strong coffee and pacing the corridors. When he was told that Cari was finally asleep, he left to go to his parents' home. His mother greeted him at the door. She frowned at his pale and disheveled appearance. He forced a smile and shrugged.

"You and father have always taught me to be a Good Samaritan, Mother. So, here I am." He embraced her and kissed her cheek.

"Is she beautiful?" asked his mother, "this wounded traveler?"

"Oui." He sighed as he rubbed the back of his neck. "And just as soon as I take a shower and get changed, I'll tell you all about her." He grinned. "What little I had the chance to find out, that is."

———————

John drummed his fingers on the armrest of his business class seat on the jet. *How could a cut foot land her in the hospital? There has to be more to the story than that.* He frowned. *But she was pretty tired when she left the other day. Maybe it's exhaustion more than anything else.* He stopped his fingers and put his hands in his lap. *Why does she work so hard anyway? Is she trying to prove that she's capable enough? Or is it still the stalker thing? And just* who *is behind that? Did they follow her down to Mexico? Why would they?* He shook his head. *This is useless. I can't figure out* anything *when I'm tenser than my squash racket.* He tilted his seat back and tried to relax. He couldn't. A certain blonde haired woman was too heavy on his mind.

———————

"I'm here to see Cari Daniels," John said as he got to the nursing station on Cari's floor. He repeated himself in Spanish and the nurse smiled.

"Right down the hall, Senor, room 205. She was awake just a moment ago." She kept smiling at him.

"Gracias." He walked down the hall, a bouquet of bougainvilleas in his left hand. He paused at Cari's door. Then he decided to knock.

"Come in." It was Cari's voice, but she sounded so tired.

John pushed at the door and entered the room.

Cari looked at him in surprise. "John? How did you know I was here?"

"Rebecca called me yesterday. I came as soon as I could. How are you doing?" She looked dreadful. Dripping fluids, machines, an ugly hospital gown, and she was deathly pale. He set the bouquet on her tray at the foot of the bed.

"I'm tired," she replied with her usual frankness. She closed her eyes and sighed. "I don't even know when they'll let me go home." She looked at him again, trying to smile. "Watch out for seashells when you walk on the beach." She pointed at her bandaged right foot, peeking out beneath the sheets. "It took a dozen stitches to close the cut, and I think I lost a pint of blood before that."

"Some vacation," he said as he dragged a chair close to the bed.

"My words exactly." She turned her head so she could see him better. "Why did you come all the way down here?"

"So I could see for myself that you're okay." He frowned. "You look far from *okay*. A cut on the foot doesn't usually end up in a medivac across the country."

She looked away for a moment. "Heart failure does," she replied very softly.

"Heart failure!" he almost yelled, stiffening in the chair. "What *happened* back at the resort?"

"A lot of things, John. I guess the combination was too hard on my body." She smiled again. "But God took care of me. I'm going to be all right. Please don't worry so much."

"Who said I'm *worried*?" he scoffed. "I only flew a thousand miles so I could sit and watch the lines on your heart monitor go up and down."

She managed to smile a little brighter. "The up and down part is good, John. You only need to worry if it goes flat."

He sometimes hated her sense of humor. This was one of those moments. He decided not to pursue it.

"Where are you staying?" she asked, "and how long?"

"I checked into a hotel not far from here. And I'm staying until they let you fly home."

Cari's eyebrows rose. "What? I'm sure you've got better things to do than that, John. Like your job at the firm." She shook her head. "You don't need to stay."

"Well, I'm *going to.* So don't argue with me."

Cari laughed very softly. "Why on earth would I waste my time doing that?"

"Smart lady," he said with a grin.

Chapter 49

John was still with Cari when Gilles arrived. The two men glanced at each other. Gilles was the first to smile, perhaps because he had brought his mother along.

"Buenos dios, Cari," he said. "This is my mother, Constance."

"Pleased to meet you, Senora Rodriquez," Cari replied. "And this is John Maxwell. He's a senior partner at the law firm that I work for. My boss sent him down to make sure I'm all right."

Constance met Cari's gaze and smiled warmly. *She is very beautiful – despite the circumstances. But it seems that Gilles is not her only admirer.* She approached the bed and reached for Cari's hand. It was cold. "Perhaps we should come back later, Senorita. You must be tired."

"True. But I'm also bored. And I would appreciate the company. Please stay."

John cleared his throat. "I think only two visitors are allowed at a time, Cari." He got to his feet. "I should go back to the hotel and have something to eat anyway. I can come back later." He smiled but it didn't reach his eyes.

"Thank you for coming, John," Cari remarked with a warm smile. "Please don't worry."

John's glance moved back to Gilles and rested there a moment. "I'll try not to." He nodded his head to Gilles and Constance. "Nice to meet you." Then he turned and left the room.

Constance sat down on the vacant chair. "He must be a good friend, Senorita. He came a long way to check on you."

Cari's cheeks filled with color, a striking contrast to the otherwise pale skin. "Yes, he is." She looked to Gilles. "I've been blessed with a few it seems." She turned her attention back to Constance. "I owe your son a debt of gratitude, Senora. And he also came a long way to check on me."

"I didn't mind, Cari. And, it would seem, neither did Senor Maxwell."

Constance smiled at the note of challenge in her son's voice. She wondered if Senorita Daniels had noticed it too. Her son might be ready to pursue this woman, but that didn't mean that Senor Maxwell would simply step aside. No, that didn't seem too likely at all. Especially after the look she had seen on Cari's face. *I think she's already in love, my dear Gilles. But perhaps she isn't aware of it herself. This could be very interesting.*

<hr />

Another bouquet came for Cari just after Gilles and Constance left her room. *Strange, it's only eleven roses. I wonder if the florist was short or something. Maybe it was just a mistake.* She reached for the small envelope and withdrew the card. Her heart rate skipped as she read the message.

"Roses are red, violets are blue,
And time is running out for you."

Cari's hands shook as the pretty flowers took on a menacing quality. She threw them to the floor as tears filled her eyes. The ribbon bedecked vase shattered and a nurse ran into the room.

"Get those out of here!" Cari screamed, her heart once more hammering. "Get them away from me!" She crumpled the card in her hand, but knew she needed to keep it. It was *evidence*. But she didn't want the flowers. Not even one of the eleven. Each was a painful reminder that she was at the mercy of someone who always knew where to find her. Someone who seemed to have plans for her. And none of them were good.

―――≈⟨◉⟩≈―――

Gilles immediately noticed Cari's reddened, puffy eyes when he entered her room that evening. She looked up at him as he drew near the bed. "You had a bad afternoon?" he asked, his tone gentle. To his dismay, fresh tears filled her eyes. "What's the matter? Is there anything I can do?"

Cari shook her head. "No," she whispered. "There's not much *anybody* can do, Gilles. But thank you for asking."

"Is it your heart problem?" he wondered aloud. She shook her head. "Then what? I can pray for you even if I can't do anything else."

She forced a smile and wiped at the tears. "Someone has been stalking me. Leaving me notes, sending me flowers, calling me. I don't know who or why. Whoever it is they're very smart. They keep changing tactics. There's no real pattern." She rubbed her forehead. "The messages are getting more threatening now. I don't know what to do."

Gilles held her clammy hand between both of his warm ones. "I'll pray for you. Pray that God will keep you safe. Pray that you or the police will discover who is tormenting you like this." He reached out and gently stroked her cheek. "And I'll pray that your physical strength will increase so that you can deal with this. Right now, you're tired. You need rest." He licked his lips. "Has Dr. Ortega told you when you can go home?"

Cari shook her head.

"All right, just let me know when he does. I'd like for you to come to my home for a few days." He smiled at her look of total confusion. "Your vacation got cut short, didn't it? Why not spend a few days with my family? We have a large home. You could sit by the pool. Walk in the garden." His smile faded. "And I promise – *no one* would come near you. My father has very tight security."

Cari laughed, but without a hint of humor. She shook her head. "You don't understand, do you? I'm the *head* of the security at the law firm. And I've still received a call at work, and flowers at my apartment. My tires were slashed in my parking area. I was even called at the resort. And flowers came *here* today. Wherever I go, this *person* knows. Even if I went to your home, somehow they would contact me." She trembled. "And, possibly, that contact will become physical at some point. I won't put your family at risk."

"What makes you think we would be?" She didn't answer. "It's *you* I'm worried about." He raised her hand and kissed it. "Please say you'll come." He smiled down at her. "S'il vous plait. Por favor."

"Are you always so persistent, Gilles?" she asked, a slight smile on her lips.

"Actually, no, but I've never met anyone like you, Cari. I'd hate for you to leave as soon as I get to know you. Please stay – even for a few days."

"I'll have to ask Dr. Ortega about it, and Dr. Wilson in LA." She shrugged. "My life is not my own."

"A Christian's life never is," he observed quietly.

"True, very true." She yawned and pulled her hand from his. "Thank you for coming, but I'm very tired."

"All right, I'll leave." He smiled. "But only until tomorrow."

"Don't you have work to do? I thought you help your father with his art business."

"I do. But that doesn't take all my time."

"You sound like John," she sighed as she closed her eyes. "He's sure he should stay down here until I fly home. And he's a senior partner at the firm." She yawned again. "You both worry too much." Her breathing evened out and her facial muscles relaxed.

Yes, I'm worried, Cari. And I can certainly understand why John Maxwell is here. A woman like you is simply too precious to leave in the care of strangers.

He rubbed his hands over his face, realizing how exhausted he was himself. Then he grinned. *I finally meet the perfect woman — and it looks as though someone has already claimed her attention.* His grin changed to a frown. *And someone else is trying to destroy her.* He looked at the ceiling. *And where do I fit into this, Lord? What can I do?*

Chapter 50

"I would not advise flying back to Los Angeles for several more days, Senorita Daniels," stated Dr. Ortega. "But it's also not necessary for you to remain in the hospital, and paying for special care." He rubbed his chin as though deep in thought. "Do you have any friends here in the city?"

Cari smiled. "Yes, Doctor, I do. Why?"

"Perhaps it would be a good time to visit with them." He gave her a stern look, reminding her of Dr. Wilson back home. "I remind you, you are to *rest* for a few more days. Whether you choose to do that in a hotel or with friends I will leave up to you. I will allow you to leave in the morning, so you should have some time to think about it."

"Time enough for me to prepare a guest room," Constance Rodriquez said as she entered Cari's room with a smile.

"But Senora --" Cari stammered. "I couldn't impose on you like that. I don't mind staying at a hotel." But she wasn't sure it would be a good idea to stay at the same one as John Maxwell.

"C'est rien, ma chere," Constance insisted. She looked to the doctor. "I will personally make sure that Senorita Daniels gets all the rest that she needs."

"Buena, Senora. Gracias." Dr. Ortega once more looked down at Cari with a smile. "It would seem that some plans have already been taken care of." He patted her hand. "Rest well today. I will see you in the morning." He left the room, leaving the women alone.

"Really, Senora Rodriquez," Cari tried again, "I appreciate your generous offer, but --"

"Then why not accept it?" Constance replied. "I'd enjoy having you in my home."

Cari closed her eyes and considered her options. She could stay at a hotel and risk offending the Rodriquez family. Or, she could go to a hotel and risk spending too much time alone with John Maxwell. In that light, being surrounded by a large family seemed the wiser choice. She opened her eyes and met Constance's gaze. "All right, I'll come. But it's only for a few days. Then I really must get back home again."

"Magnifique! I'm sure Gilles will be happy to pick you up tomorrow morning, so don't worry about how to get there." Constance sat down on the chair and moved it closer to the bed. "But tell me, what are some foods that you most like to eat." Cari rhymed off a few for her soon to be hostess. "Fine, fine. I'll have Juan go to the market later today."

"Please don't go to extra work just for me, Senora."

"And why not? I enjoy doing things like this for others. God has been gracious to me and my husband. And we receive great pleasure in sharing what He has given to us."

"Then I suppose I shouldn't try to deprive you of a blessing." Cari's thoughts wandered to Gilles' incredible smile. And his gentle touch. *Maybe a houseful of people won't make any difference. He's every bit as charming as John. And he's a Christian. So, is it just 'brotherly concern' that he's been showing so far? Nah, I don't think so. And I don't think that the impression that John got either. John! How on earth am I going to explain to him that I'll be spending several days with a family I don't even know – just because they're Christians? Oh, brother.*

"You're what?" John exclaimed, looking uncharacteristically upset. "You don't even know these people."

"John, please, calm down. I'll try to explain, okay?" Cari watched him ease himself into the chair before saying anything else. "Okay, do you remember how comfortable you were the first time that you came with me to Mike and Julie's?"

He nodded, but his expression was still guarded.

"Well, I think a large part of the reason was because they share the same faith that I do. So does the Rodriquez family. I won't be *alone*, and likely not *lonely* either. And Constance has practically made it a personal mission to see that I'll be well taken care of. You really have nothing to worry about, John."

"Oh sure, nothing except for the guy you met at the resort." He rubbed the back of his neck. "I'm sure he'll make it *his* personal mission to keep you happy while you're there, too."

"John Maxwell, are you actually *jealous*?"

"Yes." His gaze locked with hers. "And why wouldn't I be? The guy must be ten years younger than I am. And you obviously enjoy his company."

Cari made no effort to deny that.

John sighed and got up from the chair. He walked to the window and looked out. "So, I guess you'd like for me to fly home right away, and leave the two of you alone."

"I didn't say that, John," Cari murmured, her shoulders tense. "But you don't need to stay for another few days just *because* of me either. I'm sure people will be anxious to have you back at work. I flew down here alone. I'm sure I'll be fine on the way back."

He turned to face her again. "So, you're dismissing me again," he said, a slightly bitter edge to his tone. "All right. I'll head back to LA. And you can have some fun socializing with the Mexican elite." He moved towards the door.

"John, please don't leave here angry."

He faced her once more. "Why not, Cari? I already admitted that I'm jealous. So, why not leave here angry as well?" With that he stalked out of the room, his usual gracefulness totally lacking.

Cari gnawed on her lip. *Now what? It takes a lot for John to lose his temper. How could something so trivial set him off like that? And jealousy – how unlike him.* She frowned. *Then again, when has he seen another guy show any interest in me before now? He's never even met Rick Benson.* She rubbed her face with both hands. *Please keep Your hand upon him, God. Help his focus to shift to You, rather than me. Somehow, please draw him to Yourself. He needs You, God. More than he even knows.*

———————

Cari could not believe the Rodriquez home. She had been impressed by the Richards', but this one surpassed it. There were several bedrooms, a huge courtyard. The hallways of the second floor were lined with works of art. The pool was as big as the one at the resort. The landscaping was flawless. Yet, despite the imposing size of the property, Cari immediately felt at home, something that greatly surprised her.

She met some of the other children, just before they left for their various schools or jobs. The girls were as beautiful as Constance, and the younger boys took after Gilles. Each of them had a decidedly French first name. Francois, Maxine, Pierre, Henri, Collete, Genevieve, Jacinthe. They ranged in age from twenty-seven down to fifteen. Pierre and Henri were both engaged, and so was Maxine.

Constance led Cari to a guest room, while Gilles carried her suitcase for her. Though she was loath to admit it, she was already tired when she reached the room. She felt Gilles place a gentle hand on her left shoulder.

"Why don't you rest up here for a couple of hours?"

"I think I'll do that, if you don't mind, Senora Rodriquez."

"Why would I mind? But, I would like you to call me Constance." She smiled as she patted the lace edged spread on the canopy bed.

"Take a nap if you like. You won't miss anything exciting I assure you." She winked at her. "Besides, you're supposed to be *resting* while you're here. Not *touring*. I'll come back later to see if you'd like to join me in the courtyard. I like to have my lunch outside whenever the weather permits it."

Cari realized that Gilles' hand was still on her shoulder as she turned slightly. She felt her cheeks flush with color. "Thank you for picking me up, and for carrying my bag." She smiled at him as he moved his hand and set her bag on the floor. "I suppose I'll see you later."

"I'll be working with my father most of the day. But I'll be here tonight."

Cari became aware of the way that Constance was watching the two of them. She cleared her throat. "Excuse me, Constance, but could you show me where the bathroom is?"

"Certainly. It's right through that door." Cari had thought it was a closet. "Just make yourself at home, Cari. And if you need anything, just ask."

"Thank you." She felt like a coward, but she needed to get away from Gilles' warm gaze, so a quick retreat seemed a likely plan. "Excuse me." She took her purse and pushed open the solid pine door. And she stepped into the biggest bathroom she had ever seen. *If this is the* guest room, *what on earth is the master suite like?*

———⚬———

"Cari?" Constance called from the hallway. "Cari? Would you like some lunch now?" She waited a moment longer, but when she received no reply, she turned the handle very slowly and gently pushed the door open. She smiled as soon as she saw her guest curled up on the huge bed, a bright cotton blanket for a covering. She was obviously sound asleep. Constance backed into the hallway and closed the door just as quietly as she'd opened it. Then she went to inform Juan that she'd be eating alone.

————))((————

Cari shifted onto her back and stretched slowly. She gradually got her bearings as she looked around the room. *I'm at Gilles' home. I must have fallen asleep. What time is it by now?* She blinked a few times before actually checking her watch. Then she raised her brows. *Three o'clock! I slept for hours! Right through lunch. Some houseguest I am. How rude of me.* She sat up quickly and immediately regretted doing so. Dizziness forced her back to the pillow. *Why hurry? I've missed one meal, I'm sure I can wait until supper for the next one.* She closed her eyes and took several deep breaths. Then she sat up slowly, and without mishap.

After freshening up in the bathroom, Cari left the suite and stepped into the hallway. She could hear someone singing and followed the sound. She soon found Constance carrying some fresh cut flowers towards a set of open doors.

"Senora?" Cari called softly, not wishing to startle her hostess. She needn't have worried.

Constance turned around, a warm smile on her face. "Cari, you look so much better. Did you rest well?"

"It seems so," Cari replied with a slight blush. "I just woke up a little while ago. I'm sorry that I missed lunch."

"C'est rien. I'm glad you were able to sleep." Constance suddenly seemed to recall the flowers she was holding. "Would you care to join me? I'm just going to put these in water, and then I'll be ready for something cool to drink."

"If you don't mind, but I don't want to be a bother."

"You're not. Come with me." She turned and passed through the open doors.

Cari followed a moment later. "Oh my goodness! I've never seen such a beautiful room, Senora." *This must be the master suite.*

There was a huge bed, with a headboard at least six feet tall, and she was quite sure it was carved mahogany. There were two armoires, a dressing table with an oval mirror, two nightstands, and a chest of drawers. And in front of a marble fireplace, there were two leather chairs, and a low table. Lace covered French doors led to a large balcony.

Constance arranged the flowers in a crystal vase on the mantle. "Merci, Cari. I'm glad you like it. My husband may be an art collector, but I have always been fond of furniture, especially antiques or unique pieces." She went to one of the chairs and sat down. Please have a seat. I've been looking forward to chatting with you."

Cari sat down and noticed a small brass dinner bell on the table between the chairs. She watched as Constance picked it up and gave it a slight shake. Within two minutes a young man was at the doorway.

"Please bring some iced tea, Juan. And some sliced fruit would be nice. We'll have it in here."

"Si, Senora." He bowed slightly and left.

"Are you hungry, Cari? I could have Juan prepare something for you if you'd like."

"I'll be fine. The fruit will be more than enough for now. Thank you for asking."

"You must have been tired this morning. I must confess that I checked on you at lunch time, but you were sleeping soundly and I didn't want to disturb you."

"Oh, I never even noticed you come in. I suppose it was so much easier to sleep without nurses coming and going all the time. And that bed is so comfortable."

"Perhaps you'll feel up to seeing the courtyard after our refreshments."

"I'd like that very much."

"Good. We'll have plenty of time before dinner is ready."

Chapter 51

Cari enjoyed the lovely courtyard, but her right foot was throbbing by the time she sat down on a wrought iron chair on the tiled patio.

Constance frowned. "I forgot, ma chere. Your foot. I'm sorry. Just rest here for a little."

"It's not so bad, Constance, really. I'll be fine."

"Good. But rest here anyway. I want to go check on dinner."

"All right." Cari closed her eyes as Constance went into the house. She allowed herself to relax as she listened to the numerous birds which resided in the courtyard area. She inhaled deeply of the many flowers around her. And she dosed off, her chin on her chest, and her hands loosely clasped on her lap.

———⊙———

"Good evening, Cari," Gilles said, stepping close to the chair she was sitting on. He reached for her shoulder when her head jerked up. "I'm sorry. I didn't mean to frighten you. I thought you were just resting. I didn't know you hadn't heard me." He watched her shoulders relax and a slight smile come to her lips.

"I seem to be doing a lot of sleeping today, Gilles. I missed lunch the last time." She grinned then. "Please don't tell me that I've just missed dinner too."

He laughed as he gave her shoulder a slight squeeze. "No, you haven't. But it will be ready pretty soon."

"I should go and change then," she remarked, glancing down at herself. "Somehow shorts and a blouse don't seem appropriate for dinner." Then she bit her lip. "Umm, I'm not sure I could find my way back to my room, Gilles. This place is so huge. Would you mind showing me?"

"Not at all." He held out his hand as she got up from the chair. "I'd be happy to show you." He didn't release her hand as they entered the house. "And, by the way, I'm glad that you've been able to rest so well here. You should be able to regain your strength sooner."

"I suppose so."

"Not that I'm anxious to get rid of you," he hastened to add. He was pleased to hear her laugh.

"Somehow, Gilles, I didn't get that impression."

Cari was soon changed for dinner, and Gilles escorted her to the dining room. He introduced her to his father, Eduardo, and then held her chair as she sat down. There were twelve of them at dinner. Besides the Rodriquez family, and Cari, Maxine's fiancé had joined them too. His name was Julio, and he eyed Cari curiously throughout the meal.

Gilles and Constance kept Cari engaged in conversation all through dinner, but Eduardo said little. Cari was beginning to feel uncomfortable by the time she'd finished her dessert. Just as she was about to excuse herself, Constance suggested that they go into the living room to drink their coffee. Not wishing to be rude, Cari simply smiled and nodded her head.

Eduardo still had little to say. He spoke with his wife, and with Gilles. He asked Cari a few questions about LA and her work there, but that was all. She was getting edgy by the time Juan came to retrieve the cups and saucers.

"Thank you for a lovely meal, Senora Rodriquez," Cari managed to say past the tension in her neck and shoulders. "If you'll excuse me, I think I'll go to my room now." She stood, wincing at the pain in her right foot. "Good night."

"I'll show you the way," Gilles offered, his hand on her arm. He frowned when Cari shook her head.

"No, thank you, Gilles. I'll be fine. I shouldn't get lost this time." She forced a smile and moved past him. She even managed to keep her tears at bay until she got upstairs and sat down on the soft bed. She'd have cried harder if she'd heard the heated discussion going on down in the living room.

———————

"You don't even know much about her, Gilles," Eduardo ranted. "Yet you pay more attention to her than you ever did to Louisa. Are you just intrigued by her because she's *American*?"

His father said the word with such obvious distain that Gilles was hard pressed not to speak without thinking first. "And you've already decided that you don't like her – after one meal together. Why is that?"

"She's just not right for you, Son."

"And who is, Father?" Gilles asked, losing what little patience he had left. "You picked out Louisa Sanchez for me – so *certain* that we would be happy together. I was only twenty then, and I didn't want to defy you. But I can honestly say that I'm thankful that Louisa chose to run off with someone else. We would have been miserable." He shook his head. "How can you, of all people, expect me to walk into an arranged marriage, especially after the way that you and Mother met? I'm thirty now, Father, in case you've forgotten. And I'm old enough to live on my own. I'll even leave the business if you wish." Gilles clenched his fists. "But I won't sit back while you make someone I care about feel miserable while she's a guest here."

Constance no longer held her peace. "Please, both of you, stop it! Cari Daniels would hate to be the cause of an argument. It was difficult enough to convince her to come here and rest for a few days. I don't want her to leave because she's made to feel unwelcome, or a source of division." She looked back and forth between husband and son. She lowered her voice. "Please settle your differences sensibly. I'm not about to take sides." Gaining no response from either of them, she quietly left the room.

Gilles once more looked at his father. He realized how much it hurt not to agree with him. They seldom argued. Louisa had been a sensitive issue for quite a while. Gilles had resisted all efforts at romantic arrangements after that. But he normally got along very well with his father, both at home and at work. He didn't understand where this sudden tension sprang from.

"Beauty isn't enough to build a relationship on, Gilles," his father said, his tone once more even. "A pretty smile won't carry you through problems, either." He sighed heavily, as though weary of the whole discussion. "Get to know her, if you're so bent on it. But I'm not willing to give my blessing."

"I'm not asking for it, Father," Gilles replied, a chill coursing down his spine. "I'm not even asking for *approval*. Good night." He turned and left the room, not even waiting for a response from the very man who had always mattered the most to him.

———— ✦ ————

Cari's sleep was fitful at best. At four in the morning, she got up and dressed. Then she packed her suitcase, determined that it would be best for everyone if she headed home as soon as possible. She bit her lip as she thought of the stern warning from Dr. Ortega. Then she straightened her shoulders. *Well, it's not the first time I've ignored medical advice, is it? Why break with precedent?*

She wrote a note for Constance, and left it on the bed. Then she slipped from the room as quietly as possible. She made it down the staircase without incident, then hesitated, the hair on the back of her neck bristling. She swallowed as she made a concerted effort to remain calm.

She had just stepped towards the foyer when she heard someone behind her. She immediately turned.

"Please don't leave, Senorita Daniels," Eduardo requested, "at least not while it's still dark outside."

Cari noticed that he was holding a small envelope, the kind that came with flowers. "I – it's better this way, Senor Rodriquez. I knew at dinner that it wasn't a good idea for me to stay." She shrugged. "I couldn't sleep anyway, so I'll go now while I won't disturb anyone."

"Oh, but you see, I already am *disturbed*, very much." He tapped the envelope on his other hand.

"I – I don't understand," Cari stammered, quickly losing her tenuous hold on calm.

"This came for you this evening, after you went to bed. One of my men brought it to me." He passed her the envelope.

"What are you talking about?" Her hands shook as she opened it.

'Did you think I wouldn't find you? How foolish. How dangerous. I'm always closer than you think.'

"W – what came with the card?" Cari forced herself to ask.

"A box of ten red roses," he replied. "And every flower was severed from the stem."

Cari fought the rising nausea and faltering pulse. "All the more reason for me to leave," she whispered. "I told Gilles this could happen." She met Eduardo's questioning gaze. "If you could just order a cab for me, Senor, I'll leave right now. I refuse to allow anyone to threaten your family."

"I won't call a cab for you, Senorita," he said, his tone sounding angry.

"But I --"

"I'll drive you myself."

Cari shook her head. "No! That isn't necessary. I just want to leave."

"If my son found out that you left in a cab, alone, he'd very likely never speak to me again." He lowered his voice a notch. "Besides, if anyone sent a threatening message to my wife or daughters, I wouldn't allow them to leave alone either."

"But I'm not your --"

To her amazement, he laughed. Very softly, but he did laugh. "I can see what my wife meant when she said it was difficult to get you to come." He placed a surprisingly gentle hand on her arm. "But I can be just as insistent. I *will* take you myself. I assume you wish to go to the airport?"

"Yes. Please." What was the point of arguing with him anyway? She just wanted to go home. Then she shuddered. *But I'm no safer there, am I?* The envelope was still clutched in her hand. *Who are you?*

Within an hour, Cari was at the airport, a boarding pass in hand, and finding herself very grateful for Eduardo's assistance. He was still with her, insisting that he would stay until she was on the plane bound for LA. She wasn't sure if his presence made her feel better or worse.

"Please don't expect my son to ignore you, Senorita," Eduardo told her. "If he doesn't visit you in person, I'm quite certain that he'll call or write."

Cari shook her head. "He doesn't have my number, or my address. At least, I didn't give it to him."

Eduardo frowned. "I'm not sure that will matter. My son is very good at finding information when he wants it badly enough. You should still expect to hear from him."

"Please ask him not to. I'm grateful for his help at the resort, and at the hospital here. But I don't want anyone else to get involved in this mess."

His frown changed to a smile. "Ah, that may be what you wish, but Gilles is still my son. He doesn't give up easily either."

Cari couldn't help but smile at that. "So I've noticed," she whispered.

The sun was still rising when the jet took off, Cari looking out the window. She wondered if she'd ever be back, or if her stalker would ever reveal their identity. Then she closed her eyes and tried to think about home. She fell asleep before they even reached cruising altitude.

Chapter 52

Cari called Mike from the L.A.X. He was in the middle of breakfast, but he promised to come as soon as he could, and asked her for a specific place to meet her. She named one of the numerous car rental kiosks, and went to wait for him there. Despite sleeping on the plane, she was trembling with tension and fatigue when he walked up to her. She impulsively threw her arms around his neck and held on.

"It's been so awful," she choked out. "I don't know what to do anymore."

"Shh. It'll work out somehow. For the moment, I'm taking you back to our place. It was all I could do to keep Julie from coming with me. She'll have my head if I don't return with you in tow."

"All right. I just – I just can't talk right now."

"That's okay. Take all the time you need." He put his arm around her shoulders after reaching for her suitcase. "Let's go, Partner."

———◦《◎》◦———

"You were contacted *three* times while you were gone?" Mike asked in amazement.

"Yes, at the hotel, the hospital, and at the Rodriquez home." Cari massaged her temples. "I don't know what to expect anymore, Mike. I don't know if the person actually followed me to Mexico, or if they managed everything from here at home." She shook her head. "But that doesn't really matter, does it? The trapped feeling is just the same."

"We'll find this person, Cari," Mike insisted. "They're going to slip up, sometime, somehow."

"*Before* or *after* I'm dead?" She met his gaze evenly. "Come on, Mike, who are we trying to kid? They may not be death threats yet, but they sure are close. And we still don't have a blessed *clue* as to who's behind them."

He reached for her hand and held it securely. "Don't fall apart on me, Cari. Not now. You've made it through an awful lot of stuff before this. Don't let this throw you."

"I'm scared, Mike," she whispered.

"We all get scared, Cari. Please trust me. We'll find who's doing this, *before* it's too late."

She forced a smile. "What would I do without friends like you?"

"Don't ever try to find out."

Mike drove Cari to her apartment, helped her pack some things, and returned her to his home. She had agreed that she was in no shape to stay alone, and Mike offered at least some sense of safety. She settled back into the guest room, and fell asleep for a few hours. Then she made an appointment to see Dr. Wilson the next morning. She almost dreaded it. *He already knows about my trip. I'd better brace myself for the third degree.*

She was right.

"You're in terrible shape!" he scolded, after listening to her heart for a full minute. "Worse than you've been for months." He had an EKG done. He was more upset than ever. "Okay, we're back to the basics here, Cari. We'll try the external pacemaker for another month. If there's no improvement by then, you'll have to go the internal."

Cari sighed but she didn't protest. "I understand, Doctor. Frankly, I'm amazed I've lasted this long without one."

"What's going on? And I don't mean the cut on your foot either." He listened intently as Cari explained about the messages she'd received. "No wonder your pulse is so erratic." He frowned. "I'm no detective, but I'll do everything that I can medically to help you cope with this kind of stress."

"Thank you, Dr. Wilson."

"What about your job?"

"I have to go back. In all likelihood, the stalker is someone from the firm – or at least connected to it somehow. I'm not staying at my apartment, but I really do need to go to work." She forced a smile. "I'll try to be careful."

"Please do."

———⟫⟨●⟩⟪———

"Welcome back," John said when Cari entered Rebecca's office on Monday morning. "How are you feeling?" He immediately noticed that she was wearing a loose fitting sweater rather than the shirt of her uniform. His brows furrowed.

"If you sit down," Cari replied, "I'll be glad to tell you all about it."

John sat down across from Rebecca, his eyes still on Cari. To his surprise, she lifted the edge of her sweater enough to reveal a small box. It seemed to be fastened to her waist with a Velcro strap.

"What the --" he started to ask.

"It's a temporary pacemaker," Cari explained, answering John, but looking at Rebecca. She put her sweater back down over the little gadget. "Dr. Wilson insisted on it for the next month. After that, I may need surgery to have a permanent one implanted." She shrugged, looking almost casual about the whole thing. "It depends on how well my heart behaves. I've had to use it twice before." She frowned. "No, three times, I guess. I'm not sure. I just wanted you to be aware of it."

"And the fact that you may need further surgery," Rebecca remarked, her voice remaining calm, though the color had drained from her face.

"Yes. That's a possibility." Cari leaned back in her chair and sighed. "It may be the wisest option really. Cardiac arrest is not my favorite pass time."

"How can you joke about it?" John demanded.

Cari turned her head and met his gaze dead on. "What else can I do, John? Curl up in a corner and wait for death?" She shook her head. "I'm not prepared to do that. I'll be careful. I'll use this." She tapped the little box at her waist. "And I'll have surgery if I need to." She clasped her hands together in her lap. "And I'll pray a lot."

"Should you even be working, Cari?" Rebecca asked.

"Yes, I should. I need something to focus my attention on." She looked back at John. "And I don't need people feeling sorry for me either."

"All right," Rebecca said. "But don't hesitate to change your hours, or take extra days off." She smiled. "Please be careful."

"I will be."

<hr/>

"I want to know if any other employees were gone the same time that I was," Cari stated as she and John had lunch together. "If anyone on my list was away from here last week, I sure want to find out about it."

"Sounds like a good idea, and it shouldn't be too hard to check on either."

"I also want into Jerry Neilson's office."

"That could be a little harder to arrange. What are you hoping to find?"

"Envelopes, pencils, glue, numbers of florists on his Rolodex, *anything* that might tie him to the messages."

"Granted, you can get into any *office* in the building, but you can't open the desks or briefcases or filing cabinets. Can you?"

"Yes and no. Yes, I *could* open them, with a little help. But no, legally speaking, I would need a search warrant. And so far, there just isn't enough hard evidence pointing to Jerry to get one." She sighed in frustration as she reached for her drink.

"So, do you think Jerry has a strong enough motive for something like this?"

"I'm not sure. But I feel like I need to be *checking*, rather than just *waiting* for the next message to arrive." She looked up when he placed a hand over hers.

"Don't do anything rash, Cari. This is no fool you're dealing with."

She smiled at him as she looked down at his hand. "Are you referring to yourself, John? Or to the person stalking me?" She laughed at the stunned expression on his face. Then she withdrew her hand. "Trust me; I'll carefully consider any move that I make —beforehand."

"Why don't I find any comfort in that remark?" He shook his head. "A week ago you were in the hospital, and looking pretty awful I might add. Now you sit here and tell me that you want to go through Jerry Neilson's office with a fine tooth comb."

"Do I still look 'pretty awful'?" she asked, unable to resist teasing him.

John let out an exasperated sigh. "No. You look wonderful, a little pale perhaps, but as beautiful as always."

"Thank you," she replied softly. She crumpled her napkin. "We'd better get back to the office.'

"Still run from flattery, do you?" he commented. "You must be feeling better."

Chapter 53

C ari listened to the messages on her machine. The first was from Tammy, anxious to hear from her, and wondering if they could soon get together. The second was from a catalogue store, letting her know that her merchandise was ready to be picked up. The third was from the stalker.

"Welcome home, Cari. Feeling better? You won't be for long. Consider this call as nine pretty red roses – with all the petals pulled off."

She removed the tape from the machine and stuffed it into her pocket, intending to take it back to Mike's with her. She was frightened, but she was even angrier. *All these bits and pieces of evidence – but none of them are leading anywhere! But they have to, and soon!*

———◆———

"Obviously, there's some sort of 'countdown' going on," Mike stated in a purely logical way.

Cari felt like screaming. "I realize that, Mike, but until *when?* I haven't been receiving the flowers every day, but maybe I'll start to." She slammed her fist on the kitchen table. "It's so frustrating!"

Mike grabbed her by the shoulders and looked into her face.

"Get a grip, Cari. You weren't a cop for so many years for no reason. And you were very good at it too. You have to think this through. Don't let your emotions run wild. Don't make a careless mistake. Don't run in circles. Clear your head. Go over everything in order. Then change the order. See if it makes more sense backwards. Check off every date on a calendar. But don't run off half-cocked and get yourself in worse trouble. Are you listening to me?"

"April 4th," she murmured, no longer looking at Mike.

"What?"

"April 4th. The shooting was April 4th. That's next week." She focused her gaze on him once more. "Wouldn't that make sense? Maybe someone involved with the case, someone who would remember. Someone who knew I was in Mexico." Her words faded as she went over her list of potential stalkers. Then she shook her head. "It couldn't be," she mumbled. "It couldn't. I can't be that blind."

"What are you talking about, Cari? Look at me and talk some sense."

"Rebecca Richards, Mike. She would certainly have a motive. I'm one of the reasons her son is dead. She knows my address and phone numbers. She was at the inquest. Maybe she hired me because the inquest fell through. Maybe she's been planning this all along. She not only *knew* I was in Mexico – she paid for the trip. Maybe it's all been a set up the whole time." She shook her head again. "But it's just so hard to believe she would do something so cruel."

"Grieving parents can be pretty irrational, Cari. You could be dead on with this idea. Though, why wouldn't she come after me? I'm the one who pulled the trigger. Either way, you don't have any solid proof."

"I'll have to set myself up."

"What? What are you talking about?"

"Set myself up. Go somewhere alone – on April 3rd. And see who might show up."

"Are you crazy? There is no way I'll let you do something that dangerous."

"Got any better ideas?"

"No," he admitted after a moment. "But it's not April 3rd yet either. Give me a chance."

Cari was still busy thinking. "I could go up to John's cabin. Few people even know it's there. It would be a perfect place for a confrontation."

"Perfect place to get killed, you mean!" He let go of her and stared at the table. "It makes sense, Cari, too much sense. But there's got to be a safer way to go about this."

"Why? What makes you think I've been *safe* through any of this?" She reached for his hand. "Besides, I could be totally off the mark on this, and I'll get to spend a couple of peaceful days in the Sierras. What's wrong with that? And I'd come back knowing that the boss I've come to admire isn't some sort of nutcase."

"You should really go into detective work, you know. You're as determined as a bloodhound."

"I'd better be, Mike. My life may depend on it."

—•((●))•—

"Absolutely not!" John fumed. "You're not going up there alone and get yourself killed. Not at my cabin, you won't."

Cari crossed her arms and frowned at him. "Would you feel better if I got killed a little closer to home?" she asked, her voice thick with sarcasm.

"Of course not!" He rubbed the back of his neck and noticed that he was trembling. "This whole discussion is ridiculous." He went to the window and looked down at Wiltshire Blvd. "You want me to let you go up there alone?"

"Yes," was her maddeningly calm reply.

"Why won't you let me go with you?"

"I've already explained all that, John. Look, I know that you can't be the stalker, because you were in my office when I got a phone call. Remember? Well, almost anybody else is fair game. We need to make it clear that I'm going by myself. It's the only way this will work." He heard her come closer and then she put her hand on his arm. "Please? I don't know of a better place."

John turned and put his arms around her. To his surprise, she didn't resist, or say anything. He cradled her head against his chest and held her tight. He felt her arms go around his waist. "You don't play fair," he moaned. "You know I won't refuse at a moment like this." He could feel the silkiness of her hair and he raised her head so that she had to look at him. There were tears in her eyes.

"I'm not playing games, John," she whispered. Her embrace tightened. "I missed you when I got to the resort. I was so glad to see you at the hospital. But I hated it when you left angry. I don't like quarrelling with you. Please understand that."

"What about the guy down in Mexico?" he asked, wishing he didn't need to.

"Gilles? I'll likely never see him again. All he knows is my name that I live in LA." She frowned. "And that I work here. And that I used to be with the LAPD. Okay, there is a very *slim* chance that he might call or show up some day."

"And?"

"And he's a wonderful guy. Truthfully, he probably saved my life when I cut my foot." John stiffened, but Cari only held him a little tighter. "But he still doesn't turn my head like a certain forty something lawyer right here at home." She smiled, a tear slowly coursing down her left cheek. "Get the message, Mr. Maxwell?"

"Almost," he hedged. "You could try a little harder to convince me." She bit her lip and loosened her embrace. "What's wrong?"

"John, I – I still have to be level headed about our relationship. I mean, what I *want* and what is *right* aren't always the same. As long as we don't see eye to eye on spiritual things, this is a little bit like torture for me."

"Join the club," he sighed. He gave her a quick kiss on her wet cheek and stepped away from her. He cleared his throat, straightened his tie needlessly. "I'll give you the key in a few days."

"Thank you."

"I only hope that I won't live to regret this."

"So do I."

———»«(»)«———

Julie handed Cari a small package wrapped in brown paper. "This was on the front porch when I got home from the store." It had Cari's name scrawled in crayon on the paper.

Cari slowly unwrapped the paper, wondering what was in the heavy little box. She opened the gift box to find a shattered *Royal Doulton* figurine inside, in the midst of white tissue paper. It had blonde hair and dark eyes.

"Oh, Cari! Who could be so sick?"

"I don't know for sure, Julie. But I intend to find out." She didn't tell her friend the thought that was racing through her mind at that moment. *Rebecca Richards has the largest collection of figurines that I've ever seen. She could certainly spare one of them.*

———»«(»)«———

When Cari walked down the driveway the next morning, she noticed the flowers on the hood of her car. Five red roses, each stem broken in several places. A small white card was beneath her wiper blade.

"Pretty flowers, such a shame, we'll soon have to end our little game."

Cari gritted her teeth. It was March 30th — only five days left until April 4th.

—✦《◉》✦—

"You're still certain about this?" John asked as he gave Cari the key to the padlock on his cabin.

"More than ever."

"I'm coming up there myself if you're not back in 48 hours, do you hear me?"

"Yes, I hear you." She smiled as she caressed his tense jaw. "I'll look forward to it. Be ready for a batch of pancakes and a pot of coffee."

John grabbed her hand. "How can you joke about something so deadly serious?"

"Because it's the only way for me to stay sane, John. If I can't stay calm, I'll never pull this off."

"What about water? You know you can't haul it from the creek."

"I'm going to take plenty with me. Please don't worry so much." She pulled her hand free. "Why don't you try praying instead?"

"I just may do that," he mumbled. He pulled her into his arms and kissed her.

She briefly returned his embrace before pulling away from him. "I need to get going." She held his gaze for another moment. "Good bye, John."

"Just for 48 hours."

"I'll count them too," she said just before she turned and left his office.

John slumped down into his chair, staring at nothing, and wondering if he was ever going to see Cari Daniels alive again.

Chapter 54

Cari drove up to John's cabin in a 1993 Ford Bronco. The weather began to change when she reached the half way point. A light drizzle gradually became wet snow. By the time she reached her destination, she could hardly make out the cabin amongst the blowing snow. She shivered as she left the warmth of the rental vehicle and made her way to the now white porch. She got the lock off the door, put the key into a zippered pocket of her jacket and went inside.

A rush of warm memories greeted her as she hastily closed the door. Having breakfast with John was the most prominent. She shook her head. *I didn't come here to have romantic daydreams. But, if all goes well, I will be having breakfast with John in a couple of days. For the moment, I've got work to do.*

Within an hour she had a lantern lit, the fire blazing in the wood stove, and her supplies were all inside. She put the coffee pot on the back of the stove and waited for it to warm up. She went to one of the windows and looked out. Only trees and swirling snow to see. She shivered. *Well, either the stalker won't even make it here — or neither of us will be able to leave.* And that didn't entirely rest with the weather.

John paced his living room as he thought of Cari. *She must be there by now, but what about the weather? Is she going to get snowed in? Will I be able to get up there myself? Why am I so worried about such an efficient, professional woman in the first place? She knows what she's doing – I hope.*

———《◎》———

Julie watched Mike as he sat in his chair, remote in hand, staring at nothing in particular. She finally sighed, took the remote, shut off the TV and sat on her husband's lap.

"She'll be fine, Mike. We have to trust her with this. Besides, none of us could really think of a better way." She kissed his cheek.

"I just have this awful feeling that something is going to go wrong,
very wrong." He put his arms around her.

"Then keep praying, Mike, instead of worrying."

"I'll try."

———《◎》———

The howling of the wind was louder than the crackling of the fire in the stove when Cari decided to go to bed. She wasn't truly cold, but she pulled the quilt up to her chin anyway. Then she forced herself to close her eyes and try to get some rest. She wakened twice during the night and added wood to the fire, but each time she went back to sleep immediately. It was seven when she decided it was time to have something to eat.

———《◎》———

Cari stepped onto the porch and squinted against the lightly blowing snow. "It's freezing out here," she muttered as she moved towards the neatly stacked wood pile. She was just reaching for a log when an icy ball slammed into her left eye. Her head snapped back and she covered her eye with her left hand. A second snowball hit her neck, sending moisture inside the collar of her flannel shirt.

"Put your hands behind your head, Ms. Daniels," said a familiar voice, not far from the porch.

Cari shakily complied, realizing that whoever was speaking could see her plainly.

"Good. Now don't move."

She didn't. With her right eye she saw the hazy form approach her, gun in hand. "I should have known, especially after the way you treated me at the inquest."

Jerry Neilson laughed as he stepped onto the porch and came closer. "Well, I guess you just weren't smart enough, were you?" He removed her gun from her belt clip, even as he pointed his own at her face. "Now you're all out of time." He grinned at her. "Turn around and go inside. We have a lot to do today."

———⟨◉⟩———

After attending a brief memorial service for Kyle Richards with Luke and Rebecca, John returned to the firm with the master keys that Cari had left in his keeping. He headed straight for Jerry Neilson's office. It didn't take him long to find what he was looking for. A drafting pencil sat in a brass cup on the desk, along with several ball point pens. But it was the glue that caught his attention more. It had a foreign label on the bottle, and the glue itself was clear. The brush applicator reminded him of nail polish. He sighed as he recalled Cari's description of the first message from the stalker. Then he turned and headed to his own office, where he immediately called Mike Patterson.

———⟨◉⟩———

"Jerry Neilson didn't come in at all today, Mr. Maxwell," Kelly told him from her place behind the security desk. She looked from John to Mike. "I double checked with Ted in the parking area. He hasn't been in at all. Not even really early this morning. And there's no answer at his apartment, or on his cell phone."

John and Mike both frowned.

"Well," Mike said, "I guess this points to *whom*, but it doesn't tell us whether or not Cari is still safe."

"I could have the Rangers try to radio her at my cabin, but she may not have it on, and the weather is lousy." He shrugged. "Shall we try it anyway?"

"Sure. At this point I'm ready to try almost anything."

"So am I."

The phone reception was terrible at the Ranger Station. John tried to explain the situation.

"We'll try the radio, sir," remarked the Ranger. "But there's no way we can get to your cabin. Visibility is almost zero up here." John waited on the line for a few minutes. "I'm sorry sir, but no one is answering the radio."

"Thank you for trying."

"You're welcome. If your friend calls us, sir, we'll be sure to relay the message to you."

———

"Remove the battery from your pacemaker," Jerry ordered.

Cari simply stared at him. "Why?"

"Because we're going to make a swap." He pulled a small battery from one of his pant pockets. "Give me yours and you can have this one." He leveled the gun at her face once more. "Right now."

Cari opened the small box and removed the fresh battery, and handed it to Jerry.

He took it from her and put it into his shirt pocket. Then he gave her the other battery, a grin on his face. "Of course, this battery is almost dead – just like you."

Cari installed it anyway, noticing how much weaker the display was. She looked at him. "Why are you doing this, Jerry?"

"That's *Mr. Neilson* to you. And I have plenty of reasons. I'll even tell you a few – while you have some coffee."

"I don't want any."

"Well that's just too bad. Pour it and drink it."

———— ((◊)) ————

"Now you're going to go outside for awhile. Just leave your jacket in here."

Cari could feel the stuttering of her pulse after the cup of coffee. She knew that going outside into the cold without proper clothing wouldn't help either. Obviously, Jerry Neilson knew that too.

She stood on the porch and shivered for almost thirty minutes before Jerry allowed her back inside. Then he told her to drink another coffee, to warm up.

Lunch time came and went. Jerry ate a power bar, but he only allowed Cari another coffee.

"I can't drink any more."

"You will," was his cold reply.

After allowing Cari to use the toilet, Jerry forced her back outside, this time for nearly an hour.

———— ((◊)) ————

"I have to get up there," John said as he and Mike ate a supper that neither wanted. "I was going to drive up in the morning. Now I'm wondering if it'd be easier on horseback or on foot."

"I don't know, John. But you'd better not go in alone." Mike sighed. "I'm working tomorrow. And we don't have enough evidence on Jerry Neilson to truly get the Department involved with this either."

"On the contrary, Mike, I think I *should* go in alone. The less commotion the better. I don't make much noise by myself."

———— ❖ ————

"Ever swung an axe before?" Jerry asked. Cari nodded. "Good. Then you know it's hard work." He grinned. "Some nice, aerobic exercise." He lifted the axe from its bracket above the door and handed it to Cari. "And don't try anything stupid. I'm sure I could pull the trigger quicker than you could throw the axe at me. Get moving."

Cari split logs until her hands were blistered, her arms grew limp, her heart pounded, and her knees buckled.

"Get up!" Jerry ordered.

"I can't. I'm too tired." She felt the barrel of the gun at the base of her skull.

"I said to get up."

Cari managed to stumble to her feet, but only for a moment. Then she collapsed again, her breathing raspy and painful. Her shirt was soaked with sweat, and the snow was dampening her jeans.

"Get up! We're going inside." Jerry jerked Cari's left arm painfully, but she regained her feet. Then she staggered into the warm cabin and made it to the couch. "This is taking too long."

"You could always shoot me," Cari replied through chattering teeth. "That would be faster."

"You know exactly what I'm doing. You're just a little stronger than I anticipated. That'll change. You're already tired, and hungry, and thirsty."

Cari licked her chapped lips, annoyed that he was right.

"I just have to up your stress level, don't I? And I know plenty of ways to do that."

Cari closed her eyes, but she couldn't block out the sound of his voice.

"Does the name *Mark Hamilton* mean anything to you?"

With intense effort Cari kept her eyes closed. "Should it?" *How much does he really know about me?*

"Yes, considering he performed the D&C a year ago today. And," he added, touching her throat with the gun barrel, "considering you were engaged to marry him. And *especially* considering he was the father of that baby."

"What makes you think that?" she asked, her voice quavering.

"Because I put a lot of effort into that inquest," he replied. "It wasn't very difficult to backtrack and find a possible date that you got pregnant. Thanksgiving, wasn't it? And who were you with at that time – Mark Hamilton. It was common knowledge among some of your co-workers. It was very easy to piece it together."

Cari tried to get up. "I need a drink of water."

"I'm sure you do. Your left kidney must be getting a bit aggravated by now." He jabbed her in the side with the gun. "No water."

Cari felt her heart flutter and gritted her teeth. *I have to stay calm, somehow.*

"Show me the scars," he said as the gun pressed against her throat. "I can tell you the number of sutures it took to close you up again. But I think I'd like to see for myself." He laughed as Cari's pulse skipped.

Cari tried to shake her head. "No."

"Undo the buttons, Ms. Daniels – or I'll do it for you."

Cari closed her eyes and shivered. His tone was so much like Mark's the night he'd – "I can't," she whispered. "Not with that gun so close. Back up a little."

Jerry laughed just before grabbing her throat with his left hand. "I tell *you* what to do. Not the other way around."

Cari opened her eyes and stared at him. *What can I do? For all I know, the gun isn't even loaded. But can I take that chance?* She reached for the top button on the flannel shirt.

Chapter 55

"I'll go up most of the way in my Jeep," John said as he and Mike went over his plan. "Then I'll hike around through the woods, by the creek, and approach the cabin that way. I'm sure I can do it without being seen." He rubbed the back of his neck. "What I'm not sure about is whether or not to carry a gun with me."

"Would you rather go unarmed? I know I wouldn't."

"I don't own a handgun, Mike. I have a couple of hunting rifles. I couldn't hike as well if I'm packing one of those."

"I suppose not. But how else would you plan to defend yourself – or Cari, if need be?"

John sighed. "I don't know." He stood and shoved his hands into his pockets. "That's just it. There are too many *unknowns* in this whole scenario. We're *assuming* that Jerry Neilson is the stalker and that he's followed Cari to my cabin. But we don't even know that for a certainty."

"No, but it's more than we had to go on before."

"True." John gripped the chair back. "I'll take a rifle with me, just in case."

⸺⸻●⸻⸺

"So," Jerry asked, "what would happen if I gave this little wire here a tug?" He reached for the lead wire to Cari's pacemaker.

She grabbed for his left hand. "Don't touch that!"

He shoved her hand away. "Why not? What's the worst that can happen, a punctured heart, some hemorrhaging? You're not worried about that, are you?" He firmly clasped the wire and locked his gaze with Cari's. "You haven't got a prayer and you *know* it."

She moaned as she felt the wire move, ever so slightly. "Don't do this – please," she whispered. This time she reached for the gun, deciding she'd rather die fighting than helplessly waiting.

Taken by surprise, Jerry almost dropped the gun.

Cari shoved him harder and he lost his balance, his left hand still holding the lead wire. She felt it moving again, but she continued to fight.

Jerry toppled backwards to the floor, but he still had the gun.

Cari kicked at his wrist with her left foot, and he lost his hold. As soon as the gun hit the floor, she kicked it aside. Then she got to her feet and reached for the poker from the stove set.

Jerry got up and tackled her. Cari tripped and hit her forehead on the wooden chest, but she managed to regain her feet. She could barely breathe, the pain in her chest agonizing. She got her hand on the poker just as Jerry grabbed the back of her shirt. Since it was still unfastened, it slid from her shoulders, but she was able to grip the poker and swing it around as she dropped to her knees. It caught Jerry in the left hip and he staggered back a step, releasing the shirt. Cari hit him a second time, hammering his left knee.

Jerry swore as he lunged at Cari, easily knocking her to the floor. She didn't have much strength left and her heart was going wild. He swore again as he grabbed her face and slammed the back of her head against the rough planks. Amidst the pain, Cari reached up her left hand and clawed his face. Furious, he took hold of her arm with both his hands and jerked it brutally.

Cari screamed as her shoulder slipped from the socket. Desperation took over. She could still feel the handle of the poker. She picked it up and swung it at Jerry's head. The cast iron connected with his left temple and a look of surprise crossed his face. He tried to get up, but he toppled instead. He collapsed in a heap next to Cari.

⸺ ⟨⟨◉⟩⟩ ⸺

John inched his way towards the cabin. He'd known someone was with Cari as soon as he'd spotted a second rental vehicle near hers. But something was very wrong. It was too quiet. He didn't hear voices – not even threatening ones. And very little smoke was drifting up from the chimney. He got to the porch and moved along it towards the door. Still no sounds from inside. *Maybe he's just waiting for a clean shot at me. Well, here goes nothing.* His rifle ready, John kicked the door open. Two seconds later his rifle barrel was leveled at the still body on the floor.

"You're early," Cari rasped. "I was hoping."

John turned slightly and saw her. She looked horrible, even in the dim morning light, and flickering lantern glow. She was half sitting, her back propped against the frame of the sofa. Her flannel shirt was pulled together, but not fastened. Her left arm hung down at an odd angle. There was a large bump on her forehead.

"Thank God you're here," she whispered, her eyes closing in obvious pain and relief. Then she began to tremble.

John looked at Jerry once more. "Is he --"

"He's dead," was her shaky reply.

John flicked the safety back on on his rifle, and leaned it against the wall and shut the door. Then he went to kneel down near Cari. He could see the beads of perspiration on her face. Her labored breathing caught his attention. The term *respiratory distress* had been something vague until that moment. He gently touched her face, but drew back when she winced.

"I'm going to radio the Ranger Station, Cari. I'm hoping they can get a chopper into here. There's a clearing not too far away."

"I need – surgery," she murmured through trembling lips. "The pacemaker wire . . ." She took a shuddering breath. "Jerry pulled it loose."

John didn't want to consider how painful that must have been, or the implications for her heart. "If they can't get a chopper into here, I'll have to drive you out."

"I – wouldn't – make – it." She opened her eyes and tried to smile. "Sorry – about – breakfast." Her whole body contorted for a few seconds.

"How can I help you?" John asked, trying to stifle his mounting sense of panic.

"I'm cold," she replied, her eyes closing and her head dropping back against the sofa cushion.

John grabbed the nearest quilt and draped it around her, trying not to worsen the pain from her apparently dislocated shoulder. "Hang on. Please." He went to the radio, turned it on and tried to get through to the Rangers. Within five minutes he was informed that a chopper bearing medics would be dispatched ASAP. And *Cedar's Sinai* would be notified as well, Dr. Wilson in particular.

John added wood to the dying fire. He turned back to Cari when she moaned.

"When did Jerry get here?" he asked, hating the need to fill in the silence.

"Yesterday. Early." Cari bit her bottom lip, which was already crusted with dried blood. She turned her head to the side.

"I should have come sooner," he replied, regret edging his tone. "Mike and I were both pretty certain he was the stalker."

"He had – a gun," she whispered.

"So did I." He moved her hair away from her forehead. "Looks like a rough battle."

"Yeah. Last night. Late. I didn't – mean to – kill him."

"Don't try to talk anymore." He continued to stroke her hair. "I wish there was something I could be doing for you."

"You came," she mumbled, seeming drowsy. Her eyelids fluttered and then her face relaxed.

John frantically felt for her pulse. Finding it, he forced himself to remain calm. *She's exhausted. She's resting. Unconscious, maybe, but she's still alive.* He kept stroking her hair until he could make out the distinct sound of an approaching chopper.

———)•(◊)•(———

Cari woke up in the recovery room, several hours later. She was thankful to be alive, but oh, she hurt. And she was desperately tired. She closed her eyes as soon as she recognized where she was. This hospital had become almost a second home to her in the past year.

"Take it easy, Cari. You came through the surgery just fine. We'll soon take you to your room."

Cari thought the nurses' voice was somewhat familiar, but she was too tired to even open her eyes for a brief look.

———)•(◊)•(———

John sat in the waiting room with Mike and Julie. He got to his feet as soon as Dr. Wilson came through the doors. "How is she?"

Dr. Wilson smiled, though lines of fatigue creased his forehead. "She's in recovery right now. We'll take her to a private room shortly. I've seen few people come through what she has." He shook his head. "She's a remarkable woman."

"We serve a remarkable God," Mike countered. "I'm just glad that Cari's such a fighter."

"That she is. We repaired the bleeding in the heart, implanted the pacemaker. And we did an ultrasound to examine the left kidney. Given time for recovery, I think she's going to be fine."

"Thank God!" Julie sighed as she put her hands up to cover her face.

"How long will she be here?" John asked, practicalities replacing panic at last.

"Up to two weeks. If all goes well, she'll be able to return to work in about a month. By mid summer she can resume regular activities."

"When can I see her?" John realized he should have said 'we', seeing as Mike and Julie were also with him.

"In about a half hour, but only one at a time, and only for a couple of minutes. I'll be restricting her visitors for a few days yet. She needs to have complete rest."

"You can go in first, John," Mike said. "Seeing as you're the one who saved her life."

Mike's grin brought rising color to John's face. "Thanks, Mike. I'd appreciate that."

———— ((●)) ————

Cari heard someone enter the room and opened her eyes. She tried to smile at John, but she was too weary. She simply watched him approach the bed. She felt sorry for him. She doubted that he'd seen too many people so soon after major surgery. *Then again, maybe he has. He does handle insurance claims. He saw me down in Mexico, but I wasn't wired up like I am now. I wonder what he's thinking.*

"I have never been so scared in my entire life," were his first words to her as he gently picked up her right hand. "I will never let you go alone to my cabin again either." He was so pale, and his jaw line was shadowed from a day or two of missing the razor. He gripped her fingers in his own.

"Thank you," Cari rasped, hating the dryness of her throat and mouth. "I never would – have survived – without your help." She closed her eyes, annoyed at the exertion from one statement.

"You're welcome." He leaned down and kissed her cheek, then her mouth, very softly. "Expect to see a lot more of me in the future." He fingered her hair. "Somebody has to keep an eye on you. And I've appointed myself to that job."

Cari managed to open her eyes once more. She could see that John meant every word, despite his teasing tone of voice. "You're hired, Mr. Maxwell." She sighed. "Now go away – and let me – sleep."

"Yes, Ma'am."

Chapter 56

Cari was back home within two weeks, back to work within a month. And back to being busy by the end of Tammy's school year. The two spent a weekend together to celebrate. Tammy had managed to testify at a hearing against the two boys who had attacked her. Both had been sent to a juvenile detention facility. Jill Harris didn't even need to testify against Trevor MacBride. The evidence against him had been almost overwhelming. He was still awaiting sentencing, but he was expected to get between ten and fifteen years.

Max Gardener finally confessed to being the one who had slashed Cari's tires. Once Trevor had told the police that Max had been the one to arrange his entrance and exit at the firm, Max had decided that confessing would be better than the police finding out on their own. He also admitted that he'd taken numerous bribes from individuals who'd wanted access to offices in the building, just as Cari had suspected. It would still be months before a judge heard the charges against him.

Jerry Neilson was buried at the same cemetery as some of his relatives. When the police went through his office files and belongings, they found several receipts from florist shops. The glue proved to be a match to the one used in the message to Cari. And his most recent phone bill showed a call to the resort in Mexico that Cari had been at. A safety deposit box contained several bank cards, which led to various accounts, and a great deal of money.

It was Cari who had found out the motive behind his hostility towards her. She shared that knowledge with the Richards and John as the four of them had dinner together.

"Apparently, Jerry had been supplying Kyle with crack for several months, as well as some of Kyle's friends and clients. So, when Kyle was killed, and the case of crack seized from the trunk of his car, Jerry was out a lot of money – both *actual* and *potential.* Then, at the inquest, Jerry was so certain that he could discredit Mike and me. He came very close to succeeding." Cari reached for her goblet and took a sip of water. Then she continued.

"However, he hadn't really bargained on me collapsing right there in the room. And he certainly hadn't expected to be removed from the case by you, Rebecca." She looked to her employer. "When you put him on probation, you made him very nervous. He needed his connections at the firm to keep his drug dealings going well. That's why he made no moves until the six month period was over."

"Then he made up for it," John said, glancing at Cari as he cut another piece of his steak.

"True. He kept pressing until I thought I might go crazy. And, actually, that was his intent all along."

"To drive you crazy?" Rebecca asked, her fork not quite making it to her mouth.

"Not exactly, but to bring on a heart attack. You see, we all forgot just how much *research* he did for the inquest. Specifically, he had my medical files. As a matter of fact, he kept a copy of them. And, at the inquest, he saw first hand how poorly I could cope with high levels of stress. So, he just kept at me, trying to increase my frustration until I reached the breaking point. That's what he was doing at the cabin. He never intended to shoot me. He just wanted to wear down my stamina, and put my body under too much stress. He planned on it looking as though I got *careless,* and since I was supposed to be up there alone, who would have been any the wiser?"

"But his *plan* didn't quite work that way," Luke commented.

"No. He didn't think I would be able to tolerate as much as I did. He also didn't think that I'd bother to resist him while he was holding a gun on me. That proved to be a fatal mistake on his part." She looked down at her plate of half eaten food. "Though I never meant to kill *him* either." She raised her head and looked from Rebecca to Luke. "I think I understand a bit better how Mike was feeling. Sometimes you just don't have a lot of choices. I wanted to stay alive. And I tried to defend myself. I didn't realize how hard the blow was until he didn't get up again." She swallowed hard as she thought about staring at Jerry's lifeless body for hours, wishing she'd done something different.

"You did what you had to," John asserted. "Besides, if you hadn't killed him before I arrived, I might have shot him myself." He reached for Cari's hand, bringing a blush to her cheeks. "Especially if I'd known how much he'd already hurt you."

"So," Luke said after clearing his throat, "you seem to have the resiliency of a cat, Ms. Daniels. I vote we give you a raise and hold you to a contract. I, for one, would hate to lose you – to a competitor, that is." Luke gave a rather significant look in John's direction. "*Within* the firm – all's fair, I suppose."

"I'm flattered, Mr. Richards, but --"

"I knew it! Another offer already?" Luke exclaimed, a playful glint in his eyes.

"No, not another *offer*," Cari hastened to explain, suddenly realizing that John was still holding her hand. "But I've decided that if I'm going to keep getting involved in investigative work, I'd like to get my license."

"You want to become a private investigator?" John asked, obviously taken aback. "How many career changes do you plan to go through in your life?"

"Would you plan to leave the firm?" Rebecca put in, seeming

to have a better grip on the logic of the situation than the men at the table.

"Well, that depends," Cari replied. "I'd like to remain at the firm, still in charge of security. But I'd study part time to be an investigator." With her free hand she toyed with her napkin. "I thought that it might be rather convenient to have your own P.I. available to the lawyers." She smiled. "And I wouldn't have to fork out any of my own money to set up a practice of my own either." She laughed. "You see, I really can be a little selfish at times, Mr. Richards. So, what do you think, now that you've heard my whole idea?"

"I think it's wonderful," Rebecca answered. "Why haven't any of us thought of it before? I can't think of another investigator that I could trust as readily as you, Cari. When would you like to start?"

"Wait a minute!" John protested. "She nearly got herself killed just by being a cop turned security manager. Now she wants to do something even more dangerous. I'm not in favor of it at all." He squeezed Cari's fingers for good measure.

"Well, I'd say you're out voted, John," Luke replied. "I agree with Rebecca. Other companies have their own investigators. Why shouldn't we?" He leaned back and crossed his arms. "And why not Cari?"

"I have no intention of starting a feud," Cari said, half seriously. "But this is something that I'd like to do. Thank you for your encouragement. And your *input*, John. I'll find out what I can and get back to you about it." She pulled her hand free of John's. "I'm looking forward to a *lengthy* career with Richards & Richards."

⸻ ◦◉◦ ⸻

"I apologize for my outburst during dinner tonight," John said as he walked Cari to her car. "I suppose I just wasn't prepared for another surprise so soon. How long have you been considering this?"

"I guess since I went to the cabin. I realized how much easier this might have been if I'd actually been trained as in investigator. I would have had a better idea of what I was looking for in regards to both Jerry Neilson and Max Gardener." She stopped when she reached her car and turned to face him. "In case you hadn't noticed – I like to do my *best* when I'm working on something. I figure that getting my license would make me more efficient."

"But it couldn't possibly make you any more beautiful," he replied, his voice like a caress. She didn't resist as he put his arms around her. "You know something? I actually *prayed* for you when I drove up to the cabin. I realized how little there was that I could do for you. I guess God must have taken me seriously."

"Does that surprise you?" she asked, feeling so relaxed in his warm embrace.

"Maybe a little." He sighed as he gently pulled her head against his chest. "I'm still a long way from where you seem to be. Spiritually, I mean. I just wanted you to know that I've been doing some thinking about it."

"Thank you for telling me. I appreciate your honesty, John." She couldn't help but laugh. "Even when you disagree vehemently." She raised her head so that she could look at him. "You've helped to make this past year something very special."

"Likewise. Who knows what will happen during the next one?" He released her and cradled her face in his hands. "Promise me to stick around that long?"

"I've got no plans to go anywhere, John. Do you?" She placed her own hands on top of his and smiled. "Don't you usually go to St. Moritz each summer? Why are you still hanging around the office?"

"Because the *scenery* right here has improved dramatically since last summer." He lowered his head and kissed her. "Why would I want to go away?" He kissed her again, this time putting his arms around her and holding her close. It was several moments before he moved away from her. "I think if I ever go back to St. Moritz, I'd like to take somebody with me."

Cari cleared her throat before unlocking her door. John opened it for her and held it while she got seated inside, the engine running. Then she smiled at him. "Good night, John."

"Good night, Cari." He closed the door and stepped away from the car.

＞━•«◉»•━＜

Cari was still in a bit of a daze when she entered her apartment. It seemed that no matter how hard she tried, she just couldn't set John Maxwell aside. Even knowing that he wasn't a Christian didn't make him any less attractive. *Or caring, or responsible, or gentle, or handsome, or a wonderful kisser.* She shook her head as she went to check her answering machine. The light was flashing. She flicked the switch and listened.

"Buenos Dios, Senorita Daniels. This is Gilles Rodriquez, in case you've forgotten. It's taken me months to find you again. Please get in touch with me. How are you? How is your health? Did the police find the person who was stalking you? As you see, I have many questions that need answers. Please call me. I'm in Los Angeles for a few more days. Would you have dinner with me? Or lunch? Or breakfast? You can reach me at 555-9937 until Friday. I haven't forgotten you, Cari. Please call me. A dios."

Cari sat down on the nearest chair and tried to clear her head. *Gilles? Now? It's been four months since I was there. And he's been trying to find me ever since? What on earth should I do? Maybe arrange to meet with him at Mike and Julie's? That would be better than a hotel or restaurant, I think.* She frowned. *What about John? His feelings for me are getting more obvious all the time. But he sure didn't like Gilles when he met him before. Should I just not mention that he called? No, I told John that I appreciate his honesty, so I should probably just tell him.*

She got up and began to pace the room. *Why is it that every time it seems like life is settling down, a curve ball is thrown my way? My health is finally stable. My job couldn't be better. John is even giving God some consideration these days. Gilles, your timing is positively lousy. But I can hardly wait to see you.*

The End

Printed in the United States
147584LV00003B/15/P